FRANKENSTORM

FRANKENSTORM

RAY GARTON

PINNACLE BOOKS
Kensington Publishing Corp.
www.kensingtonbooks.com

PINNACLE BOOKS are published by

Kensington Publishing Corp.
119 West 40th Street
New York, NY 10018

All Kensington titles, imprints, and distributed lines are available at special quantity discounts for bulk purchases for sales promotions, premiums, fund-raising, educational, or institutional use.

Special book excerpts or customized printings can also be created to fit specific needs. For details, write or phone the office of the Kensington special sales manager: Kensington Publishing Corp., 119 West 40th Street, New York, NY 10018, attn: Special Sales Department; phone 1-800-221-2647.

This book is a work of fiction. Names, characters, businesses, organizations, places, events, and incidents either are the product of the author's imagination or are used fictitiously. Any resemblance to actual persons, living or dead, events, or locales is entirely coincidental.

PINNACLE and the P logo are Reg. U.S. Pat. & TM Off.

First printing: May 2014

ISBN-13: 978-0-7860-3407-9
ISBN-10: 0-7860-3407-6

10 9 8 7 6 5 4 3 2 1

Printed in the United States of America

First electronic edition: May 2014

ISBN-13: 978-0-7860-3408-6
ISBN-10: 0-7860-3408-4

PART ONE
Severe Risk

Prologue

"It's starting to rain. You two need a ride someplace?"

Will looked with suspicion at the young Latino smiling from the open window of the van's passenger door. A grinning cartoon man held up a wrench on the side of the van beneath the words MINUTEMAN PLUMBING. There was a phone number below that, and then, 24 HR. SERVICE! The van had pulled up to the curb next to them just seconds ago.

He didn't like being suspicious of people when they tried to do good things, but Will knew it was stupid not to be, at least a little. As much he wanted to think that people were basically good and decent, he knew there'd been a rash of disappearances lately among Eureka's homeless population and from what he'd heard, the police weren't all that interested in doing anything about it.

"We're heading across town," the man in the van said. He was young and had a pleasant, smiling face.

Will looked down at Margaret. She was in pain, though she'd never say a word about it. He looked at the man in the van again. He didn't set off any of Will's alarms.

"We're going to Halvorsen Park," Will said.

"Oh, yeah, just up the road. Slide that door open and hop in."

Will stepped over to the van and opened the door for Margaret.

Fifteen minutes earlier, Will left the Old Town Shelter with Margaret and they headed along the sidewalk with stomachs full of beans, cornbread, and hot coffee. He had a backpack and Margaret carried a large, bulging, cloth bag that made her list to the left.

"Cornbread was awful dry," Margaret said. Her voice was hoarse.

"You think so?"

She nodded. "But it was awful good."

They'd managed to sneak out before the sermon. He didn't know Margaret well, but he remembered that her attitude toward that stuff matched his.

The cloudy, late-October day was ending and growing shadows darkened 2nd Street in Eureka's Old Town. The Carson Mansion loomed over the shops even though it stood a couple of blocks away. It was an enormous Victorian mansion that towered over everything like some fairy-tale house from a faraway land, as if it had dropped out of the sky and plopped itself in the grubby surroundings of Eureka, California. But Will knew it had been built by a pioneering lumber baron for his wife, a gift of beautiful excess, a work of art, but most important, a safe and warm home for a family, the kind of home many people no doubt dreamed of when they thought of coming to America. Even when it was still a home, it also served as a monument for what could be achieved in America with enough determination and hard work. But now it was owned by a private club for rich men who held meetings and social events there. The club preserved the mansion and kept it looking as beautiful as it had the day it was finished. A monument, no longer a home. The public was not allowed on the premises.

Will didn't know where they were going, but he didn't ask because he didn't even know if they'd be sticking together. All he knew was that they were walking together now, as they had a couple of months ago. He hadn't seen Margaret since then because he'd been hanging around McKinleyville and Arcata, traveling on foot, sometimes hitchhiking, catching a bus if he had a little money. New laws were making it harder to stay in one place for very long. He had to keep moving.

He was thirty-one-years old and had been on the street for one year and five months. It felt like a lot longer. He'd been homeless before, but never for such a long stretch. Each time he looked in the mirror of some public restroom or homeless shelter, he found his reflection more unfamiliar. Older and hairier, thinner and more weathered. His once sensitive but pensive eyes—"The eyes of a worried little boy," Kim used to say—had filled with a cloying desperation that he found difficult to look at for long. He knew the day was coming when he would not recognize the face that looked back at him, when all traces of himself finally would be gone.

He'd met Kim at AA. He'd been attending for months when she showed up looking lost and frightened. She remained silent through two meetings, and at the end of the second, he introduced himself and offered to buy her coffee. After thirty minutes in a Burger King, he had her laughing. They spent that night together and were married a month later. Will worried that they'd been too impulsive, a common problem among addicts. But the next four years proved it hadn't been a mistake. Both of them had come from troubled, abusive backgrounds and long ago had severed family ties to go it alone in the world. They saw in each other the anchor their lives had been missing.

They barely scraped by, of course. He was a high school dropout, and neither of them had any marketable skills. But they managed. He got hired to work the loading dock at a trucking company, a position in which he'd flourished. Kim did a lot of waitressing before lucking into a steady job at a rental car company. For the length of their time together, they remained sober. They focused their energies on each other, drew strength from each other. Then Will lost his job, and Kim got sick.

She didn't seem sick at first, she simply started to lose weight. They thought it was a good thing, because she was a little overweight, something that had started when she stopped drinking. But the weight loss progressed rapidly and it soon became apparent that it was not a good thing. Abdominal pain followed. She went to a doctor, he ordered some tests, and she was diagnosed with pancreatic cancer. It all happened quickly, and the next thing Will knew, the anchor he'd found in Kim was gone and he was alone again.

He tried to find work, but with no success. In their four years together, he and Kim had lived from paycheck to paycheck and had been able to save very little. Will soon had to leave the apartment he'd shared with Kim because he couldn't pay the rent. He stayed with a friend for a while as he looked for work, but he found none.

Now he was homeless, penniless, and futureless, walking through the dusky shadows with a fellow homeless woman almost twice his age.

"What have you been up to, Margaret?" he said as they walked. She'd aged in the months since he'd seen her. She looked wearier and was limping slightly.

She shrugged her bony shoulders. "Tryin' to stay outta jail. Tryin' to keep from starvin'. The usual. Where you been? Ain't seen you in a few months."

As they walked, Will told her about his wanderings.

Before Will had left Eureka, he and Margaret had spent a good deal of time together. They felt comfortable with each other. Instead of the camaraderie one might expect to exist between homeless people, there was a great deal of distrust. Being alone on the street instilled a feeling of vulnerability that never went away. But Will and Margaret had connected quickly. He knew nothing about her because she'd offered no information, and Will hadn't talked about his own background much, either. The companionship was enough.

"It's gonna rain tonight," Margaret said. "I can feel it in my bad hip."

"Too late to get beds for the night. Where do you want to go?"

She shrugged again. "I know a spot in Halvorsen Park." She held out her hand, palm up, as it began to sprinkle. "Gonna get wet no matter what, looks like." She reached into her bag and removed a compact umbrella which she extended and opened. "Ain't you got an umbrella?"

"Used to. I sold it to an old guy in Arcata who needed it more than I did."

"What'd you get?"

"Couple of candy bars and a pretty nice flashlight."

Will was taller by more than a foot, so she lifted the umbrella high enough to cover both of them.

"Storm's a-comin'," she said.

"You think?"

"Oh, yeah. A bad one."

"What are the cops up to around here these days?" Will said. "I thought they cracked down on Halvorsen Park."

"They did for a while. It's calmed down now. I know a spot."

"Is your hip up to the walk?"

She waved a bony hand and said, "My hip can live with it."

But Will could see that her limp had worsened since they'd left the shelter.

As they walked down 2nd to I Street, it quickly grew darker and the sprinkle turned into a modest downpour.

Traffic had been thin, with only an occasional car passing

by in either direction, so Will noticed the sound of a vehicle slowing down as it approached them from behind.

That was when the white van with the cartoon man on the side pulled up next to them.

As Margaret got in, Will took off his backpack, then he got in and hugged it to his lap. He closed the door and the van pulled away from the curb.

There was a cardboard box at the other end of the seat, so they were a bit cramped. Will looked over his shoulder at a black drape that separated the backseat from the rear of the van.

The man at the wheel was older than the passenger. Heavyset, balding, brown hair speckled with grey. He looked at Will in the rearview and his eyes smiled.

"I hope you got a dry place to stay," the passenger said, "'cause it's really starting to come down."

"I know a spot," Margaret muttered.

When the driver made a U-turn on I Street instead of turning onto Waterfront Drive to go to the park, Will knew something was wrong.

He started to lean forward and say something when Margaret began to struggle and kick beside him. Before he could turn to see what was wrong, a hand holding a white cloth filled his field of vision. The cloth was pressed to his face and his nose filled with a harsh chemical odor.

Everything melted away into blackness.

1

"They're calling it Frankenstorm," the boisterous male voice on the radio said, "because it's just damned *spooky*. A hurricane like this on the West Coast? Get outta here. But it's happenin', folks, it's happenin' in the morning. Climate change is really kickin' our butts! It's created a freak set of meteorological circumstances, and the result is Hurricane Quentin, which will be dancin' our way tomorrow morning, Saturday, to the tune of two hundred mile-per-hour winds, which means you'd better tie your butt down or kiss it good-bye. I'm not joking, kids, you've got to be prepared for this. Have plenty of candles ready because we're gonna lose power. Have water and nonperishable foods on hand, and for crying out loud, stay indoors. *I'm* ready! I've got my baby-duck swim ring on and the Classic Rock 97 studio is loaded with Red Bull and Doritos, so *bring it on*, baby! Here's The Doors singing about what we're all gonna be in the next twenty-four hours, 'Riders on the Storm.'"

Dr. Fara McManus had stopped chewing her fingernails in college, but now she couldn't find a nail to chew on because she'd gnawed them all away. Wind raged outside and driving rain rattled against the single window in her office in what used to be the Springmeier Neuropsychiatric Hospital. Today, the office felt smaller than usual.

Fara sat at her desk, but with her chair turned around so she could look out the window. She sat with her right ankle resting on her left knee, right foot bobbing nervously. Her insides were knotted with dread. It wasn't a new feeling. She'd been feeling that dread long before Hurricane Quentin was announced. She'd started feeling it by the end of her first week working for Corcoran. The storm only made it worse. The grey world outside her window was blurred by the wind-blown rain that dribbled down the glass.

Why isn't this window boarded up yet? she wondered.

It would be if someone responsible were in charge.

A knock at her door made her jump. She swiveled the chair around as Dr. Jeremy Corcoran pushed the door open and leaned into her office.

He was a tall, lanky man in his late sixties, balding on top with a wild explosion of long, frizzy, silver hair all the way around his head, a matching goatee, and thick horn-rimmed glasses. His nose was narrow and prominent and his mouth looked too small for his face. In the white lab coat he always wore, Fara thought he looked like a mad scientist from an old movie.

He is *a mad scientist.*

Corcoran was the reason she had taken the job. He was also the reason she desperately wanted out of it.

"Hope I'm not interrupting anything, Fara," he said with that little chuckle that seemed to punctuate everything he said.

Fara said nothing, just waited for him to go on.

"I'm having a little gathering in my quarters this evening." Chuckle. "Nothing special, just some drinks, some music. I thought we'd have a little party to greet the storm." Chuckle. "Like I said before, I think it's a good idea if everyone stays here for the duration. So I thought a little party would help everyone relax." Chuckle.

"A party?" she said. "Is that a good idea?"

"Well . . . I don't think it's a *bad* idea."

She stood. "Dr. Corcoran, I don't know if liquor is wise when we're about to get hit by a—"

"Please," he said, still smiling as he closed his eyes in frustration for a moment. "Jeremy. I wish you'd call me Jeremy. I've told you, after all this time, I don't see why you insist on being so formal when—"

"And as I have told you, Dr. Corcoran, I think we could use a little *more* formality around here. This is not just a storm we're talking about, it's a hurricane, and I'm not sure we're prepared for it. Getting *drunk* doesn't strike me as a very good idea right now when we're about to—"

He cleared his throat loudly to interrupt her and said, "Look." His fists clenched at his sides for a moment, but quickly relaxed.

Corcoran hated confrontation. And she was pretty sure he was eager to get back to enjoying his high. Pills, she suspected, but nothing would surprise her. She could tell because his pupils were dilated and his eyes were wide instead of his lids being at half-mast as usual, and he seemed hyperalert.

"I know you have some problems with the way I've been running this project," he said, "but let's keep one thing in mind. I'm still in charge. I know you've reported me more than once and yet, in spite of that, I'm *still* in charge. That should tell you something, Fara. Vendon Labs put me here to do a job and, apparently, they like the way I'm doing it. I'm not going anywhere."

"You're here because of your government connections, Dr. Corcoran. This is a government project and they want you on it because of your past work in—"

"You are free to leave, Fara. I would hate to see you go because I think you've been an asset, you do very good work, and I appreciate your contributions to the project. But no one is holding a gun to your head." Chuckle. "Personally, I hope you'll stay. But if you do, then I suggest you . . . *relax* a little. Please come to the party this evening. Socialize. You've been here all this time and nobody knows you. Everyone suspects there's an interesting person behind that stiff, professional demeanor, but nobody's seen her yet. Quit being such a"—chuckle—"a stick in the mud. All work and no play, as they say."

Before she could say anything more, Corcoran turned and started out, then stopped in the doorway and looked over his shoulder at her.

"Remember, testing soon. See you downstairs in a while."

That feeling of dread inside Fara threatened to become nausea as she lowered herself back into the chair.

Wind rumbled and rain spattered against the window as shrubbery just outside was violently whipped about. It was as dark as dusk at a few minutes after two in the afternoon.

She reached down into her purse by her feet and removed a cigarette, lit it, and blew smoke loudly. Another bad habit she'd resumed since coming to Springmeier.

Fara had been recommended for the job by Dr. Delia Urbanski, one of her former professors at Stanford. It did not sound appealing at first—in fact, she had to stifle a mocking laugh when Professor Urbanski described the project to her—but it came along at a time when she was looking for any escape.

After finally ending a long, bad relationship in Tucson, where she'd had a tedious job at a small pharmaceutical company, Fara moved back home to northern California and got a job in San Francisco as a hospital microbiologist specializing in infectious diseases. She knew that, in that position, she would be spending more time with patients than in the lab and she thought it might be good for her to do something outside her comfort zone. She enjoyed the work itself and, for a while, thought she'd made the right choice.

It crept up on her. She was able to dismiss it at first, tell herself it was simply part of the landscape, an unavoidable consequence of providing health care to the masses. Looking back on it, she realized she'd pushed the subject out of her mind often the first eight or nine months, not wanting to acknowledge it to herself so she wouldn't have to deal with it. But it crept up on her.

The patients were powerless numbered assignments given to nurses and staff. They were poked, prodded, and drugged by people who saw them as nothing more than work. Day after day, Fara heard the nurses talk about their patients as if they were lab rats or something growing in a petri dish. Week after week, she saw people who existed as nothing more than numbers with diseases.

Fara recognized that this was a ridiculous way of looking at a hospital—how else were nurses supposed to deal with so many patients? Most hospitals were understaffed and most nurses were overloaded with work, but even when that wasn't the case, this was how hospitals worked. She understood that. To think otherwise was unrealistic and maudlin, but there it was, in her head, persisting. Underneath it was the fear that she would come to do the same thing.

All of that was made even worse by the thing that Fara knew dominated and virtually ran every hospital—politics, which did not even take the patients into consideration. From the inside, everything felt so cold, impersonal, and businesslike. And ultimately, that's what it was, what it had to be. It *was*, after all, a business.

But those thoughts persisted, and before she knew it, they had become feelings and she had slipped into a depression that clutched at her quietly, trying to drag her down and hold her back.

When Dr. Urbanski called, Fara was thrilled to have an alternative. It was the kind of job she never thought she would consider taking, but Dr. Urbanski's arguments were compelling.

"This would be fantastic experience for you, Fara. It would look good on your CV, you would learn a great deal, and how many opportunities do you think you'll get to work with Corcoran?"

"I thought you said Corcoran was crazy."

"I did, and he is. Most people would call him eccentric because of his notoriety, but I know him, and I say crazy. He's a bundle of quirks, and that was fifteen years ago. By now, he's probably bouncing off the walls. But most brilliant people aren't wired like everybody else. Look at you."

"*Me*?"

"Drop the false modesty, Fara. You're a brilliant woman, one of my best students, and if you had some ambition to go with your intelligence, you'd be rich by now. Think about it. How well do you fit in with average people? Do they see you as . . . odd? Does casual conversation with them come easily to you? How did you get along with people at the last, say, wedding shower or baby shower you went to?"

"Well, I . . . I've never been to either."

"See? I rest my case. You know what I'm talking about. Jeremy Corcoran is a brilliant man, a genius, great leaps ahead of everyone else in his field. But he's crazy. An utter loon. An emotional mess. Frankly, I'm not sure he *has* emotions. He has a great mind, but it's in the possession of a man whose emotional and psychological development froze somewhere in late middle school. And to maintain access to the great mind, everyone puts up with the spoiled, self-obsessed, hedonistic asshole."

Fara knew the type, but she wasn't sure she wanted to work for one.

"Look, Fara, *you'd* be crazy to turn this down. The connections you'll make alone will be worth it. One job like this can lead to other government work, and that's always a good thing. If you want it, I think I can get it for you. I know a couple of people. But you need to decide soon. And you need to say yes."

Fara was still thinking about Dr. Urbanski when she left her office half an hour later. She turned left and headed down the corridor as Emilio, one of the janitors, wheeled a bucket into a utility closet, mop in hand. He was soft-spoken, a tall, heavy, black man in his mid-thirties with short-cropped hair.

"Hello, Dr. McManus," he said, smiling.

"Hi, Emilio."

"While I'm down here, you want me to do your office?"

"Yes, go ahead. I'll be out for a while. I've got some work to do."

"Anything I can help with?"

"No, I'm doing some work down in the . . . well, with Dr. Corcoran. Go ahead and do the office, Emilio. And thanks."

Her shoes clicked on the tiles as she walked past him and reverberated in the broad, otherwise empty corridor.

Fara knew she should have thought about the job longer when Dr. Urbanski told her about it. She should have asked more questions. Once she knew what the project entailed, she should have asked for certain assurances. But she did none of those things.

And now, she was in the former Springmeier Neuropsychiatric Hospital, making her way down to the basement, where she would engage—and not for the first time—in performing deadly experiments on human subjects against their will.

Most of what Fara was doing there would never show up on her CV. Not even if she survived.

2

The closing music of Ivan Renner's Internet radio show began to play. It was "Tangerine Dream," a cut from the *Miracle Mile* soundtrack album.

"That's it for another Friday edition of Red Pill Radio," he said. "This weekend, everybody here in the Redwood Empire will be hunkering down for the big storm that's set to hit the West Coast tomorrow morning. Normally, we don't get full-blown hurricanes here on the West Coast. We get tropical storms, what's left of the hurricanes, because the water's too warm and the current runs in the wrong direction. Or *some*thing like that, I'm not a meteorologist. But climate change is doing some weird things to our weather and the storm coming in is a good example of that. A lot of people are wondering, though, if HAARP is being used to disrupt our weather. Is it possible it's being used to control *us* by controlling our weather? We'll be doing a show about HAARP next week. And we'll have a guest who's written a new book about the US government's history of experimenting on citizens without their knowledge or consent, too, so keep tuning in. If you missed a show, you'll find it in the archives at our website, Red Pill Radio dot com. Until Monday, stay safe and be calm, because we're all in this together."

He wrapped up the show in the small room he used as a studio. It was in what used to be his garage; six years ago, he'd added onto it and converted it, in part, into the small room where he sat for three hours, five days a week, and broadcast to the world via the Internet. The show's audience had grown rapidly in recent years. Ivan was getting more requests for interviews in publications and on other shows with each passing month, and a New York publisher had shown interest in the book he was writing.

The door opened and his assistant Mike Dodge stepped into the studio as Ivan stood and stretched his arms above his head.

"Ollie just called and he's not happy," Mike said.

"When is Ollie ever happy about anything?"

"He says he's coming in to speak with you."

Ivan sighed with more than a little dread. He stepped around Mike and stood in the doorway. The small room, which had a table with Ivan's laptop and a couple of microphones and was only big enough for him and a guest, should he have one, began to feel a bit cramped by the end of the show. "Remind me, Mike—after this storm's over, I need to have a window put in here so it's not so claustrophobic."

"You know, you can do the show from your office if you'd just—"

"I know, I know. I just like the idea of having a separate place for the show, you know? A *studio*. Even though this isn't a *real* studio. But it's the closest I'll ever get to my boyhood fantasy of being a radio DJ." Ivan stepped out of the studio and through the small alcove that opened on a room full of desks. Julie was on the phone, Rudy was busy typing at his keyboard, and the other desk was unoccupied and piled with books and papers. "Ollie didn't say what he wants?"

"No, but he sounds more upset than usual." Mike looked and sounded nervous. That always happened when Ollie showed up. Mike was gay, and Ollie, who was loud and often obnoxious and never hesitated to loudly criticize things he did not approve of, made him jumpy.

"Great. Probably something about the hospital. Ever since I mentioned a possible connection to those missing homeless people, that's all he ever wants to talk about. I don't know what he expects from me. Send him in when he gets here." Ivan went into his office and closed the door.

It was more of a walk-in closet than an office. A desk, two chairs, and a single file cabinet left room for no more than two people, three if comfort wasn't a priority. But unlike the studio, it had a window behind the desk that looked out on Ivan's backyard. It was dark out there and the pyracantha bush outside his window was being whipped around by the wind. The weather was bad, but it wasn't anything too unusual. He knew the storm that would hit in the morning would be a lot worse, and he still needed to get the windows boarded up. Ivan seated himself at his desk with a sigh and mentally prepared himself for a visit from Ollie.

Ollie Monk was something of a local celebrity. He was loud, opinionated, sometimes paranoid, and he'd been kicked out of more than one City Council meeting for angrily disrupting the proceedings. He was a regular listener to Red Pill Radio and often called in to make bombastic comments or argue with guests. He wore a lot of camo and drove around in a black F-150 with two rifles on racks in the back window.

Ivan knew little of Ollie's background other than the fact that he was a veteran of the first Gulf War and he'd inherited a handsome sum from the uncle and aunt who'd raised him. His aunt had invented some kind of powdered adhesive for fabrics—or something like that, Ivan wasn't sure of the details. Ollie had used a lot of that money to buy a little over a hundred acres of wooded land east of nearby Blue Lake, and he'd invested the rest well. The "Monk Compound," as it was often called, was the source of a great deal of speculation.

Protected by fences, walls, security cameras, and men with guns, no one got in who wasn't allowed in.

Most of the local gossip and speculation focused on what everyone referred to as "Monk's Militia" (as far as anyone knew, the group had no official name), made up mostly of capable homeless veterans Ollie had recruited right off the streets in Eureka, Arcata, and McKinleyville, as well as San Francisco, Sacramento, and other cities and towns in northern California. Some were concerned that Ollie had created his own private army and worried about how he might choose to use it.

Ivan was the kind of person who tried to find the good in everyone, and Ollie made that difficult with repugnant views that went beyond politics, which he all too often voiced, views about women and ethnic groups and gay people and most religions other than Christianity ("The Mormons may be fulla Satan and apeshit crazy, but they take care of their own as long as everybody follows the rules!"). But Ivan had managed to discover a real person behind the camo clothes and macho behavior.

Ollie's interest in the homeless went beyond recruiting men for his militia. The only time he was known to keep his opinions to himself and behave like a perfect gentleman was when he volunteered his time at local homeless shelters, which he did regularly. Although his political leanings went quite far to the right, he was unfailingly sympathetic toward the homeless. When it came to them, he did not subscribe to the old pull-yourself-up-by-your-bootstraps attitude that was so prevalent among conservatives.

Ivan did not know the reasons behind Ollie's apparent need to help the homeless, but he was convinced it was genuine and selfless. It clashed with the rest of his personality, but it was enough of a redeeming factor to keep Ivan from simply telling him to go away.

Ivan did not have to be told Ollie had arrived because he

heard his booming voice, even with his office door closed.
He got up and opened the door as Ollie hung his dripping,
dark green raincoat on a coat tree.

"Would you like some coffee, Ollie?" he asked.

"No, thanks."

"Come on into the closet and have a seat."

Ollie was forty-three and stood five feet, seven inches tall,
and was shaped like a bullet. He wore camo pants, and carried
a closed, dark blue umbrella. A black baseball cap with a
small American flag on the front covered his buzz-cut head.
He had a stern face and a loud voice.

"I'm sorry I haven't returned your last couple of calls,"
Ivan said as he went around the desk and sat down. "The last
few days, I've hardly had time to stop and think."

"I came to talk to you one more time about the old hospital," Ollie said.

"What about it?"

Ollie lowered himself slowly into the chair facing the
desk. "Ivan, I just can't shake the feeling that you know more
about what's going on there than you're telling."

"I'm not keeping any secrets, Ollie." But that was a lie. In
the last few months, he'd learned some things about what was
going on in the old Springmeier Neuropsychiatric Hospital,
ever since he'd managed to get a pair of eyes and ears inside
the place. Ivan was afraid to tell Ollie what he'd learned for
fear of what he might do about it.

"The last time we spoke," Ollie said, "we talked about the
possibility that there was a connection between what's going
on in the hospital and the homeless people who've disappeared around here. You even mentioned it on your show."

Ivan nodded. "I mentioned it. As speculation."

"Yeah, because Vendon Labs is involved. At least, that's
what you said."

"That's right. Apparently, the hospital was the kind of facility they needed to do whatever it is they're doing in there."

Ollie cocked a brow and leaned forward slightly as he said, "And you don't know what that is."

Ivan had always been a terrible liar, mostly because he always tried too hard to conceal the fact that he was lying. He cleared his throat, shifted in his chair, and said, "If I knew, I would've talked about it on the show by now."

Ollie's eyes narrowed slightly and he slowly leaned back in the chair. "Yeah, see, I don't believe you. I've got an ear for lying, and I think you're lying."

"Why would I do that?"

Ollie shrugged. "Maybe you're afraid. Or maybe you found out and they bought you off. Or scared you into not talking. I don't even know how you found out about this in the first place, so for all I know, you're *working* for them."

Ivan rolled his eyes. "Come on, Ollie, you're sounding paranoid again."

"Yeah, well, people say I'm paranoid all the time." He smiled. "I figure if that's what they want, that's what I'll give 'em."

"You must not have been listening the day I talked about stumbling onto the activity at the hospital. It was an accident."

"Tell me about it."

"It was a year and a half ago. No, more than that, closer to two years. I was being interviewed by this guy named P.J. Burnett for *Shadow Journal*. Are you familiar with it?"

Ollie shook his head.

"It covers the whole conspiracy spectrum. P.J. was a young guy, early twenties, pudgy, looked like he didn't get out much. But he asked some good, clearheaded questions. First we had breakfast at Cuppa Joe's that morning. I eat breakfast there almost every day. And then I go for a walk, usually through the woods across the street from the diner. I didn't think he'd want to go with me because I take a long brisk walk every day and he didn't look like he could keep up. But he said he wanted to. While we walked, he kept asking questions, even though he was huffing and puffing before long. He recorded it all on his phone."

As they walked through the woods that morning, Ivan heard something odd and stopped walking to listen. Somewhere in the woods, he heard vehicles. He left the trail they'd been following and began walking toward the sound, and P.J. followed. The farther they went, the louder the sounds became: the rumble of vehicles, the unintelligible chatter of voices, the beeping of a truck backing up, the sound of hammering.

P.J. said, "Sounds like some kind of construction to me."

"But what kind of construction would be going on here in the woods?"

As they continued to trudge through ferns, vines, and other shrubbery, Ivan told P.J. about the area.

"There used to be a hospital up ahead. It was the Humboldt County Mental Hospital for ages, long before I was born. When I was a kid, they used to take some of the patients on outings into town, to the beach or the park. I used to see them once in a while, and they always scared me. They were so . . . different. Scary to a little kid who didn't know any better. Some of them would grin and babble. Others walked funny. Like hunchbacks, or something. Some were like great big children. Used to scare the piss out of me. But other than those occasional field trips, the hospital kept a very low profile.

"In the late 1980s, it went private and became the Springmeier Neuropsychiatric Hospital, a pretty exclusive facility for those who could afford it. They stopped the field trips and after that, it was like the hospital didn't even exist anymore. Springmeier finally closed its doors in 2001 and it's been abandoned ever since. They boarded it up to keep people out, but even so, I've heard that homeless people use it for shelter and kids mess around in there a lot. I'll be damned, look at this," Ivan said as they approached a chain-link fence that stood about ten feet high.

Beyond the fence, the ground sloped gently downward. The hospital rose like a blocky grey ogre from the center of a large clearing that had become overgrown with weeds and shrubbery. Spidery vines clung possessively to the walls, and windows with no panes stared like dead, black eyes. To Ivan's right, a cracked and broken parking lot stretched out in front of the hospital, its white lines faded to ghostly streaks.

There were four enormous old oak trees visible from where they stood—two in front of the hospital, one in the rear, and one on the western side, the one closest to them. That one was old and grey and gnarled, split in the center into two fat, twisted trunks.

Workers were busy everywhere, clearing brush and vines, working on the hospital itself. A cement truck stood near a rear corner of the building, its mixer drum turning slowly, and a dump truck carried a load of cleared rubble away from the hospital and down a gravel road that disappeared into the woods behind it.

"P.J. suggested that they might be reopening the hospital," Ivan said to Ollie, leaning forward at his desk. "But that didn't make sense. I drive by the hospital's front gate almost every day, and it's still locked and overgrown with weeds. They cut a new road through the woods *behind* the hospital."

"Yeah, I've seen it."

"You have?"

"Sure. I've been out there. Several times. Been all around it."

"Why?"

Ollie shrugged. "Just lookin'."

"Well, the road in the back is less visible. If they were reopening the hospital, why wouldn't they use the front entrance? Why try to hide it? Besides, if the hospital were reopening, it would be all over the news."

"Did you talk to any of the people working on the place?" Ollie said.

"No, they didn't even notice us. P.J. was going to take some pictures, but he leaned on the fence and it knocked him on his ass. It was electrified. I took him to the hospital and he was okay, but obviously they wanted to keep people out. So I started doing some research."

In 1987, the hospital and the property on which it stood had been purchased from Humboldt County by the Springmeier family. Ivan learned the Springmeier estate still owned it but had leased it to DeCamp Pharmaceuticals, who then rented the facility to Vendon Labs, a wholly owned subsidiary of DeCamp. Vendon was a biochemical company that popped up often in the world of conspiracies because of its history as a government contractor.

Both DeCamp and Vendon had been involved in Project MK-Ultra, a covert US government research operation begun in the early 1950s. The program experimented in the areas of mind control and effective interrogation and torture tactics, and it was carried out at universities, hospitals, prisons, and pharmaceutical companies using drugs, electroconvulsive therapy, sensory deprivation, and physical and sexual abuse, among other techniques. The experiments were performed on mental hospital patients, students, and private citizens, usually without their consent or knowledge, leaving many with permanent mental and physical damage.

Outside of conspiracy buffs, few people were familiar with MK-Ultra, although it had been made public in the 1970s by a US Senate committee investigating illegal activity by the CIA. Due to its connection to MK-Ultra, any mention of Vendon Labs grabbed the attention of the kind of people who were drawn to Ivan's show. People like Ollie Monk.

Ivan said, "All we could get out of Vendon was that they're using the hospital to develop new antibiotics to combat infections that have become resistant to standard antibiotics. They didn't want to talk about it at all, but when they finally did, that's what their PR person told us. And she wouldn't tell us any more. She stopped taking our calls. And *that's* how I found out about it, Ollie. Nothing suspicious."

Ollie nodded once, then thought for a moment, looking around the office. Finally, he turned to Ivan and said, "They started working in there a little over a year ago, right?"

"Longer than that. A year and a half."

"The disappearances have been going on for about nine, ten months, or so. I was the first to notice. I'm the one who brought it to the attention of law enforcement. I know some of the people who've disappeared."

"I know, Ollie. I don't want you to think I'm dismissing it. I'm not. But I don't know what you want from me."

"I want to know everything *you* know."

"You do," Ivan lied.

Ollie stared at him for a long moment, eyes narrowing again. Then he slowly turned his head from side to side. "I don't think so. I think there's something you're not telling me."

"And what do you *think* I'm not telling you?"

"I don't know. That's why I'm here. To see if you'd open up about it before I decide to act."

"Act? What do you mean?"

Ollie stood and slowly paced in the short space behind his chair. "Homeless people don't just up and leave, y'know? They may be homeless, but this is their . . . home. If that makes sense."

"It does."

"Sure, there are drifters, but they're easy to spot. They come, they go. But I know the homeless around here. They might move around the area, y'know, from Eureka to McKinleyville to Arcata, that kinda thing. But they don't just up and leave. Some of the folks I know have been around here for a while. Now a bunch of them are gone. I got two eyewitnesses say they saw a plumber's van picking up a couple of homeless people a little over a week ago, and that's the last time anyone's seen 'em. Minuteman Plumbing. That's what was painted on the side. I've asked around and over the last few months, other people have seen that van on the street, just driving around. There's no Minuteman Plumbing around here. I checked. Doesn't exist."

"Have you told the police? The sheriff?"

"Of course, I have. But try getting them to give a good goddamn about the homeless. If they found out somebody was tryin' to get 'em to disappear, they'd probably give him a fucking grant, or something. They don't care." He stopped, placed both hands on the back of the chair he'd been sitting in, and leaned forward. "But I do. A van with a fake plumbing company painted on the side tells me somebody's up to something. With Vendon Labs working here, it's hard not to make the connection."

"I agree, but that doesn't mean it's true."

"You don't think so?" Ollie removed his phone from his pocket, thumbed a couple of buttons, then handed it to Ivan. "Google Earth. That's a view of the old mental hospital."

Ivan recognized the bird's-eye view of the hospital. In front, the parking lot was empty, but the lot in back had several vehicles parked in it. One of them was a white rectangle. He felt a small chill when he realized what it was.

"It's a white van, Ollie."

"That's right."

"You know how many white vans there are? Everywhere? This proves nothing."

"It's enough for me."

"Have you shown this to the police?"

Ollie nodded. "Sheriff Kaufman. Said he's already been there and talked to them. He said the same thing you did, that they're developing new antibiotics. He believes that story and said he had no reason to think they were experimenting on homeless people. 'Lotsa white vans out there, Ollie,' he said."

"Well, he's right." Ivan handed the phone back to him and

Ollie put it in his pocket. "It doesn't mean anything." He felt his voice quaver a little because he was lying. It meant plenty. "What did you mean when you said you were going to act?"

"I mean if nobody else is gonna do anything about this, we will, and we aren't waiting around any longer."

"We?"

"Me and my men. We all know Vendon Labs doesn't have any qualms about experimenting on people. And homeless people are perfect. Nobody'll miss 'em, right? Wrong."

"You're making assumptions, Ollie, and that's dangerous. You can't just—"

"Look, you sit in your little studio and you *talk* about this stuff. But I'm not a talker."

"Be serious, Ollie. You're the loudest and most prolific talker I know."

"Yeah, okay, I talk a lot, I know. But I'm not a talker, I'm a *doer*. Nobody else is doin' anything about this. We're going to. If you've got something more you want to tell me, Ivan, you'd best do it today, and soon. You've got my number."

He turned and left the office, even though Ivan tried to call him back. Ivan got up and followed him, but Ollie just kept walking, grabbing his raincoat on the way out.

"Oh, shit," Ivan muttered.

"What was that about?" Mike asked.

"I'm not sure, but I don't like the sound of it." Ivan went back into his office and sat down at the desk. If Ollie knew that Ivan had managed to plant someone in that hospital, he'd want to know everything Ivan knew. And Ivan was afraid if Ollie knew everything he knew, he'd do something crazy. Like trying to storm the place with his militia. From what Ivan knew, that could be very dangerous, not only for Ollie and his men, but for everyone around that hospital.

He decided to call Sheriff Kaufman and reached for the phone on his desk, but his cell phone vibrated in his pocket. When he looked at the phone's screen and saw who was calling, he felt a jarring rush of adrenaline.

3

"How do you feel, Will?"

"Feel?"

"Yes. How do you feel? Right now?"

As he waited for a response, Corcoran glanced at Fara, as if to make sure she was paying attention.

Will was thin and wiry, face creased with premature lines, head and face shaved clean, and he wore only the pale blue hospital gown and slippers provided him. He stood in the tiled chamber they called the Tank, facing the glass through which Fara and Corcoran observed him, but he could see only his reflection. He stood erect, almost defiant, not intimidated or cowed by his strange surroundings or Corcoran's disembodied voice.

"I feel, uh . . . shaky. A little shaky. And, uh, kinda achy."

"Anything else?"

"Well . . . kinda cold." He folded his scrawny arms across his chest.

"Sounds like maybe you've got the flu?"

"Could be, yeah."

"How long have you felt this way?"

"Just started."

"Just now?"

"Few minutes ago, yeah."

Will kept squinting at the reflective glass, as if trying to see if he could make out anyone on the other side.

A moment later, Corcoran said, "And how are you feeling now?"

Will slowly looked around at the tile floor and walls, at the cameras on the ceiling, and the drain in the floor. It looked like a big shower room, but with no showers.

"Same," he said. "Only . . . worse." He hugged himself and his body shuddered as his face tightened into a deep frown.

The door through which Will had come opened and a woman stumbled into the tank.

"Hello, Margaret," Corcoran said.

She was already hugging herself in the flimsy hospital gown and shaking all over. She was scrawny and weathered and looked at least a decade older than her actual age of sixty. Her head was shaved, and she looked more annoyed than frightened.

"How do you feel, Margaret?"

"Not good."

Corcoran checked his watch, leaned over and muttered something to Holly Im, his young assistant, who stood on the opposite side of him from Fara.

Fara could feel the muscles of her shoulders and back tensing, neck stiffening, palms becoming moist. Her insides shifted like a knot of sleeping snakes. She stole a look to her left at Corcoran. He watched Will and Margaret intensely, with anticipation. On the other side of him, Holly jotted notes on a glowing tablet cradled in her left arm. Fara tossed a look over her shoulder to see if anyone had joined them, but they were alone in the basement.

She did not want to be there and had to fight the pressing urge to turn and run out of the room. But she knew Corcoran had more planned that afternoon. He seemed all but unaware of the coming storm. The fact that a hurricane was heading straight for them did not seem to concern him in the least.

Fara tried to look at Corcoran without being too obvious. He held his left forearm across his chest and rested his right elbow on it, his right hand absently stroking his cheek as he watched Will and Margaret. His lower lip was slightly tucked inward along the edge of his upper teeth. He was waiting.

It happened more suddenly than in past tests.

Both of them stood there looking increasingly uncomfortable, and Will began to scrub his palms up and down over his face, then rub his eyes with the heels of his hands, and then he was on her like an animal, making a high, shrill sound that first seemed to be fearful, then became enraged.

Fara's entire body stiffened and she clenched her eyes shut. But she opened them after a moment. She did not *want* to watch, but she felt it was an obligation. This was her handiwork. These people were suffering the effects of something she helped create. It seemed wrong to look away simply because it disturbed her. But it made her stomach churn, her throat tighten. The blunt tips of her nail-chewed fingers pressed into her palms.

Will threw Margaret down on the floor and began to beat her with his fists as she struggled and kicked. Blood spattered the tiles in crimson blossoms and speckles. She screamed hoarsely as he wailed with rage and Fara thought it would be over quickly.

Margaret sat up with a furious shriek and managed to grab Will's arm with both hands and bite into his wrist like an ear of corn. He roared in pain and tried to pull his arm away from her, but her hands and teeth were tenacious. He reared away from her, but she stayed with him and did not let go. Blood bubbled up around her lips and streamed down her battered face, her eyes impossibly wide. Will ended up on his back with Margaret straddling him, her sharp knees jutting up on both sides as she clawed and punched, then leaned forward with her bloody mouth open. She was about to bite his face when Will lifted his head and closed his yellow teeth on her left cheek.

Fara pressed her lips tightly together and sucked in a sharp breath through her nose as Will tore a strip of flesh away from Margaret's face, revealing her remaining bloody molars. Margaret released a long, gargling scream.

Fara turned away from the gory struggle, toward Corcoran, and croaked, "I have to go."

His head jerked toward her and frowned. "But we've just started, we've still got more to—"

"Dr. Corcoran, in case you're not aware of it, we're going to be hit by a hurricane in the morning." She intended to speak more forcefully, but her voice was weak because her stomach was so sick and she was so horrified. Once again. Not only by what she'd seen in the Tank, but by what she was doing there. By what she had done and was continuing to do.

"Don't worry, I've got Emilio on that." His attention was torn between Fara and the screaming activity in the Tank.

She turned and headed for the door, saying over her shoulder, "Bullshit. I just saw Emilio. He's mopping floors."

"This is your *job*, Fara," Corcoran said angrily.

I'm ruining his high again, she thought as she left the room and rushed back upstairs, hands trembling, heart hammering in her chest. *And his fun.*

She reached the first floor, but stopped in the stairwell and vomited in a corner.

She had reported Corcoran three times, and the last time, she had included the fact that he was testing on homeless people taken off the street. The first two reports received aloof responses assuring her the complaint would be investigated. The third received no response at all. She took from that the message that any further complaints would only cause problems for her.

Fara had stayed this long only because she was afraid if she left, something disastrous would happen. She no longer cared. She had to get out. The nightmares, when she was able to sleep, were already bad enough, and she knew if she stayed, nightmares would be the least of her concerns.

She leaned on the wall in the stairwell for a moment to catch her breath and calm herself. Then she headed down the corridor, still taking slow, deep breaths.

The hospital was big, but Corcoran's entire staff was comparatively small because they weren't utilizing the entire hospital. Such high-ceilinged corridors seemed cavernous with no activity in them. They were drafty—especially with the wind battering the building outside—and those drafts whispered around corners and through open doorways like restless ghosts. Most of the time, Fara felt as if she were all alone in the building. It gave her the creeps.

She passed Emilio's utility closet, which was closed now. The fact that her door was closed meant Emilio had finished cleaning up her office and had moved on. Fara turned the knob, pushed the door open, and gasped as she stepped inside.

Emilio stood at her desk, hunched over her computer, with a cell phone held to his left ear, speaking into it quietly. He lifted his head but did not straighten up.

Their eyes locked and stared for a long stretch of time, and the wind and rain battered against the window.

4

"Authorities are advising everyone in the state's coastal areas to stay home unless absolutely necessary," said the steady, professional-sounding woman on the radio. "While Hurricane Quentin is not expected to make landfall until tomorrow morning, driving conditions are bad throughout most of northern California right now, and they get worse as you near the coast. A massive pileup has closed the westbound lanes of I-80 near Fairfield, and more closures are expected as conditions worsen."

As Latrice Innes drove north on 101 toward Humboldt County and her destination in Eureka, she began to wonder if she'd made a terrible mistake. After leaving work early, she'd figured she could make the drive to Eureka and be home by eight that night. If Leland was right and all she had to do was drop the package off, collect her payment and leave, she'd thought that, even in the rain, she could get home before the weather became dangerous.

Now she wasn't so sure.

She hoped Leland was right. He *had* to be right. She needed the money he'd promised. She had a scared, sick little boy at home and didn't know what was wrong with him.

More tests were needed, tests that would cost more money than she had. She tried not to think about it because it always sent her into a chest-tightening panic and she couldn't afford that right now, not on the road in this weather.

The powerful wind buffeted her Toyota Highlander and the windshield wipers weren't doing a very good job of keeping up with the pouring rain. During the entire drive so far, the woman on the news station had been telling people to stay indoors and stay off the roads. And it was too late for Latrice to take her advice.

Her phone began to play "Hangin' Tough" by New Kids on the Block. People laughed at Latrice's ringtone and her affection for New Kids. But it was *genuine* affection. Their music had loomed large in her youth and she'd become emotionally attached to it. She knew a lot of people who had Bruce Springsteen ringtones, but did she tell them she thought he sounded like a gorilla having a stroke and accuse them of having bad taste? No, she ignored it and moved on like an adult. She wished they would show her the same courtesy. One of these days, someone would make a crack about New Kids and her musical tastes and she would give in to the temptation to tell that person to kiss her taint.

The call was coming from her mother's house. For a moment, her blood chilled. She feared the call was about Robert. He'd gotten worse, maybe. She thumbed the button on the phone in its dash mount and said, "Hello!" She had to shout to be heard above the din of the rain.

"Mom?" It was Tamara, her oldest. "Robert is being mean to me and Grandma won't make him stop."

"Sorry, honey, but I'm driving in a storm. Tell Robby if he doesn't stop doing what he's doing, he'll lose Internet privileges for a week. Put Grandma on."

"Grandma's on the other phone."

"How's Robert? Is he okay?"

"He's okay, he's just being *mean*."

"How's his leg?"

"He says it's tingly and it shakes sometimes. The same."

"Well, if there's no emergency, honey, I've got to go."

"When are you coming home?"

"I'll be back tonight, unless I'm in a terrible car crash because I'm being distracted by the phone."

"'Bye, Mom."

"Love you, honey!"

She looked down at the package in the passenger seat. It was a cardboard box wrapped in brown paper and taped up well. It was about the size of an old VCR, the kind her parents had when she was a kid, but not nearly as heavy. Latrice didn't know what was in it, but she knew it was illegal. The only reason she was driving it from Sacramento was that she desperately needed the money she would be paid upon delivery.

The dark sky flashed with lightning. She felt the rumble of thunder as well as heard it. The Highlander vibrated with its force.

Latrice took in a deep breath, clutched the steering wheel tightly in her fists, and kept driving.

5

"Gotta go," Emilio said, then put the phone in his pocket and stood up straight without taking his eyes from Fara.

"What are you doing?" Fara said, speaking deliberately and with quiet anger.

Emilio stared at her, his mouth open, as if frozen in place, like a giant child caught doing something wrong.

"I'm not going to ask the question again."

"Are you going to call Dr. Corcoran?" he said nervously.

"Are you going to answer my question?"

"I'm here because . . . well, I thought you'd be gone longer."

"What are you *doing*?"

"That's a longer answer."

According to protocol, she was to alert security and Corcoran immediately. But it was Emilio, the only person there with whom she'd had any friendly interaction. She'd felt comfortable around him because he was a funny, amiable man and she knew he was not involved in the work they were doing there for Vendon Labs and the government. But he obviously was involved in *something*.

"Who are you working for, Emilio?" she said.

"That's . . . part of the long answer. I'm not here for any, uh . . . un-American reasons."

"Un-American?" She chuckled without smiling. Everything they were doing there was un-American. She used to think so, anyway. Now she wasn't sure. She was starting to think it might be very American. "You mean a foreign government?"

"Yeah. Nothing like that. Look, a lot of people are pretty suspicious about what you're doing here. I probably don't have to tell you that. I've been here long enough to know you don't want to be here, Dr. McManus. I know you don't like what's going on here. Neither do I, and I'm not even sure exactly what it is yet. And neither will a lot of other people."

She nodded once. "You work for that local guy with the paranoid Internet radio show? What's his name? Renner? He's talked about this place a few times."

He stared at her silently.

Fara knew she should have security on the way by now and be on the phone with Corcoran, telling him to get his ass upstairs. But she didn't move from where she stood just inside the door. Instead, she continued to stare at Emilio as she thought about what he'd said.

Before either of them could speak again, Fara heard movement behind her and spun around as Corcoran stepped into the open doorway.

"Fara, I'm going to have to insist that you come back downstairs with me until we're finished," he said, trying to sound firm and authoritative. It did not come naturally to him.

Fara turned to Emilio. "Dr. Corcoran says he gave you the job of preparing for the storm," she said. "Is that true?"

Emilio frowned as he looked back and forth between them. "Prepare for the storm?"

"I think we're safe, Fara," Corcoran said. "This hospital is a fortress. Even after being abandoned for a decade, this place is solid as a rock."

"Dr. Corcoran, *nothing* around here has been 'solid' the whole time I've been here."

Corcoran licked his lips. His mouth was dry. He set his jaw and raised his voice slightly as he said, "Unless you want to lose this job and seriously damage the future of your career, you should come with me so we can get back to work."

"Emilio and I are going to do what we can to prepare for this hurricane, Dr. Corcoran."

Corcoran turned to Emilio. "I *told* you to bring in all the garbage cans and—"

"Emilio, we have this afternoon to board up windows, make sure our generator is in working order, and see that we have everything we need here before the storm hits." Fara turned to Corcoran. "I'm afraid you'll have to work without me today, Dr. Corcoran. Oh, and you have a party to attend tonight, don't you? Have fun. Now, if you'll excuse us, we have work to do."

Corcoran's nostrils flared as he gave her a long, fiery glare. Then he turned around and left the office.

Fara closed her eyes long enough to take in a deep, steadying breath and let it out slowly. Then she turned to Emilio again and looked at him silently for a moment.

He said, "You're not . . . turning me in? Throwing me out?"

She did not answer his questions. "I was serious about getting some work done around here. We've got a hurricane to prepare for and if we don't do it, it won't get done."

6

"Shit," Ivan said when his connection with Emilio was severed. He hung up the phone and sat back in his squeaky chair, hands locked together behind his head.

There were two quick knocks at his door and Mike Dodge walked in. Ivan nodded at the door and Mike closed it, then sat down in front of the desk.

"I was just talking to Emilio," Ivan said. "He hung up. Abruptly. I think someone walked in on him while he was snooping around in a computer."

"Oh, damn." Mike leaned forward in his chair. "You gonna call him back?"

"No. Not yet. I'll give him a chance to call again. I wasn't able to tell him about Ollie before he hung up."

Mike's face darkened as he leaned back again. "What about Ollie?"

Ivan told him what Ollie had said during his visit earlier. Mike's eyes slowly widened as he listened. "I think he's planning something. I'm afraid he intends to do something at the hospital."

"He'll probably get himself killed," Mike said. "Is he that stupid?"

"He's not stupid. But he's extremely misguided." Ivan reached for the phone. "I'm going to call Sheriff Kaufman. I think he'd love an excuse to put his foot down with Ollie. I was going to tell everyone to go home early today, but . . . well, stick around a little longer."

Mike got up and said, "I'm not going anywhere until Emilio calls back."

He left the office and Ivan called the sheriff.

7

After leaving Ivan's office, Ollie drove a truckload of cots over to the Old Town Rescue Mission. Earlier, he'd delivered a load of folding chairs. They would be overrun with people taking shelter from Hurricane Quentin and would need all the help they could get. In spite of any evacuation attempts by the authorities, the homeless would hide away in their secret places until the weather got so bad that they needed some protection, and then they would converge on the shelters.

Now he was on his way back to the compound, driving through pouring rain and buffeting winds. He would have preferred to make the rounds to all the local homeless shelters—two in Eureka, one in Arcata—but he had more important things to do.

It wasn't often that Ollie considered anything more important than helping at the shelters. Nearly everything he did was, in some way, connected to helping the homeless. But he didn't think of it as charity, and he didn't expect any praise. In fact, whenever someone commended him on his efforts for the homeless, he replied, "Thanks, but I'm not doing anything special here. I'm doing what we *all* should be doing. So why the hell aren't *you* doing it?" But this was more important than usual

Oncc hc arrived at the compound, he went to his quarters, cleaned up and changed his clothes. Then he made a call and ordered all the men to gather at the mess hall for an urgent meeting. He got in his pickup and drove over there, running the plan through his head again and again.

Because Ollie was an outspoken conservative on most issues, people expected him to complain about the homeless and call them bums and deadbeats. They expected him to say the homeless should get jobs and quit expecting a free lunch. But he didn't say or think any of those things.

Ollie's father had not been a bum or a deadbeat. He had not been a lazy man. He'd fought for his country in the Vietnam War and had forfeited his life doing it. He didn't die in the war, but it killed him. He came home in one piece, but he was never the same. That's what everyone had told Ollie, anyway. He'd been a baby when Dad went to war. But he saw firsthand what it had done to him. It made it impossible for him to relax, to feel joy, to express love. It left him with a constant, throbbing anger just below the surface, always ready to explode.

Ollie remembered nights when he woke to the sound of Dad screaming in the other bedroom, followed by Mom's gentle voice and his sobs. He remembered the days when Dad's anger would explode and he would break things, shout and roar. Dad usually left the house when that happened to keep from taking it out on them. But there had been a few times when he didn't leave soon enough. Sometimes, Ollie still had nightmares about those times, though not as often or as vividly as he used to.

Dad had tried to fight those problems by drinking, but that only made him worse, of course. He'd left them when Ollie was eleven years old. He just disappeared. At first, Ollie had been glad. He'd come to hate and fear Dad by then. But Mom would not allow him to speak a word against his father in her presence.

"He's broken," she'd told him. "He was different before the war, I've told you that. He was kind and funny and he didn't even raise his voice back then. But the war broke his mind. He had to do and see all kinds of horrible things. Ever since he got back, he's been trying to learn how to live with those things. But he can't. Because those things broke his mind."

It took a couple of years for that to begin to sink in. Watching some documentaries about the Vietnam War on TV helped. What he saw in those movies gave him nightmares, but Dad had experienced it up close; he'd been *in* it. He'd lived it. The older Ollie got, the more he understood Dad's behavior, the less he hated him, and the more he pitied him. And even missed him.

A year after Dad disappeared, Mom got sick. Lung cancer. She got worse fast and Ollie went to live with Aunt Joan and Uncle Edward in Tiburon, a suburb of San Francisco. Aunt Joan was Mom's sister, and she took him to visit Mom often. With each visit, she looked thinner, paler, sicker, and there seemed to be less of her personality left, too.

During one of those visits, Mom told him that she had tried to keep track of Dad. Last she knew, he was living on the street in San Francisco, homeless and drunk, possibly addicted to drugs, as well.

"I want you to always remember," she told him that day, "that he loved you once and was so proud of you. Before he was broken. If you can, try to keep track of him. And if he'll let you, try to take care of him a little."

He'd been clinging to the hope that Mom would get better, but when she said that, he knew she was going to die.

Aunt Joan and Uncle Ed had no children of their own and they welcomed him into their lives warmly. They had a much larger, nicer house and lived in a much better neighborhood because they had a lot of money. Even so, it never quite felt like home to Ollie, even in the years after Mom died.

After he graduated from high school, Ollie went to San Francisco to find Dad. It didn't take long. He looked a lot like Mom had before she died, only older and greyer and with fewer teeth. He didn't recognize Ollie at first, but once he did, he quickly displayed a variety of emotions. First, he got up from the sidewalk and stood in front of Ollie bouncing like a little boy on Christmas morning. He hugged him and cried through his smile, thrilled to see his son. But that stopped abruptly and was replaced by horrible shame and sadness and an inability to look at Ollie. That finally passed as he became calm and asked about Ollie and his mother in a tone that was more like himself, almost familiar to Ollie. When he learned his wife had died, he collapsed sobbing to the sidewalk.

Ollie tried his best to care for Dad. He got him a room and some clothes and tried to get Dad to settle down and make a home for himself. He wouldn't do that. He stayed for a week and then disappeared. His broken mind had been so eaten away by drugs and booze that he couldn't even pretend to function in a conventional way. He could not take care of himself, but he could not let anyone else take care of him, either.

The last time Ollie had seen his father, he was running down Eddy Street screaming his head off, flailing his arms. Ollie returned to San Francisco several times to search for him and finally found someone who knew him. Ada, who ran a halfway house, told him Dad had shown up a few times over the years, but never stayed long. The last time he'd shown up, he'd died in his sleep on a porch swing.

Ollie had been devoting his time and energy and most of his resources to helping the homeless ever since. Jesus said to take care of the poor, and these, Ollie decided, were exactly the people he was talking about. He focused on homeless veterans because they were twice fucked. They were homeless and penniless, *and* they were veterans of wars that had broken them for a country that kept trying to come up with ways to do less and less for them in return. Ollie didn't care if they were men or women, what color their skin was, whether they were liberals or hebes or fags or atheists or feminists. If they were homeless and they were veterans, they were his helpless brothers and sisters. They were his helpless father. He would do everything he could for them.

That was why he'd called the men to gather in the mess. They were going ahead with Operation Vendonectomy, and they were doing it that night.

With the weather so bad, the cops were going to be busy, and everyone else would be huddling at home to wait out the hurricane, unless they lived in an area that had been evacuated, in which case, they weren't going to give a good goddamn about a dark old hospital in the woods because they had enough problems. There would be heavy duty security, of course, but they were prepared for that. They had been planning this for months and they were prepared for everything.

The government and military could experiment on all the soldiers and citizens they wanted to, just like they could do anything *else* they wanted and there wasn't a goddamned thing Oliver Bradley Monk, Jr., or anybody else could do about it. He knew, he wasn't that naive. He'd almost come to peace with the fact that his government wasn't his government anymore—it was in business for itself and he and everybody else were just useful meat. As long as he was left the hell alone, he could come to live with that. It sucked, it spelled the end, every bit of it was biblical retribution that people managed to bring on themselves, but he wasn't going to succumb to the demons of his father, let the weight of all of it crush his mind. He'd chosen to enlist and go to the Gulf so he could see and live what his father had seen and lived, what had broken him and so many others, and tell it to go fuck itself. He had no qualms about telling everybody else the same thing, including the government, and going his own way. But when they came into his town and set up shop and started kidnapping homeless people so they'd have somebody to torture . . .

Well, that was a different fucking story altogether.

On the hardwood floor of the mess, the men's footsteps were a low rumble that gradually decreased until there was utter silence. They stood between and around the long tables. A tall, slender, pot-bellied man leaned against the buffet wearing a white apron and chef's hat, arms crossed over his narrow chest, his long, silver hair in a net below the cap. He had bushy black eyebrows and eyes set deep in his craggy face.

"We're going through with our plans this evening," Ollie said. "We've been going over and over this for months, and we're going to do it exactly as we've planned. It's after three right now, which means we're going to have to get moving. Team One, the tree."

There was a good-sized tree on the western side of the hospital that was going to fall on the fence, which would short out the current flowing through it and render it harmless.

"Team Two, the eastern fence."

That would allow his men to scale the fence on the other side of the hospital without getting shocked on their asses like the guy who'd interviewed Ivan Renner. Ollie would lead Team Two.

"Team Three, the tunnel. And we've got Ricky Jessom to thank for that," he added, turning and gesturing toward the man in the apron leaning against the buffet.

Ricky was a recruit, but he was seventy and would not be participating in Operation Vendonectomy. He was, however, an experienced cook who'd worked in restaurants, diners, bars, and hospital and school cafeterias, so Ollie had put him in charge of the kitchen a few years ago. He had worked in the kitchen of the Humboldt County Mental Hospital for most of the 1970s and he'd become quite familiar with the place.

During his time there, he'd learned about an underground tunnel that went from the hospital to the old boiler house behind it. Back in the old days, the management didn't like to upset or offend those visiting family members in the hospital. The tunnel had been designed to conceal any patients brought to the hospital during visiting hours whose behavior might be disturbing to the visitors. One of the hospital's janitors—a crotchety old black man named Merian who'd been there forever and simply hadn't gotten around to retiring—had told Ricky about it one evening when they went outside and walked a good distance away from the hospital to smoke a joint on their lunch break. He'd taken Ricky into the old boiler house and shown him the rickety stairs that led down into the tunnel. It had been a mess, but it was still there, and it ended in a rear section of the hospital basement that was never used anymore, not even for storage. The tunnel did not appear in the hospital's floor plan or blueprints, and when Ricky learned of it in 1972, he and Merian were the only people at the hospital who knew about it, as far as he could determine. Ricky had made a point of asking around, but nobody was aware of any underground tunnels, and he hadn't told them about it.

The old boiler house was outside the electrified fence that now surrounded the hospital and late one rainy night six months ago, Ricky had taken Ollie down into the tunnel. It wasn't safe, but it was worth the risk to get into the hospital before anyone even knew they were there.

There was a moment of raucous applause for Ricky and he took an exaggerated bow.

"I think I've outfitted you pretty good," Ollie said when it was quiet again. "Those of you going inside have your Batman utility belts. A knife, small bolt cutters, your cell phone, all that other stuff. You've got night-vision goggles, your weapons, your training, including the ability to improvise, which is going to come in handy, I'm sure. No radio communication because we want stealth, silence, no talking back and forth. You know the drill by now, so you know your jobs when you get in there. And don't forget to use your cameras. That's important. Get video of everything you can, especially the people. Remember why we're there and who we're looking for. If we find them, we get them out through the tunnel and into the vans behind the boiler house. Everybody else there is . . . just in the way."

8

In the Cuppa Joe diner, Andy Rodriguez reversed the sign on the door so CLOSED was facing outward. May was at the register tallying up the drawer. The dull, grey light coming in from outside was gradually disappearing as Grady and Norman boarded up the windows. The hammering wrestled with the sounds of the wind and rain and filled the empty diner with noise.

Andy wandered around straightening chairs and absently wiping off a table here and there with a towel. May stood at the register with her head down, counting money, but her eyes kept peering at him through a few stray strands of her brown hair.

"What's going on with you, Andy?" she said.

"What?" He hadn't understood her through all the noise. He turned and walked to the register.

"What's wrong? You're . . . nervous. You're making *me* nervous."

"Yeah, I guess I'm worried about the storm."

"Is everything okay, though? I mean . . . everything with you. How about Donny? How's he doing? I haven't seen him in here for a while."

"No, he's been, uh . . . with his mother."

Thinking about Donny made Andy's stomach knot up, but before he could change the subject, May said, "What about that sheriff's deputy?"

"Who? You mean Ram?"

"Yeah, you had him in here last week, ate with him, bought him lunch. I didn't think you liked him. Didn't you say he was a big bully back in school?"

Andy chuckled. "Yeah, he was. And I didn't like him. I was terrified of him. But he's changed. He's got kids of his own now. That makes you see things a little differently, I guess."

"You sure you're okay?"

He looked at her and tried to push a gentle smile onto his face. "I'm fine. I've just been—"

His phone vibrated in his pocket. He took it out and checked the screen. Ram was calling.

"I'll be back in a minute," Andy said as he hurried around the coffee counter and pushed through the door into the kitchen. He put the phone to his ear and said, "Yeah."

"Tonight's the night," Ram said.

"Okay. Tonight's the night . . . we do what?"

"I told you I'd think about the problem and come up with something. Well, I have. And we do it tonight. Everybody's distracted by this storm, getting ready for the hurricane in the morning. It'll be the perfect cover. When you get off work, go home and wait for my call. Sound good?"

"Uh, sure. Sounds good."

Andy couldn't believe he was having this conversation with the guy who'd caused him so much misery during his school years, the guy he'd hated so intensely for so long, the very sight of whom used to make Andy sick to his stomach. He also couldn't believe he was agreeing to do it. Although Ram wouldn't tell him how he planned to change Jodi's mind,

Andy had a pretty good idea, and he hoped it didn't end badly. But he remained focused on Donny's safety. That was all that mattered.

Andy said, "Just tell me when to be ready. And I'll be ready."

9

The old hospital stood oblivious to the wind and rain that continued to assault it. The front half of the building was dark and invisible in the black, stormy night. The Vendon Labs team occupied the rear half of the hospital, and in back, bright lights illuminated the gravel parking lot and part of the new road that had been cut through the woods. The road passed through the gate by the small guardhouse where security guards gave authorized personnel entry to the grounds within the fence, and on past the old boiler house and the woods. There was no movement or activity back there, just several parked cars.

There was movement, however, at the western fence. A small group of men were helping a tree to fall. The ground around it was already wet and soft after many days of continuous rain. Ollie had spent a day searching for just the right tree to suit their purpose. Now they shoved the tree with the front bumper of a Cadillac Escalade.

When the tree fell, it took down the fence.

A short time later, there was movement on the eastern side of the hospital. Dark figures materialized out of the night and scrambled over the fence, then gathered together on the inside.

A figure made three sharp gestures with his right arm and four men wearing night-vision goggles hurried through the rain to the oak trees within the fence and climbed the trunks. More arm gestures sent the rest of the men fanning out in both directions around the building.

The downpour and raging wind covered whatever sounds they made, and they quickly disappeared in the darkness, leaving the night undisturbed.

A full three minutes passed before the first crack of gunfire sounded. It was not the last.

10

The old Springmeier Neuropsychiatric Hospital was as prepared as it ever would be for a hurricane, and Fara was ready to go home and hunker down. For the duration of her stay in Humboldt County, she'd rented a lovely little cottage in McKinleyville, where she would much rather be. McKinleyville though was under an evacuation order, like every other town along the coast. A crescent-shaped slice of the western end of Eureka was ordered to evacuate, the part closest to the bay, while the rest of the city was not. But it was strongly urged by officials. The hospital was located at the eastern edge of Eureka in an area known as Batten, and nobody in it was going anywhere for the weekend because it was probably one of the safest places to be.

Fara was of the opinion that Dr. Corcoran was crazier than a shithouse rat, but he was right about one thing: the old hospital *was* a fortress. It was built over a century ago and had been built to last by people who knew what they were doing. Back in a time, apparently, when there *were* people who knew what they were doing. It had an enormous basement and sub-basement. The place was like something out of those Edgar Allan Poe movies directed by Roger Corman. Driving toward it on a foggy morning would give chills to the most diehard skeptic. If this place were in a movie, Fara would be cast opposite Vincent Price as Dr. Corcoran.

Normally a thought like that would make her smile, but she hadn't smiled all day and saw no reason to start out in the evening. Besides, she had no reason to smile because she was about to do something that could—no, it *would* get her into a lot of trouble.

The security was top-of-the-line. It was a government-funded operation, which was obvious, but that funding came mostly through CIA front companies. Officially, this was not a government project and had no connection to the government or military whatsoever. Having military personnel around would make that claim pretty unbelievable and draw as much suspicion as attention. Fara knew nothing about the security team protecting the hospital except that it was not a typical security team. They were like ghosts.

As far as the storm went, the hospital was probably the safest place to be. But it wasn't safe at all. Aside from the fact that Corcoran, who was a disaster waiting to happen, was overseeing a potentially deadly project even though he did not display any of the necessary qualities—like leadership, integrity, good judgment, sobriety, a conscience—it was unsafe for Fara because of what she was about to do.

Her office window had been boarded up, but wind and rain battered it like an angry mob. The darkness had deepened as night fell.

When Emilio came into her office, she closed and locked the door. She told him to have a seat in the chair facing her desk, then went around the desk and sat, as well.

"Well, Emilio, was I right?"

"I'm sorry?"

"You work for Renner, don't you?"

He nodded.

"And you're trying to expose the project, aren't you?"

He blinked several times, surprised that she was getting down to business immediately. "If there's something to expose."

"Have you found anything that you feel should be exposed?"

Emilio chuckled. "You kidding?"

"The problem is, nobody will believe you."

"Plenty will believe me."

"Your boss's listening audience? What good would that do? I'm guessing most of them are already considered paranoid nut jobs by those who know them because they believe aliens built the pyramids, or the moon landing was faked, or something. Am I right?"

"Some. But not as many as you think. Ivan Renner's not like the other conspiracy guys. He tries to appeal to practical, commonsense folks. He doesn't go along with the alien stuff, or all that Satanic Illuminati crap. He has a slightly different audience than Alex Jones, or even *Coast to Coast AM*. He appeals to the people who don't believe in any of that sci-fi supernatural stuff, but who think something's going on that they don't know about, something under the surface of . . . just about everything. And he's getting real popular. If he breaks this story, more reasonable people will believe him than any other conspiracy guy. More than you probably think."

"Especially if you've got someone from this project corroborating your story."

"You? You're sure about this? It'll cause a world of trouble for you."

"I can't live with it anymore. I can't live with *myself* anymore. But I want to do it right away. Now. Can your phone do video?"

"Sure," he said, removing his phone from his pocket.

"I'll give you all the information you need. When I'm done, I want you to send it to your boss right away. Then get out of here."

Emilio held up his phone and centered her on the screen. "Go ahead," he said.

"I'm Dr. Fara McManus, a microbiologist currently employed by Vendon Labs here at the former Springmeier Neuropsychiatric Hospital in Eureka, California. I am going to tell you the truth about the work that's being done here."

Emilio was so excited, it was difficult to hold his hand still as he recorded the video with his phone. Ivan was going to fall over when this showed up on his phone. *If* Dr. McManus was honest and gave them something juicy.

"We are not developing new antibiotics here," Fara said to Emilio's phone. "We have been creating a virus that will be used for military application. A bioweapon. I can provide no documentation to support that claim because none exists. We have not been told by anyone in charge that this virus will be used as a weapon, but it's very obvious to anyone here who's privy to the details of the project and is capable of critical thought."

Holy shit, Emilio thought. He wondered if this would break outside the conspiracy bubble, or if the fact that it came from a conspiracy guy with an Internet radio show would make everyone turn a deaf ear and a blind eye, as Fara had suggested. No, he had a feeling this was going to get some mainstream attention.

"Worst of all," Dr. McManus said, then stopped, took a deep breath, and let it out slowly. "We have been testing the virus on human subjects. This was not part of the original plan. It was the brainchild of the man in charge of this project, Dr. Jeremy Corcoran, who claims to have done this before and who—"

Fara stopped talking when a series of sounds outside cut through the noise of the storm. Four popping sounds. *Pop . . .*

pop-pop-pop. Frowning, she cocked her head and listened for more.

"Did you hear that?" she said.

Emilio had been tense with shock ever since she'd said they were working on human subjects—*It's MK-Ultra all over again*, he thought—and sent a splash of ice-cold water over his lungs. Now he snapped out of it with a jerk of his head. "What?"

"That popping sound outside."

"Nuh-no, I didn't."

"It sounded like gunfire."

"You serious?" He listened closely, but heard nothing but the wind.

Emilio's whole body jerked when he heard an explosive sound somewhere in the hospital. It sounded like it came from the corridor outside the office, but some distance away. And it sounded like a gunshot.

Their eyes locked and Emilio said quietly, "The hell was that?"

Emilio slipped the phone back in his pocket and went to the door.

Fara's hands clutched the plastic armrests of her chair as she watched Emilio go to the door.

Someone, a man, shouted, and his voice echoed down the corridor.

Another gunshot.

Fara shuddered with an overwhelming feeling of dread, and she sucked in a breath to tell Emilio to stop as he opened the door and stepped outside.

A male voice in the corridor shouted, "On the floor! Now! On the floor!"

Emilio tossed her a frightened glance, then dropped face-down to the floor, lay flat, and spread his arms out at his sides.

Fara shot to her feet with a quiet gasp.

The intruder was tall and lean and wore dark clothes and a black ski mask over his head. He raised his right arm and aimed the Ruger SR40 in his hand at her face.

"Who are you?" he said.

Fara grew dizzy and swayed a bit before catching herself. Her head was swirling with thoughts. Who was this man? Some kind of activist? A terrorist? The shock of the situation had made her world stop revolving for a moment, but now it continued in the opposite direction. Suddenly, nothing seemed quite real.

"Who *are* you?" he said again.

"I-I'm Dr. Fara McManus."

"Are you in charge here?"

"Yes. *No*. I mean I-I-I—no, I'm not in charge, no."

"Who is?"

Before she could reply, another voice spoke in the corridor and drew Fara's eye to the open door.

"Emilio? Is that you?"

The man holding the gun on her shifted his position so he could see the door without taking his attention from her.

Emilio lifted his head from the floor and looked up at someone standing just out of sight.

"What the hell are *you* doing here, Emilio?"

Emilio said, "I could ask the same of you."

He knows these people? Fara thought, feeling dizzy again.

The man she couldn't see said, "Get up and don't try anything or my men *will* shoot you."

As Emilio got to his feet, the man stepped through the doorway. He was dressed like the first man, but short and stocky. He held a gun at his side in his right hand.

"Dr. Fara McManus," said the man aiming the gun at her. "She's not in charge, but she's in a position of authority."

"Good, thank you," the shorter man said as he walked toward her. "Who *is* in charge?"

She glanced at the gun leveled at her head and said, "That would be Dr. Jeremy Corcoran."

He nodded. "They'll find him."

"They?"

Another nod. "My men. They're all through this hospital right now. Looking for your victims."

"The test subjects?" she said.

He moved so quickly that she felt the slap before she saw it coming. His left palm struck the side of her face so hard that she spun to her left, toward the other man, and fell to the floor.

The man who slapped her said, "Get up."

Never forgetting the two guns in the room, Fara ignored the fiery pain in the right side of her face and scrambled to her feet.

"They're not test subjects," the man said, voice soft and level. "They're human beings. And we're here to get 'em. I suspect my men have probably found them by now."

"You can't," Fara said, timidly and with a cracked voice. Then she lost the timidity and said with urgency, "I'm serious, you *cannot* do that, you'll—"

He used the other hand this time and hit her with the gun.

Fara lost consciousness before she hit the floor.

PART TWO
Hurricane Quentin

11

"Some experts are predicting that Hurricane Quentin will make landfall significantly earlier than we've been told," the woman on the radio said. She still sounded professional and calm and oblivious to the wind slamming into Latrice's Highlander.

"Earlier?" Latrice said, glancing at the radio. "How *much* earlier?"

The drive had taken longer than Latrice had expected because the weather had been worse than she'd expected, which made her wonder what the hell she'd been thinking, anticipating anything less than the worst possible weather with a hurricane on the way. It helped that she knew the route.

When she was nineteen, Latrice had driven that route a few times to visit a guy she was seeing at Humboldt State University. They'd met in Sacramento, where he lived before enrolling at Humboldt. His name was Geoff and he was studying oceanography so he could become the first black Jacques Cousteau, and he was the best sex Latrice had ever had. She couldn't understand why he kept asking her to come back for more, why he was drawn to her. When she looked in the mirror, she did not see the kind of young woman she would expect to be with someone like Geoff. She'd dropped in on him unannounced once and found him in bed with a stunningly beautiful blonde, all legs and tits, creamy tan skin, bright white teeth. Latrice was crestfallen and began, for just a moment, to cry, something she hadn't allowed herself to do since she was a very little girl. But she stopped herself, sucked it up, and turned around to leave.

"Wait, Latrice!" he shouted as he came after her. She slowed her pace a moment when she realized he sounded *happy*. He stepped in front of her, naked and with an erection, grinning like a happy child. "Come join us!" he said.

And Latrice's life had not been the same since. That was when she learned that monogamy wasn't for everybody, that some people were more suited to having multiple partners— sometimes at the same time!—and she learned that she was one of those people. Latrice had little self-confidence in life and her self-image was a work in progress, but when she was in bed with someone, she felt sexy and not only assured but assertive, even brazen. It was the only time she ever felt strong.

Every therapist she'd ever had told her that she was repeatedly trying to win her father's love and approval, that her promiscuity was an attempt to resolve their relationship. There probably was some truth to that, Latrice conceded, but as far as she was concerned, her relationship with her father had been resolved long ago. He'd been a mean, hateful, drunken prick and she'd cut him out of her life like a tumor. Relationship resolved.

She loved her mama, a sweet and selfless woman, but she'd never managed to find it in herself to respect Mama's decision to stay with Dad. Latrice had tried many times to talk her into getting a divorce, but Mama's religious beliefs didn't allow that. Because it wasn't enough that she had a mean, violent drunk in her life; she also needed a bunch of crazy-ass religious rules to live by. The best thing that had ever happened to Latrice's mama was the death of Latrice's dad. But by the time he finally fell over dead in the kitchen while pouring vodka into a little Sunny D at nine-thirty in the morning, he'd already done plenty of damage to his family, especially Latrice, the youngest of their three children.

The verbal abuse had been so relentless and had started so early that she quickly grew accustomed to it as a little girl and stopped reacting or responding. But she didn't stop absorbing. Dad never had anything good to say to or about anyone, but he seemed to store up venom for Latrice, criticizing every-thing she said and did, telling her she was stupid, fat, useless. He hit her a few times, but that didn't stand out in Latrice's memory. The things he said, however, never went away.

She reached the end of her tolerance at the dinner table one evening shortly after her seventeenth birthday. She and Mama were quietly discussing Latrice's future when Dad made a sound like coughing. He was laughing. He'd been staring at his plate as he ate, and now he lifted his head somewhat and aimed his bleary eyes at Latrice over the top of his glasses, which had slipped down his nose.

"Here's why you ain't got no future," he said.

"Clifford," Mama said pleadingly.

He ticked them off on his fingers: "First, you're black. Second, you're female."

"*Clifford*," Mama said scoldingly.

"Shut the fuck up. And next, you're fat. You got no future. Might as well open your wrists right now." He scooped some mashed potatoes into his mouth, chewed noisily, then raised his right hand and wagged it urgently as he gulped the food. "But for Christ's sake, go do it in the tub, or something, okay? We just cleaned the carpets."

"What's this *we*?" Mama said.

"Shut the fuck up." He continued eating, head down, staring at his food.

Something happened inside Latrice at that moment. It made a sound inside her head: *Snap!* Like a great big rubber band that had been stretched too far. Next thing she knew, she was on her feet with a knife greasy from rib meat in her hand, blade jutting from her fist, and in her mind she heard her own voice shouting, *What are you doing? What are you doing? Whatareyoudoing?* She honestly didn't know and her lungs filled with panic, but on the outside, she was perfectly calm and steady, without so much as a tremble as she walked around the table.

Dad raised his head at the sound of movement and his eyes grew large and suddenly alert and he sat up straighter and straighter as Latrice closed in on him, until finally, she stood beside him and towered over him.

"I'm not just fat, Daddy. I'm big. Almost half a fuckin' foot taller than you." It was true. Dad was a squat five feet five. "You might want to remember that, you human mistake." He flinched. "Yeah, that's right. You waste of space. You drunken piece of shit." His eyes began to narrow. "You ever speak to me that way again, I'll take your fuckin' head off and shove it up your ass where it belongs. You understand me?" He glared at her. Latrice bent down, pressing her face toward his, and he nearly fell off his chair trying to back away from her. "Do. You. Understand?"

His eyes were wide again as he nodded.

Latrice walked out of the house and never went back inside for the rest of her father's life. She had her girlfriends Lizzy and Kate pack up her things and bring them to her. Kate still lived with her parents, but Lizzy was a couple of years older and had an apartment. She offered to put Latrice up until she found a job and got on her feet, but after five months of enjoying the hell out of each other, they found a bigger apartment together.

But that was a long time ago, when there was a lot less worry and responsibility in her life. Now she had Tamara and Robert, who made her life better than she'd ever thought possible. But along with them came all the responsibility that caused so much worry. She rarely heard other parents talk about that—the weight of being solely responsible for whole human beings, keeping them safe from the stormy sea of dangerous possibilities that awaited them every day beyond the front door. She supposed they didn't talk about it because, if they were anything like her, they didn't like thinking about it for very long at a time. If she thought about the weight of that responsibility for very long, she started feeling it. It was a lot less stressful to focus on one thing at a time.

That weight was heavy enough when everything was going well, and everything had been going well for them lately— they were broke as hell, but they had the things they needed and they were healthy and still together. Latrice knew plenty of people who were unable to have everything they needed and weren't healthy. A couple of them recently had become homeless and no longer had much of anything beyond the goodwill of their relatives. Everything had been going well for them. Until four months ago.

Robert complained of numbness in his left leg. As it worsened, it became accompanied by weakness and tremors. To Robert, it was an annoyance, but it terrified Latrice. She didn't let him know how much it worried her, though. She made an appointment with their family doctor.

Latrice couldn't afford insurance and she made too much money to qualify for Medi-Cal on her own. Because she was a single parent, her children automatically qualified regardless of her income, but she chose not to apply for it. She was still trying to build a life for herself and her kids after divorce and she didn't want to do that by relying on any kind of assistance unless she absolutely needed it.

She had managed to make sure they all had annual physicals and dental check-ups, including her mother, by going to a community health clinic that charged on a sliding scale according to income. As long as they were healthy, that was enough.

The doctor told her that tests would be needed to determine the cause of Robert's symptoms. It could be a number of things, including multiple sclerosis, muscular dystrophy, a spinal problem—he did not want to speculate until the tests were done and he knew more.

Latrice knew she could not pay for the tests and applied for Medi-Cal immediately. But the process took time. Robert began to have the same symptoms in his left arm, numbness, weakness—"Like I slept on it all night and now it's just starting to wake up again," Robert said.

To apply for Medi-Cal, Latrice had to provide a pile of paperwork within twenty days, but her work schedule made it impossible for her to deliver it in person. She mailed a package of bank statements, pay stubs, copies of her and her children's social security cards, and other forms of ID. All of it would be imaged into the system, and then destroyed. Ten days later, she received a notice from the Department of Health and Human Services that they did not have the material they needed. She called them on her lunch break and explained that she had sent it in. Two days later, she learned that her material had been imaged into the system and destroyed, and then it had disappeared. She would have to resend all of it, which would take more time. Meanwhile, Robert was rapidly getting worse. Then Leland Salt had offered her an opportunity to make five thousand dollars very fast.

Latrice had been doing a lot of temp work lately because full-time jobs had gone the way of four-leaf clovers and virgin brides. The last one she'd had, senior grievance coordinator at an insurance company, had been eliminated in a fit of downsizing. For the last few weeks, she'd been working at Instant Liberty Bail Bonds. She'd been employed there for a week last year and they had been pleased enough with her work to specifically request her this time. A flu virus had ripped through the office, sending half the employees to bed, and Latrice had been doing the work of two, sometimes three people. The boss, a round little bald man named Ed Cooper, had told her twice how impressed he was with her work and had hinted at permanent employment, so Latrice worked even harder.

She'd met Leland the first time she'd worked there. He'd come in twice in one week, but Latrice suspected the second time was to ask her out, which she'd declined. He was still a regular client at Instant Liberty, and he was still trying to get her to go out with him. She'd had lunch with him a couple of times at a Subway across the street, but that wasn't a date because she was still working, just on her lunch break.

Leland was on the high side of fifty, thin, with silver hair neatly combed, parted on the side, thin mustache carefully trimmed. He claimed to have some Native American blood, and it showed in his cheekbones and nose. He always wore a sport coat, slacks, and shiny shoes. But in spite of how presentable he was, he still managed to look like trouble, like he might be up to something.

He'd told her he was a thief by trade but had gotten too old for that kind of work, so now he mostly did odd jobs. Bailing friends out of jail was one of them. Leland managed to manipulate every topic of conversation with Latrice, no matter how obscure, back to his favorite, which was his intention of getting her into bed, always playful and sweet about it, but always blunt, too. And Latrice always declined. She thought Leland was a sweet guy, but she didn't find him attractive, and even if she did, she wouldn't get involved with a former thief who was always bailing his friends out of jail. But she couldn't deny that she enjoyed Leland's attention. She enjoyed his company, too. She'd told him how afraid she was for Robert, that she feared his problem was something serious. He was a good listener and could make her laugh when she didn't feel capable of laughter.

Yesterday morning, he'd come into the office looking rushed and harried. He told her to meet him for lunch at Subway, then left. He was late for the lunch, and when he showed up, he looked weary and distracted.

"I'm gonna have to cut out of here," he said.

"You just got here. Aren't you going to eat?"

"I mean Sacramento. California. Hell, the country."

"Why? What's wrong?"

He shrugged. "There's always *some*thing wrong, I guess. But this is because I took advantage of an opportunity that'll get me killed if I stick around."

"What have you done?"

"One last score, that kinda thing. Unplanned, spur of the moment. I saw an opportunity and jumped on it. Anyhow, I've gotta get out of here today, but I've got a job I committed to doing tomorrow. I won't be able to do it if I leave. I thought you might be interested. It'll make you an easy five grand."

"Are you serious?"

"Yes. All you gotta do is deliver a package to Eureka."

"A package? What kind of package?"

"You know, a cardboard box. That kind."

"I mean, what's *in* it?"

"Yeah, I know what you mean. You don't need to know. Look, it ain't gonna blow up or hurt you in any way, that's all you gotta know. Just take it to the address I'll give you, give it to the guy, and he'll pay you."

"What's he going to do when I show up instead of you?"

"Don't worry. I'll make sure he knows you're coming. I called him a little while ago, but he didn't answer. By the time you get there, he'll be expecting you, not me."

"That's all there is to it?"

"That's it, nothing else."

"And he'll give me five thousand dollars?"

"In cash. You can get those tests going on Robert while

you're waiting for the Medi-Cal people to pull their heads out of their asses."

She nodded. "I'm in."

After work, she'd met Leland in the parking lot of a nearby Denny's and he gave her the package.

"Who'd you steal from, Leland?" she said as they stood between their cars.

"Somebody who will end my story soon as he figures out I'm the one did it. But that might take a few days. I'll be long gone. Don't you worry about me, Latrice, honey. I'm just sorry we never got horizontally acquainted."

Now she was driving slowly down a road flanked by tall redwoods, clutching the steering wheel in tight fists as she steered against the force of the wind. Her windshield wipers were slashing at the rain at top speed and still couldn't keep up with it. Streetlights were rare on this road, but she saw one coming up and considered pulling over near it and then hoping the rain would lighten up a bit.

She sighed, shaking her head. "Hurricane's on the way. The rain's not gonna lighten up, you dummy. Jesus."

The streetlight was in front of a small clapboard building on the right with a sign that read CUPPA JOE'S DINER, which appeared as a brief flash of civilization in the utter blackness all around her. Her headlights didn't reach very far in the storm and she saw nothing else ahead but more road, more darkness.

A few minutes later, the voice of her navigation system told her to take the next right. She had to slow way down to *find* the next right because there was no light or road sign. That turn put her on a narrow dirt road that went through the dark woods. There were lights ahead, but she couldn't tell what they were until she got closer. The road had ruts and potholes, so she drove slowly. She came to several trailers on both sides of the road, tucked away as if hiding. For all she knew, that was what they were doing.

At the end of the road was a two-story redwood house that blended nicely with the rich greens and rusts and browns around it. The porch light was bright, but the windows were boarded up for the storm. There were a couple of SUVs and a pickup truck parked in front of the house and a few other cars parked by the trailers. Latrice parked her Highlander and killed the engine. She got out, leaned in and grabbed the package and her umbrella, then stepped back and closed the door, revealing the barrel of a shotgun which a hooded man was aiming at her face.

"Who are you," he said, "and what do you want?"

12

Andy paced the length of his living room, waiting for Ram. Trees creaked as they were blown by the wind outside and rain was a dull roar. Every now and then, Dickens released a shrill series of barks from the bedroom.

He'd boarded up the windows and cleared the front and backyards of anything that could cause damage while being blown around. His miniature schnauzer, Dickens, hated loud noises, and when there was a storm, he hid under Andy's bed, where he spent much of his time barking at the sounds of the weather.

Now Andy waited, pacing, feeling strangely numb. Nothing about the situation felt real. It had the texture and scent of a dream, the feeling of something that was happening inside his head. He could not believe what he was about to do, and that he was doing it with Ram made it even weirder. More than weird—hallucinatory.

His full name was Ramsey von Pohle. Back in school, whenever a new teacher mispronounced his last name—and they all did, usually pronouncing it "von Pole"—Ram would say with a glare, "It rhymes with 'holy.'" He hated the name Ramsey and would allow it only once. If someone called him Ramsey after being told to call him Ram, his face would become dead. All the features would relax, his eyelids would lower halfway, and he would stare at that person for a long moment with no expression on his face, no emotion in his eyes. It was a frightening thing to see, and if that look was aimed at you, it meant that you'd better stay out of Ram's way if you knew what was good for you. If you didn't, he might humiliate you in public or beat you up when he knew none of the teachers were looking. But he didn't need a reason to do any of those things.

He had killer looks back then: golden blond hair and a sullen, pouty face the girls loved, and he was the school's star quarterback, so he got away with all the bullying and harassing. When Andy learned he'd become a cop, he wasn't surprised. It was a job that would allow Ram to continue bullying and harassing people with impunity.

Andy had been the kind of boy that Ram, and every guy like him, loved to torment. His father had died of a heart attack when Andy was only four years old. Heart disease ran in his father's family, and even though Andy had been adopted when he was only a few days old, his mother feared that he would have the same fate. She became obsessed with his health and micromanaged his life. She made him take several doses of vitamin supplements a day, and if he forgot to take them to school in his lunchbox, she would show up in the middle of a class and give them to him. She prohibited him from doing anything that might result in sickness or injury, which included virtually everything. She was afraid to let him play any sports, so he never learned how, and he didn't get much exercise because she didn't like him to play outside, so he got fat. She was afraid of every possible sickness or wound, and that made *him* afraid, too.

Whenever he spotted Andy, Ram's brooding face lit up and he headed in Andy's direction. "Hey, mommy's boy!" he'd call, and his entourage would laugh as they came toward him. The entourage unfailingly included the most beautiful and coveted girls ever to walk the halls of Eureka High, and they always laughed as Ram gave him titty-twisters, or wedgies, or pulled his hair, or dragged him to the bathroom to wash his face in the toilet.

Ram seemed to enjoy picking on Andy more than any of his other targets. Looking back on it, Andy supposed it was because of his fear. He was afraid of everything back then. An unexpected noise could make him jump out of his seat. It was probably quite comical to everyone else, which would explain why Andy was laughed at so much while he was growing up.

Andy had spent his whole life working on himself, trying to make improvements, strengthen his weaknesses, and undo what his mother had done. He did not want to go on being that weak, frightened boy who, if allowed, would have lived the rest of his days jumping at every noise and flying into a panic with every ache or pain.

He was in high school when it became clear that his mother was the source of his problems. He loved her, but he had to get away from her. Andy became determined to get into a college out of town. That turned out to be Berkeley, where he studied business and spent any free time he had adjusting to a life his mother did not control. After graduating, he stayed in the Bay Area and lived in an apartment that never felt like home and worked a series of jobs in which he never felt comfortable. He stayed in the Bay Area for a few years, but never felt like anything more than a visitor whose life had no direction.

He went home for Christmas one year and learned that the Cuppa Joe Diner was for sale. It was a popular breakfast and lunch spot and the owner was selling only because he'd been diagnosed with cancer. Andy became captivated by the idea of owning and operating that diner and leading a quiet life in the town where he'd grown up, but as an adult, not as his mother's little boy. He ate lunch there every day while he was in town, and that was where he met Jodi, a waitress at the Cuppa Joe.

She was everything he wasn't—attractive, charming, funny, and she was a talented musician who could play both guitar and piano, among other instruments. She had long, wheat-colored hair, a crooked smile, and squinty eyes that always had a sparkle.

In the next year, it all came together with startling ease. He got the diner, moved back to Eureka, and started seeing Jodi.

She was a drug addict. She was clean when he met her, but that was something new for her, and it was a daily battle. She'd recently broken up with her boyfriend, Vic, who was also her dealer. She stopped seeing the friends with whom she got high because she wanted to stay clean and knew that would be impossible with those people in her life. It was clear to Andy from the start that she wanted to be free of drugs and stay clean, and he wanted to help her. Jodi needed him, and Andy discovered how desperately he needed to be needed.

Andy's mother was opposed to all of it and warned him that buying the diner, and later, marrying Jodi, would result in disaster. That convinced him that he was doing the right thing.

Andy and Jodi ran the diner together at first. She had a couple of relapses, but they were brief and Andy encouraged her to move past them quickly and focus on staying clean. She got pregnant and had a baby boy, whom they named Donald, after Jodi's brother, who'd died of pneumonia when they were kids.

Having a son made Andy feel like a new man—it made him feel the *need* to be a new man, anyway. A more responsible and aware man. He had a son to raise, an entire human life to launch, and he wanted to make sure he was up to the task. He began exercising, taking better care of himself, lost thirty pounds, bought some life insurance, and tried to learn as much as he could about football and baseball and other sports because he wanted his son to enjoy all the things he hadn't as a boy.

Andy found much joy in being a father, but there were a few perils. He often found himself thinking like his mother, being overprotective, paranoid, wanting to control every aspect of Donny's life from top to bottom in order to keep him safe. It was disturbingly easy to fall into that kind of behavior and he had to fight it. It helped him understand his mother a little better. Fortunately, she wasn't around to encourage Andy's inclinations because the year after Donny was born, she'd moved to Oregon to take care of her older sister, who'd broken her back in a car accident.

For a while, Andy had a good life. It was so good that he forgot it had ever been otherwise. He seemed to forget that his wife was a recovering drug addict. He'd become wrapped up in the business of running the diner alone while Jodi stayed home with Donny, and he did not see the changes taking place in her. He could see them in hindsight, which was always so infuriatingly crystal clear, but it was too late by then. He didn't notice her restlessness and agitation, her weight loss, the change in her temperament. She started spending a lot of time with her sister Leah in the evenings, staying out later and later.

One day, he came home from work to find Donny watching TV alone. Jodi was gone, as were most of her clothes. Donny had no idea where she'd gone because she'd left while he was in his bedroom doing homework, and she had not left a message of any kind. When he called Leah, he learned that Jodi had not been spending any time with her sister lately, and Leah had no idea where she'd been going, or where she might have gone. But they both knew she was using again.

Jodi had gone back to Vic. Andy was surprised when she filed for divorce, and shocked when she asked for full custody of Donny. He was certain she'd never get it with a history of drug addiction and a live-in boyfriend who was a known drug dealer with a record. But Jodi had done nothing to show that she was using again, and she wasn't living with Vic. She'd been set up in a nice two-story house that she couldn't possibly afford on her own, and she suddenly had a good job at a law firm. Jodi didn't know anything about law and had no interest in it. But it seemed Vic's fortunes had improved since he and Jodi were last an item, and he was now in a position to pull a few strings and help Jodi get full custody of their son. That included hiring for her a killer of a divorce lawyer who specialized in custody cases. And it worked. Andy got supervised visits every two weeks.

It made Andy sick. He became an insomniac and, for about six weeks, he started to drink too much. He put a quick stop to that. For more than a year after the divorce, Vic was nowhere in sight. Andy hired a private investigator to keep an eye on Jodi's house for a while, then to check back regularly to see if she was still living alone. A couple of months ago, he reported that Vic had started spending a lot of time at the house. A month later, Vic moved in, and after that, the house was never quiet. People came and went at all hours of the day and night, and parties lasted for days. Neighbors complained to the police twice, once about loud music, and a second time about what sounded like gunshots.

The news about gunshots scared the hell out of Andy because it meant Donny was in danger. He talked to his attorney about filing for full custody, but was told it would be a long shot and very expensive because her attorney would drag it out. If Andy wanted something done, he would have to do it himself, but he had no idea what that should be. He needed advice.

A few days after Andy met with his lawyer, he had to go to the courthouse to fill out some paperwork for his business license renewal and on the way in, he ran into Ram coming out. Andy cringed inside when Ram headed toward him, expecting to hear, "Hey, mommy's boy!" But he was left speechless when Officer von Pohle smiled and offered his hand to shake and said, "It's been a long time, Andy. You'd think we'd run into each other now and then in a town this small. It's good to see you. How have you been?"

Andy had seen Ram often enough since moving back to Eureka, but he was always careful to avoid an encounter. He would have avoided this one if he'd seen it coming. He'd seen Ram on the job and in his off hours with his wife and children, and he appeared to be a perfectly civilized family man. But Andy had always suspected he was still a sadist and probably tormented his children or beat his wife, or something. Ram did nothing to confirm that suspicion and was warm and jovial and seemed genuinely happy to see Andy. He said he'd been meaning to come to Andy's diner for a bite, but he worked the other side of town and hadn't gotten to it yet. Andy was so impressed with Ram's friendliness that he invited him to come for lunch the next day, on the house.

Ram showed up and Andy seated him in a booth. Once he'd ordered, Andy asked Ram if he'd mind some company and sat down across from him.

Ram looked a lot different these days. He'd gained weight and lost his looks. His face was puffy rather than pouty, and his blond hair surrounded a bald spot on top of his head. But there was no menace in his face, no cruel delight in his eyes, just a relaxed smile. Andy said he needed some advice, and then told Ram about Jodi and Donny, the divorce, and the custody battle, and the most recent developments. Ram's bacon cheeseburger arrived and he went on listening as he ate.

Andy began to get concerned when he saw some dark shadows fall over Ram's eyes as he listened to Andy's story. A frown and a vague look of anger settled into his face.

"Are you talking about Vic Delko?" Ram said when Andy was done.

"That's the guy. You know him?"

"You kidding? Word is he's made some distribution deal with somebody in Sacramento. I thought he'd mellowed out, but I think he's just gotten smoother. He's busier than ever and making a lot of money. And a lot of connections, I think. But I don't think he's doing anything here in town, or even in this county, not anymore. Unless he's made some kind of deal with Giff Clancy. He's the drug source around here and he gets real cranky when there's competition. Sorry to hear about your wife, Andy. Really. I mean, of all people to hook up with. Hearing this makes me angry. Because of your son. Kids have no control over their lives, so it's the responsibility of adults to take care of them. She's not taking care of your son. That pisses me off."

"I don't know what to do. My attorney tells me I'll never get custody through the courts, but I don't know what else I can—"

"The courts are stacked against fathers," Ram said, shaking his head. "Even if the mother is a piece of shit on toast, she's got a strong chance of getting custody. It stinks, but that's the way it is. Forget about court. You just need somebody to convince your wife that the boy doesn't belong with her and her boyfriend and to give up custody."

Andy chuckled coldly. "Yeah, like that's a service you can find on Google."

"Let me take care of it, Andy."

"What? I mean, I don't expect you to—"

"It would be nothing. Really. And I owe it to you. For all the times I was so hard on you in school."

Andy was speechless. He stared at Ram with his mouth hanging open and felt a twinge in his chest, surprised by how powerful those simple words were, hearing Ram admit that all that torture was not business as usual because Andy deserved it for being different and not fitting in, but that it was wrong and done out of cruelty.

When he saw the dumbfounded look on Andy's face, Ram

smiled and said, "I know it took a long time, but . . . well, growing up and having a family of your own . . . it makes life look a lot different."

Andy said, "Thank you, Ram. That means a lot. But I don't understand. What can you do?"

"Let me think about it. I'll get back to you. Okay?"

He'd finally gotten back to Andy that afternoon.

Andy's phone vibrated in his pocket. It was Ram.

"I'm pulling up to your house right now," he said. "Get out here."

Andy put on his raincoat and flipped the hood over his head, then hurried out the door and locked it. He turned to face the stormy night. Ram's police cruiser waited in the driveway. The front passenger's side door opened and Andy rushed through the wind and rain and got in.

"Listen to me closely, Andy," Ram said. "We're going over to your wife's house. We'll go to the door and you'll knock. Soon as we get in, you find your son and take him out of the house and wait here in the car. Got that?"

"What if she won't let me in? What if somebody else answers the door and won't let me in?"

"Don't worry, we'll get in." He smiled briefly. "I'm a cop."

"Okay, then what?"

"Then I'll convince your wife that she needs to do the right thing and transfer full custody to you."

"And . . . how will you do that?"

"Leave that up to me, okay? Don't worry about it."

He said nothing more as they drove through the storm. But in spite of Ram's instruction, he worried.

13

Dr. Corcoran loved science women. Always had. Especially young science women. He loved them even more now than he had when *he* was young, because when you're young, you don't appreciate what you have. He wasn't young anymore, but unlike most men his age, he was still fucking them. He used to call them "science chicks" but some of them hadn't appreciated that—although it was an improvement over "science pussy," a phrase he'd used in high school, back when he was the leader of his clique of one and had no chance in hell of gaining access to *any* pussy, "science" or otherwise. But those days were long gone.

He was especially fond of young Asian science women, like Holly Im, a delicious copper-skinned goddess of Korean descent with what might be—he hadn't quite decided yet, but they *might* be—the most beautiful breasts he'd ever seen. He chewed on his lower lip and made a groaning sound as he watched those breasts sway while Holly bent at the waist and snorted a couple of lines of white powder he'd put on the bathroom counter for her. She'd removed her top just a moment ago and hung it from the knob of the closed door. Her breasts jiggled with each snort and, from his angle, he caught glimpses of the dark, erect nipples. He passed his eyes along her body to the top of her jeans, which hugged her round ass so nicely, down to her delicate bare feet, and then back up again.

He chuckled and muttered, "Science pussy." As he watched her, he moved his hips to the beat of the music from the other room. He didn't recognize it—something new that Eileen had put on, probably, and he just wasn't interested in new music—but he liked that beat.

Corcoran had made the white powder himself, his own concoction. Drove women crazy. Made them wet almost instantly. He'd already imbibed and was flying high, but it wouldn't be a party until she'd had some. It was the perfect snack for hanging out in the bathroom with a hot, young freak like Holly. And she *was* a freak. She needed no help from drugs. The drugs turned her into an animal, made her crazy. Without the drugs, she'd be game for an orgy. With them, she'd start one. That's why he'd brought her into the bathroom. He wanted her all to himself after those first couple of lines.

Holly suddenly stood upright, back rigid, face upturned, eyes clenched, fingers splayed, and said, "Oh, *fuck*, yeah!"

Corcoran grinned. "That's my girl."

"Who're you callin' *girl*?" she said, spinning around to face him. "It's chick, remember? Science chick." She gave him a naughty smile as she moved close, ran her hands up his arms to his neck and slid her fingers through his frizzy hair as she rubbed her body against him.

"Oh, yeah, that's right," he said. "I'm so used to that being politically incorrect."

"I like it. *Girl* is politically incorrect, too. But I don't like it, so I wouldn't care if it wasn't." She spoke just above a whisper, breathing hard.

Corcoran turned to the big mirror over the two sinks and watched Holly rub herself against him, passing her hands up and down over his body. He liked the way the side of her breast bulged when she pressed it against him hard enough. He wore a black T-shirt with a picture of Einstein sticking out his tongue on the front, a pair of camo scrub pants, and sandals.

"Uh-oh!" Holly said with a throaty laugh. Her right hand had made its way below his waist. "Feels like Einstein's got a new theory," she said as she squeezed his erection through his scrubs. She slithered down his body until she was on her knees.

Oh, how Corcoran loved young Asian science chicks on their knees. Especially in the bathroom. Doing it in the bathroom just made it dirtier somehow, and the dirtier the better, Corcoran always said. He watched her in the mirror as she tugged on the tie of his scrub pants, and then pulled them down. His cock popped up out of the descending pants and she caught it in her mouth and pushed her face forward, making a little growling noise that he could feel to his balls.

Corcoran had taken the doctors' lounge as his living quarters during his stay at the hospital. Others on the team rented apartments or houses, but he preferred to live where he worked, because his work was his life. Especially tonight. He began to thrust his hips forward, gently at first, smiling.

He looked down at her and watched her head move from above for a while, then turned to the mirror again. He was amazed by her fluid movements as she got off her knees and squatted in front of him with her legs spread wide without taking her mouth off of him, the way her hands constantly fondled and caressed him, the way her right hand snaked down between her thighs and clawed at the taut denim over her pussy. She was like a pro, like a porn star, and watching her only excited him more.

There was a quick knock on the door. Todd Hinkle walked in. He was a slightly nerdy lab tech. He froze, then pushed his black-framed glasses up on his nose and smiled. "Looks like the party's in here," he said.

Startled, Holly released Corcoran, stood, and turned around. "Oh, hi, Todd," she said rather groggily. She turned to Corcoran, wrinkling her nose, moisture glistening around her mouth. "It's hot in here. Or is it me? Is it hot in here? I'm hot." She unbuttoned her jeans and pushed them down her legs along with her panties, then stepped out of them.

"Hey, Dr. Corcoran," Todd said, "we've been hearing noises that sound a lot like gunfire."

Corcoran smiled, anticipating a punch line, but Todd simply stared at him, awaiting a response.

"Wait, what?" Corcoran said. "Are you serious?"

"Well, that's what it sounded like. They were outside at first, but what we just heard a few seconds ago sounded like it was inside the building."

Corcoran realized he was standing there with his pants down and his erect penis pointed at Todd. He bent down and pulled up his pants.

"It's just the storm," he said. "There's no gunfire around here. If there was a problem, security would be on it and somebody would have called me by now."

"This room is too small," Holly said. She went to the door, leaving her pants on the floor, and smiled as she gently patted Todd's cheek. Then she left the bathroom.

Corcoran smiled. "Okay, *now* it's a party," he said as he followed her out.

There were half a dozen other people in the room, the same group that always showed up for his parties, a small segment of the staff, kindred spirits who enjoyed good company and a good, friendly fuck. Corcoran was glad Fara had not come—they all were—because she would have stifled the whole evening. He knew she wouldn't, but he'd invited her, anyway. She couldn't say she hadn't been invited. And if she had come, they could've slipped something into her drink. She needed loosening up. He'd decided he'd had enough of her moralizing and stern disapproval. He intended to boot her off the team. She just wasn't any fun.

Unlike, say, Eileen Waxner, a short, plump, adorable virologist with enormous breasts who'd already doffed her top and sat on Ira Goldman's lap wearing only a bra and skirt. Ira, a fifty-four-year-old biochemist who was pretty plump himself, had a beefy arm around Eileen and was grinning like an idiot as he ogled her prodigious cleavage just inches from his face. The two of them made the recliner Ira was sitting in look overtaxed.

With a dramatic flourish of his arm, Corcoran said in a stentorian voice, "Eat, drink, and be merry, for tomorrow, we get a hurricane!"

"The TV says it's coming tonight," Eileen said.

"What?" Corcoran said, dropping his arm.

"Yeah, just before I came, I had the TV on and the news guy said the hurricane is hitting earlier than expected. Tonight."

"Hey, I really think that was gunfire we heard," Caleb Tan said. He was a twenty-five-year-old whiz kid aero biologist from Singapore who looked like he hadn't started shaving yet. He stood by the table where all the booze was, making himself a drink.

"Yeah," Ira said. "Sounded like machine gunfire. Some of it did. To me, anyway."

The words "machine gunfire" cut through Corcoran's high like a hot knife. "Machine gun. Are you serious?"

Ira nodded.

"That can't be," Corcoran muttered. "If there were something happening, someone would have called me, I'm sure." He reached for his pocket to check his phone and make sure it was charged and operational. "Besides, that's what we have security for." He realized he was wearing scrub pants that had no pockets. "Has anyone seen my phone?"

Before anyone could answer, the door flew open so hard, it hit the wall with a sharp crack, and two men in black wearing ski masks and carrying guns burst into the room and aimed their weapons at everyone.

14

Hank Clancy hugged his knees to his chest in the corner of the small room, the tile floor hard under his bony ass. He squinted as he looked around at the walls. Had it grown smaller?

Don't be an idiot, Hank thought. *Rooms don't get smaller.*

He was cold and shivering and felt sick. He'd wrapped himself in the blanket from his cot, but it didn't help. This had come suddenly only a couple of minutes ago and felt like a fever, like the flu, or something. Hank shook his head and chuckled. No, not the flu. It was probably something those bastards had *given* him with their needles and swabs, something they were whipping up right there in Eureka, right under everybody's nose.

He'd seen them coming and going in their protective suits with their syringes, disappearing into one of the other rooms, then leaving. Later, they would come back and get that person and take him or her away. Once taken away, that person didn't come back.

One of them had come to Hank's room. He wasn't sure how long ago, that was the scary part. With no windows, there was no day or night. With no clocks, time didn't exist and he'd lost track of it a while ago . . . although, he didn't know how long. But it hadn't been too long—at least, it didn't *feel* like it had been too long. He'd been given an injection, then the space-suited person had left. He'd been waiting for them to come get him, but no one showed up. He waited and waited . . . but he didn't know how long.

Hank's ears were ringing loudly and a headache was coming on pretty fast. He heard distant noises, but wondered if they were real or just part of the irritating ringing. Earlier, he'd heard what sounded like thunder, and then a sound like wind rising up and then falling away, over and over. But now he heard . . . popping noises. Like gunshots, maybe. But that didn't make any sense. Unless he was hallucinating. Had they given him something to make him hallucinate?

Whatever it was, they'd given him *something*. The protective suits were pretty telling, as far as Hank was concerned, and they didn't tell anything good. But it didn't tell anything he didn't already know, either. He knew what was going on. He knew the other people they'd brought in off the street probably were confused, scared, and wondering what the hell was happening to them, but not Hank. He'd seen all of this coming. No one would listen to him, of course. Who listens to anything a homeless old man says? What sane person in America would take a homeless old man seriously?

Hank regularly prowled the woods around the old Springmeier Hospital, sometimes living there for days at a stretch, and he'd seen all the activity as they moved in and began working on the place. The back half of it, anyway. They'd breathed new life into that decrepit old hospital building, like some voodoo priest reviving a corpse. They'd carted in a lot of machinery and made a lot of noise, and then it was quiet again, but alive, working, breathing. Up to something. Hank didn't know who they were, but they had erected an electric fence to keep people out or in or both, and they'd avoided attention by cutting a new road through the woods off of an old road that had been closed over a decade ago. They'd reawakened the dead building for their own purposes. He'd watched them bring it back to life, wondering what atrocities would be committed in its halls, never suspecting that he would be taken there and held like a criminal.

Hank suspected his son was behind the kidnapping. He'd tipped them off about Hank, targeted him, and they'd taken him right off the street in a ridiculous plumber's van. Gifford, his son, had gotten tired of waiting for him to die. Living on the street gave Hank the freedom to pop up in Gifford's life whenever he wanted, and disappear whenever he wanted, and Gifford didn't like that. He used to tolerate it, back when he thought Hank would leave him some money. Once Gifford knew that wasn't going to happen, he had no use for Hank, who had decided not to leave anything to anyone and revoked his will. That was when Hank decided to get off the grid.

He'd lived outside the law his whole life. He'd been *born* outside of it. His pappy had been a moonshiner, a thief, and a pimp, and his mother had been one of the old man's girls. Hank didn't know anything else. He discovered early that he had some talent as a thief and a liar, and he built on those. He started out as a cat burglar, but by the time he was twenty, he'd moved up to stealing cars, then selling and distributing them. Later, he added guns to that. Then drugs. He was reluctant to get into the drug trade, but it was too tempting. He was so good at it that he abandoned all the other stuff and focused exclusively on drugs.

It all ran beautifully for so long. Smooth, quiet, no trouble, lots of money. Then Hank started dipping into the inventory. Some told him that was the biggest mistake he ever made, but Hank disagreed. It changed his life. Marijuana, cocaine, acid, meth, ecstasy—he tried it all, then kept using the stuff that made him see the world so differently, so clearly. The story was that drugs ruined Hank Clancy's life, but that wasn't true. Seeing things clearly ruined his life. He saw too much, and the horror of what he saw only made him want more drugs.

He saw two different worlds existing simultaneously. There was the world most people lived in, where everybody got their news on TV, found out what to wear on TV, what to think, who to hate—and thought it was real life. The other world was made up of what was *really* going on, the stuff that didn't get reported on the news, the *real* life that was occurring all around them but out of their sight. Because it wasn't on TV.

Then the Internet came along and was supposed to make all the information in the world instantly accessible and improve everyone and everything. But that didn't happen. What *did* happen—and Hank saw it instantly—was that everything bad about life on planet earth escalated. People started becoming more divided, more isolated, and all the insanity in the world seemed to move to an express lane. That's when he began thinking about getting out of the asylum.

Gifford thought he was crazy, of course, and said the world was only getting better. Like he was under hypnosis, or something. Like everybody else. In a trance. Gifford was too preoccupied with being a big shot to pay any attention to the world.

He hung around with lowlifes he could ingratiate himself with, then use. Gifford had always worked for Hank and as long as his instructions were clear and thorough and not delivered too fast, he was pretty reliable. But that changed when Hank started giving him more responsibilities and teaching him the business. Then he started bringing his friends around, showing off to them, giving them drugs, letting them crash at the house, playing the big shot. Hank had never met Gifford's friends before, but he recognized them— punks, all of them, nothing but trouble. He'd been trying to avoid people like them as much as possible his whole life, and he didn't want them around now. He kicked Gifford out, and his friends with him. Gifford just moved into the mobile home Hank had behind the house for guests. It wasn't some trailer park dump—this one was big, and as mobile homes went, pretty damned luxurious. Gifford and his friends turned it into a dump in three months.

Useless prick and his useless prick friends. Nothin' but punks and whores who can't hold their drugs and want 'em for free, sons-a-bitches.

Hank felt a surge of anger as he thought about Gifford and his friends. He still felt cold and shivery and was starting to ache everywhere, but he stood and paced the small room. He was angry and tense and he couldn't remain still any longer.

Shortly after the incident with the mobile home, Hank started tucking his money away in small neighborhood banks all over northern California using phony identities. Some people collected stamps; Hank collected phony identities. He made his preparations quietly and went on with business as usual, which included arguing with his son. It was all they ever did.

"You're crazy, Dad," Gifford would say. "We all know where computer technology came from."

"I just seem crazy to you because, like everybody else, you don't recognize sanity anymore. You know, it wasn't very long ago when all this stuff was science fiction! Computers, iPads, the Internet, cell phones, all of it. Then out of nowhere, it *exploded*! Where do you think that came from? You really think some geeks in garages whipped up all that shit?"

"What's so crazy about that? Somebody invented the light-bulb, the telephone, the car—why not all this other stuff?"

"Because it's too big a leap. They've been working on this stuff for a long time, since Roswell, deconstructing the alien technology, then putting it back together again. Then they dumped it on us, made everybody love and crave it, and they're gonna use it to control us all."

"You gotta lay off that shit you been doin', Dad. It's fryin' your brain."

"My brain's fine! Your brain's been washed."

When he was finally ready, Hank just disappeared. He felt safer alone in the woods in the middle of the night than he felt on the street in broad daylight. He preferred wild animals in the dark to human beings in any light. He knew how to deal with animals in the woods, but he was never sure with human beings. Hank believed that living with other human beings caused insanity, that all of them were carriers of the disease, and all of them, in one way or another, suffered from it, gave it to each other in a long cycle of people driving each other and themselves monkeyfuck crazy that went all the way back to whatever witch-cursed pond humanity crawled out of. He preferred isolation and detachment, and that made all those insane people think he was crazy. It was a fucked-up world.

He shivered and hugged himself as he paced unsteadily, sweating now, and angry that he was cold. *Really* angry. He was breathing heavily and clenching his fists. His skin felt too tight. He felt ready to explode.

Hank stopped pacing and threw himself at his cot. He tore the thin mattress from it and threw it across the room, knocking the pillow to the floor. He picked up the cot itself and threw it against the wall.

He stopped and stared at the mess while he caught his breath. It wasn't enough.

Hank stopped breathing when an explosion of sound came from somewhere outside the ward. It sounded like gunshots.

Gunshots again. Am I hallucinating? Or is something happening?

He went to the window in the front of the room. The reinforced glass looked out on the round ward outside, with a small, derelict nurses' station in the center, like the hole of donut. All around the large circle were rooms like his with windows looking out on each other. To Hank's right, an archway opened on a short hall, and at the end of that hall was a door, but he couldn't see it from that angle.

That was where the sound was coming from. And it *was* gunfire. There were a few pops, some shouting and then the loud, sustained sound of a machine gun, followed by a big crash. Then two men dressed in black and wearing ski masks, each with a pistol in hand and one with a compact black machine gun strapped to his shoulder, rushed into the ward.

Hank felt weak and leaned against the wall as he looked out the window, trying to retreat as much as possible so they wouldn't notice him. Still thinking he might be imagining things, he rubbed his eyes with the knuckles of both hands, then looked out the window again.

They talked quietly, then one of them reached beneath his black jacket, still wet from the rain outside, and produced a small camera.

Had they come to execute him? Torture him? Experiment on him?

Fear and adrenaline coursed through him and swirled with his growing anger, and his lips peeled back over his yellow teeth as his entire body tensed. Hank would not go without a fight.

15

Tyler Bursell adjusted his headlamp as he and Edgar Castillo descended the narrow, dark staircase that went below the basement.

They had entered the hospital through the underground tunnel from the boiler house. While the others were to go upstairs and spread throughout the building to look for the missing homeless people, Tyler and Castillo had been instructed to stay behind and explore the basement. The first thing they found was a room with a large rectangular window that looked into a much smaller room with tile on the walls and floor, a drain in the center of the floor, and cameras mounted on the ceiling.

"I don't like the look of this," Castillo had said.

"Me, neither."

They moved through the entire basement but found nothing else of interest except the stairs to the subbasement. But the stairway was dark and the light switch by the door produced nothing, so they turned on their LED headlamps.

Ty hadn't been with Ollie as long as Castillo, who was in his thirties, about ten years ahead of Ty, but he was every bit as loyal. He came home from Afghanistan to learn that his wife was divorcing him to move in with his best friend, he couldn't get a job, couldn't sit still, couldn't sleep, couldn't think straight because of all the noise in his head, and he couldn't get through the iron bureaucracy of the Veterans Administration to get the help he needed. Once he started self-medicating, his descent was swift and blurred by drugs and alcohol. During a brief moment of clarity, he realized he was living on the street, that he'd become one of those crazy-looking street people he always tried to avoid. He would have died that way if it hadn't been for Ollie.

Ollie had a friend who ran a rehab clinic in Eureka and all of his addicted recruits were sent there, including Ty. Once he'd gotten through the nightmare of withdrawal, which would have been much worse had it not been for that doctor and his staff, Ty was presented with a choice. Go back to life on the street or commit to "Monk's Militia" until he got back on his feet and could function on his own. There was no conflict for Ty, who gladly signed up. Ollie helped him clear up his problems with the VA and he was able to get the medical attention he needed. He got back into shape while going through Ollie's training program and working at and around the compound, and he had a reason to wake up in the morning.

"Hope there's lights down here," Castillo said. They'd been speaking in whispers since they'd arrived.

Grit crunched under their feet on the concrete stairs. At the bottom, a doorway opened on the right. Castillo found the light switches and started flipping them, but nothing happened.

"You gotta figure," Ty said, "this place has been abandoned for a decade, and who knows how long before that they stopped using the subbasement for anything?"

They walked over an uneven dirt floor as their headlamps cast light across the pipes overhead, the concrete floor someone had never finished pouring, the rusted old file cabinets against one wall.

An explosion of squeaks and squeals made Ty freeze and look down in time to catch several long, skinny rats dashing away from his light and running for cover in some dark crevice or hole.

"Jesus fucking *Christ*!" Ty shouted as a he stumbled backwards, away from the fleeing rodents.

"Shouldn't take the Lord's name in vain."

"Hey, the Lord shouldna made *rats*. I fuckin' *hate* rats."

Castillo turned off his headlamp and told Ty to do the same.

"What the fuck *for*? Didn't you see them *rats*?"

Castillo reached over and turned off Ty's headlamp, and a moment later, he saw why.

On the other side of the spacious subbasement, beyond the pipes and pillars and long-abandoned crates, a faint glow came through a small square glass.

They turned their headlamps back on and unholstered their Ruger SR40s, then headed in the direction of the light. Things skittered away from them in the dark outside the reach of their headlamp beams. The light came through a small window in a door. When he looked through it, Ty saw a clean room with a tile floor, a table, some chairs, a refrigerator, a sink and counter. But that room was dark. The light was coming from an open door on the other side of that room.

Ty and Castillo held very still and listened. There was a sound coming from somewhere beyond the door, and probably beyond the door through which light was shining. Someone was wailing, possibly a woman's voice, a high and hopeless wail of misery.

Ty expected the door to be locked and was surprised when Castillo opened it with ease on the first try. They turned off their headlamps as they entered the room. Castillo led the way in, and as they passed through the room with the table and chairs, he gestured to the right.

Ty saw the half-open door Castillo had pointed out and went to take a look. It was a small, empty bathroom. By the time he was done, Castillo was already passing through the doorway into the lit room, and a moment later, he groaned, "Oh, Jesus! Oh, my God Jesus Christ!"

Ty hurried to join him.

16

"This is a *bad* idea, Ollie," Emilio said.

"No names, please."

"No names? *Fuck* no names, Ollie. You lost my courteous side when you did *that*," Emilio said, pointing at Dr. McManus, who lay on the lumpy couch in her office. He'd put her there after Ollie had knocked her unconscious and placed a cold cloth on her forehead. She had a bump just above her temple, but it wasn't bleeding too badly. Emilio stood beside the couch, facing Ollie and feeling his anger growing. "Which was totally fucking unnecessary, by the way. What the hell was that, hitting her with your fucking *gun*? She was trying to tell you—"

"Hey, hey," Ollie said quietly, stepping up close to Emilio. "Don't make the mistake of thinking that because you know us, you're one of us. You're not. You're still on the wrong end of the gun, and in case you hadn't noticed, we're not here to take prisoners—we're here to *free* 'em."

"And you'd best put the brakes on *that* idea because they're not prisoners, they're *test* subjects. Stop and think about what that means, Ollie. I don't think you have yet. I don't know exactly what they're working on, but I know it's some kind of weapon, a biological weapon, and it's probably contagious. I don't know how it spreads—or even *if* it spreads because I don't know the details yet, but she was *giving* them to me when you and your posse rode into town."

"What kind of weapon?" Ollie said. His eyes had narrowed, though, and Emilio could tell he was frowning beneath the ski mask.

"You need me to say it again? I don't know the specifics. But I know what I've told you. A bioweapon. Are you starting to do the math?"

Ollie nodded slowly.

"Then what the hell you waiting for? Can't you—"

"I know the specifics," Fara said.

Emilio turned to Fara as she sat up on the couch, conscious now, but groggy. The cold cloth dropped off her head to the floor.

"It's a virus," she said, looking at Ollie. "It alters behavior."

Hoping no one noticed, Emilio reached into his pocket and removed his phone, holding it down at his side as he started recording. Then he slipped it into his shirt pocket, hoping it would pick up their conversation better there than in his pants pocket. He was afraid if he kept holding it, someone would notice.

"The virus creates and maintains a state of violent rage and paranoia," she continued. "It's not airborne, but it's not like most blood-borne viruses. An exchange of bodily fluids isn't necessary. You get the blood of a carrier on your skin, the virus is absorbed quickly."

"Through the *skin*?" Emilio said, frowning. He didn't think that was possible.

"Yes, through the skin. That's what sets this apart. The virus works swiftly. It will turn you into an enraged psychopath. If you let those people out, you will let the virus out."

Emilio turned to Ollie. "Holy shit, man, stop 'em."

"Yeah, yeah, I'm calling." Ollie reached into a rear pocket, took out a cell phone, thumbed a couple of buttons, and put it to his ear.

Emilio realized how fidgety he was. He was shifting his weight back and forth from foot to foot, rubbing the back of his neck nervously. He went to the couch and sat down beside Fara.

"How you doing, Dr. McManus?" he said.

Blood was drying in her hair and on her temple. "Call me Fara, for Christ's sake. We've bonded."

"How's that cut?"

"It's nothing. He nicked me. But he gave me one hell of a headache."

"I was gonna beat him up for it."

"Oh, no, please, not in the office. You'll break something."

Emilio looked over at Ollie, who was pacing across the room, talking quietly but urgently into the phone. He stopped abruptly. "Hello? *Hello*? Jesus Christ, what the hell is—" He took the phone from his ear and switched it to speaker, then turned toward Emilio and Fara.

Two sounds: gunfire and screaming.

17

There was no shouting, no rushing around—one look at those guns and nobody moved. Corcoran was vaguely relieved by that, but he was too busy trying to control his own terror to give it much thought.

"Who's in charge?" one of the masked men said.

Corcoran had to swallow a gasp when he saw each of the people at his party point a finger at him without hesitation.

The man who had spoken stepped over to Corcoran and aimed the gun at his face. "Who are you?"

He stammered his name.

"You're in charge of this place?"

Mouth hanging open, he nodded.

"Where are the homeless people you've taken off the street?"

Corcoran snapped his mouth shut. He couldn't stir up enough saliva to swallow. He kept his eyes on the gunman, but he heard the rustle of movement that passed through the small group as everyone turned to him. Most people at the facility were unaware of the test subjects, and even Fara McManus didn't know about the ones in the subbasement.

"The-the-the . . . the what?" Corcoran said.

"You know who I'm talking about."

"No, I-I don't."

"We're not alone. The rest of our team is moving through the hospital right now. We're going to find them. If you tell me now, maybe it'll keep some of your people from getting hurt in the process."

"Find them? Who are you? What do you want?"

"I told you what we want. You took them. We're here to take them back."

"Back? Take them . . . *back*?" The initial shock was wearing off and Corcoran's head reeled with questions. *This* was the gunfire they'd heard. Where was security? What did they want with the test subjects? Could this man mean they want to set them free? Is *that* why they'd come? He couldn't let that happen. "Take them back to where? To what?"

"What is he talking about?" Caleb said to Corcoran, barely above a whisper.

Eileen frowned at him. "*What* homeless people?"

He ignored them.

"Where are they?" the gunman said.

Corcoran took in a deep breath, tried to steady his voice. "Look, um, listen to me, you can't . . . those people can't leave here. They're test subjects. They're infected."

Eileen slipped off of Ira's lap and stood. "You're using *human* test subjects?" she said after a collective gasp from the others.

"Infected with what?" the man said.

"A virus. A virus that I created, that we developed here. If you let them out, that virus . . . it'll spread. You can't do that."

"*What* virus?"

Corcoran was horrified to hear himself laugh. It was a tense, frightening sound. "We don't have time to go into that now. You have to stop your team. They can't let those people out or we could *all* get the virus."

The man tossed a glance at his companion. "Should I call him?"

"Call him, dammit," the other man said. *"Right now!"*

The man turned away from Corcoran as he got on his phone.

The other man turned to Corcoran and said, "Where are they?"

"Second floor."

Corcoran finally steeled himself and looked at his party guests. They were all staring at him in shock. Not at the men with the guns, but at him, at Corcoran, as if he had eclipsed the fact that they were all being held at gunpoint.

Corcoran said to the masked man standing in front of him, "You say your team is going through the whole hospital?"

"Yes."

"Does, uh . . . does that include the basement?"

"Already there. The basement, subbasement."

"Jesus Christ, the subbasement?" Corcoran said in a tremulous whisper.

The man's attention was on his partner, who was speaking quietly on the phone.

"You've got to stop them," Corcoran said. "Keep them from going into the subbasement. You *have* to!" The man did not seem to be paying that much attention to him. "Do you hear me? I'm serious, you can't let them—"

The man turned on him angrily, raised his gun, and touched the barrel to Corcoran's cheek. "I *will* shoot you."

Corcoran found himself out of breath, as if he'd been running. He turned to his party guests and met their shocked gazes, their looks of condemnation.

He turned away from them and lowered his head.

He wasn't sure how or why, but suddenly, everything seemed to be falling apart.

18

Hank quickly turned off the light in his room, got down on his knees and peered over the bottom edge of the window. He hoped they wouldn't notice him right away so he could watch them, see what they were up to.

As the man with the camera turned slowly and captured the whole ward on video, the other man shouted, "We've come to help you! You're the reason we're here. We've come to get you out of here. Please cooperate so we can get you out of the building as quickly as possible."

Help? They'd come to *help*? Well, it seemed to Hank, as he shuddered at the chills that passed through him in waves, that these boys were just a tad fuckin' *late*. And the way that guy was talking, you'd think he expected them to do a happy dance because they were there. Who the fuck did they think they were, anyway? Shooting their way in after Hank had been there for—

He didn't know how long he'd been there. Others were already there when he arrived. Some of them had been taken away by the people in the protective suits and had never come back again. Who knew how long they'd been locked up in this place, given pills and injections, treated like some kind of deadly poisonous snake. Hank didn't think these guys were going to be too popular in the ward.

The man who had spoken went to the first door on his right and discovered it was locked with a simple dead bolt. He turned the latch, opened the door, then went to the next one. He made his way all the way around the donut to Hank's room.

No one came out of the rooms. They were in there, Hank could see some of them, dark shapes in the small, shadowy rooms, but they didn't come out. Not yet.

Hank dropped down below the window and drew his knees to his chest, his back to the corner.

The lock made a *clack* sound, and was pushed open. But no one came inside.

Hank waited and listened as his fingers dug into his knees.

One of the men made an inarticulate sound of surprise, then said, "Oh, no, no, wait, we're here to *help* you. We're not going to— Hey! No, wait, don't—*hey*! Call for some backup!"

The other man was already talking to someone. His voice stayed low at first, so Hank couldn't understand what he was saying, but he spoke to someone rapidly.

The first man shouted, "Hey, no, *no, NO*! Goddammit, you're gonna—"

He fired his gun once, then screamed. It was high and shrill and full of terror first, then pain, too, and it seemed it would go on forever, until it came to a strangled halt.

The other man began to shout. "Just get somebody up here now for Chrissakes *right now* or we're gonna—" Then he cried out in pain and there was another gunshot, and another. He screamed for a moment, but his voice was cut off sharply.

There was a rush of movement then, and a bit more screaming, although it sounded garbled and distorted. And shuffling, rattling sounds. Hank suspected they were taking all the weapons from the men in black. That was what he would do. It went on for some time, but he had no idea how long. It went on until it stopped.

Hank realized he'd been digging his fingernails into his knees. When he pulled his hands away, he could see in the light from the window four crescents of blood on each kneecap.

After it had been silent for a long moment, he peeked out the window and saw no movement, no sign of anyone remaining on the ward. To his right, not far from the door, he could see two black legs, the toes of the boots pointing upward.

He got to his feet with the blanket still draped over his shoulders and left the room in a rush. The adrenaline surging through him made him feel fast and deft, even though he was freezing cold and feeling sick, and he jogged to the right, toward the door, but stopped when he saw all the blood spattered around the two men in black.

One lay on his back, the other on his side with his left arm pulled up and back at a disturbing angle. Their masks had been removed, and so had their faces, for the most part, leaving behind ghoulish red masks with exposed teeth, dangling strips of flesh, and at least one empty eye socket.

Hank hunkered down beside the dead man lying on his back to see if his fellow inmates had missed anything useful. He winced when he looked at the torn and mutilated face. It would seem that all that screaming and struggling he'd listened to had gone on longer than he'd thought. There was a great deal of blood, and not all of it had come from his face. Hank noticed the empty knife sheath on his belt, then the blood on his black clothes coming from the many stab wounds. He spotted the headlamp. It had come off when the man's ski mask had been removed. Hank snatched it up. The ski mask, too.

Hank eyed the man's black boots. They were fine boots, Hank recognized them immediately. Bates. Maybe not top of the line, but damned reliable footwear. Hank thought that shoes were perhaps the most important thing in anyone's daily life. He knew shoes and boots, and he never hesitated to spend extra money for something that would make his feet comfortable. He stood and walked on his feet all day; the boots were a wise investment.

He looked down at the flimsy foam slippers he wore and thought those boots would feel damned good on his feet. Then he looked at the thin hospital gown he wore and wondered why he was limiting himself to the boots. He let the blanket over his shoulders drop to the floor.

The guy in front of him was too short and stout, but the other one, the one lying on his side, was pretty close to Hank's height and build. That man had been stabbed as well, and his throat had been cut. Hank knew he wouldn't have much time before someone came in and checked on the two dead guys. He undressed the man as quickly as he could, then shed the gown and slippers and dressed. All the while, he shivered and ached. Anger surged in him when he had difficulty undressing the dead man.

Hank found a snub-nose .38 strapped to the man's ankle. It was fully loaded. He placed it on the floor beside the body, and then dressed in the dead man's clothes. Hank was thinner than the man on the floor so the clothes were a little baggy, but they fit. He slipped the gun in the small of his back under the waist of his pants. He put on the ski mask, then the headlamp, and then he released some of that anger bubbling inside him by kicking the stripped dead man in the face. He did it once, then a second time, a third. Then he lost track because he lost control. Kicking, kicking, kicking. He turned around and stomped on the other man's face with the heel of his boot, making a low groaning sound in his chest as he stomped again and again, enjoying it, even releasing a growling laugh, until each stomp created wet crunching sounds.

Then he got the hell out of there.

19

The storm was rapidly getting worse and it was making Andy nervous. Ram's police cruiser quaked under the growing force of the wind. Stray newspapers, bags, and boxes flew through the car's headlight beams like missiles, and the heavy rainfall did not provide much visibility on the road. Ram's police radio occasionally burst to life with voices, and then fell silent for a while before doing it again.

"I thought the hurricane was supposed to hit tomorrow," Andy said, realizing he was digging his fingers into the seat as if hanging on for life.

"Nah, they changed that," Ram said. He had to speak loudly to be heard above the rain. "Now they're saying it's going to hit sooner than they thought. Meaning tonight. Heard it on the radio earlier."

"*When* tonight?" Andy said, alarmed. He'd planned to be holed up in his house when the hurricane hit, safely tucked away on the far eastern edge of Eureka with plenty of candles, Dickens, and some beer, where he'd probably spend all of his time in agonizing worry about Donny.

"They didn't say." He smirked. "Probably worried about getting it wrong again if they're too specific. But don't worry,

I think we've got time to do what we're gonna do and get you and your boy back home before the worst of it hits."

They were in Jodi's neighborhood. The windows on all the houses they passed were boarded up and the residential streets were dark between the glowing halos of the streetlights. Ram took a right turn, drove a couple of blocks, then pulled over to the curb.

"Jesus Christ," Andy said when he saw her house. Bright light glowed from the windows, which had not been boarded. There were a few cars parked in front of the house. "Do they *know* there's a hurricane coming?"

"Okay, Andy," Ram said, killing the engine, "are you ready for this?"

"Ready as I'll ever be."

Ram reached over, opened the glove box and removed a pair of black gloves. As he put them on, he said, "Don't expect this to be easy. You might see and hear things in there that'll piss you off and make you crazy. You've gotta keep your cool and just focus on getting your boy out of there as soon as possible so I can get to work."

Something about the words "so I can get to work" disturbed Andy, but all he said was, "Yeah, okay."

When he got out of the car, he was almost knocked flat by the wind. The cold rain hit his face like pebbles and stung his skin. He ducked his head down and struggled to walk up the driveway to the house.

The thumping beat of loud music came from inside the house. The sound of a dog barking, then howling somewhere nearby threaded through the roar of the wind.

The porch light was on and he and Ram cast long shadows backwards as they climbed onto the covered porch.

Andy rang the doorbell, and, to be safe, knocked hard on the door, then waited.

20

In Fara McManus's office, Emilio watched Ollie return his phone to its pouch on his belt. Before he could speak, the phone trilled and he put it to his ear again and said, "Yeah." He listened, and then said, "Corcoran?"

Fara looked up at him.

"That's the guy in charge," Ollie said. "I want you to bring him here to—" He looked at Fara. "What's your name again?"

"Fara McManus."

"Bring him to Fara McManus's office. He knows where it is. Bring him here and keep him here, along with Dr. McManus. And listen to me. Abort the mission. If you find anyone who's being held here, do not—I repeat, *do not* set them free. They carry a virus. You need to—no, no, it's not like that. You're safe as long as you don't get any of their blood or fluids on you, understand? Do *not* get their blood on your skin. Tell as many of the others as you can. And get Corcoran here right away." He ended the call, went to the other masked man in the room, and stood close, whispering, "Stay here and keep an eye on these two, Craig. They do *not* leave this room." The man nodded. Ollie turned to Fara. "I've got a lot of questions for you and your boss. I'll be back."

After Ollie left, Emilio turned to Fara. "Is there someplace where I can get some ice? You should have ice on that."

"No ice," she said. "We're just going to sit here and talk quietly until your friend comes back."

"He's not *my* friend."

"You obviously know him."

"Well, yeah, but that's different than being friends. He listens to the show, calls in a lot, comes by to talk with Ivan sometimes. Especially since you guys got here and homeless people started disappearing. He's been like a dog with a bone. I'm not surprised by this. He finally found something for his militia to *do.*"

"What do you do for—what's his name again?"

"Ivan? I've got a few jobs. I handle some of the advertising sales for the website and his radio show. I'm also a researcher, and a doer of odd jobs. Like this one. This one's pretty odd."

"Here's another odd job for you. Go to my desk and open the bottom drawer."

Emilio went around her desk, opened the drawer, and knew immediately what she wanted. There was an unopened fifth of Jack Daniels in the drawer. He held it up and turned to her. "Is this what you're looking for?"

"That's it. While you're over there, grab my purse."

He took the purse from the floor beside the chair.

"Oh, and grab the ashtray, too," she said. "I don't have glasses, but if you don't mind my cooties, we can share the bottle."

Emilio handed the purse and ashtray to her, sat down beside her on the couch, removed the cap, and handed her the bottle. She tipped it back, took a couple of swallows, then exhaled loudly.

"None for me," Emilio said when she offered him the bottle.

She took a pack of cigarettes and a lighter from her purse, shook a cigarette out and lit it. "I stopped smoking almost five years ago. I come back here and bang, I'm a smoker again. How did you come to be a janitor, Emilio?"

"Oh, I've been a janitor, a mechanic, flipped burgers and painted houses. I've been all kinds of things. When Ivan learned you guys were going to be using Humboldt Janitorial Services, he asked if I'd be willing to apply for a job there and see if I could get in. It was a long shot, but I got lucky. And here I am."

"Clever. But the joke's on you. It's not safe here. You've been in danger the entire time." She took another puff of her cigarette, then tapped it over the ashtray.

"Then why are you still here?"

"I've been afraid to leave. It's Corcoran." She shook her head, sighed, then took another pull of whiskey. She held the bottle out to him and said, "Here, get it away from me. I'm such a lightweight, I'll be drunk in no time, and I don't need that. I just wanted a few sips of that because I've run out of fingernails to chew."

Emilio put the cap back on the bottle, took it to the desk, and returned it to the bottom drawer.

"Unless you want some," Fara said to Craig, the masked, armed man standing silently in the room with them.

He shook his head.

Fara said, "I got this job because an old professor of mine at Stanford told me about it and then pulled a couple of strings to help me get it. She said it would look good on my CV and I'd have the opportunity to work with the brilliant and renowned Dr. Corcoran. She's known him for ages and said he's always been crazy and infuriating, but brilliant. But she hasn't seen him in years. She doesn't know what a drug addict he's become, what a . . . *lunatic*. The man is a mess. All he cares about is drugs and fucking. I've heard he holds orgies in his room. Can you believe that? That's probably what that party was tonight. Must have been an interesting discovery for the masked intruders." She laughed and shook her head. "The man's a highly respected scientist in his sixties and he's still trying to make up for being a geek in high school. But he's still brilliant. What he's done here is pretty amazing, if you ignore how immoral and horrifying it all is. But he's too careless.

"The homeless people were his idea. Vendon Labs would never go along with something like that. Not officially, not on paper. But when you've got a star like Corcoran working on a project the government wants done ASAP, you look the other way and wash your hands of it. He didn't want to work on rats or monkeys, which is what we're set up for here. 'We'll be altering *human* behavior, not rat or monkey behavior,' he said. 'If we're going to have any hope of succeeding at this, we'll need human subjects.'"

She reached up and rubbed her forehead with four fingers, wincing a little in pain. "But we're not set up to deal with infected *people* here, and it's not like he could ask Vendon to equip us for people, because, of course, we *had* no human subjects here. So he's got them on an observation ward on the second floor. They're locked in, but there's no security, there's no—there's *nothing*. I mean, this is a deadly virus we're talking about, here, and they're just up there, locked in their rooms. Everyone who deals with them uses protective suits, but that wouldn't do much good if one of them decided to get violent and attack. And that's exactly what we *want* to make them do. It's insane."

"How many do you have?"

"I don't know. I'm not about to go up there and look around. I've tried to keep as much distance from it as possible. Corcoran was making noise about keeping the infected survivors of the tests to see what kind of long-term effect the virus had, but if that's what he's done, I don't know where he's keeping them. I suspect he'd put them in the basement, but I haven't looked around down there to see, and I'm not going to."

Emilio took the phone from his shirt pocket. It was still recording, but he stopped it, then thumbed a few buttons and sent it to Ivan. He said, "I appreciate your talking to me like this and—"

He stopped when the lights went out, and for a moment, they sat in the dark and listened to the furious storm outside.

21

Ty didn't understand what he was seeing at first. It looked like a prank. It looked like a room in one of those Halloween spook houses. But they weren't in a spook house and this wasn't a prank.

Large cages stood along three of the room's walls, six on the right, six on the left, and four in the rear. Nine of the sixteen cages had people in them, one to a cage, and each was locked with a padlock. The occupants of the cage stood or squatted in back corners, silently watching Ty and Castillo. Harsh fluorescent lights glowed overhead, casting the interior of each cage in shadow.

"What . . . the fuck," Ty whispered as he and Castillo stood just inside the door, gawking at the cages.

"Oh, man, these bastards," Castillo said angrily through clenched teeth. "These fuckin' *bastards*. You know, I didn't believe Ollie at first, I thought maybe he was just being paranoid, but . . . *fuck*."

"We gotta let 'em out."

Castillo nodded slowly. "That's why we're here," he said, as if to remind himself, calm himself. "Yeah. Okay, let's get these things open and let them out."

They worked fast, using the bolt cutters on their belts to cut the padlocks. Because the cutters were small, it took some effort to cut through the shackles. As they worked, Castillo talked.

"You folks are gonna be fine," he said. "We've come to get you out of here. We're gonna get you to safety, don't you worry. You need any medical attention and we're gonna get it for you, you hear? We've come to help you."

When Ty opened each cage, he looked in at the occupant and found they were all doing the same thing: squatting in a corner looking tense and ready to spring to their feet and flee. Some were muttering to themselves rapidly, even angrily. By the time he opened the last one, it occurred to him that maybe they weren't ready to run away—maybe they were ready to attack.

When they were done, Ty and Castillo turned and looked at the open cages. No one had come out.

"If you can walk, it's okay to come out," Castillo said. "If you can't . . . well, let us know and we'll help you out of—"

The lights went out.

"Oh, shit," Ty said under his breath as he stood in complete darkness, unable to see anything. As he reached up to turn on his headlamp, there were quiet sounds of movement all around them.

The people in the cages were coming out.

Ty turned on his headlamp and found himself face to face with a pale, bony woman whose face had a skull-like appearance. An instant later, Castillo turned on his headlamp and illuminated more faces, all standing close.

"Don't worry," Castillo said, "the power's out, that's all. We're still going to get you out of—hey, don't do that. You need to come with us and—*hey*!"

Ty turned to see one of them attacking Castillo, all flailing arms and dancing shadows in the light of Ty's headlamp. Castillo raised his gun, but it was knocked out of his hand.

The faces moved in fast.

Both men were shouting when their headlamps were knocked off, and Ty fired his gun into the dark.

After that, there was only shouting. Then screaming.

PART THREE
Category 8

22

The barrel of the shotgun looked like a gaping black mouth about to close on Latrice's head. Her umbrella slipped from her suddenly slack right hand while her left arm hugged the package.

"Leland sent me," she said, frozen in place, afraid to move. "Leland Salt. In Sacramento."

"Where's Leland?" the man said. "*He's* supposed to be here."

"He had to leave the country."

"He had to—the fuck you mean, the *country*?"

"I . . . I mean . . . well . . . the country. He had to go to another country to live. That's what I mean. And he had to do it right away. He asked me to bring your package and said he'd let you know I was coming."

The man slowly lowered the gun. "Goddammit, Leland!" he said with more frustration than anger. "He'd let me know, huh? Well, he *didn't* let me know." He took the package from her. "Who're *you*?"

"Latrice Innes."

"You Leland's girlfriend, or somethin'?"

"No, just friends. I work in the bail bonds office he frequents." She stood between her Highlander and another SUV, somewhat protected from the wind, but she was getting soaked by the rain.

"I guess you should come on in outta the rain. Unless you got somewhere else to go. The hurricane's gonna hit tonight and they're tellin' everybody to take cover. It's all over TV." He reluctantly turned around and headed for the house, glancing over his shoulder to see if she was coming.

Latrice bent down and groped for her umbrella on the muddy ground. She found it, but got her hand muddy. She didn't care, was too scared to care, and shook the mud off. She'd never felt such strong wind in her life. Had she opened her umbrella, it would have been destroyed.

The first things Latrice saw upon entering the house were two dark, beefy pit bulls rushing toward her out of the dark, their claws clicking on the hardwood floor. She held up her hands defensively and started to back up when she saw their pink tongues flopping from their snouts and heard the excited, puppylike whining sounds they were making. One reared up, put his paws on her hip, and tried to lick her face while the other rolled over on her back and peed a little as she excitedly wiggled over the floor.

"Get down," the man ordered the dog as he closed the door. He leaned his shotgun in a corner, stomped his foot, and shouted, "Go on, you two, get outta here!" When the dogs ignored him, he kicked the one rolling on the floor. "Get the fuck out!" The kicked dog squealed and scrambled to get out of the foyer. The other followed and tossed back a single wounded glance on the way out. He shouted, "Hey, Marcus! Put the dogs in the garage, will ya?"

She heard movement deeper in the house then and a man's voice called the dogs.

"Take your coat off," her host said, nodding at the coat tree as he removed his own. "Sorry about the dogs. They always get excited when we have company. They're not very good watchdogs. Somebody broke in here to rob the place, they'd probably just play with him."

He was tall and somewhat pear-shaped. He pulled back his hood as he removed the coat to reveal a thick shock of red hair, which matched the freckles on his round, puffy face.

It was cloyingly warm in the house and Latrice wanted nothing more than to remove her coat, but she didn't want to stay.

"Look, I've really got to get back home to my kids," she said. "If you could pay me, I'll just get back in my car and—"

"*Pay* you? The fuck you talkin' about, *pay* you? For *what*?"

Latrice felt panic swelling upward from her gut. It had never occurred to her that she might not get paid. She'd trusted Leland. But at that very moment, she had no idea *why* she'd trusted him because she hardly knew him.

The only thing you know for certain about Leland Salt is that he's a charming old fart who wants to fuck you, and that's all. You're too damned trusting, always were. Mama always said that. And you never listened because how could you take her seriously while she was married to that asshole? But she's right, you're just too trusting, too fucking trusting. Now, how long have you been standing here staring at this angry ginger like you're in a trance?

She remained calm and quiet, in spite of her panic, as she said, "Leland told me you would pay me for the delivery."

"Oh. Well . . . you want, I can cover your gas."

"Leland said it would be five thousand dollars."

His facial expression became almost cartoonlike in its shock. "Five thou—what the fuck is he—when did Leland start doin' drugs? 'Cause he musta been doin' some good shit if he told you I was gonna pay you five thou—oh, wait."

He frowned down at the floor for a moment and scratched his head, deep in thought. Then he cocked a brow and studied her with suspicion.

"Leland said he was gonna call me and explain all this?" he said.

"He said he already had, but he'd missed you, so he left a message."

"Yeah, he left a message, left me a *couple*, but he didn't *tell* me nothin'. Just that there was some kinda change in plans and we needed to talk. Well, uh . . . it just so happens I owe Leland some money. Comes to about five grand. But I ain't givin' it to *you* till I talk to Leland. I mean, he wants me to give it to you, I will, but he's gonna have to tell me himself. I'll try to get him again, but he hasn't been answerin' and it's pissin' me off."

Latrice felt guilty for doubting Leland. He'd tried to cover up the fact that he was giving her five thousand dollars owed him by his friend. She was touched by his generosity, and his attempt to avoid embarrassing her with charity. But at the moment, she wanted to kick him in the junk for sending her to this place. There was a torchiere lamp glowing in the foyer, but through the archway ahead, she could see nothing but darkness with occasional flickers of light—a television playing somewhere in the next room.

"Take your coat off and I'll try to reach Leland again," he said.

Once she'd hung up her coat, he led her into the living room, which was lit only by the fifty-two-inch flat-screen TV on the wall, where two voluptuous, naked women were mud-wrestling in a ring surrounded by a screaming crowd. Two young men slumped on a couch watched the TV with heavy-lidded eyes. In front of them, a coffee table was cluttered with boxes of crackers, bags of potato chips, a few handguns, beer bottles, and a lot of drug paraphernalia. A young woman was curled into a sleeping ball on a love seat and sitting next to her was a fat, stubby Japanese guy with long hair and thick glasses, wearing sweatpants and a T-shirt, reading a book.

There was a brick fireplace in the corner that looked like

it hadn't been used as a fireplace in a long time. Instead, it was being used a storage space. Books and magazines were sloppily piled in the fireplace as if wearily waiting to be burned for outliving their usefulness. At the right end of the hearth stood a four-piece set of black iron fireplace tools— poker, shovel, broom, and tongs—hanging on a rack.

"I'm Giff, by the way," her host said as he sat down in a recliner and put the package on his lap. He nodded toward the love seat. "That's Jada, but she's wasted. Next to her is Tojo, but he's reading. He's always reading." He turned on a lamp beside the chair, produced a pocket knife, and cut the box open. Once he looked inside, he closed the box and put it on the floor, saying, "Yeah, that's the shit Leland was supposed to bring." Removing a cell phone from his pocket, Giff waved toward the men on the couch. "That's Jimmy and Marcus, by the way. Turn that fuckin' thing down, guys."

Jimmy aimed a remote at the TV and lowered the volume. He was so small and wiry that, at first glance, he looked like a boy, especially in the torn jeans and plain white T-shirt he wore. Marcus filled out his snug wife beater undershirt with plenty of muscle. His sandy hair was short and mussed, and he had tattoos on his arms and neck and metal in his face. He seemed unaware of Latrice's presence.

This is not the kind of company you wanna be keeping, girl, Latrice thought, looking at the guns and drugs on the coffee table. She stood there feeling stupid, wondering if she should sit down in one of the two empty chairs in the room or stay where she was and wait for Giff to make his call.

He leaned back in the recliner as he put the phone to his ear.

Marcus suddenly noticed Latrice and jolted to his feet as if he'd been poked with an electric cattle prod. He turned to Giff and said, "What the *fuck*, dude?"

"Shut up, Marcus, and deal with it," Giff snapped. Then he shouted, "Hey, Rosie! We got company!" He listened to the phone, then said, "Goddammit, Leland, where the fuck are you? Your friend is here and she wants your fuckin' money! Call me back right away and explain what the hell's goin' on, here, goddammit." He put the phone on the end table and turned to Latrice. "He say where he was goin'?"

Marcus stood beside the couch, silently glaring at Latrice. She tried to ignore him.

"Only that he was leaving the country," she said.

"He say why?"

"He said he stole something from somebody who's going to kill him for it if he sticks around. This was yesterday, and he said he was leaving right away. But if he hasn't called you back by now . . . well, I hope he's okay."

She glanced at Marcus. He had not moved nor taken his eyes from her.

"The fuck's wrong with you, Marcus?" Giff said.

"Well, who the fuck *is* she?" Marcus said.

"She's a friend of Leland's. You can shut the fuck up and watch your show or go back to your fuckin' trailer."

All three men were about the same age—late twenties, early thirties—but Giff spoke to Marcus as if he were a child.

Marcus stalked out of the room saying, "You gonna be bringin' niggers around, Giff, I'm outta here." A moment later, the front door opened and the sound of the storm rushed into the house until the door slammed, shutting it out again.

Giff looked at Latrice and shrugged. "That's just Marcus. He don't like your kind, is all."

Oh, yeah, Latrice thought, *this is a fun evening waiting to happen.*

She had to get out of there.

A moment later, a young woman walked in and stepped in front of Latrice, grinning.

"Hi, I'm Rosie," she said, smiling. She had thin, stringy, blond hair, extremely pale, splotchy skin, and a black patch over her left eye. Her face was gaunt and her sweatshirt and sweatpants seemed to be a few sizes too big for her. She appeared to be made of sticks, unable to hold still, constantly twitching or turning or slightly bouncing. "Who're you?"

"Uh, I'm Latrice."

To Giff, Rosie said, "Who's Latrice?"

"She delivered a package for Leland. I need to reach him but he ain't answerin' his goddamned phone."

Although neither sentence answered her question, Rosie seemed satisfied. She turned to Latrice and said, "C'mon in the kitchen, I'll get you something to drink."

Just us girls, Latrice thought. She followed Rosie, wondering just how weird the night was going to get.

23

The door was opened by a man who filled the doorway. He was tall, broad, black as midnight, with a head as smooth as an egg, and he wore a black sweatshirt, dark pants, and sunglasses. He was so unexpected that, for a moment, Andy wondered if they'd come to the wrong house.

The pounding beat of hip-hop music became louder when the door opened and, combined with the noise of the storm behind him, was a distraction for Andy.

"Uh, I need to see Jodi," he said.

"Jodi who?"

"Jodi Rodriguez. My ex-wife."

His eyes were invisible behind the dark glasses. "Jodi ain't here."

"Is my son, Donny, here?"

"No, Donny ain't here."

"Where are they?" Ram said.

The man did not move his head, just kept staring straight ahead, but Andy knew he was looking at Ram. "You got a warrant?"

Ram laughed. "I'm not here to search anything. We'd like to see the home owner, please."

"How you know I'm not the home owner?"

Ram smiled pleasantly. "You gonna make trouble? I'm not here for trouble. The man wants to see his son, that's all. What's the problem?"

He stared at Ram for a moment from behind those opaque lenses, then said, "Hang on a sec."

He started to close the door, but Ram reached out and stopped it, saying, "Hey, there's a storm going on out here. Mind if we wait inside?"

The man's mouth tightened for a moment and he seemed about to shove the door closed, anyway. He thought better of it and pulled it open to let them in.

The strong smell of marijuana filled Andy's nostrils and he immediately thought of Donny. Anger rose up in his gullet like bad seafood, but he held it down.

An entryway to the left opened onto a sunken living room where several people, black and white, were sitting around listening to music and talking. There were two black men and one black woman, and a white couple. Every head in the room turned to Andy, then shifted to Ram just behind him. They stiffened and the two black men stood up abruptly. Andy recognized none of them—they weren't part of Jodi's old crowd.

"Don't worry," Ram said, smiling, "I'm not here to bust anybody. That's not what this is. Andy, here, is an old friend of mine and I'm just helping him out, that's all. Nobody panic. I don't want any trouble."

The two men remained standing for a moment, watching Ram. One was small, skinny, boyish, and wore a fedora pulled low in front. He said something to the other one, who sat down, then came across the room to Ram. Up close, he was obviously older than he'd first appeared, probably in his late thirties, with a rugged face and a thin scar across his throat. He was quite short, not much over five feet. "What can we do for you, officer?" he said in a low, raspy voice.

"This is my friend Andy Rodriguez," Ram said. "His

ex-wife and son live here. He needs to see the boy as soon as possible."

"Yeah, well, they around here someplace." The little guy didn't hold still. He shifted his weight from foot to foot, bobbed his head, fidgeted with his hands. He turned to the big guy who had answered the door and said, "Get 'em down here. I think they upstairs." To Ram, he said, "I'm Anton. We just visiting from Sacramento. Vic's a business associate of mine. We came for the tornado."

Still smiling, Ram said, "You mean the hurricane?"

"Yeah, yeah, hurricane, that's it. We never been in no hurricane before, figured that'd be some real sick shit, y'know?"

Ram looked around the room. "Well, with all these windows unprotected, you're going to have the hurricane right in here with you before it's over." His smile never faltered.

"Ain't comin' till tomorrow."

Ram shook his head. "Now they're saying it's coming tonight." He looked at the windows again. "And I wouldn't want to be in here when it hits."

The little guy looked nervously at the windows, then turned to the others. "You hear that? The tornado's comin' tonight."

"Hurricane," one of the women said.

"What the fuck ever. Where's Vic?"

A moment later, a tall white man with shaggy dark hair that fell to his shoulders and a neatly trimmed beard and mustache walked into the room. In the cream-colored kaftan he wore, he looked a bit like Jesus Christ. He looked at Ram nervously and said, "Is there a problem?"

Ram's smile became a grin. "Vic! You look real good. A lot better than the last time I saw you. Remember that?"

Vic frowned suspiciously. "I don't think so."

"Yeah, I arrested you on a DUI, remember? Well . . . maybe not. You were pretty drunk, and it was a while ago. Anyway, my friend Andy here needs to see Donny."

Vic turned to Andy and said, "Who're you?"

"I'm Donny's father. Jodi's ex-husband."

Vic's eyebrows rose. "Oh, yeah, yeah." He turned to Ram again. "You're not here to bust us, or anything?"

"No, just helping Andy out. Can he see Donny?"

Vic continued to stare at Ram. He obviously didn't believe him and was wary.

"Hey, Vic," Anton said. "He says the tornado's comin' tonight, man, you gotta do somethin' about these fuckin' windows."

"What are *you* doing here?" Jodi said as she entered the room.

Andy was startled by how thin and pale she was as she hurried to his side looking at once surprised and angry. Her blond hair had been cut short and was flat and lifeless, and the sparkle was gone from her squinty eyes.

She said, "You're not scheduled for a visit today You're not supposed to *be* here!"

"I came to see Donny."

"Well, you *can't* see Donny because it's not your day to—"

"*Dad!*" Donny said from the entryway.

Andy turned and smiled at his son. The boy was wearing a sweatshirt and a pair of jeans. Andy knew they wouldn't have a chance to get his coat because he was just going to get Donny and leave without pausing for anything, but once he got in the car, he'd be fine. He hurried to his son with arms spread and said, "Hey, kiddo, how's it going?"

They hugged and Donny said, "How come you're here tonight?"

"Because I needed to see you."

Ram was suddenly beside him. "Take him and get out to the car," he whispered to Andy. "Now."

"Come on, big guy," Andy said, turning Donny toward the front door.

"Hey, wait, what do you think you're doing?" Jodi said. "Where are you going? It's not your scheduled time!"

Ram intercepted her, still smiling as he said, "He just needs a minute with the boy, that's all."

"But he can't *do* that!"

Ram nodded. "Yes, he can. The boy's in danger. You got drugs here. I can smell the weed, and your windows aren't boarded up, which means when that hurricane hits soon, you're gonna have a mess here. You've put your son in danger."

"But-but-but—"

"It's gonna be just fine, don't you worry. While he talks to your boy, I want to have a word with you." Ram went over to the front door to see Andy out. He whispered, "I'll be out in a minute, just sit in the car and wait."

"Where we going, Dad?" Donny asked as they went out the door.

Andy said, "We're going to sit in a police car for a minute, Donny, how about that?"

He glanced back just in time to see Ram closing the door with one hand and reaching under his raincoat to draw his gun with the other. Putting his arm around Donny, he said, "Okay, let's run to the car!"

They ran down the steps and into the wind, down the front walk, feet splashing in puddles, to the cruiser parked at the curb. Andy opened the car's rear door and let Donny dive in, then followed him and pulled it closed.

"What's happening, Dad? Why are you with a policeman?"

"He's here to help me get you home."

"Home? You mean your place?"

"Yeah. How would you like that? Would you like living with me full time?"

"Really?"

"Sure. I'll fix up the spare bedroom for you. We can get a basketball hoop for the backyard."

"And it'll be quiet, too, won't it?"

Andy put his arms around the boy and held him close,

chuckling. "Yes, it'll be quiet. Is it noisy like this most of the time here?"

"Yeah. Mom's friends like music. A lot. But they don't like cops." He looked out the window at the house. "I bet they're not very happy right now."

Andy followed Donny's gaze and looked through the window at the house. Water cascaded down the glass and made the house look like it was melting. He wondered what was going on in there. Ram had refused to tell him how he planned to convince Jodi to transfer custody, and Andy had been worried about that ever since. After seeing the people in the house, it seemed even less likely that Ram would be able to convince Jodi of anything. In her current mood, Andy doubted he'd be able to talk to her at all. The longer Ram stayed in there, the more worried Andy became.

Up the street, Andy saw a clump of shrubbery rolling and bouncing over the pavement, driven by the wind like a tumble-weed through a ghost town.

"How long is he gonna be in there?" Donny asked.

"I don't know. I'm not sure what he's—"

Andy's body jolted when he heard the first gunshot from inside the house, and again when the second fired. Then a woman screamed. Andy's insides turned to ice.

He turned to Donny to reassure him, but the boy looked unfazed. He did not seem at all surprised by the gunshots. He casually said, "They prob'ly shot him. They've all got guns."

Three more shots, almost overlapping each other. Another scream. As the wind blew harder, the windows of the house, along with the entire neighborhood, went dark.

24

Ollie was running up the stairs when the lights went out and plunged the stairwell into blackness. It startled him and his toe hit the top of the next stair and he went down, cracking his forearms against the edge of a step, then slid most of the way back down the stairs. He cursed as he reached up and turned on his headlamp, then got to his feet. His breathing was loud in the stairwell, and his heartbeat was loud in his ears.

He pulled the door open and stepped into the second floor corridor. He looked to the right, the left, stood there and listened a moment. It was drafty, and he could hear the storm outside, but he neither saw nor heard anything in the corridor. He knew that didn't mean much.

He turned right and moved swiftly but quietly down the corridor toward the rear of the building. He knew some of his men were on the second floor and was tempted to shout for them, but after the screams he'd heard on the phone, he decided to exercise caution.

A whispery sound behind him made him spin around. Rapid, rhythmic slapping noises—bare feet running on the tile—grew distant somewhere in the darkness beyond the reach of his headlamp. Someone was running away from him.

Ollie began running after the sounds, his heavy footsteps reverberating in the corridor. He saw nothing ahead. He stopped, listened, heard nothing. Turned around, listened again, then hurried back in the direction he'd originally been going, past the stairwell, farther into the darkness.

He came to another corridor that branched to the right, stopped and listened. Nothing. He took the cell phone from his belt to call one of his team leaders, but his foot struck something solid and heavy and he went down again, cursing. The cell phone slipped from his hand and shattered into a few pieces that skittered over the floor.

"Goddammit to hell," he muttered as he got up. Then, when he turned to see what had tripped him: "Oh, fuck."

One of his men, Sean Ferguson, lay sprawled on the floor on his back in a large puddle of blood, his face badly slashed, throat cut. His eyes were wide and his mouth yawned open, as if he had died mid-scream.

Head down, Ollie examined the floor around his feet and saw dark, wet smears and some distinct footprints. Some of the prints were clearly of bare feet. They had come from the direction in which he'd been headed.

"Blood," he whispered, stepping back. He remembered what Fara McManus had said about what she called the "test subjects."

You get the blood of a carrier on your skin, the virus is absorbed quickly. . . . The virus works swiftly. It will turn you into an enraged psychopath.

Goose bumps rose on his flesh under his clothes and the hair on the back of his neck stiffened. He had no way of knowing whose blood besides Sean's was all over the floor, so he made sure he avoided it as he moved slowly down the corridor, heading back to the footprints' point of origin. He made a mental note to remove his boots when he left the building, just to be safe.

The light from his headlamp fell in a pool on the floor and

moved along with him, passing over the shattered pieces of his cell phone, smeared with blood. He did not pick them up.

He came to another body, this one a woman in a pale hospital gown lying facedown on the floor. Blood stained the back of her gown and a section of the back of her head was a black, bloody hole. She'd been shot.

Ollie heard a sound up ahead, lifted his head, and saw light glowing through a doorway on the left, sweeping this way and that, and he heard a quiet voice.

"Jesus . . . Christ. Jesus fucking *Christ*."

He hurried forward, calling, "Who's there?"

"Ollie? It's Mack." His voice was hoarse and tense. He stepped through the doorway and turned toward Ollie, head-lamp flashing brightly.

"Don't move," Ollie said. "Stay right where you are."

He went toward him, watching where he stepped. He knew he already had blood on his boots and that he was safe as long as it didn't get on his skin, but after what McManus had said, he didn't want to touch any more blood if he could help it. Just being near it made his skin crawl.

"What the hell is going on?" he said.

"Sean and me, we were down the corridor going through all the rooms," Mack said, "when we heard gunshots and screaming. As we were running down here, the lights went out. We came around the corridor and there were these . . . these . . . *people*. A bunch of 'em. In, like, hospital gowns, or something. They just came out of the dark, a bunch of faces rushing toward us, a bunch of angry, crazy faces, and a couple of 'em had knives and they went for Sean. I mean, they just *jumped* on him like animals, like *savages*, and started stabbing and slashing. I started firing. I got a couple of 'em, killed one, I think, and then they came after me. I panicked, I lost it, and I just ran. Down here, into this room."

Ollie moved toward the doorway.

"Nothin' in there but Mikey Holt and Lester Cabot, and

they're both dead. They found the people we were looking for.
Shot their way in there"—he turned and gestured toward the
doorway through which he'd come—"Blew the fuck outta the
door. And they rescued 'em. Just like you said. They found
'em, let 'em out, and then . . . far as I can tell . . . those people
killed 'em, killed Mikey and Lester like they hated them,
cut 'em all to hell, stabbed 'em. They took Lester's clothes.
Those people, they were like, Jesus, like angry savages, or
something."

"Where the hell did they go?"

"I don't know. They came outta nowhere, I ran, and then
they were gone."

"You get any blood on you?"

"Blood? I-I don't know, I—"

"Any of *their* blood, I mean. The people who attacked you."

"I don't know."

"Jesus Christ. Who else is on this floor?"

"It was just me and Sean, Mikey, and Lester."

Ollie shook his head slowly as he stared at the open doorway. "We've gotta find them. We've gotta find the people they
let out of this room." He spoke the next sentence in a tight and
angry voice. "Before they get out of this building."

25

Hank found an emergency exit in the rear of the building, and when he pushed it open, it was caught by the wind and slammed against the outer wall. The wind nearly knocked Hank over when it hit him and he braced himself against the doorjamb. Rain blew in through the open door as he pulled the dead man's black coat together in front and stepped outside.

He thought it might be a good idea to cover his traces as much as he could. He pulled the door away from the wall with both hands and shoved it closed. Then he turned around, leaned back against it, and took in his surroundings.

After making his way through the dark hospital, his eyes had adjusted to the lack of light and he saw dead bodies lying in the gravel parking lot. They were dressed in dark clothes, but not the same clothes as the men who'd let Hank and the others out of their rooms. No ski masks. He saw four of them sprawled on the ground amid the parked cars. Another lay on the hood of a Toyota Corolla, the windshield of which bore three bullet holes, each at the center of a web of cracks in the glass.

Hank sucked in a deep breath of cold, damp air and blew it out with puffed cheeks, trying to calm himself. He was so angry, his hands shook and his knees felt weak, and he did not understand why. He should be glad to be out of that little room, out of that round, donutlike ward. But he was clenching his teeth and his fists as he stood in the rain.

It was the first time he'd been outside in what felt like a small eternity. The ski mask protected his face from the stinging rain and the heavy clothes kept him warm. Now all he needed was a car.

He scanned the cars until his gaze fell on a deep-red Jeep Wrangler hard top with black fenders. Hank had always been fond of the Jeep brand. Sturdy, long-lasting vehicles that were built to take a lot of crap. This one couldn't have been more than a year or two old and appeared to be in great shape.

With one more quick look around to make sure there was no one in the area to see him, Hank staggered through the wind and rain to the Jeep. He thought he would have to break in, but the door was unlocked. After all, it was parked in a secure facility that was fenced and gated, so why not leave it unlocked?

Before getting in, he looked across the parking lot at the single chain-link gate. It would be risky, but he thought he could crash through it without damaging the Jeep too badly.

He got into the Jeep, pulled the door closed, and took a moment to collect himself. He wanted to relax, but he couldn't. His heart pounded in his tight chest and his throat felt constricted. Maybe he'd feel better once he got away from the hospital and the people in it.

He'd started stealing cars when he was a kid. He hadn't done it in a while, but it was like riding a bike. He pushed the seat all the way back, spit on each of his palms, rubbed his hands together, then leaned forward to reach under the steering wheel.

Gifford was going to be so surprised. And he was going to pay for what he'd done.

26

Ivan's living room was thick with an air of nervous anticipation. He sat in the golden light of the popping, whispering flames in the fireplace with Mike Dodge and Julie Falk, eating popcorn, drinking coffee, and listening to the radio.

"We shouldn't be here," Mike said. "We should've gotten out of town." He sat in a club chair and rocked back and forth, his hands wringing, fidgeting, wringing.

"Would you like a Xanax, Mike?" Ivan said. "If so, I've got one. You really need to relax. I mean, Jesus, you're making me antsy." He had watched Mike grow increasingly anxious as the evening wore on and it was becoming irritating, even a little alarming.

Mike winced and shook his head. "I don't like pharmaceuticals. Got any weed?"

"No, sorry. I haven't had any in a while."

"I might have a joint in my purse," Julie said. She opened the bag and rummaged through the contents.

"Whatever you do," Ivan said, "don't drink any more coffee, Mike. You don't need it. I've got some wine. Would you like a glass of wine?"

"I don't drink," Mike said. "But this seems like a perfect

time to start. I've never had wine before. Maybe I should have a glass."

"We're going to be fine, Mike," Ivan said. "We're far enough inland here so we won't—"

Mike popped out of the chair like a toaster pastry, saying, "It's not the hurricane. That's just weather. The longer Emilio doesn't call, the higher my blood pressure goes. If Ollie and his soldiers have raided that hospital, and if what we suspect about what they're doing there is true, this could be . . . *disastrous*." He began to walk aimlessly around the living room. He didn't pace, he wandered.

"Found it!" Julie said, raising her hand with a joint between thumb and forefinger. "Do you need a lighter?"

Mike crossed the room, took the joint and the lighter she offered, and lit up where he stood.

Julie had just turned twenty-one, but she looked like an all-American high school cheerleader. Petite, with long, wavy, blond hair and a sunny disposition, she was the most unlikely of Ivan's Red Pill team. His radio show and website were more appealing to downbeat people who were inclined to have a darker outlook. She seemed much too conventional and wholesome to be interested in such things, but Julie was a walking encyclopedia of conspiracy lore.

Her grandfather had lived with her family when she was growing up and he had been, by all accounts, a complete loon who'd firmly believed *all* the conspiracy theories, even the ones that contradicted each other or canceled each other out. Julie had adored him and spent a lot of time listening to him talk, and reading his books and magazines. She'd absorbed all of it and remembered every detail, but she believed very little of it.

"I didn't believe Grampy's stories back then," she'd told Ivan, "but I loved them because they were such *great* stories. They were at least as good as fairy tales, or Harry Potter, or any of the comic books I read. I didn't believe any of those, so why should I believe Grampy's stories? For a long time, I didn't know *he* believed them. I just thought he was telling me stories, you know? But as I got older and learned he and a whole lot of other people believed them, I looked at them differently. They still work as stories, but as reality? No. I had to admit to myself that my grampy was . . . well, a little nutty."

When he asked her if she believed *any* of them, she said, "I know there are lots of real conspiracies and always have been. I don't know how anyone could know anything about history and not know that. Wherever there's power, there are conspiracies. I just don't believe in extraterrestrial lizards or the antichrist or witches and Satanists trying to rule the world. That's why I was so happy to find your website, because neither do you. You only focus on the stuff that makes sense. Nobody else is doing that. They either think the Illuminati is using the Freemasons to usher in the antichrist's rule, or they dismiss any mention of the word 'conspiracy.' You're in the middle ground, and that's usually where the truth is."

Julie had gone through high school in nearly half the usual time and started college early, where she'd earned a degree in literature and was working on another in anthropology. She believed the crazy conspiracy theories were myths in the making that served as a kind of camouflage for *real* conspiracies swirling in the halls of power, many of which were threats to life and freedom, all of which had as their goals money and power for a minutely small few.

She had never been, nor had she ever wanted to be, a cheerleader.

Julie and Mike were still at Ivan's house because they'd gotten stuck there. Ever since Ivan had heard from Emilio that afternoon and the conversation had been abruptly interrupted, they'd been waiting anxiously for him to call back. They'd done busywork around the office as they waited, but no call came and Emilio himself did not show up. When Ivan saw the news on the Internet that the hurricane would be hitting earlier than expected, later that very night, he'd told them to go home, but the weather had become so furious that he decided not to let them leave.

"I've got plenty of room and food," he'd said. "You can stay the night. We'll make popcorn and tell ghost stories."

And then they'd received Emilio's recording. They listened to it again and again, their mouths hanging open in a combination of shock and delight.

But still, there was no call from Emilio.

"I think you should call him," Mike said.

"I'm afraid to do that. If he were capable of talking on the phone, he'd call. I don't know what kind of situation he's in, I just know it's one in which he can't talk on the phone."

"Then you should call the police," Mike said.

Ivan shook his head. "I don't think they'll be too receptive, not when they've got a hurricane to worry about."

"Are you going to smoke that whole thing by yourself, Mike?" Julie said.

"Oh, damn, sorry, Julie, I wasn't thinking," Mike said, quickly offering her the joint.

"You're thinking too much," Ivan said, standing. "Sit down and relax and I'll get you a glass of wine."

He was on his way to the kitchen when his phone trilled in his pocket.

Julie and Mike gasped.

Ivan looked at the screen. "It's Emilio." He turned on the speaker. "Jesus, Emilio, we've been worried sick."

"I can't talk long, just listen," he whispered.

Ivan turned up the phone's volume

Emilio said, "Ollie and his crew have taken this place and seem to have taken out all the security guys doing it. There was a lot of shooting earlier, and since then, Ollie seems to have the run of the place. They came here to release the test subjects, but damn, is *that* a bad idea. Did you get the recording I sent you?"

All three of them said at once, "Yes!"

"Emilio, it's fucking amazing," Ivan said.

"Last time I saw Ollie, he was in a panic," Emilio said. "They're keeping the test subjects on the second floor. Once he learned what they were about to set free, he called one of the guys on the second floor and tried to stop them. Didn't work. Over the phone, we heard screams and gunshots. I think they've let them out. Some of them, anyway. Fara thinks there's more in the basement."

"Fara?" Ivan said. Emilio had told him about Dr. Fara McManus in the past, but he'd never called her Fara before.

"Yeah, we kinda bonded. You gotta get her, Ivan. She's ready to talk. Far as I can tell, she knows *everything*, and she's ready to spill it all."

"Is there anything we can do to get you out of there?"

"Talk to Ollie. Talk some sense into that crazy fucker. He might listen to you."

"He didn't listen to me this afternoon."

"You shoulda seen his face when he heard those screams. He knows he's made a big mistake, I think, but he doesn't know how to deal with it. He likes you, Ivan, in spite of your differences. He knows you're fair with him, which is more than you can say about most of the people in this town. Maybe you can help him rationalize his way out of this, give him some way to get out of it without losing too much face. Just tell him anything to get him to call this shit off so we can get the fuck outta here."

"Where are you now?"

"The bathroom in Fara's office. The guy Ollie's got watching us wouldn't let me go down the hall. And he doesn't want me making any calls, either. So I gotta go. Get to Ollie. Talk to him."

"Can I call you?"

"No, don't. I'm afraid they'd take my phone away. I'll call again when I can. I hear the hurricane's hitting tonight. We might be in the safest place in town here, but I'd rather be home, tell you the fuckin' truth. Back at my house, ain't nearly as many people gettin' *killed*. I'll call again soon as I can."

27

The bathroom in Fara's office was so small, it made him feel claustrophobic and a little short of breath. She had given him her small flashlight so he didn't have to relieve himself in the dark. He put the phone in his pocket and flushed the toilet. There was no sink, so he opened the door and went back into the office.

"The sink's over there if you want to wash your hands," Fara said, pointing to the sink in a dark cubbyhole in the opposite corner of the room.

"Sit down," Craig said. "Wash later." He stood near the closed door to the corridor, hands joined in front of him.

As Emilio was returning to his chair, Dr. Corcoran entered the office with another masked man right behind him with a gun. He was surprised to see some genuine emotion on Corcoran's face. Normally, the man walked around deep in thought, or with a smirk, or he was talking a mile a minute to someone as he hurried down a corridor, or he looked half asleep. But as he stood in Fara's office, Corcoran wore fear on his face like foundation makeup.

"I hope this didn't interrupt your party, Dr. Corcoran," Fara said.

His eyes narrowed. "I think the fact that you can find humor in this is disgusting."

"That was sarcasm, not humor. I'm not laughing. We have no power because our generator is shit. It looks like these geniuses have let out our test subjects, something they never could have done if you'd installed the proper safeguards."

"This is as much your doing as it is mine," Corcoran said.

Fara's eyes wandered in the direction of nothing in particular as she slowly nodded her head. She seemed to drift away for a moment, then turned back to Corcoran.

"Yes, you're right. I've got a lot to make up for, and that's what I intend to do."

"What are you talking about?"

Ollie walked in before Fara could answer. He went to Fara's desk, turned around, and leaned his ass on the front edge. He pointed his gun at Corcoran, then turned it on Fara, then back to Corcoran.

"I want answers from you two," he said. "This project, this whole thing, with your human test subjects and everything, this is for the government? The military? It's Uncle Sam–approved, and everything?"

Corcoran looked down his nose at Ollie with unconcealed disdain. "I have no obligation to explain any of this to you or—"

Ollie pressed the barrel of his gun to the corner of Corcoran's left eye. "I got your obligation right here. Don't fuck with me, pal. I *will* shoot you. We came here with the idea that everybody other than the people we came for was expendable, just in the way. Now I've found a use for you, so you'd better take advantage of it. Answer the fucking question."

Corcoran licked his lips. "The work we're doing here is for Vendon Labs."

"Vendon Labs is a government contractor, don't bullshit me. This work is for the government, yes?"

"Yes, it is," Fara said, "of *course* it is. We're developing a biological weapon for the military. A virus. I told you that already."

"I'd like to hear *him* say it," Ollie said.

A sudden explosion of sound and movement in the dark made everyone jump. A figure ran into the office through the open door shrieking, jumped in the air, and latched on to Corcoran's back. Corcoran released a ragged yelp as he went down, hitting the floor with a grunt.

Fara screamed as she lunged from the couch and hurried to Emilio's side in the corner. Emilio stood so suddenly that he knocked his chair over as he shouted a string of obscenities.

The figure was a skinny man with a shaved head, wearing a bloodstained hospital gown. Blood was spattered and smeared on his bare arms and legs, too. He straddled Corcoran's prone body and began repeatedly punching the back of his head.

28

"I'm making cookies for the kids," Rosie said as she led Latrice into the kitchen.

It was a beautiful kitchen. The floor, walls, and counter-tops were all tiled in a mottled tan and brown. There was a big sub-zero refrigerator built into the wall with a shiny stainless-steel door, dark wood cabinets. But it was a slovenly mess. Dirty dishes, pots, and pans filled both sides of the sink and covered most of the counter space. Spilled food littered the floor, along with a couple of children's toys, some pet toys, and scattered bits of dry pet food. An archway opened onto a dining area, but it was dark in there. On the floor in the arch-way was what looked to Latrice like a dog turd. She was grateful that cookies were baking. The delicious aroma prob-ably covered other smells.

"I got hot coffee, if you want," Rosie said. "And we got lotsa booze."

"Coffee would be nice." Latrice wanted to see if Rosie could find a clean cup.

Rosie opened one of the cupboards. It was empty except for three lonely coffee mugs. "You want cream? Sugar? Or just black?" She took in a sharp breath and turned to Latrice with big eyes. "Um . . . no offense."

Latrice surprised herself by laughing. "No offense taken."

"Oh, good." She poured coffee into the mug. "I just never know what's supposed to be offensive anymore." Rosie was so jittery that she spilled some of the coffee as she handed the mug to her. "You're lucky to be here tonight, you wanna know the truth. The storm's knockin' the power out all over the place, but Giff's got a great big generator. We got all the power we need. Where you from?"

"Sacramento. I was planning to drive back tonight, but—"

"Oh, no, you don't wanna do that. The hurricane's coming tonight. They screwed up. Or the hurricane got faster. Something. You might get stuck here for the night."

Latrice could not conceal her chagrin.

"Oh, that's okay, we got room. It don't look like it from the front, but this is a big-ass house. Giff's dad, Hank, had it built a long time ago. Hank's gone now, though. I mean, he's not dead. Well . . . not that anybody knows for sure. See, Giff's dad is kind of, you know, mentally unhinged because he's been doing drugs for so long, and years ago, he went off and decided to be a homeless bum. Lives in the woods, eats at homeless shelters. Only *now*, nobody knows *where* he is, 'cause he's disappeared, like a bunch of other homeless people. Giff thinks they're being experimented on in the old mental hospital, but only because he listens to a crazy fuckin' show on the Internet."

Rosie seemed to be a sweet girl under all those meth symptoms, but she had a harsh voice and Latrice found herself unable to keep up with her chatter. She sipped her coffee and turned down the volume on Rosie's voice.

She couldn't be stuck here for the night. But she knew Giff might never get in touch with Leland. Latrice had the sinking feeling she would be going home empty-handed.

"—want some of these cookies, Latrice?"

She was startled out of her thoughts. "I'm sorry, what?"

"Cookies are almost done. Want some?"

They smelled delicious and Latrice was hungry, but she'd decided she could not stay. If she got out of there right away, maybe she could beat the hurricane. She couldn't take Highway 101, though, because it ran along the coast. There was another route that would take her to Redding and she could catch Interstate 5 from there, but she didn't know what that route was. She'd have to Google it. But she could do that in the car.

Before she could respond to Rosie, an explosive crash made the entire house rattle.

Latrice and Rosie stared at each other a moment, paralyzed by the shock. Rosie shouted, "What the *fuck*?" and ran out of the kitchen.

As Latrice followed, she heard excited voices ahead.

Giff shouted, "Sounded like somebody drove into the goddamned house!"

When Latrice got to the living room, it was empty. Rosie was looking out the front door, struggling to hold on to it as powerful wind pounded into the house. She leaned out of the door for a moment, then came inside and shoved it closed against the wind.

"God*damn*, somebody drove a Jeep into the corner of the house!" she said.

Two gunshots cracked outside, then someone shouted, and the shouting got louder until the door flew open and Giff stumbled in.

"Jesus fucking Christ," he was shouting, "he shot me! Dad fucking *shot* me!" He had not put on a coat and his clothes were soaked. His left arm dangled uselessly at his side as he grabbed the door with his right hand and tried to close it.

"It's your *dad*?" Rosie said.

"He shot Jimmy! In the *head!*"

Giff almost had the door closed when it was shoved from the outside.

"Open this door, you cocksucker!" It was a man's voice on the other side of the door.

Giff threw himself against the door and slammed it shut.

The gun fired again and Giff hit the floor, frantically crawling away from the door.

It flew open again and an old man dressed in black, with a pale, shaved head, burst into the house, shouting and shooting.

29

Andy could not remember ever being so afraid. He and Donny huddled together in the backseat of Ram's police car, peering out the window at Jodi's house after hearing gunshots and screams. The wind assaulted the car, which bounced on its shocks under the force of the storm.

"What's he doing in there, Dad?" Donny whispered.

"I don't know anymore."

Another gunshot was accompanied by a brief flash in the dark front window.

Andy's palms were wet, his hands were shaking, his mouth was dry, and he felt nauseated. Somewhere in the back halls of his mind, his mother called for him to come take his medicine, and his hands clenched into fists.

"I need you to stay right here in the car, Donny," he said.

"You're going in there?"

"I have to. Your mom's in there and we want to make sure she's okay, right? Don't we?"

Donny nodded, but his frown did not support the gesture. "But what do I do if *you* get shot?"

"Ram is—that police officer is a friend of mine, he won't shoot me."

"What about Vic and Anton and them guys? They'll shoot anybody."

"Just stay right here, Donny. I won't be long. I just want to make sure that—well, just stay right here and I'll be back in a minute."

He gave Donny a tight hug, then ignored his own fear and opened the door. The wind snatched it from his grasp and swept it open wide. Andy got out, closed the door, then ducked his head, leaned into the wind, and went up the front path, up the porch steps to the door.

His heart throbbed in his throat, choking him with each beat.

You're going to give yourself a heart attack with all this stress!

He clenched his eyes shut against the sound of his mother's voice.

You're fine, he told himself. *There's nothing wrong with you. There would be something wrong with you if you weren't afraid right now.*

He went into the house.

Once he closed the door against the bullying wind, he stood in the dark and listened.

The house seemed eerily silent after the music that had pounded so loudly earlier. Through the howling of the wind, he heard a voice speaking quietly, but angrily. It sounded like Ram.

He moved to the archway to the left and looked into the living room. There was a small sphere of light at the other end of the room, but before Andy focused on that, his eyes paused over the still shapes in the dark. Three were on the floor, shapes of deeper darkness within the darkness. Another was half-sprawled on the couch and another lay on the floor beside the couch. Still another was slumped in a chair.

Andy's eyes moved to the light and saw Ram on his knees, shining his flashlight into Anton's face. Anton was sitting on the floor with his back against an ottoman that had been

shoved against the wall. Blood glistened on his face. Ram
straddled Anton's outstretched legs and held the flashlight in
his left hand. In his right, he pressed the barrel of his gun to
Anton's cheekbone. He was speaking to him in a low, breathy
voice, but angrily, sometimes spitting as he talked.

Andy gulped and tried to stir up some saliva in his mouth.
He said, "Ram?"

Ram moved with frightening speed as he rose to his feet
and turned around, aiming his gun at Andy.

"Hey, it's me, it's *me*!" Andy said, raising both hands.

"Oh, Andy," he said, smiling as he lowered the gun. He
turned to Anton again and kicked him hard in the face.
Anton's upper body flew sideways and hit the floor. After that,
he remained still.

Ram came to Andy, stepping over the bodies on the floor.
His left arm swung at his side, sending the flashlight's beam
sliding wildly across the floor and onto the walls.

"Did I lose track of time?" he said. "I do that sometimes."

"Whuh-what, uh . . . what are you doing?"

Ram frowned. "Doing? What I told you I was going to do.
Set things straight. Make sure you got custody of your son."
He sounded defensive and a little offended. The he added,
with a smile, "And hey, I did the world a few favors in the
process. These people? Scum. All of them. Your ex-wife was
hanging out with some bad people, Andy, *bad* people. Drug
dealers, pimps. Niggers! And she was exposing your son to
all of it."

"Where . . . where is she?"

He lifted the flashlight at his side and pointed it at the
couch.

The beam fell on Jodi, who lay with her upper body on the
couch, legs hanging off to the side, feet resting on Vic's head.
Jodi's cheek rested on her right arm, which was extended
across the cushion. Her eyes were open and seemed to bulge
from their sockets. A strip of glistening red started at her

nostrils and covered most of her mouth, chin, and right cheek. There was a black hole nearly centered in her forehead.

Andy's lungs turned to ice and he could not inhale or exhale. He could not move his limbs. Even his eyes would not move from Jodi's corpse.

She'd served him corned beef and hash the first time they met. She had cried when she'd confessed to him that she was a drug addict, fully expecting that to be the end of their relationship. She'd cried and laughed at the same time when he'd asked her to marry him. She'd wailed in agony and delight as he watched Donny come out of her. He'd seen her at her best and worst and everything in between, and during the years she'd managed to stay away from drugs, she'd been the best wife anybody could hope for, the best lover and mother and friend.

Now her dead eyes stared at him in the beam of a flashlight because he had sent Ram to kill her.

But he hadn't! He *never* would have gone along with it if he'd known Ram's intentions. How could he have known the man would turn it into a mass killing? How could he have known?

Hey, mommy's boy!

Then his lungs of ice shattered and he gasped for air as he rushed to the couch, arms outstretched, saying in a high wail, "Jesus *Christ*, what did you *do*?" He dropped to his knees beside Jodi, reached both hands out to touch her, but he couldn't do it. His trembling hands stopped a fraction of an inch from her body, then pulled away. He turned to find Ram towering over him, the light on his face.

"You changed your mind about her, did you?" Ram said. "Since we last spoke? Huh?"

"Changed my—"

"Because you came to me, remember. You came to me with that story about how your wife was endangering your son. Isn't that right? Am I misremembering that?"

"No, no, you're not, buh-but I-I-I didn't want to—"

Ram hunkered down and leaned his forearms on his spread knees, hands dangling between them, the flashlight's glow coming up from the floor. He leaned close to Andy and whispered, "You can't let the cunts get away with that. You just can't, Andy, because if you do, they'll just keep it up. And in the process, they fuck up the kids. I see it again and again."

Andy felt like he was sinking. Like the floor—even the earth under the floor—was dissolving and he was sinking down into the kind of nightmare from which it is impossible to wake up.

"But the whole world's against you, Andy. The laws, the courts—everything's against you. Because this country's turned into one big, fat, stinking vagina."

Andy thought of all the times he'd seen Ram with his family—a lovely, plump, blond wife, two blond kids, a boy and a girl—in town shopping, or sitting in a restaurant, or coming out of their church on Sunday as Andy drove by. While Ram might no longer have his youthful good looks, they made a handsome family, the kind of family you might see in a travel brochure, or in a prescription drug commercial. But the Ram Andy had known did not fit into that picture, so each time he saw them, Andy had told himself that Ram probably was a rotten husband and a nightmare of a father, that he probably cheated on his wife and treated her like a slave, and took all of his problems out on his kids.

"So you gotta look out for yourself. I'm tellin' ya, Andy, you *gotta*. Nobody else is gonna look out for you. Unless you happen to be one of those lucky few who has a friend . . . a *real* friend . . . who has your back. I was trying to be that kind of friend, Andy."

All it had taken to change Andy's mind was that single, brief meeting with Ram in the courthouse. That had convinced him that Ram the hateful, sadistic boy had grown into a responsible man. Ram was so friendly and genuine, he'd made Andy *want* that to be true. He *wanted* to believe that the monster of his youth had been melted down into a decent, friendly human being.

But Andy had been right the first time.

"I wanted to be the kind of friend who would look out for you. To . . . well, like I said . . . to make up for the way I treated you in school." He rose up to his full height again, extended his arm, elbow locked, and held his gun a couple of inches from the top of Andy's head. He shouted at the top of his voice, "*Are you tellin' me I made a fuckin' mistake?*" The corners of his mouth were pulled down and he glared at Andy.

Hey, mommy's boy!

Andy's mind, barely coherent, babbled at him: *Go along just tell him go along what he wants to hear go along with whatever he says!*

"No, Ram, no, no, no." He repeated the word "no" quietly, over and over, as he slowly got to his feet, holding up his left hand, palm out. "No, you didn't. I'm, I'm—" For a moment, the words caught in the soft, moist tissue of his throat like shards of glass. He coughed once. "Grateful, really, I'm grateful for what you've done. Are *you* okay? They didn't hurt you, did they?"

Ram slowly lowered his gun. He seemed confused by Andy's response. "Uh, no. They didn't hurt me."

"Good, I'm glad. We were worried."

He frowned. "We?"

"Donny and me. Out in the car. We heard the gunshots and we were worried."

"About . . . me?"

"Yeah. Donny's still out there and the storm's getting worse. Don't you think we should get out of here?"

Ram thought about that for a moment, then slowly nodded. "Yeah, we should go. We should. It wouldn't be good to stick around here." Still nodding, he said, "Hang on just a second."

Ram turned and walked back over to Anton, who still lay

on his side, unmoving. Pointing his gun at Anton's head, arm
rigidly extended downward, Ram leaned forward slightly and
fired. Then again. He stood upright and turned to Andy.

"This was a good thing we did here tonight."

Jesus Christ, we?

Andy wondered vaguely if Ram had always been like this,
or if something had triggered it. If he did *this* sort of thing
with any regularity, it seemed he would get caught. He had
killed everyone in the room—did he expect to simply walk
away and be free of any consequences? As a cop, he should
know better. He didn't seem to care if he got away with it or
not. He didn't even seem to be considering that.

"These people wouldn't have changed," he continued.
"They don't rehabilitate. They just reproduce." He released
one cold, steely laugh. "These won't. Now, your boy is with
you, and that cunt, that traitor to her own son, is gone. I know
it's harsh, Andy, but it's the only way to deal with them. I
know. My wife was gonna take our kids. She was gonna take
'em away from me. That fucking cunt was gonna take our
kids and leave town and divorce me and keep me away from
my own fucking flesh and blood."

His voice was getting tighter and his upper lip began to
pull back as he spoke. He was making himself angry.

"She's been fucking somebody else. Can you believe that?
Some other guy, some cocksucker. I don't know who yet, but
I'm gonna find out, and I'm gonna take care of him. But I had
to take care of her first. And I did."

He winked at Andy and suddenly broke into a bright smile.

"Took care of her tonight. That cunt ain't gonna pull that
shit with *me*, nofuckingsiree. So I know what I'm talking
about, Andy. From personal experience. There's only one way
to deal with them, and it's harsh, but when it has to be done,
you've just gotta fuckin' *do* it." He turned and headed for the
archway. "Let's go, Andy. Let's get you and your boy home."

Andy was afraid his legs would collapse beneath him, but

he tried to move with confidence as he followed Ram. He had to keep himself steady, stay calm, and play along until he and Donny got home. Somehow, he would have to signal to Donny to say nothing once Ram was behind the wheel.

As they went out into the storm, he feared for Ram's wife and children, hoping they were safe. And he feared for Donny, and for himself. Because Ram was clearly insane.

30

"Get it off me!" Corcoran screamed. "Get it off me!"

Fara pressed her back to the wall and watched Corcoran struggle under the angry man punching him in the back of the head. She looked around at the others. No one would move. They were all thinking the same thing, she was certain—that the blood on that crazed man could infect them.

Everyone was frozen in place, in a position that suggested they were trying to back away even farther.

Corcoran struggled and screamed.

Fara thought, *I should do something. This is my responsibility. I should help him, but I don't know how, and I'm afraid, holy shit, I'm so afraid.*

All she wanted to do was run from the room, run to her car, and get as far away from Springmeier as possible.

Time seemed to stretch like warm taffy as they stood there and watched that angry, bloody man pound on Corcoran's head forever and ever.

But only seconds passed, just under three, and the man Emilio called Ollie stepped forward confidently, pulled back his right foot and kicked the bloody man in the ribs. The man grunted and fell off of Corcoran, landing on his side, but he did not let go of him. Ollie stepped over Corcoran's legs and kicked the man in the back. He cried out in pain and lost his grip on Corcoran.

Ollie nudged Corcoran with his toe and said, "Get up, get up."

Corcoran crawled on hands and knees away from his attacker, straight toward Fara. He got to his feet and turned around as the bloody man was trying to get up.

Ollie aimed his gun at the man's head and fired. He dropped flat and stopped moving. Ollie stood there and stared at him for a long time, his back to the others, head down, arms at his sides.

No one moved. Fara, Emilio, Corcoran, Ollie, and his two men—they all stared at the dead body. Fara felt something new in the air, something that hadn't been there just a moment ago: dread.

A life had just ended in front of them because of all this, and suddenly, it became real, the scope of the threat became real, and they were all in great danger.

Ollie turned around and locked a withering gaze onto Fara, then Corcoran.

"I knew that man," he said in a quiet, trembling voice. "Killing him has not put me in a good mood, so I don't want any shit from you two. You got some kind of antidote to this?"

Corcoran did not seem to notice Ollie. He continued to stare at the dead body. His lower lip trembled and his eyebrows pressed together above wide eyes.

"No," Fara said.

Ollie squinted at Corcoran as he approached them slowly. "The hell's wrong with him. Is he sick?" He looked at Fara. "Does it kick in this fast?"

"I'm sure it's drugs."

"Drugs?" Ollie's eyes were disbelieving. "What kind of drugs?"

"Who knows. Pills, cocaine."

"He's been running this place on drugs?"

"I'm afraid so."

The quivering in Corcoran's lower lip spread over his face and he appeared to be near tears. He was shaking all over as he continued staring at the dead body.

Ollie turned to Corcoran. "How many are there?"

Corcoran's head began to turn back and forth, slowly at first, but steadily faster.

To Fara: "Do you know? How many of these *test subjects* are there?"

"I'm not sure. At least a dozen, but beyond that, I don't know." She turned to Corcoran. "Dr. Corcoran, you need to snap out of it," she said firmly. She stepped in front of him, closed her fists on his scrub shirt, and shook him, saying, "Goddammit, *snap out of it!*"

Corcoran pushed her away limply, turned and staggered to the couch, where he dropped down into a slumped position, a look of pain and terror on his face.

"A dozen upstairs," he said, his voice a croak.

"What about the survivors?" Fara said.

He looked as if speaking were painful. "Nine."

"Where are they? Where are you keeping them?"

"The subbasement."

"How did you get them down there?"

"I . . . had help."

"Who? Who else knows about them?"

"Just . . . Holly. And Caleb."

"Tell me something, Ollie," Fara said. He flinched at her use of his name, but she ignored it. "Do we have *any* security team left?"

"They were very aggressive, and we were very determined. There may be some still alive, but they aren't functioning."

"Then this is going to be up to you and your guys."

"What is?"

"We can't let those people get out of the building. They are going to be angry and violent and irrational."

"Those are the people we came here to help."

"Yes, well, that wasn't a very good idea, was it? Now you're going to have to help everybody else by finding them and killing them. Maybe next time you want to raid a facility like this, you'll give it some thought first."

Ollie's eyes stared icy daggers at her for a moment. He said, "I need to borrow somebody's cell phone. I lost mine upstairs."

Fara took her purse from the couch, got her phone out of it, and handed it to Ollie. He took it and punched in a number, then turned away from her.

"You hearing that storm out there?" Emilio whispered to her.

She listened for a moment. The wind roared outside the walls like an army of banshees. She heard the faint crash and clatter of things blowing around outside, slamming into the building.

"I think Quentin has arrived," Emilio said.

Ollie finished his call and said to Fara, "I'm gonna have to keep this phone while I'm here."

She nodded.

"Are the only exits in the rear?"

"Yes," she said. "Everything is locked up pretty tight except for the entrance and one emergency exit in the rear."

"Okay, I got a couple of men on that." He turned to the two masked men, waved toward the door, and started to lead them out. He stopped and turned to Fara and Corcoran, mouth open to speak, but an explosion went off somewhere in the hospital. Everything shook and the explosion dissolved into the sound of heavy things collapsing, sounds of destruction and collapse.

After that, the storm somehow became louder.

31

Hurricane Quentin arrived on the northern California coast at 9:14 p.m., more than thirteen hours earlier than originally forecast. The storm already in progress suddenly became infused with malicious intent as its strength doubled, then tripled as Hurricane Quentin roared into Eureka like a demon. Trees bowed to it, and some snapped and went down forever under its force.

The Pacific Ocean seemed to take notice of Humboldt County for the first time in recent memory and rushed in to see what these industrious upstarts were up to, do a little damage, put them in their place.

The community of Samoa, in the northern peninsula of Humboldt Bay, was a collection of residential neighborhoods, with houses lined up in neat rows on clean streets. The hurricane slammed into them like the tantrum of a god. Fences were ripped out of yards and sent cartwheeling through the air. Trees were toppled and sent into empty, evacuated living rooms and bedrooms and kitchens. Tool sheds and pool houses were flattened. Lawn furniture and garbage cans that had not been put away traveled through the air like missiles.

The vast, barn-red Samoa Cookhouse—the only authentic cookhouse remaining in the West, which had fed the workers from the Hammond Lumber Company at the beginning of the twentieth century and now fed hungry tourists who belched their eggs-and-sausage breakfasts as they wandered through the historic museum and gift shop after eating—was flooded by the storm surge, and the wind tore off great segments of its peaked roof, flinging them into the night.

When the old man staggered through the front door, shouting, and firing his gun, Latrice turned and hurried back the way she'd come. As she put the living room behind her, she glanced at the love seat to see Jada still curled up on her side. Latrice found herself in the kitchen again, with Rosie scurrying in behind her, moving in short, staccato steps, her head down, as if she were ducking bullets.

"You said there are kids in here somewhere?" Latrice said.

"They're in their rooms playing games."

"Well, Jesus Christ, girl, who's taking care of them?"

"They won't come out. They know better."

"Fuck, what kind of people *are* you?" she said as she rummaged in her purse for her phone.

There were two more gunshots in the living room and a lot of shouting.

Latrice held her phone in a shaking hand as she pressed three buttons.

"Who you callin'?" Rosie said.

"The police."

Rosie's gasp was loud as she lunged toward Latrice and reached with both splayed hands for her phone. Latrice stepped backwards, but Rosie's hands latched on to the phone, one on each side.

"No, you can't do that!" she hissed. "Giff'll be so *pissed*! Don't call the cops, Latrice, *please*!"

As she pleaded with Latrice, she tried to pull the phone from her hand.

Another gunshot exploded in the other room.

A man screamed, "No, goddammit!"

A deranged cackle rose and fell a few times.

Another gunshot.

Latrice feared the old man would run out of people to shoot and come in here.

"Let go of the phone or I will fucking deck you," Latrice said, her voice surprisingly calm as she struggled with Rosie.

"No no no, you can't he'll be so mad please don't—"

She heard more screaming from the living room, a man shouting, "Jesus, no, get him off me, get him off me!"

Adrenaline surged through Latrice and made her ears ring and her own terror overwhelmed her desire not to hurt Rosie. She punched her in the face.

Rosie immediately stopped talking and collapsed to the floor like a skinny, multijointed marionette whose strings had been cut, limbs splayed, eye patch askew.

When Latrice put the phone to her ear, a woman was already saying, "—your emergency, please? Hello? Is someone there?"

"Hello, yes, I'm here. I need help. I'm trapped in a house where some guy has gone crazy and is shooting people."

"Where are you?"

Latrice had memorized the address on the drive up and recited it.

"Who's shooting?"

"I don't know, some old man who—"

Another gunshot startled Latrice so badly that she almost dropped the phone.

"Is that more gunfire?" the dispatcher said.

"Yes. I'm in the kitchen, he's in the living room."

The dispatcher didn't say anything for a moment and Latrice heard silence in the other room.

The voice said, "I'll have someone there in—"

He came through the doorway, his dark clothes soaked,

his face and bald head bloody, holding the gun in both hands, arms outstretched, elbows locked, and he ran toward Latrice shrieking.

It slammed into Old Town and wailed down its narrow streets and alleys. Shingles leapt from the roofs of the shops and two of the decorative, sculpted trees planted along the sidewalk did a dance down Second Street, bobbing and tumbling.

The Carson Mansion, constructed in 1886 by lumber baron William Carson for his wife, Sarah, stood in Old Town like an enormous Queen Anne music box, emerald green and intricate in its baroque design, ready at any moment to become animated as it played its delicate, tinkling tune. In a town filled with cakelike Victorian mansions, this one was considered to be one of the most grand in the world.

The wind tore at it like a thousand talons, ripping and scratching and pounding, clawing at shingles and slats and eaves and ornate pieces of carved wood, slashing pieces from the extravagant old house and sending them flying into the storm like pieces of old dead skin sloughing off. Finally, a segment of the roof lifted up like a great mouth opening until the top part was sheared away by the wind and tumbled into the night.

While the wind assaulted the old house, the ocean surged into the bay, attacking the marina, sending docked boats slamming into piers and each other. Water rushed up over the land and flooded First Street, then covered the green grounds around the mansion, gushing through the bars of the wrought-iron fence and washing away the sign that identified the mansion as the headquarters of the Ingomar Club, before rushing the house itself and splashing against its green walls.

* * *

Andy had insisted that Donny put on his seat belt because Ram was driving much too fast for the weather, which rapidly grew worse. He watched Ram carefully through the Plexiglas divider and tried to determine where they were going. It would be a mistake, he thought, to assume Ram was taking them home. He had no idea *where* they were going, and he was afraid to ask, afraid to do anything that might divert Ram's attention from driving.

Every time a voice crackled over Ram's radio, he tipped his head toward it and listened, and when the voice stopped, he held his head upright again. He did not appear to be a man who had just killed a room full of people. He seemed to be in thought as he drove, sometimes frowning, but relaxed and calm.

Donny whispered nervously, "Dad, where we going?"

Andy touched a vertical finger to his lips. He especially didn't want Donny to get Ram's attention.

Outside, the storm was on a rampage. As they drove through the residential neighborhood, Andy saw shingles and pieces of siding flying off of houses on both sides of the street while trees were bent and twisted by the storm

Ram slammed on the brakes when a mailbox, still attached to its post, tumbled into the street and clattered and banged to the opposite sidewalk, crashing into a house.

Andy was afraid they were in more danger from Ram's driving than from Ram himself. He didn't want to speak to him, but he feared Ram was so lost in thought that he wasn't paying attention to what he was doing.

"Uh, Ram, I think the hurricane has arrived," he said.

Ram glanced at Andy in the rearview mirror and barked a single laugh. "Yeah, sure looks like it, huh?" He was friendly, jovial, and relaxed, with a smile Andy could see in his reflected eyes.

"Where, uh, where are we going, Ram?"

"Well, I was thinking. Maybe you and your boy oughtta

come to my house. I got a basement, you know. We can go down there and sit it out. I got a TV down there, too. And a generator, of course."

Andy was painfully aware that Ram's references to the house made it sound like he lived alone now. And after what he'd said about his wife earlier, Andy thought he might. But he found himself wondering if Ram's wife was still in the house somewhere, and what had happened to his children.

"Well, Ram, that sounds great, and I really appreciate the offer, but I need to get home. I, uh, have to take some medication. It's a nightly thing."

Ram frowned in the mirror. "You sick?"

"No, I'm not sick. But I will be if I don't take the medication."

"Oh, I see. Well . . . yeah, sure. I can take you—"

There was a burst of chatter from the radio and Ram stopped talking, inclined his head, and listened.

Andy caught a word here, a number there, but other than that, he couldn't understand what the dispatcher was saying.

The radio fell silent and a moment later, Ram barked that single laugh again and said, "Well, hot damn, that's the Clancy place! Sounds like maybe Giff's having some problems tonight. And we're really close."

Ram suddenly took a sharp left turn and increased his speed. He hit a button and red and blue light began to dance in the darkness in a swirling pattern around the car as it drove through the night.

"You two just sit tight," Ram said. "I gotta take this call. You two stay in the car and you'll be fine, okay?"

Andy turned to Donny, who looked afraid. Andy knew exactly how he felt. He could not believe Ram was taking them on a call. He really *had* lost his mind. But Andy said nothing.

When he got no response, Ram shouted at the top of his lungs, "*Okay*?" It was a sharp, piercing sound in the small space and it made Andy's ears ring.

"Sure, Ram, sure, okay," Andy said quickly, because there was nothing else he could say, nothing else he could do. Like it or not, he and Donny were in Ram's hands.

Simon Granger stood on a fat, sturdy branch and hugged the trunk of the oak tree he was in to keep from falling as it tossed and swayed in the raging wind. He wore night-vision goggles over his ski mask and his Remington 700, equipped with a suppressor, was strapped to his shoulder. He'd been soaked to the skin for so long now, it was almost easy to forget he was wet.

Upon entering the hospital's fenced-in grounds with the others earlier, he and three other men had climbed the enormous oak trees that stood like great sentries around the hospital. Simon stood in the tree on the western side. The trunk split into two fat arms that spread apart, as if it were going to hug the building, its tentaclelike branches extended in all directions.

As Ollie's men had headed for the back of the building to get in, Simon had watched the Vendon Labs security team as they were caught completely off guard. They'd come from the guardhouse at the gate, from the building's rear entrance, and some had materialized out of the darkness that had concealed them. They were fast and silent and Ollie's men did not hesitate to shoot them. Now their bodies lay scattered around the grounds. The guardhouse stood dark and empty and the chain-link gate was twisted and broken and standing open.

Earlier, he'd watched someone crash a Jeep through the gate and speed away down the gravel road. He should have called Ollie and told him about it, but he'd been too busy hanging on to the oak's trunk to keep from falling out of the tree. His only job was to cover the others as they went into and came out of the building.

The storm had intensified in the last several minutes and now the tree in which Simon stood was flailing in the powerful wind, creaking and groaning, threatening to throw him to the ground. A sound came up from beneath him, one he could not identify at first—a cracking, popping sound. It came in bursts and reminded him of the sound of popcorn popping in a microwave oven.

The wind attacked the hospital like an angry beast. The windows on the ground floor had been boarded up, but apparently not well enough. The boards over some of the windows in the rear began to come loose. One of them flapped noisily in the wind for a while, then tore away with a crunching sound and flew into the darkness. Others began to follow.

Simon was afraid that Hurricane Quentin had arrived early and was ready to party while he was still in this tree, waiting to cover the others when they came out. But when would that be? He didn't think it would be a good idea to stay in the tree to wait and find out. Even if there were any security guards left to protect them from, Simon knew he would be useless in that tree. He had to get down. But he didn't feel right climbing down without calling Ollie first.

As he reached down to take his phone from its sheath on his belt, the crackling sound continued below and suddenly grew louder. Simon did not grasp what was happening until the tree was already falling toward the building.

The hospital's western wall rapidly grew larger until it swallowed up Simon's field of vision. He made no sound before his skull was crushed in an avalanche of plaster and wood and glass and metal and oak. Simon died inside the building.

PART FOUR
Deranged

32

Quentin ripped through Humboldt County like a horde of demons.

The roof of the café and gift shop at the Sequoia Park Zoo was peeled off the building. The roar of the wind could not drown out the cries of the animals in the zoo—the hooting and howling of gibbons, the shrieking of birds. The storm destroyed much of the Barnyard petting zoo, flattening fences and tearing down porticos.

The Old Town Shelter was the only part of Old Town that had not been evacuated. The police knew they wouldn't be able to get all the homeless out of the area. They had hiding places where they would lay low to avoid having to move. Most of them were scared of the police and hid from them. They were suspicious of relocations and especially evacuations. The shelter remained open for those who would inevitably come out of their hiding places and need food and shelter from the storm.

It was in a white clapboard building in a First Street storefront. It had been a flophouse back in another time. Now it stood between a restaurant supply store and FleshArt Tattoos and Piercing in the most consistently disheveled and run-down part of Old Town.

It was dark and crowded inside. Much of the light they had came from kerosene lanterns and battery-operated lights positioned here and there, stable and unwavering, but the rest came from flashlights and handheld lanterns and flew all over the place as the lights were moved around. Someone led them in singing old campfire songs they remembered from Boy Scouts and summer camps, while waxed paper cups of hot chocolate were handed out.

Something crashed into the front of the building with a sound that some would later describe as a bomb going off. It was a power pole, but it did not fall into the building—it was *hurled* into the building like a missile. It slammed into one of the front pillars in the old building as sparks flew from two overturned kerosene lanterns. The explosive crash was immediately followed by the screaming of voices in pain.

Flashlight beams cut through the dark and converged on the damage.

Someone shouted, "Get that lantern! It's *burning*!"

And then there were flames, and screaming, and a frantic explosion of movement.

The steeple of St. Bernard's Church was sheared off at the base and thrown several blocks, where it crashed through the roof of a sewing machine store and repair shop.

A twenty-three-foot-long Airstream Flying Cloud was lifted from the Redwood Empire RV and Motorhome Park and flung a distance of two miles by the storm, until it crashed and slid loudly through a Safeway grocery store parking lot, spraying sparks as it gouged the pavement.

It was a night when more than rain was falling from the sky and the wind was out for blood.

A single pair of headlights moved cautiously through the street, slowly up one block, then down another, fighting the wind, easing through the downpour, as if searching the streets for something. . . .

33

Sheriff Mitchell Kaufman worried about his blood pressure as he drove through the storm. He was so tense at the wheel that the muscles of his back, neck, and shoulders burned and his chest felt tight. His blood pressure was probably high and climbing. His cholesterol level probably felt pretty good about itself in comparison.

His patrol car was rocked and jostled by the wind as he drove slowly through the eastern part of town. Farther west, closer to the bay, much of the town was already flooding. Even here, the gutters had become creeks.

Kaufman had lived in Eureka his whole life. With a population of a little more than 27,000, it was the biggest coastal city in the state north of San Francisco, but it was still a rural town more than a 160 years after its founding. As sheriff, Kaufman's responsibility was the entire county of Humboldt, which was home to nearly 135,000 people. Tonight, with the power outages and flooding and other damage done by the hurricane, all of those people would be a lot more stressed than usual, which meant that Kaufman's department and Eureka's police department were going to be busier than usual.

Kaufman was old enough to remember the Columbus Day Storm of 1962. His little brother had been born only a month earlier and Kaufman was almost six years old. It turned out to be one of the most powerful cyclones ever recorded in the United States in the twentieth century. He remembered his father driving them to Grandma and Grandpa's house, a big Victorian in McKinleyville with a dark, musty basement that young Kaufman refused to enter alone. They spent the entire storm huddling in that drafty basement in the flickering light of kerosene lanterns. It was fun and terrifying all at once—fun because it was a new and exciting experience and terrifying because of the constant, violent sound of the howling storm trying its best to get at them. As he listened to that sound, Mitchy, as he was then called, imagined the storm as a giant, black monster that blended in with the night as it stomped and slashed its way through towns and neighborhoods. And yet, he didn't truly believe anything bad would happen to them because he was with his family and he was confident they would keep him safe.

Now, even though he was old enough to know better, he found himself imagining the same thing again as a blue-and-white-striped canopy from a porch swing slapped onto his hood, clung there for a moment as if resisting the wind, then blew away in a blur. It was easy to imagine the storm to be a living thing. Unfortunately, he no longer had the luxury of being a little boy in the arms of his family, and he did not feel confident that he would be safe.

Hurricane Quentin promised to be worse than the 1962 storm, which had become known as the Big Blow. He knew he wouldn't be able to drive around like this much longer, but he didn't want to go back yet.

In the last hour, there had been looting in Old Town, with shots fired between police officers and three subjects. There were power lines down all over the place and live wires were squirming like electric snakes over the ground, spitting venomous sparks. A car had driven into a house in Willow Creek and a fight had broken out in which someone had been stabbed. There was a report of shots fired in a mobile home park just outside of McKinleyville. A little girl was missing in Arcata. It was like a big disaster party that was getting too crowded.

Kaufman was listening to the radio on his way to the old Springmeier hospital, but his eyes scanned the night as he drove, searching for Deputy von Pohle's car. The drive to Springmeier was mostly a cover story. He had something else on his mind as he took a wandering, indirect route, eyes scanning, searching. He'd told no one about the real reason he was driving around in such a bad storm because he had no proof, only suspicions, and a sick feeling in his stomach that he knew wouldn't go away until he'd either proved or disproved those suspicions.

Something had been up with von Pohle for months. Kaufman had watched his work performance gradually deteriorate, as well as his behavior. He'd become increasingly withdrawn, distracted, and temperamental. He'd been reprimanded a couple of times for using unnecessary force, and once he was caught drinking on duty. He was quick to anger and was abusive and even threatening toward his coworkers more often and with less reason all the time. He'd been a deputy for almost thirteen years, and although he was a little loud and overbearing at times, he'd exhibited nothing but model behavior until recently.

Kaufman had called him into the office about ten days ago and asked him what was going on.

"Going on?" von Pohle said.

"I don't have time for that. You know what I'm talking about. I've been paying attention, you're chewing on something, or it's chewing on you. Is everything okay at home?"

He got a tired, faraway look in his face and slowly slid down to a slumped position in the chair. "No. It's not."

"What's up?"

"My wife. She's been fuckin' some guy. Some guy who

runs a nursery. Can you imagine that? A fuckin' *gardener*," he said through clenched teeth. "He's even a spic! And he's younger than her!" His fists were clenched, and even though he was slumped in the chair, he was taut. His lips trembled a little when he spoke the last two sentences.

"Look, Ram, you need to calm down, okay?" Kaufman said softly. He'd seen this kind of behavior in cops before and knew it was unpredictable and dangerous. "Just . . . calm . . . down. Take a deep breath, okay?"

Although irritated by the direction, Ram took a deep breath, let it out slowly, and readjusted his position in the chair a little, making a clear attempt to try to get more comfortable and relax.

"You never seem to be very far away from rage these days," Kaufman said.

"Why shouldn't I be? Now she's talking about divorce."

"You need some time off?"

"No."

"You sure?"

"No, I couldn't handle this shit if I couldn't come to work every day."

"Maybe you should think about it. Maybe work isn't where you should be focusing your attention. We'll get you some counseling, you take a week off and try to start fixing the problem."

He tilted his head back slightly. "Fixing the problem?"

"Yeah. Is there anything I can do?"

"Well . . ." His big body shook as he laughed silently. "You wanna kill her or should I?"

Something about that silent laugh jolted Kaufman. He'd never known von Pohle to do that before. He was a loud, unabashed laugher. Seeing him shake with laughs he kept inside was somewhat disturbing.

"You serious, von Pohle?"

He remained slumped there for a moment, grinning at

Kaufman, saying nothing. Then the grin fell away as he sat up straight, stiffened his back, leaned forward slightly, and got serious.

"No, sir. Just letting off some steam."

"You want to be careful how you do that. It's gotten you into trouble before, and if you keep it up—I'm serious about this, von Pohle—it's going to kick you in the ass. If you don't want to take time off, I want you to get some counseling."

"Look, I'm fine, really, I don't think I need coun—"

"*I* think you need counseling, and that's all that matters. And you are *not* fine. Infidelity, divorce—those are traumatic things. They fuck people up. I'm going to make the call right away. So be ready. When you're told when to go, you go. Understand?"

He nodded.

"Now, what about your wife? Is this going to be a problem you can handle?"

"I never said I couldn't handle it."

"I know you didn't, but I'm asking. Can you?"

He slumped in the chair again. "Yeah, I can handle it. You kidding?" He shook again as he laughed silently. "Goddamn right I'll handle it. I'll handle 'em both."

"Jesus Christ, do you hear yourself? Should I be worried? You aren't going to do anything stupid, are you?"

He turned his head slightly back and forth. "No. I'm not."

But by then, Kaufman was not prepared to believe him. He insisted on counseling and decided to go on keeping a close eye on von Pohle. If counseling didn't help, or if he got worse, Kaufman would reassess the situation and act accordingly.

Neither von Pohle's work nor his behavior got any worse, but he became more withdrawn and isolated. He stopped going out for drinks with other deputies after his shift. But he did not step out of line. He showed up on time and did his job.

Kaufman was not sure if that was a good sign. Did the fact

that he was exhibiting decent behavior at work mean that he was giving his rage an outlet elsewhere?

So far, Kaufman had not encountered any other cars on the streets. Unlike him, most people seemed to be smart enough to stay inside where it was warm, dry, and safe, rather than out and about, driving around in this hellish weather.

As he watched for von Pohle's car, he listened to the radio, keeping track of everyone and everything: downed power lines secured outside of Fortuna . . . missing girl's parents being interviewed . . . looting quashed . . . mobile home park shooting being investigated . . .

Earlier that day, Ivan Renner had called to warn him about Ollie Monk.

Kaufman thought what Renner did for a living was nuttier than a Christmas cheese log, but he liked the guy. It was rare to meet someone who was exactly what he appeared to be, said exactly what he meant, and did the things he said was going to do. Kaufman had listened to his show and was surprised by how much of it *didn't* sound crazy, but that was only because Renner didn't sound crazy and was a pretty likable guy. He couldn't buy all the things Renner believed, but Kaufman knew he was sincere and that he really believed it and wasn't just trying to sell books, videos, website memberships, and post-apocalypse survival equipment. Kaufman had a lot of respect for Ivan Renner, enough to listen when he called or showed up for a chat.

Several months ago, Renner had gotten it into his head that the government was up to something in the old Springmeier mental hospital. He gave Kaufman all of the research he'd done on Vendon Labs, told him about the secretive back road they'd cut through the woods rather than reopening the front gate. Kaufman had agreed to pay an unannounced visit to the old hospital, but he would not let Renner accompany him.

The new road was exactly where Renner had said it would be, and it led to a gate in the fence that had been erected around the hospital grounds and electrified. He told the guard at the gate that it was a friendly visit and he had some questions for the person in charge. The guard made a call, then let him in.

Kaufman was greeted at the hospital by Dr. Jeremy Corcoran, who was in charge of the project. They went to his office and had coffee, chatted for a while. Corcoran was happy to answer Kaufman's questions, and he answered each one thoroughly and without hesitation.

What were they doing there? Developing new antibiotics to fight new infections that had become resistant to standard antibiotics.

Why there? The hospital perfectly suited their needs. More accurately, it *over*suited their needs, because they used only small section of the enormous old building. Most of the hospital was completely closed off because it was no longer structurally sound. They had refurbished only one section on the ground floor in the rear of the hospital.

Is this a government-funded operation? Corcoran claimed he didn't know because he never concerned himself with that end of any project, but it was very possible that there was some government money involved because antibiotics-resistant strains of infection were a major concern and it was in the country's best interest to combat them.

Corcoran was no different than any other brainy type Kaufman had encountered, and the county was full of them thanks to Humboldt State University—academics, scientists, geniuses, and brilliant students who had more intellect than sense were all over the place. Kaufman had nothing against them and recognized that they were an important part of society, and he wasn't one of those morons who was suspicious of anyone intelligent and well educated, but the exceptionally brilliant types tended to put him off.

They were odd, distracted, and quite often rude and dismissive. Most of them were socially awkward and always seemed uncomfortable. They often seemed to be in a hurry, which, in Kaufman's line of work, was usually seen as a deliberate tactic of evasion. Maybe that was why they always gave him the feeling that they were up to something they didn't want him to know about. Corcoran was quite pleasant and happy to answer Kaufman's questions, but he was also odd in appearance and manner, distracted, awkward, uncomfortable, and unrelentingly twitchy. It was the kind of twitchiness common to drug addicts, but in Corcoran, it came off as an elaborate series of nervous tics.

Corcoran introduced him to Dr. Fara McManus, a woman whose smile and polite manner could not conceal her general crankiness. While she gave the impression she would rather be anywhere else, McManus was helpful and informative during a tour that took about ten minutes.

Kaufman had no reason disbelieve anything Corcoran and McManus told him, or to believe they were doing anything other than what they claimed to be doing. He took his conclusions to Renner, who was frustrated. He asked if Kaufman would mind if he brought in any further evidence he uncovered, and Kaufman said he'd be happy to consider it, but as things stood, there was nothing suspicious going on at Springmeier.

After that, Renner showed up every couple of months with some new piece of information that he felt increased the likelihood that his suspicions were accurate. Then he brought up the possibility of a connection between the Vendon Labs people and the disappearing homeless people.

Kaufman told Renner that he was barking up the wrong tree. Renner understood Kaufman's frustration with his regular visits, but he felt strongly about it and did not want to give up. Kaufman respected his sincerity and determination, but he thought he was dead wrong and there was nothing he could do for him. But no matter how strongly they disagreed, they always remained civil and reasonable and thought no less of the other for the disagreement. That was so rare and Kaufman missed it so much that he actually thanked Renner for it once. These days, everyone seemed so eager to find some reason to be offended and vent their outrage that the simplest conversations had become minefields.

Ollie Monk, on the other hand, was not civil or reasonable or even entirely sane. He did not engage in conversations, he made declarations and proclamations and then expected everyone to accept them as facts. He seemed blissfully unaware of the fact that he was paranoid about every aspect of his life, sometimes for reasons that were not bound by reality. He was a proud and open bigot and because he had a lot of money—something about which Ollie was inexhaustibly arrogant—most people let him get away with it.

Kaufman couldn't do anything about the fact that Ollie Monk was an obnoxious, bigoted asshole, but he'd be damned if he was going to let him step out of line with that militia of his, or whatever it was. He'd become sheriff just a year after Ollie had begun what he referred to as "working with homeless veterans." He'd asked Ollie for a tour of the place, just a friendly visit so Kaufman could become more familiar with what Ollie was doing out there in the woods.

"Tell you what, sheriff," Ollie had said. "If you want to come out some evening, after business hours, as a citizen and not a sheriff, I'd be happy to give you a tour of the facilities."

Ollie seemed pretty confident that Kaufman wouldn't do that. But he did. He showed up one Friday evening in jeans, a blue chambray shirt, and his favorite cowboy hat. Ollie was unusually quiet and stammered a lot. He gave Kaufman a tour, but it was brief and hardly complete. It was the only time he'd seen Ollie nervous and uncomfortable, squirming like a caterpillar being held by a pair of tweezers. Kaufman's visit was unexpected and Ollie was unprepared, not entirely in control of the situation. It was gratifying. After that, Kaufman made one visit a year in his street clothes. He always brought a cake or a pie. He could tell Ollie hated the visits, but he always went along with them, smiling the whole time. Each time, Ollie took him on a drive around the property and introduced him to some of the men.

Kaufman was impressed. Ollie not only had managed to get some serious drunks and drug addicts cleaned up, he had them in good spirits, as well. They looked healthy, vigorous, and happy. Kaufman did not think Monk's militia was as much of a threat as Ollie Monk's proud ignorance and stupidity, but there was nothing he could do about that. He still thought Ollie was an asshole, but he was doing good work with the homeless.

Then Ollie got the idea that the homeless people who had disappeared had been kidnapped by the people at the old mental hospital. They worked for Vendon Labs, which had been involved in some kind of drug testing, which meant that experimenting on kidnapped homeless people would be business as usual.

Renner had told him about that, and then he'd looked into it himself. He remembered the hearings back in the 1970s, but he hadn't paid very close attention to them back then. He found the whole thing very disturbing, something he would prefer was just a spooky conspiracy theory. It was the kind of thing that made being patriotic a little bit harder than it already was. It also made it perfectly reasonable to be suspicious of shady government projects.

But Kaufman did not see that happening at Springmeier, and he told Ollie he was wrong. Several times. When he got tired of saying it, he threatened Ollie with arrest if he kept showing up or calling to complain about it. He also threatened Ollie with arrest if he were to take it upon himself to do anything about his crazy suspicions.

After that, Ollie was pretty quiet. So quiet that Kaufman nearly forgot about him. Then he'd gotten the call from Ivan Renner earlier in the day.

"Look, I don't have any solid proof that he plans to do anything . . . problematic," Renner said. "But what I just told you is exactly what he told me, and he wasn't very happy when he said it. He didn't get specific, only that he and his men were going to *act*."

"That's good to know, Ivan. I'm glad you called. Did he happen to mention *when* they were going to—"

"No, he didn't say when. I'm really worried, sheriff, that he's planning something . . . dangerous."

"Dangerous how?"

"Well, let's say that—um, you're gonna have to humor me for a few minutes, okay?"

"I humor you all the time, Ivan, you know that."

They both had a quick, nervous laugh.

"Let me give you a hypothetical situation. Let's say that Vendon Labs *is* doing some secret and shady work for the government up there in the old hospital."

Kaufman sighed. "Yeah, okay. Hypothetically. Let's say that."

"And let's say the work they're doing is developing a new biological weapon."

"Oh, Christ. Are you serious? Are you trying to tell me that's what they're—"

"I'm not telling you anything. This is just a hypothetical situation. I'm trying to make a point. Give me a chance, okay?"

Another sigh. "All right."

"Ollie and his men storm the place to rescue the people he believes are being held captive there, and in the process, something goes wrong with this biological weapon they're working on. In all the chaos, all the violence, maybe shooting—"

"Yeah, okay, I get your point. And?"

"Well . . . think about that for a second, sheriff. Ollie and his men, who knows what kind of damage they'd do with all their righteous indignation. Think about what could happen.

And really, we don't know *what* they're doing in there, but if it's—"

"They're developing antibiotics, goddammit! There's no reason to think otherwise!"

"What if I told you we have evidence to the contrary?"

"I would say, '*Again*, Ivan?'"

"Hey, at least I've always had evidence. You can't say I haven't. Just because you aren't convinced by it doesn't mean it's not evidence."

"Look, Ivan, I'm glad you called about Ollie. I'll keep that in mind. Maybe if I have time, I'll swing by the hospital and make sure everything's okay. But this other stuff—I just don't have time for it right now, Ivan. I've got other things to do."

Then a few hours later, shortly before he left the station, while he was still trying to come up with an excuse to drive around looking for von Pohle's car, Renner had called again.

"When you dropped by Springmeier, didn't you say it was Dr. Fara McManus who gave you the tour?"

"Yes, that was the one. McManus. Why?"

"I've got a recording of Dr. McManus talking about what they're really up to in Springmeier."

"What they're really— Jesus, Ivan, I don't have time for this."

"You have to make time. Listen, we've had somebody in there for a while, and he's been—"

"Wait, in where?"

"In Springmeier."

"I don't understand, what do you mean?"

"Somebody who works for me also works at Springmeier and he's been gathering information for us about—"

"A spy, you've got a *spy* in there? Is that what you're saying? Jesus Christ, are you crazy? They could sue you. And *win*. What the hell do you think this is, *Mission: Impossible*? If I'd known *that* was what you were up to, I would have—"

"Sheriff, you have *got* to let me finish. The guy who works for me sent me a recording tonight of Dr. McManus talking about what they're really doing. She's having a fit of conscience and she's ready to go public. And, sheriff, they *are* experimenting on homeless people in there."

Kaufman opened his mouth to respond, but Renner just kept talking without giving him a chance to speak up.

"You need to listen to this. I don't know how good it'll sound over the phone, but just listen to this, sheriff."

Then a woman was talking. Her voice was a bit tinny because he was listening to a recording over the phone. But the more he listened, the more familiar the voice sounded. Dr. McManus had a way of talking in a quick burst, then pausing, then talking in another quick burst. He recognized the rhythm, the cadence. And then he listened to what she was saying.

A burning nausea settled into his stomach as he listened, and before long, he was afraid he would vomit up a bellyful of acid.

Then Renner was saying, "Dr. McManus and my guy and everybody else in there are being held at gunpoint right now by Ollie and his men."

"What? Are you shitting me? We haven't gotten any calls—"

"They can't call you, that's why *I'm* calling you. It sounds like Ollie and his men have let out the test subjects."

"Test subjects? I don't under—"

"The homeless people infected with this virus."

For a moment, Kaufman felt like his chair was spinning around. Then he remembered something: He was talking to Ivan Renner, who was a nice guy, but who believed some pretty crazy things, and this might be one of them. Kaufman had listened to Renner's show, he'd listened to his guests, and he knew that much of Renner's information came from sources that were unreliable at best and crazy or creepy or both at worst. Renner himself might be convinced that the voice in that recording belonged to Dr. Fara McManus, but that didn't necessarily mean it was, and Kaufman had to keep reminding himself of that fact.

"What do you want me to do, Ivan?"

"Do? Get some deputies up there and—"

"I'll drive by and take a look."

"*What*? You mean . . . by *yourself*?"

"Yes, by myself."

"Didn't you hear what I just told you?"

"Yes, I heard it. And I have no doubt you believe it. But let's be honest, Ivan. You aren't exactly a good horse to bet on at the moment, you know what I mean? We're up to our eyes in trouble right now because of the hurricane and I'm not going to send a bunch of deputies to Springmeier just on your say-so. Your record so far just wouldn't support it. Even in good weather. But I'll take a look myself. If there's a problem, I'll call for backup. Now, if you don't mind, I'm on my way out."

Now he made his slow way to Springmeier, taking a meandering route so he could search for von Pohle's car. He'd called von Pohle's home number to talk to his wife, hoping she'd know where he'd gone, but no one answered. Kaufman occasionally grabbed his radio mike and called for von Pohle. He never got a response.

34

It took a long time for all the noise to stop. After the initial explosion—what sounded like an explosion, anyway—shook the entire hospital, the extended sounds of collapsing, of something large falling apart, went on for a while, the crashing and banging and shattering sounds of destruction in progress. Fara backed into Emilio and pressed against him. She was trembling. He put his hands comfortingly on her shoulders, hoping she couldn't tell that he was trembling, too.

"One of those trees," Fara said.

Emilio leaned close to her ear and said, "What?"

She turned her head toward him and said, "One of those huge oak trees outside. They're as old as dirt. I think one of them fell into the building." She pointed. "Sounded like the one on the western side."

The sounds of the storm seemed to be inside the old hospital now, echoing up and down its corridors, shoving on its doors. Emilio noticed the room suddenly felt colder.

"If that's what it was," Emilio whispered, "sounds like it knocked the shit outta that side of the building."

"Yeah, I'm afraid that was a breach," Ollie said. "Which means there may now be other ways for those people to get out of this building." He turned to one of his men. "Leave a man on each exit, but get the rest together in the corridor intersection ASAP."

The man hurried out.

Ollie turned to Emilio. "Are you gonna give me shit?"

"What do you mean?"

"I mean if your only interest is to get us out of here without spreading this goddamned doomsday plague, I could use your help."

Emilio nodded. "Yeah, at this point, that's my only interest."

"Can you shoot a gun?"

"I've been to the range a few times."

Ollie turned to Craig, who'd been standing silently with them all night, and said, "You got a handgun you can give him?"

The man removed his pistol from its holster and handed it to Ollie, who turned and offered it to Emilio.

"Can you handle that?"

"A Ruger? Sure." Emilio took the gun.

"We might need some muscle, too. Whatever happened out there, it sounds like a mess." He glanced at Fara. "I think you're right about that tree. I had a man in that tree, goddammit."

Ollie started to head for the door and Emilio began to follow him, but Fara's hand clutched his elbow and pulled him back.

"Don't leave me here," she whispered.

"Well . . . I don't think he's gonna want you to come with us."

"Don't go out there. I'm scared. I'm serious, Emilio, I'm very scared, I don't feel safe in here." She folded her arms across her stomach and looked at their masked guard, then at Ollie, then at Corcoran. "From anyone." She moved close, pressed herself against Emilio, and he put an arm around her. "And that dead man on the floor over there keeps reminding me that we're all in a pretty shitty situation. You know?"

"Yeah, okay," he said, turning to Ollie. "Look, I'm gonna

stay here for now. If you really need my help with something, let me know, but right now, I don't think I should leave her."

Ollie nodded once, then held out his hand. "In that case, give me the gun."

Emilio handed him the gun and Ollie handed it back to its owner. He looked at Fara but spoke to Emilio. "Is she sick?"

"No, she's just really upset. She's been through a lot and—"

Ollie barked an unpleasant laugh. "*She's* been through a lot? Imagine what she's been putting all those homeless people through, huh? Why don't you imagine *that* for a minute or two?" Then he turned to Craig. "Come with me. We're gonna need all the men we can get out there, I think."

"What about them?" the man asked.

Ollie turned to Emilio, Fara, and Corcoran, who now sat in the chair behind Fara's desk. "Where are you gonna go? There's a storm outside and a bunch of crazy, virus-carrying people in here. Safest thing you could do would be to stay right here in this room."

Ollie and Craig left the office.

Fara pulled away from Emilio, shaking her head. She spoke quietly, just above a whisper. "I couldn't. I wanted to, but I couldn't."

"Couldn't what?"

"Stop it. I tried. I reported him three times. I kept thinking I should leave, but I didn't because I *couldn't*. I couldn't just walk away from this, I kept hoping I'd find a way to *do* something. What I did with you today, that recording—I should have done that months ago. *Months* ago. But I just . . . I was afraid of ruining my life, or something, of becoming this, this, I don't know, public whipping post. My whole life plastered all over TV and the Internet."

"People will say you're a hero, Fara," he said.

"Some might," Corcoran said.

They turned to see him sitting in Fara's chair at her desk.

He had his feet on the desk, ankles crossed, and he was leaning back in the chair, holding his cell phone to his right ear. He'd been a trembling wreck earlier, but now he appeared quite relaxed and comfortable. He was watching them with a smile. In the candlelight, the smile had a ghoulish appearance—the small mouth elongated and surrounded by the deep lines of Corcoran's face. His glasses were pushed up on his forehead and his eyes, even in the poor light, were red and puffy and gleaming. But his smile was warm and cheerful and he sounded rather chipper when he spoke.

"I'm making a call," he explained, "and I'm on hold."

"Who are you calling?" Fara said.

"An associate." He kept smiling. "Look, some might say you're a hero. For a while. You'd probably get a book deal right away, be on all the talk shows. Half the country would despise you and want to string you up, but you'd have those who say you're a hero. Until they find out you've got real fur in your closet. Or that you like veal and foie gras. Or that you don't like Lady Gaga, or some dumb thing like that. Until they find out you're human. Then they'll just throw you under the bus. Or worse!" he said, his eyebrows rising high up on his spacious forehead. "They'll hand you over to the people who want to string you up!" Then he laughed loudly until his laughs became coughs and he had to drop his feet to the floor and sit up straight as he hacked and coughed and wheezed, still holding the phone to his ear. When it stopped, he took his glasses off his head, put them on the desk, and scrubbed a hand down his face. Then he put the glasses on his nose and pushed them back up on his forehead again. He chuckled quietly as he settled back in the chair and put his feet back up on the desk.

"You seem awfully happy," Fara said.

Corcoran, still smiling, said, "Who, me? Well, Dr. McManus, if you'd taken the opportunity to get to know me during our time here, you would know that I am generally a happy person.

I am optimistic, upbeat, and good-natured, and there's very little that can get me down."

"Even this? A hurricane? A raid by a private militia? The discovery of your kidnapped human subjects, and the potential spread of the deadly virus you've created? To say nothing of a possible career-ending scandal that could land you in prison? None of that troubles you?"

"I remain singularly untroubled."

"Well, that could be the drugs."

His smile opened and he laughed quietly. "You could be right."

"You're wasted," Fara said. She spoke quietly, but with contempt and anger. "Like some teenager. Completely wasted."

"I'd hate to be in this situation without *some* chemical assistance," Corcoran said with a chuckle, "but I assure you I am quite sound." He smiled at the ceiling.

"How can you call yourself a scientist and do the things you've done here, conduct yourself the way you have, I mean, the drugs, the parties—"

"Dr. McManus, I call myself a scientist precisely *because* I do the things I've done here. Your morals and your righteous indignation are admirable, but science does not share them, nor does it give a damn about them. You're free to express them as long as you continue to allow me to do things that ultimately save lives. Possibly millions of lives."

"I'm sorry, but I don't see any lifesaving being done with this virus."

"It will be used in the defense of this country. In the defense of freedom. It's very possible, even likely, that it will do work that our young men and women will then not have to do, and they won't need to risk and lose life and limb in combat."

"I bet you have a justification for everything you've done here, everything you've done before this. You've got it all worked out in your head, don't you, in some way that makes you blameless?"

He nodded his head slightly, still smiling. "Go ahead and tell yourself that if it makes you feel better."

"Do you know what I'm going to do, Dr. Corcoran?" Fara said. "I'm going to do everything I possibly can to make sure that your career and reputation are destroyed and that you go to prison for what you've done here."

He lifted his head slightly and smiled at her for a moment. "Do you know what *I* think *you're* going to do, Dr. McManus? I think you're going to commit suicide. Or I think you're going to fall ill and be diagnosed with a very rare, fast-acting cancer, and in a few weeks, you'll be dead. Or I think your brakes will fail one day soon and you'll go off a cliff and into a ravine and your skull will be crushed. Or I think you're going to quietly die in your sleep one night soon. Or . . . something like that. Do you get the picture, Dr. McManus? You want to tell the world what we're doing here? Fine. But everything has consequences. As you can see, I'm not too concerned, am I? Do I appear worried to you? I've been down this road with underlings like you before, underlings who suddenly discover they have a conscience and simply cannot live with themselves anymore. I've been down this road before and I'm still here. The same thing cannot accurately be said of them. You're not in any position to destroy anyone or anything, Dr. McManus, and based on my past experiences in this line of work, I'm of the opinion that you won't even have time to try."

That seemed to deflate her, shrink her.

Corcoran suddenly dropped his feet to the floor, leaned forward in the chair, and spoke quietly into the phone. "Yes, it's Corcoran. We have a big problem that will have to be dealt with immediately." He turned the chair all the way around so the back of it faced them.

Fara went to the couch and slowly lowered herself onto it. Emilio noticed that her knees were bobbing up and down because she was shaking all over. He was afraid she was going into some kind of panic attack.

He sat down beside her and put an arm around her. "Look, I know you're feeling a lot of bad crap right now, but you've gotta do me a favor and hold yourself together a little longer, okay?" He took both of her small, pale hands between his big, dark ones and rubbed them vigorously. "Until we get outta here. Then you can knock yourself out. But right now, we all need clear heads, and we need *you* to be clearheaded. You know this place better than any of us. We need you right now, Fara. Do you think you can keep it together a little longer?"

She nodded emphatically as she sat up straight and took a few deep breaths. She pressed the heels of her hands to her eyes and swept them outward, wiping her tears.

"Yeah," she said, sniffling. "Yeah, I think I can do that."

"Thank you. After this is over, you can go out and get shit-faced. I'll be your designated driver."

"That . . . actually . . . sounds like fun."

"Yeah, it'll be fun. We can go dancing. You like to dance?"

"Me? Oh, God, I haven't danced since high school. And even then, I wasn't any good at it."

"Get drunk enough, it won't matter."

"That's true."

"That's what we'll do, then. You can go out and get as drunk as you want, and I'll be your driver and bodyguard."

"Would that be . . . a date?" She had gone from quivering and looking deflated and in pain to relaxing on the couch and smirking.

"Well, it can be, if you'd like. But if it's gonna be a date, I think both of us should be drinking."

"Sure. Even better." She smiled. "Who'll drive?"

"We can always take a cab."

She laughed quietly.

"You feeling better?"

"Yes."

"Good." He stood. "Look, I'm gonna join Ollie and have a look around out there. You gonna be okay?"

She stood, too. "Yes, because I'm going with you." She turned to Corcoran, who still had his back to them. "I'm going to go see what happened, Dr. Corcoran."

He ignored her.

Emilio turned to the masked man. "Why don't you give me that gun now. I'm gonna go out and join Ollie. And she's going with me."

He thought about that a moment, then handed the gun to Emilio. Fara went to get her coat, put it on, then got the mini-Maglite from her purse. She removed something else, too, but slipped it quickly into the pocket of her coat. Then they left the office and went out into the dark.

35

Latrice turned to stone as she watched the old man rush toward her shrieking and aiming the gun between his hands directly at her. She was paralyzed because, in that moment, she knew she was going to die. He was going to start firing that gun and she would feel the bullets tear into her one at a time and then she'd be dead.

But he kept coming and he didn't fire the gun.

He got closer and closer, mouth open as he screamed at her, but he didn't fire the gun.

Latrice dropped her cell phone because she forgot she was holding it, then reached her left hand out toward the sink piled high with dirty dishes and closed it on the first thing she touched—something hard and cold, long and round, a handle of some kind—but when she tried to lift it, there was resistance, so she pulled hard, then gave it a strong jerk, and the pile of dishes and pots and pans collapsed in a loud clatter, some of them falling to the floor and scattering. A plate shattered on the tiles.

She threw the pot at the man as hard as she could and gasped loudly with surprise when it struck him on the forehead. That sent his feet flying upward and the gun flying from his hands and tumbling into the air.

Latrice watched all of this in slack-jawed amazement, as if it were a movie in which she was deeply involved, a movie that just kept surprising her.

He hit the floor ass first, but he never stopped moving. His arms and legs flailed, a giant spider on its back, as the gun slowly spun on its upward journey just a few feet from her, then hung suspended in the air for a moment before starting back down again.

Latrice snapped out of that weird, dreamlike state and started grabbing for the gun. Her hands clapped together on empty air once, twice, and on her third try, her hand hit the gun and sent it flying away from her and toward Rosie's motionless form. Her attention was diverted by a sudden change in movement on the floor from the old man.

He was getting up, scrambling to his feet, chattering to himself. He broke into a clumsy run toward her, kicking the dishes and cups and saucers that had fallen onto the floor from the sink. Halfway across the kitchen, he bent at the waist so his head was level with her abdomen.

"Motherfucker," Latrice said behind clenched teeth as she tried to kick him, only to find that she was no better at kicking than she was at grabbing.

His head butted her in the stomach and emptied her lungs as she went down on her ass with a loud grunt. Pain exploded from her coccyx and she cried out, but she didn't stop moving, either. She knew he would go for that gun and she couldn't let that happen. Fortunately, pain only made her angry. None of the people who knew Latrice well wanted to be around her when she was in pain, no matter how much they loved her, and she knew that and understood. Pain made her pissed off at the world.

"Mother*fucker*!" she said loudly and firmly as she got to her knees.

The old man, still looking like a spider somehow, was on

hands and knees now, crawling frantically toward the gun on the floor. It had landed in the corner by the neglected dishwasher, beneath a row of drawers, in the triangle of space between the corner and Rosie, who still lay unconscious where Latrice had put her.

Latrice grabbed the lip of the counter with her left hand and got to her feet, then reached into the dirty dishes with her right hand and groped for a different kind of handle this time.

When he lunged for the gun, the old man landed on top of Rosie, and she stirred. He grabbed the gun from beneath the overhanging edge of the cabinet and drawers and backed away on hands and knees, moving quickly but clumsily.

Rosie screamed. The piercing sound went into Latrice's ears like a couple of hatpins as she closed her hand on a thick, heavy, wooden handle and drew it from the mess.

Rosie kicked and thrashed her arms as she continued to scream and the old man cried out in surprise at her sudden outburst. He raised the gun and fired it into Rosie's confused and terrified face.

The scream was cut short and Rosie went limp.

The old man went even crazier as he stood and angrily kicked Rosie's lifeless body, his foot moving so fast it was nothing but a blur as he growled gibberish. For a moment, Latrice was mesmerized. He seemed to be punishing the young woman he'd just killed, enraged and wailing, kicking and kicking.

Then, still bent at the waist, he started to turn and aim the gun at Latrice.

She'd pulled from the sink a large butcher knife caked with old food. She drew her right arm back quickly, then rushed toward the old man and swung it upward, the blade projecting just above the thumb and forefinger of her closed fist. As she was swinging upward, he was turning toward her, chin jutting as he screamed at her again.

The blade met the soft underside of his jaw, pierced the flesh and stabbed upward into his mouth.

Before he was aware of what had happened to him, he raised the gun and fired at Latrice.

It clicked impotently.

Not wanting to lose her weapon, she jerked the knife out of the old man as he started to move backwards, away from her, pushed by the impact of the blade under his chin. As she withdrew the knife, his eyes bulged as he made a gurgling sound. Blood spewed from his mouth and spattered Latrice's face, warm and clinging. She gasped and stumbled backwards so that they were suddenly falling away from each other.

Giff staggered into the room with blood running down his left arm, a large gun in his right hand. He was the color of flour and looked drained of energy. He saw Latrice first, then turned to his right and saw his father lying faceup on the floor, legs kicking as his hands slapped at his chin in a clumsy attempt to stop the blood that was spilling freely from his wound.

"Jesus Christ, Daddy!" Giff shouted as he rushed toward the old man, dropping to one knee. "What happened? Jesus, what the fuck hap—"

Then he saw Rosie. He stood up slowly as he stared down at her, then staggered toward her, croaking, "Who did this?" Standing over her, his head turned toward Latrice. "*Who did this?*" he shouted.

She pointed at the old man writhing on the floor. "He was gonna do the same to me, I swear. I had to defend myself."

Eyes bulging now, Giff returned to his father's side and bent down close, putting the barrel of his gun to the old man's forehead.

"'Zat why you came back, you miserable old fuck?" he said. "To kill my woman? 'Zat why you disappeared for a couple weeks? Huh? So you could plan this, huh, you cocksucker?"

The old man rolled and kicked and continued to make desperate gargling sounds, spitting blood into the air, into Giff's face.

Giff fired. The old man stopped moving and made no more sounds.

Giff stood and began to pace the length of the kitchen, breathing heavily and fast, muttering to himself incomprehensibly and occasionally making high whining sounds.

A child cried somewhere in the house.

Latrice watched Giff pace, still clutching the knife tightly in her right fist, now wet with the old man's blood. She felt a shudder move through her and her head began to spin. She grabbed the edge of the counter with her left hand, then leaned against it as the room grew steadily darker.

Still holding the edge of the counter, she squatted down and lowered her head as much as she could. She didn't want to lose consciousness, not here, not now, but all the blood in the room was getting to her. She took a couple of deep breaths and gulped a few times as she began to feel steady again.

When Latrice finally stood, slowly and cautiously, she found that Giff was still pacing and muttering.

"I-I'm sorry," she said.

He stopped and looked at her, surprised, as if he'd forgotten she was there.

"Really, I'm sorry," she said again. The room became blurry and Latrice realized she was crying.

Giff looked at her with a confused frown. "Sorry? You kiddin'? I hated that fucker. *Hated* him!"

"Um . . . is everybody else okay? What about the kuh-kids?"

The child was still crying somewhere.

"Kids? Oh, shit. Yeah." He immediately turned and hurried out of the kitchen, leaving Latrice there with the dead.

In the living room, he shouted, "Goddammit, Jada, will you wake the fuck up and help with the kids? Hey, Tojo! Go over to Miguel's trailer and tell him and Mia to come in here and give us a hand. *Go!*"

Latrice looked around her for a moment, then down at her hands, the right one covered with blood as it held the knife. She opened her fist and let the knife fall to the floor, where the blade sang against the tiles. She had to clean up and get that blood off of her before she puked. She could *smell* it. She had to find a bathroom and wash in some scalding hot water and get clean. Clean. Everything would be better once she got clean.

But she couldn't move. She leaned against the counter and just stood there, looking at nothing in particular, thinking nothing in particular, just staring, unable to take a single step. She stayed that way for what felt like a long time.

Then the small window over the sink flashed a faint red and blue, and a single, loud *whoop* came from the siren of a police car.

In the living room, Giff shouted, "What the *fuck*? Who called the fuckin' *cops*?"

Latrice looked down at her bloody hand, shaking now. With blue and red flashing in her peripheral vision, she felt cold with the fear that her life was over.

36

Andy did not think he would ever stop hating himself for getting Donny into this.

How could he be so stupid? Why would he believe, without hesitation, that Ram von Pohle was now a great guy, a real humanitarian, a family man? Only because he wanted him to be.

Andy got the impression that Ram had reached the end of his ability to pretend to be somebody he wasn't. Maybe it was his wife's infidelity that had set it off, or maybe something else, but whatever it was, it had cut the ribbon on the old Ram, the Ram that Andy knew and despised and feared. That Ram was back and open for business, and he was not fucking around. No more Mr. Fake Nice Guy. He was back and worse than ever, back and in charge.

And what did Andy do? He managed to get his son trapped in the backseat of that psychopath's patrol car. Jesus Christ, every rotten thing Jodi had said about him during the divorce was true.

He looked down at Donny, who was preoccupied with the passing scenery. Either he was quite contentedly unaware of the danger they were in, or that was his way of swallowing his fear and insecurity and burying it deep. Andy hoped the boy was as easygoing as he seemed and stayed that way. It would serve him well.

Andy felt the need to speak to Ram. He was afraid that, if left to sit there and drive silently, Ram might sink deeper into whatever insanity was pulling him down.

"Hey, um, Ram?"

"Yeah?" He turned his head and glanced back through the Plexiglas. He had a big smile pushing his cheeks up and it looked genuine. He looked like he was having a grand old time.

"Everything okay?"

"Well, sure, everything's okay. Are *you* okay? You guys need anything?"

"Do we need . . . um, no. We're fine. I just want to make sure you're okay. You weren't hurt back there, or anything, were you?"

"Oh, hell, I'm fine," he said, laughing. "I may have gotten older and fatter, but I'm still tough as nails. 'Member that time on the field when I fell and broke my arm? Holy shit, man, the bone was stickin' right outta the skin, there, 'member that?" He laughed loudly, nodding his head with enthusiasm.

Andy never played football because his mother prohibited it, so he had no memory of Ram's broken arm. But Ram seemed to think he would. That made Andy wonder if Ram was sure of who he was talking to in the backseat. He decided it was best to simply go along with everything Ram said. He laughed, nodded, and said, "Yeah, that was something. Hey, Ram, how are your wife and kids these days?"

"Oh, I told you already, I took care of them. Weren't you with me when—oh, no, I guess you weren't. Yeah, I don't have to worry about them anymore. All taken care of."

Andy wanted to pursue that line of discussion, but he couldn't bring himself to do it because he was afraid he knew where it would lead—if it led anywhere.

"Where are we headed, Ram?"

"I thought you knew! We're going to Batten. That's a CDP on the easternmost edge of town. You know what a CDP is? A CDP is a census-designated place that's part of unincorporated Eureka, which is why it's in my jurisdiction, 'cause it's outside the city limits. This is county out here. Yeah, this is all mine."

Of course, he knew what and where Batten was, Cuppa Joe's was in Batten, Ram knew that. What was wrong with him? What was he thinking?

"We're going to the Clancy place. Just up the road a little here where—" As they passed Cuppa Joe's, Ram stopped talking. His eyes locked on to the restaurant as it passed, then he turned his frown to the rearview mirror and looked at Andy with confusion for a moment. Then he nodded slightly.

"Well, then, you know the Clancys," Ram said. "You've had some trouble with them, haven't you? Yeah, that's right. You have."

"A little. They like to hunt on my land."

"Well, hell, they're not supposed to be hunting anywhere out here. But that's the Clancy family for you." He wore a big smile as he said, "Bunch of scum-sucking white-trash parasites. They should all be gassed, far as I'm concerned, every last one of 'em, right down to the snotty little kids they keep poppin' out. You ever been to their place? You'll be there in a minute. Jesus, it's like a little trailer park in the woods, and it's nothing but trash. Trailer trash, white trash, meth trash. Just trash."

Oh, Christ, Andy thought, *is this going to be another slaughter?*

Ram was watching him too closely in the rearview—he'd notice if Andy took out his cell phone and made a call. He felt helpless, and yet he was overwhelmed by the urge to do something, anything.

He leaned back and turned to Donny, who was watching him. He'd been following their conversation. He looked like he wanted to say something, ask a question, maybe, but he kept it to himself because Andy had told him to say nothing, so he said nothing. He was such a good boy, so reasonable and relaxed. Given the fact that his mother was a drug addict and his father was Andy, how was that possible?

Andy leaned forward again. "That's what the radio call was about? The Clancys?"

"Yeah. Some woman called in about shots fired at the Clancy place. Something about a crazy old man. You know, I think the hurricane is hitting. Or it's just about to. This storm's getting a lot worse real fast. We're gonna be surrounded by a bunch of trees, you never know what could happen. I don't want to leave you in the car. You and the boy should come in with me. I'll make sure you're kept out of danger."

Oh, Jesus, he's taking us inside. No, I have to come up with a reason for us to stay in the car.

Ram looked at Donny in the rearview and grinned. "How would you like that, huh? You can watch a real police officer at work, dealing with some real bad guys, how 'bout that, huh?"

Andy turned to Donny and tried to tell him how to respond by smiling slightly and giving a subtle nod of his head. Donny picked up on it immediately. He looked at Ram and gave him a genuine smile and a nod and said, "Yeah, sure. Yeah."

He looked at Andy in the rearview. "Hey, do you remember Miss Fisher? Our science teacher? Remember how hot she was?"

Andy rifled through his memories. He'd never paid much attention to the teachers or faculty at school. None of them seemed engaged in what they were doing and, in fact, seemed miserable. They bored him and he didn't trust them, so beyond whatever he needed from them to complete his classes, he ignored them.

He vaguely remembered a young blond teacher in a white lab coat. That was when they were busy dissecting things, something he did not enjoy. He remembered her being young and funny and pretty, but not hot. There always seemed to be something bothering her and her distraction, her nervousness, and discomfort kept her from being hot. In Andy's mind, anyway. If he remembered correctly, she'd committed suicide just a few months after Andy and Ram graduated.

"Yes, I remember her. The pretty blonde."

"Pretty?" Ram said, glancing at him in a kind of triple-take. Then he shouted, "*Pretty?*"

Startled by Ram's shouted question, Andy quickly said, "Well, yeah, she was, like you said, she was, um, hot. She was really hot, I remember. She even made that lab coat sexy, didn't she?"

"Fuckin' A, she did. An amazing fuckin' piece. I used to fuck her, you know."

"Really?"

"Oh, yeah. The first time—well, no, it wasn't the first time 'cause we didn't really do it, but we got each other off through our clothes in her office after school. I was supposed to be making up a test." He laughed loudly. It was a forced, exaggerated laugh with no real joy in it.

Why is he telling me this? Adam tried not to let the question show in his face or eyes and kept a smile plastered on his mouth like a big pair of red Halloween wax lips.

Why is he even thinking *about this now? He just killed a house full of people, isn't he worried about that? Isn't he thinking about his next steps? About how he's going to avoid his fellow deputies and other law enforcement now that he's—*

No, no, no, he interrupted himself. *You've abandoned your first thought, which was a mistake, because you were right the first time. He's crazy. He's just goddamned* crazy*, and you cannot figure out crazy. Just keep smiling and nodding.*

"Then I had to sneak to her house," Ram went on, "'cause we couldn't be seen together, Jesus, she'd lose her job and I'd probably end up in therapy for the rest of my fucking life, or

something, I mean, can you imagine that? Can you imagine
how fucked up I'd be by now? Anyways, there was a big, steep
hill behind her house and on the other side of that hill there
was another neighborhood. I'd park in that neighborhood in
front of an empty lot between two houses and I'd climb up
that hill, trying to stick close to the trees, 'cause there were
some oaks up there, and I'd go to her back gate, where she'd
be waiting for me. The gate was in this really tall fence that
went all the way around her backyard, which was huge, with
a big aboveground pool—we fucked in that pool a few
times—and a pond full of gigantic goldfish."

   Ram was talking slower now and his grin had melted into
a vague smirk. He laughed again, but this time, it was
warmer, quieter, more genuine. "And then I'd go in and
we'd—oh, Jesus, we'd fuck like rabbits on steroids. To this
day, I never met a woman who was more into sex and more
ready to try, Jesus, anything, she'd do *anything*. That bitch
loved cock."

   Andy didn't know if Ram was telling the truth, but as he
remembered Miss Fisher, he could believe his story somehow,
it seemed right. She was always eager to please her students
and wanted everyone to like her. As he remembered her, Miss
Fisher's need to be the cool teacher was obvious. Even a little
desperate. Coupled with the fact that she always seemed troubled by something, she'd struck Andy back then as a neurotic
person who probably needed help. But what the hell did he
know? He was just a kid. He'd never told anyone about that,
but he remembered it well because—now that he was rum-
maging through memories long unexamined, things were
coming back to him—he remembered fantasizing about finding Miss Fisher in some undefined, isolated place in some
distress, crying, sobbing, alone, vulnerable, and sitting down
to talk to her, asking if there was anything he could do, and
from there, it always descended into the kind of lurid, wildly
unlikely masturbation scenario for which teenage boys have

always been so well known. At some point, he'd decided that Miss Fisher was indeed hot.

"She was fucking other guys, I think, but I never found out who. Horniest woman I ever knew. She was always wet. *Always*."

Andy turned an apologetic expression to Donny, who was looking out the window, pressing his lips together hard, and trying to stifle his laughter. That relieved Andy a little. Donny was holding up well.

"But *Jesus*, she got so fucking weird," Ram said, shaking his head. "First, she got real clingy and needy and that wasn't so bad, I mean, it was pretty nice, you know, because, hey, who doesn't enjoy being wanted?"

Andy remembered not being surprised by news of Miss Fisher's suicide and being puzzled by the fact that so many were—or claimed to be, anyway. It had seemed obvious to him that she was disturbed by something, maybe a touch unstable. He had no logical reason to back up those conclusions and certainly wasn't qualified to render such an opinion—that was why he'd kept it to himself—but he saw it in her face, her eyes, her behavior. Maybe others didn't see it. But it was there. Had it been pills? Had she overdosed?

"But then she got so weird and . . . possessive," Ram said. "She wanted us to keep seeing each other the summer after graduation and we did for a while, but I had other things to do. I was looking for a job, and I finally got one, remember? Over at that tacky tourist-sucking cavern, the Samoa Cookhouse. You remember?"

Andy had no idea where Ram had and had not worked throughout his life, but he kept smiling and nodding as Ram talked.

"But she kept wanting me to come over, or meet her someplace, and I couldn't always do that. It was nothing personal, didn't have anything to do with her at all, not at first, I just had other shit to do, that's all, shit I *had* to do. But she didn't believe me. Said I was seeing some other woman. Then she said I was seeing some *guy*." He sighed.

No, it hadn't been an overdose. Miss Fisher had shot herself. She'd put a handgun to her temple and squeezed the trigger while lying on her bed. Later, Andy had heard that she'd been wearing sexy black-and-red lingerie when she ended her life, including fishnet stockings, crotchless panties, and a peekaboo bra. It was a titillating fact back then, but now it seemed extraordinarily odd that a woman would dress herself in such a way before blowing her brains out.

"She just got weirder and weirder," Ram said, "until she started making threats. But her threats didn't make any fucking sense. She said she'd tell everybody about us, which would probably land her in jail because I was underage at the time and she was my teacher. It was crazy, so I didn't take it seriously, and then she said she'd kill herself and she showed me the scars on her wrists where she'd tried before, and I said she didn't seem to be very good at it, so I wasn't too worried, and *boy*, did *that* piss her off! She went crazy. Said she'd kill herself and make it look like I did it, you know, *frame* me, and, well . . . I couldn't let that happen." He shook his head slowly then, his eyes pensive in the rearview. Then the look was gone and he was smiling again. "Yes, had to take care of *that*, couldn't let *that* happen. She didn't know who she was fucking with. She was crazy, but . . . not prepared. Just like Grandpa. And the coach." Another laugh, this one through clenched teeth as he slowly shook his head. "That coach," he said. Then he screamed, *"That goddamned fucking coach!"*

Donny turned to Andy with wide, frightened eyes.

Coach? What coach is he talking about? Probably Kowalski, the football coach.

Coach Kowalski had claimed to be "prematurely grey," a phrase which became a punch line at Eureka High. He was fleshy and had a paunch, with little piglike eyes that looked out from beneath folds of flesh, rosy cheeks, and with his perpetual smirk, he always looked at you like he was imagining you naked and found it funny. Andy considered himself fortunate to have gotten through that school without ever having a single exchange with Coach Kowalski. No one liked him, everyone avoided him, he was loud and bossy and rude, and most of the time, he was downright creepy.

Andy looked at Ram, who appeared hunched, tense, uncomfortable. But he said nothing more. Andy found that a little disappointing because now he wondered what memory involving a coach had made Ram so angry.

About five years after Andy and Ram graduated, the same year Coach Kowalski announced his plans to retire to a life of sun and luxury in Florida, the coach was killed while hiking at Patrick's Point, where he fell off a cliff. Andy reached back in his memory for details.

It was a trail Kowalski had been hiking weekly, no matter how bad the weather, for twenty years. An autopsy proved the fall had killed him, and he hadn't had a heart attack or stroke.

It was a big story in Humboldt County because Kowalski was such a prick and so many people hated him that, if someone had pushed him off the cliff, it could have been virtually anyone in the county. Kowalski's wife said he'd gone to Patrick's Point alone, as always. Three people in the park told police they had seen Kowalski walking the trail with a young blond man in a yellow T-shirt and jeans, and two others claimed to have seen a young blond man in a yellow T-shirt and jeans coming the opposite direction on the trail later, by himself. But police had no reason to believe there was foul play and his death was declared an accident.

How long has Ram been doing this? How many people has he killed?

Andy didn't want to think about it anymore. Maybe he was thinking about it too much and overanalyzing it. It didn't matter now. He could think about it later. Keeping Donny safe was all that mattered right now.

"What the fuck was I talking about?" Ram said. He glanced at Andy. "Huh? What was I talking about?"

Andy didn't think it was a good idea to take the conversation back to the coach. "You were, uh, talking about doing it with Miss Fisher."

"Oh, yeah, she was, oh, fuck, she was such an amazing piece of ass."

"I can only imagine."

"What?"

"I said, I can only imagine."

"Well, yeah, sure. Of course." Ram chuckled. "You can only imagine, Andy, because"—he turned his grin toward Andy as he shouted—"you're a *mommy's boy!*" Then he bellowed with laughter.

Andy pulled away from the Plexiglas and pressed his back against the seat, pressed hard, trying to break through and fall out of reality and disappear. The words "mommy's boy" being spoken in that sickeningly familiar voice, in front of Andy's son—it was like a shovel that scraped out his insides and left him empty.

"Mommy's boy, mommy's boy!" Ram chanted, then he laughed some more. "Those were the days, huh, Andy? And you were a good sport, too. You took a lotta shit like a real sport, you deserve respect for that. A lotta guys? They'd cave. Not you, Andy. Hey, look, we're almost there."

Andy remained slumped in the backseat, trying to press himself through the upholstery. The car turned right, off of Emerald Canyon.

"And here we are," Ram said.

Suddenly, Donny's face appeared in front of Andy's eyes. "Dad?" he whispered. "We're there. What're we gonna do?"

That is the question, said a dramatic, Shakespearean voice in Andy's head. *What. Are you. Going. To do?*

Andy sat up and looked out the windows. They were in the woods and passing several mobile homes and RVs parked among the redwoods.

"You know, Ram, to be honest, I don't think it's a good idea for Donny to go in there. I mean, with this being police business, and everything."

"Not police business. I'm with the sheriff's department."

"Uh, yeah, that's right, sure. With this being sheriff's department business, and everything, I think we should stay in the car while you answer the call."

"Is that what you think?" Ram said as he parked the car and killed the engine. Then he unfastened his seat belt and turned and smiled at Andy through the Plexiglas. "Huh? Is that what you think, Andy?"

"Yes, I really think it would be best. Would you have a problem with that?"

Ram laughed as he faced front and reached for his door. "Get out. Both of you. We're going inside."

37

"What did you put in your pocket back in the office?" Emilio said.

Fara reached into her purse, found the cold metal of her snub-nosed .38 revolver and removed it, then turned her flashlight on it so Emilio could see it.

He stopped walking and faced her. "You mean to tell me you had that in your purse when that crazy guy came into the office and attacked Corcoran?"

"Oh, please, be realistic. I'm not going to fire this in a crowded room like that. I probably would have shot Corcoran, or even *you*. I have this for protection, not wholesale slaughter. And only for protection in situations where I have any hope of protecting myself, not when I'm—"

"Okay, okay. Jesus."

"Well, *you* have a gun, why shouldn't I?"

"I'm not saying you shouldn't, I'm just surprised you'd— never mind. Really, just never mind. Let's go." He tucked the Ruger under the waist of his pants in the small of his back.

So many of the men with whom Fara got along well came completely unraveled when they learned she had a gun. Those who reacted to her gun with enthusiasm and delight usually were men with whom she did not get along.

It got windier and colder as they walked past the door to the stairs that led down to the basement. Fara closed her eyes as they passed that door, and in the darkness of her mind, she saw the Tank, spattered and smeared with blood after a test, and snapped her eyes open.

The wind was deceptive. It made all kinds of sounds, some of which strongly resembled footsteps coming toward them, or coming up behind them. The sounds made Fara glance repeatedly over her shoulder.

They came to the main first floor corridor, usually broad and well lit at this end, and turned right. Now it was just a wall of darkness beyond the beam of her flashlight, and a rush of wind slammed into them hard enough to make both take a steadying step backwards. Paper and books and leaves and chips of plaster and wallpaper and other debris skittered over the floor, rushing toward them like a horde of mis-shapen spiders, and swept by their feet and into the darkness behind them.

There were small orbs of light in the darkness up ahead, floating and bobbing in the dark. There was movement, too, and voices garbled by the wind. The orbs of light were head-lamps.

"Looks like the cafeteria," Emilio said.

Fara nodded and said, "That tree stood right beside the cafeteria." She was surprised he heard her because her voice was so weak and shaky.

She was relieved the tree had fallen on the cafeteria because no one would have been in there. In that case, it was doubtful that anyone was hurt.

Up ahead, men were shouting at each other.

"Ollie, I'm tellin' ya, the best thing is just to get out! Right now! You guys shouldn't even be standin' in there now, I'm tellin' ya. I was a carpenter back in the day, y'know, I know what I'm talkin' about, goddammit!"

There was shouting from inside the cafeteria.

"We'll just post guards out here! Nobody's gettin' out through this mess, Ollie. And if they try, it'll probably fall on 'em!"

There was an urgency in the man's voice that made Fara slow her pace as they neared him. They could see the open door of the cafeteria now and two men standing outside. There was more yelling from beyond the open door.

The sound of a gunshot behind them cut through the howling wind. Fara and Emilio spun around.

A man's voice cried out in inarticulate fear and the gun fired again. There was another sound. Another voice down there in the dark. Low, speaking rapidly. Angrily.

"The hell's goin' on?" said a man behind them—the man who had been shouting through the cafeteria door.

Emilio said, "Gunshots and—"

The man screamed down there in the dark and the fear was replaced by pain.

There was more shouting inside the stormy cafeteria and the man standing behind them shouted, "Go help him, for Christ's sake!" Then he went back to the cafeteria's open doorway.

Somehow, Fara could not imagine herself going down that corridor, into that inky blackness with her tiny flashlight and revolver, and helping the man who was still screaming in pain. The Fara McManus who had not come to Springmeier, who had not applied for the job at Dr. Urbanski's urging, who had done something else with her life and had not been tainted by all of this—*that* Fara McManus would run into the dark without thinking, that was the kind of person she was. But she wasn't that woman anymore. She felt beaten down, dominated, cowed, and she couldn't move.

"Stay right here," Emilio said. "Right here with these guys."

"Take my light!"

"Keep it," he said. "They won't see me coming. Stay here!"

As he jogged away, he reached back and took the gun from under his shirt.

Fara did not like the idea of Emilio leaving her. If he didn't come back—

"No, no!" the man behind her shouted into the cafeteria doorway. "I'm tellin' ya, that section of the ceiling's gonna come down any minute, and when it does, it's gonna bring that—oh, *fuck*! Get out! *Get the fuck outta there*!"

Suddenly, there was a big arm around Fara's waist and she was being shoved forward in the corridor and men were running past them from behind, shouting in panic. She couldn't breathe for a moment as her feet scrambled to keep up with the man who was pushing her, and at times dragging her, away from the cafeteria. She still clutched the flashlight in her left hand and the .38 in her right.

A growing roar came from the cafeteria, a sound made up of cracking wood and shattering glass and loud crashing. But it got even louder and spilled out into the corridor with a sound that grew so loud, Fara was certain the ceiling was coming down on them.

And then the loud noise was gone and she was surrounded by dust that clouded her flashlight beam and made her cough. It swirled in the beams of four headlamps.

"Who's here?" Ollie said. "Sound off!"

Three voices called out three names between coughs.

"That's it?" Ollie growled. "Where's Jacobi? Where's Washington?"

Everyone turned around. The headlamps were bright, but they could not cut through heavy dust. They all stood there for a moment as it slowly dissipated.

The corridor ended quite abruptly now, at about the spot where the doorway of the cafeteria had stood open only a minute ago. The wall that ran the length of the cafeteria had collapsed and had brought down part of the second floor with it. Half of the corridor's ceiling had collapsed. The half that had not collapsed went along for only a short distance before it, too, had fallen in.

Ollie was angry about missing two of his men and paced back and forth shouting obscenities at himself, and one of the men asked how old the building was, anyway, and as they talked and even argued, Fara tuned them out and turned her back on them. She looked in the other direction down the eldritch corridor and listened for something that would tell her Emilio was safe. The beam of her miniature flashlight seemed feeble against that wall of onyx. She heard . . . something.

At first, she thought it was something being blown over the floor by the wind and rattling against the tiles. But it was something else. Not an object, but a . . . voice.

"—and I've said it before . . . probably have to say it again . . . nothing's fair in this life, but goddammit—"

Fara took a few steps forward, away from the men talking behind her, toward the ebony murk from which she heard the voice. It was growing louder. Rapidly becoming clearer. And through the shifting dust that clouded the darkness, she saw a speck of light getting brighter. Getting closer.

"—given my whole fucking life and what do I get in return? Has anyone even fucking *noticed*?"

A man's voice, but not too loud. His words were almost blown away by the wind. He was getting closer. Fara assumed he was one of Ollie's because he had a headlamp.

"I've had it up to *here* and I'm not taking this shit anymore, do you fucking hear me, I'm just not gonna *take* it, goddammit!"

Fara bent her right elbow and aimed the gun without raising her arm from her side. The jittery headlamp grew brighter. Closer.

"I'm fucking *done* and anybody who doesn't like it can just fuck off, understand me? Just fuck off! Shit! Shitfuck! Fuckshit!"

A figure oozed out of the ebony fog. Tall and slender and

bald with silver stubble on his scalp, and so pale, with the tattered, bloody remains of a hospital gown dangling from his mostly naked body. Blood was glossy around his mouth, on his chin, and down his chest, shoulders hunched as he continued forward in a fast, steady walk, angrily chattering, arms close to his sides, elbows bent, one fist clenched around a blood-streaked knife and the other around—

As soon as she saw the gun, Fara squeezed her .38 and it fired.

The man stumbled to a stop and bent forward a moment, crying out. He looked down at himself and saw the crimson bloom in the right side of his abdomen. Then he stood up straight and glared at Fara with wide, gleaming eyes.

"You think just because you shoot me I'm gonna roll over?" he said as he kept coming. "Huh? Like a killer whale at Marine World? Huh? What the fuck you think I am, some kinda fucking *communist*?" He lifted his gun and fired.

Fara squeezed the .38 again, and kept squeezing.

The pale, ghostly figure went down hard, and a moment later, she realized she was still firing an empty gun.

And she had killed someone.

Heavy, clopping footsteps ran toward her out of the dark. "Jesus Christ, are you okay?" Emilio ran around the body on the floor and came to her.

Her arms and hands shook and she panted like a runner. She turned the trembling flashlight on herself and looked for wounds. "Did he shoot me?" she whispered. "Am I shot?"

"I think you're fine," Emilio said. He grabbed her wrist and took the gun from her, but she tugged it away from him and stared at it. Frowned at it.

"I think I killed him," she whispered. She took a step to the left and looked beyond Emilio at the still body on the floor. "Jesus Christ, I . . . I killed a man."

"You had to. You had no choice. You're shaking pretty bad, are you gonna be okay?"

"I . . . I . . . don't know."

He put an arm around her shoulders, then looked behind her, pointed down the corridor, and said, "Hey, Ollie. One of your guys is down there and he's hurt. He was attacked by"—he pointed to the body on the floor—"that guy. He was bitten."

"*Bitten?*" Ollie said. "Oh, shit."

"Yeah, he was pretty shook up, too. He's just sitting down there, leaning against the wall. Said he was afraid if he stood, he'd pass out. He said he'd be fine if he just sat there for a while, but I don't know."

By now, the men Ollie had summoned were gathering at the corridor intersection. He stepped in front of Fara, leaned close, and spoke quietly. "I want straight answers from you. You said it could be contracted from a carrier's blood. What about a bite?"

"Yes, that would transmit the virus."

"How do we know we've got it? What are the symptoms?"

"The initial symptoms are flulike," she said. "Achiness, chills, headache, maybe some nausea. A while after that will come the rage. Violent, furious anger for no reason. When I say violent, I mean it. The time varies from person to person. Anywhere from ten to thirty minutes."

"And after that?"

Answering questions was calming her. "We're not sure, but we're going to find out. Apparently, Dr. Corcoran was keeping surviving test subjects—"

"Surviving?"

"Most of our tests involve putting newly infected test subjects together two at a time in an observation chamber. We watch as the symptoms progress, record how long it takes them to become violent, the levels of violence, that sort of thing."

Fara stopped talking for a moment and wondered if she

was going to get punched again. The anger in Ollie's eyes as they peered out of his ski mask was hotter than lava and it was aimed directly into her eyes. But he made no move and said nothing. He simply glared pure hate at her.

"One of the two usually kills the other," she continued, "although on two occasions, even the survivors died of their injuries. It seems Dr. Corcoran has been putting the survivors in the subbasement. Unless your men have let them loose, in which case they could show up anytime, couldn't they?"

"You said there's no antidote. What are my options if my people get this thing?"

"I'm sorry, I don't understand the question."

"If my men start showing symptoms, what can I do?"

"With the goal being to prevent it from spreading further?"

"Yes, of course."

There was only one answer to that question, but she could not say it out loud. Not directly. "What are you doing with the test—with the homeless people, Ollie?"

He nodded slowly, grimly. "If that guy down the hall has been bitten, then he's bleeding. And if he's got this virus and somebody gets his blood on his hands—well, you know how this works, you invented the goddamned thing. Along with being as careful as we can about getting blood on our skin— or any other bodily fluids, for that matter—do you have any suggestions?"

She turned to Emilio. "Can you get some gloves out of one of the closets?"

"Sure," Emilio said.

"Bring a whole case."

He turned and hurried down the side corridor as if going back to Fara's office, but he stopped and opened a storage closet and went inside.

Ollie stepped away from Fara and returned his attention to his men, but she watched him and listened.

As he looked around, Ollie said, "Okay, where's my brain? Delgado?"

"Here," said a small, young-sounding man as he hurried out of nowhere to Ollie's side.

"Aside from the guys in the cafeteria, who are we missing so far?"

"Nobody's seen Bursell and Castillo. I mean, not since we *got* here."

"Anybody know where they went?"

"They came in through the tunnel, and when the others came up, they stayed down there to look around. And nobody's seen 'em since."

"Jesus Christ. Bursell's pretty easily distracted. Go down there and see if you can find them. Bring them back up here."

"Yes, sir."

"If you don't want to go alone, pick someone to take with you."

"I don't mind going alone."

"Report back to me when you're done. And stay the hell out of the subbasement."

"Well, they were going to check that out, too."

"Bursell and Castillo?"

"Yes, sir. Those were your orders."

"Well, on second thought, they weren't very good ones. If you can't find them in the basement, come back up here and I'll send a couple more guys with you. I might even go myself. If what I've been told is true, I want plenty of cameras down there."

"Yes, sir."

"And listen to me, Delgado. If you find anyone locked up down there, do *not* let them out."

"Yes, sir."

Fara thought he sounded like a boy, a teenager. When he hurried away, he moved with eagerness and youth.

Emilio returned carrying a large case of individually

wrapped pairs of latex gloves. He put the cardboard box on the floor beside Fara and Ollie joined them as he tore through the tape and cardboard to open it.

"No one should deal with an open wound without a pair of these on," Fara said. "The gloves aren't a guarantee, but they're a good safety precaution."

"They're already wearing gloves."

"Then they should wear these under them."

"I'll make sure of it." He took a package of gloves from the box, turned to his men, and held it up. "These are latex gloves. You are not to go near blood or an open wound without a pair of these on your hands. Listen very closely to this because your life depends on it. When dealing with the homeless pe—uh, the people we came here to—the, uh, test subjects, when dealing with the test subjects, do not, I repeat, *do not* get their blood on your skin. They are carrying a deadly virus. If their blood gets on your skin, you will contract the virus."

He lowered his head a moment, cleared his throat, then continued.

"This isn't a garden variety virus. It was manufactured by the fine folks from Vendon Labs to be used as a biological weapon. The test subjects were infected with the virus. We released the test subjects. Now we, uh . . . we don't have any choice. We have to kill them. To be safe, I want everybody to put on a pair of these latex gloves under the gloves you're wearing. Once you've done that, Rubens, I need you to go down that corridor there. I'm not sure who it is, but somebody was bitten and he's wounded down there and needs some first aid."

Rubens peered into the black cave that was the corridor Ollie had indicated and said, "He's just bitten? Well . . . can't he come here?"

"I'm fine, I'm fine, quit talking about me like I'm not here." The voice came out of that dark cave, and it was followed shortly by one of Ollie's masked men.

"Aguilar?" Ollie said.

"Yeah."

"You were bitten?"

"On the arm."

"Did it break the skin?"

"Break the—well, yeah. Why?" He stared at Ollie a moment, then said, "Why, Ollie? Should I be worried?"

"Uh . . . c'mon over here and let's talk," Ollie said, waving him over.

Emilio moved to Ollie's side. "You want us to stick around, or should we go back to the office?"

"You've got guns, why don't you stick around and help us? We could use all the help we can get." He nodded toward Fara. "And she knows her way around this place, which would be a *big* help."

"Okay. What kind of help do you need?"

Ollie laughed and shook his head as if it were a stupid question. "The hell do you think? We need help killing them."

38

Jeremiah Delgado was happy to be doing something by himself. He was happy to be going down a dark stairwell to the dark basement of an abandoned mental hospital because it meant he wasn't in a drunk tank, or an alley, or a gutter.

He was not a veteran like most of Ollie's men. Delgado was nineteen and had been rescued by Ollie at a low point in his life. His mother had given him an ultimatum: Get out of the gang or don't come home, and if he tried to come home while he was still gangbanging, she would shoot him. Then she changed the locks on the doors. He didn't want to be in a gang anymore, but he was afraid to quit. He'd known guys who quit and got killed for it. His mother wouldn't let him in the house and would start shooting at him if he showed up, he didn't want to go back to the gang, and he had nowhere else to go. So he went to the streets and just blended in and disappeared. Ollie found him in a sweep of San Francisco's Tenderloin district and brought him to Eureka. For that, Ollie had Delgado's undying loyalty. He also had a valuable resource in Delgado, who Ollie said was the smartest, sharpest, most intelligent person he had brought to the compound. His sixth-grade teacher had told Delgado that he had something called an eidetic memory, and ever since Ollie learned that fact, he'd called Delgado his brain.

The stairs opened on a corridor in the basement. The door was bent on its hinges and hung all the way open, unable to close. Delgado stopped and listened.

Somewhere in the dark, he heard voices. Or was it just one voice? It was coming from the left. He ambled down the narrow corridor.

"Hey, Bursell! Castillo! Ollie wants you guys up top."

He stopped and listened again. The voice was closer, talking fast. Sometimes it sounded like more than one voice. Complaining, angry voices, closer still and getting closer.

Delgado kept walking.

Kaufman had no luck finding von Pohle's car, but he found the new road that led to Springmeier. It had been cut off of Ogden Pass, a road that was closed years ago because, just a mile along, it had slid into a ravine and wasn't there anymore.

While he was searching for von Pohle's car, he'd had dispatch look up Ollie's cell phone number for him. If he had a problem finding the road or getting onto the grounds, he would give Ollie a call. But Kaufman preferred to show up unannounced.

Large tree branches flew through the air and bounced across the road. Unidentifiable debris swirled and danced madly at high speeds through the night. There were moments when it felt like the wind was about to lift Kaufman's car off the ground and toss it into the night like a toy. He drove slowly, but his wipers were on high, flapping back and forth at a blur.

The gravel road curved and his headlights passed over the hospital's old boiler house, a dark, sagging structure that had already lost part of its roof. It was such a weary-looking building that Kaufman doubted it would survive the night. Parked near the boiler house were three empty vans.

Sudden movement in his headlight beams made him step on the brake pedal. The car jerked to a halt as a slender figure stumbled in from the right, struggling against the wind, then stopped and squinted at Kaufman. A skinny, black, androgynous figure with short hair, wearing a blanket around the hunched shoulders and some kind of long, baggy T-shirt, or something—

Is that a hospital gown? Oh, Jesus, a hospital *gown? That can't be good.*

—which was now soaked and clinging like skin. The slight frame wavered against the force of the blowing storm, the bare feet shifting position. Then the figure seemed to lose interest and stalked farther into the light, crossing the gravel road with head low, shoulders slightly hunched.

"What the hell now," he muttered as he put the car in park and yanked the parking brake. He opened the door, put one foot on the ground and stood with his right foot in the car and both arms on the car, one leaning on the top edge of the door and the other on the roof. The wind sounded like a thunderstorm in his ears. He reached into the car, flipped a switch on the steering wheel, hit a button on the console under the dashboard, then grabbed the radio's mike. His voice was amplified over the speaker between the roof lights, which were now flashing red and blue. "This is the sheriff. Are you injured? Do you need an ambulance?"

Kaufman still couldn't determine the sex, but the person was talking quite rapidly to him- or herself. He noticed the hands. They closed into fists, released, the fingers extended rigidly for a moment, then clenched into fists again. That was repeated over and over as he watched, then the arms came up and the hands clawed furiously at the air, as if scratching someone's eyes out. They were thick wrists. He decided he was dealing with a very skinny man.

He lifted the mike to his mouth and depressed the button again, but he didn't speak. He looked beyond the skinny man crossing the road and saw the hospital's gate. It stood open outward, but not quite all the way, and it was bent and twisted.

A voice shouted from Kaufman's right and he turned to see another figure similar to the first one—thin, wearing a denim coat over what might have been a flimsy hospital gown—was pointing at him. Behind him, another one appeared from a door in the boiler house.

Why are they coming out of the boiler house? Why are they in the boiler house? What the hell is going on here?

The man who was pointing at him was also shouting at him, but Kaufman couldn't make out the words. Suddenly, he quickened his pace and when he was on the verge of breaking into a jog, Kaufman noticed that the man was not simply pointing at him, he was pointing a *gun* at him.

Kaufman moved to duck into the car a fraction of a second before the gun fired.

The bullet struck the windshield and a tiny web of cracks appeared, and Kaufman dropped the mike as he pulled his leg into the car. Then they were running toward him, both of the figures approaching from the boiler house. The one with the gun kept his arm extended and fired again as Kaufman pulled the door closed.

A crashed gate, strange people wandering around in a hurricane—there was definitely some kind of situation at Springmeier, and he needed backup immediately. He started the engine, then reached for the mike. It wasn't in its holder. He'd dropped it as he was getting into the car. The cord stretched down to his legs. He clumsily reached for it, but the guy with the gun was now in front of the car and aiming at him.

Kaufman put the car in gear and slammed his foot on the accelerator.

The man jumped onto the hood as the car lurched forward and for the first time, Kaufman heard what he was shouting.

"—not gonna let you get away with it, you cocksucker! I saw her first, you son of a bitch! *I saw her first!*" He looked and sounded like an escaped mental patient, but this hadn't been a functioning mental hospital in over a decade.

Kaufman remembered the voice of the woman who identified herself as Dr. Fara McManus talking about the virus they'd created and what it would do.

Kaufman hit the brake and the man on the hood slid off as another one began to pound on the passenger side window with something hard and heavy. Kaufman suspected a rock.

The one who'd crossed the street had turned back and was pointing at him, glaring at him through the side window, and shouting at him in a hoarse, roaring fury.

He hit the accelerator again. The car surged forward and humped over something on the ground, first the left front tire, then the left rear tire. Up and over, up and over.

"Shit," Kaufman muttered, his voice tight, as he thought of things like being fired, or charged, or sued, and the inevitable crucifixion in the media no matter what happened.

He reached down with his left hand and tried to find the mike. The curled cord ended at the bottom of the door. The mike was hanging out of the car.

"Shit!" he shouted.

Suddenly, two fists were pounding on the windshield and an upside-down face was screaming at him and suddenly Kaufman, whose nerves had been stretched tight, was screaming, too, and the car swerved to the right.

The patrol car crashed into the guardhouse.

"Bursell! Castillo!"

They had to be able to hear him because Delgado could hear them. Or him, if it was just one voice. He still couldn't tell. But it was closer.

He'd passed a lot of doors, closed and opened. The beam of

his headlamp finally fell on a wall up ahead as he approached a T intersection. The voices were coming from the left. He rounded the corner.

A face lunged toward him out of the dark, a face so white and stark that Delgado first thought it was a mime. Another emerged right behind it, and a hand holding a knife slashed across him diagonally, and Delgado felt the blade cut his skin as he jogged clumsily backwards and started to fall, mouth yawning open silently, arms flailing—

Don't fall don't fall that's all just don't fall don't fall!

—and the hand slashed again and Delgado felt the blade cut, and he got his footing and threw himself to the left. Then he was running back the way he'd come.

They were behind him, chasing him, shouting angrily, cursing, even growling like animals, and they were fast, their bare feet slapping on the tile floor, fast enough to get closer. And closer. He fumbled for his gun as he ran, but his hand seemed to be a piece of dead meat at the end of his arm.

He came to the stairwell door and pushed through it hard, then spun around and threw himself against it to shut it. It wouldn't close. His two pursuers hit the door on the other side and shoved, gibbering furiously.

Delgado looked over his shoulder at the stairs. As soon as he stepped away from that door, they were coming through. He unholstered his Ruger, steeled himself, then turned and ran up the stairs, shouting, hoping they would hear him up there.

"They're down here!" he shouted. "Down here!"

He made it up the first half, grabbed the rail and spun himself around to go up the second half, hearing their feet behind him. As he rounded that rail, he raised his right hand, aimed the gun in their direction and fired once, twice. There was a scream of pain behind him. He didn't stop moving. Up, up, his shoes clopped on each step.

"They're down here! Down here!"

Hands on the backs of his legs, grabbing his pant legs, clutching.

He was almost at the top, he could see the door up there, the door that opened on the corridor that led to Dr. McManus's office to the left and the gathering at the intersection on the right.

"Down here!"

A hand got a solid hold and pulled hard.

Delgado tripped on the stairs and went down.

"Down here!"

They were on him and he felt the knife entering his back, his arm, his neck, again and again, the fist hammering, the blade stabbing into him—

"Down here!"

—pulling out, stabbing in, pulling out, stabbing . . .

PART FIVE
Chaos Theory

39

"I'm alone now, so I can speak freely," Corcoran said as he leaned back in the chair again and put his feet back up on the desk. "Things have gone straight to hell. A disaster, top to bottom."

"What kind of disaster?"

"Well, I told Sylvia about some of it, and—"

"You haven't told me. What kind of disaster?"

"The worst. These, these, I don't know what to call them, these lunatics, these vigilante militia *lunatics* come bursting in here and hold everyone at fucking *gunpoint* while they release the test subjects."

"The monkeys?"

"No. The, uh . . . the off-the-books test subjects."

There was a long silence on the line, then: "I see. And how did they know about them?"

"I have no clue! None!"

"None at all? You have no idea whatsoever how this could have happened?"

"Look, there are a couple of guys who do nothing but make trouble for us. Or try to make trouble for us. One is that Internet radio host I told you about. He does a show about conspiracies and, I don't know, the Illuminati's plan to enslave us all, or whatever, and he got it into his head that something suspicious was going on here at Springmeier because Vendon Labs and DeCamp Pharmaceuticals were involved with and have a long and fruitful relationship with the government, and—"

"Breathe, Jeremy. Are you high?"

"Don't be ridiculous, I haven't been doing anything."

"I know you too well. That you haven't been doing any drugs would be ridiculous. Go on with your story."

"Well, the show is on the Internet, so it's heard everywhere, but it stirred up all the paranoid nutballs here, and apparently this militia, this armed, paramilitary group of gun-loving thugs just broke in. As far as I know, they've killed our entire security team! Just *killed* them!"

"You're sure about that? The entire team?"

"According to the leader of that mob. His name is Ollie. One of our janitors seems to know him."

"Is that so? One of your janitors?"

"Yes. That's not important, though."

"You don't think so? You've had a catastrophic security breach and your janitor is friends with the man who leads the team that pulled it off and . . . you don't think that's important?"

"Well, I certainly didn't think—"

"That's becoming a problem, Jeremy, the fact that you don't think. The fact that you do drugs and throw sex parties and you're becoming more and more careless all the time. I'm afraid we're going to have to reevaluate your relationship with Vendon Labs, Jeremy."

Corcoran laughed. "Be serious. Where are you going to find anyone who can do what I can do for you? Nobody else could have done for you all the things I've done over the years. That includes *this*. Yes, this project may be fucked, but I've been doing what you were paying me to do, and with more time, I would have finished. What do you care if I do drugs or have a party now and then as long as I get the job done?"

"Getting the job done includes maintaining the security and safety of your facility, you know that. I strongly suggested that you let me send someone in to manage things, but you wouldn't—"

Corcoran lowered his feet to the floor and sat up straight in the squeaky chair. "I don't work *under* anyone. After all the years I've—with the career I've had, you want me to—I shouldn't *have* to work under anyone."

"Are you done sputtering?"

"Well, I don't think I'm being unreasonable to think that someone of my status—"

"Your status, Jeremy, is as follows: You are a sixty-eight-year-old man who still tries to pass for sixty-five, who's rapidly falling apart, but who insists on living like a twenty-year-old and who takes drugs like a rock star. All of those things have begun to outweigh any talents you have. Talents that are slipping, I might add, because the drugs are destroying your brain. *And* your mind. You used to have a *few* leadership qualities in addition to your talents as a scientist, but not anymore. You've made that clear with this disaster."

"You are *not* going to lay this at *my* feet! The biggest problem here from the beginning has been Fara. And now she's talking about going public with her story. She claims she's sent some recording to that radio host I told you about. If you want to blast somebody on this team, it should be *her*."

"She's not in charge of the project. You are. You should stop thinking of yourself as irreplaceable. You're not *that* Dr. Jeremy Corcoran anymore."

"Then . . . then what Jeremy Corcoran *am* I? I'm still the Jeremy Corcoran who did all those great things for you, those things others laughed at when you told them what you wanted. And some of those things . . ." He leaned forward, put an elbow on the desk and his forehead in his hand. When he continued, it was in a whisper. "Some of them were terrible things. What I did to those people in that little Italian village. The things you've had me do to our own soldiers. And those children. My God, what you had me to do to all those children you kept in cages. *Cages*! I mean, Jesus, it's almost funny, it's almost *hilarious*"—he giggled—"that you're ragging on *me* for doing some *drugs*!" More giggling. "It doesn't make sense. You guys? Children in cages, drugging people, messing with their minds without their knowledge, putting things in the water supply. Me? I like drugs and I enjoy sex with one or more people at once, as much of it as possible, preferably *while* using drugs. But *I'm* the bad guy here? *Me*?"

"You're looking at it the wrong way. No one is saying you're a bad guy. We never minded the drugs as long as you remained useful to us. But now the drugs have destroyed in you whatever it was that was useful to us. Do you understand? It's simply a matter of . . . moving on. And there's plenty of young talent out there, don't make the mistake of thinking there's not. Most of it is coming from Asia, but it's out there in abundance. You are no longer able to fulfill our needs, so we have to look elsewhere. In fact . . . I think it's time for retirement, Jeremy."

Gooseflesh crawled across Corcoran's shoulders and upper back and the small hairs on the back of his neck stood erect and his scrotum shriveled up tight until his testicles were snugly tucked away. He had been working for these people most of his adult life. He'd done plenty of other work as well, of course, but working for Vendon and DeCamp was how he'd made most of his money, and it was on that work that most of his reputation was based. He knew these people, he knew how they thought, how they worked. He knew about enough of the cold, cruel things they did to get what they wanted to know that all the stuff he *didn't* know about was far worse.

When dealing with these people, the word "retirement" could be taken in more than one way.

"What, uh . . . what kind of retirement do you mean . . . exactly?"

"What kind of retirement do you *think* I mean, Jeremy?"

When he did not respond, the voice at the other end chuckled.

"Have the test subjects been contained in the building, Jeremy?"

"As far as I know. So far."

"Encouraging. That must be the goal of everyone there, do you understand? Keeping those people inside the hospital until we get there."

"We? You're coming here? When?"

"You're in the middle of a hurricane right now, but the moment the weather calms down sufficiently, we'll be sending in a team to solve the problem and . . . clean up this mess."

Corcoran found that he had no saliva left in his mouth. He rolled his tongue around, then tried to swallow, but gulped loudly instead.

"The problem?" he said.

"Yes."

"Which . . . problem?"

"The problem we've been discussing, of course. You see? You're difficult to talk to when you're on drugs, Jeremy. It makes you . . . foggy and unreasonable. You can no longer afford that."

Drugs had nothing to do with it. Corcoran was paralyzed with fear. He was wondering if they would be sending a team to solve the problem of the released test subjects . . . or the problem of Dr. Jeremy Corcoran.

"Is there anything else you want me to do until you get here?" he said.

"Just keep everyone inside. Including yourself, Jeremy."

The connection was severed.

Corcoran always became clumsy when he was nervous and afraid, and he nearly dropped the phone three times before getting it back in his pocket. He pushed the chair back, leaned down, and started opening Fara's drawers. He knew she smoked, she had to have cigarettes around here somewhere. The craving for a smoke was suddenly pawing at Corcoran's throat. He found an unopened pack of Pall Malls in the bottom drawer on the left and began digging at the plastic wrap on the box. When he couldn't peel it off, he clawed at it with his fingernails, tearing it off the box. He opened the box, pulled out a cigarette, and put it in his mouth. He hadn't smoked cigarettes in a long time, but he always carried a lighter in his pocket. He lit the cigarette with a trembling hand, sucked the smoke into his lungs, and went into a fit of hacking coughs. He looked around for an ashtray and snuffed the cigarette out in the potted plant on the end table by the couch.

What he needed was a joint. But he didn't have one. Everything was in his quarters. He was freezing his ass off in scrubs and his coat was in his quarters. He didn't want to go back there. Even his car keys were there. But should he feel the need to make a quick exit, he always kept a spare key in a small magnetized box under the left rear fender in case he found himself without access to his keys.

He paced the office in the candlelight and wondered if he could drive through the storm. Even if he could, where would he go? He lived there at Springmeier. He had no friends in the area, he knew no one because he hadn't wanted to know anyone. It was a rural area filled with pot farmers, potheads, artists, and nut jobs waiting for Armageddon. The only locals who interested him were the college students, of course. He'd spoken at the university a couple of times and managed to lure a couple of them back to Springmeier for a tour of the facility. Not a *real* tour, of course, but something that would pass for a tour. Then an offer of Dr. Corcoran's magic dust, and like the horses in the Kentucky Derby, they were off.

Those days were over. This whole project was over. And now Vendon Labs was sending a team to clean up. That was the fat lady singing. That meant things were *really* over. For some people, anyway. But this time, Corcoran was certain he was one of them.

The possibility had never entered his head. He'd always known he was safe because he was too valuable. If that was no longer the case, then this project wasn't the only thing that was over. His whole *world* was over, because that had been the only thing in his whole life that he could rely on. That value had been his security.

Now it didn't come to him as a possibility, but as a certainty, because they were talking retirement. Not censure, not suspension, none of the disciplinary measures, no, they leaped way over all that in a single bound and went straight to *retirement*.

They were not going to give him a gold watch or a box of Cuban cigars.

"I've got to get out of here," he muttered as he paced. "Now. Go now, take my chances with the storm . . ."

But having no destination in mind made him pull away from the idea. He had never done anything unless he had a destination or a goal in mind, an outcome, a place to go, *something*. Without that, he wouldn't know what he was doing.

Maybe the problem was that he'd always known what he was doing. He'd always tried to control his environment so everything worked out the way he wanted. He was able to do that in a lab, but doing it in real life was a different proposition altogether. That did not, however, keep him from trying. Maybe it was time to simply jump into the abyss and leave here with nowhere to go, no living family, no real friends.

Corcoran's mother and father had been great scientists who, among other accomplishments, had helped found

DeCamp Pharmaceuticals. Corcoran had grown up knowing that he would become a great scientist who would do great things for the world, but he would do it through DeCamp.

As a boy, he'd sailed through school, leaving everyone else in his dust, and had degrees before most boys his age had kissed a girl. Everything he had done, every decision he'd made had a specific goal. He reached that goal significantly sooner than the average scientist, and before long he was doing work that other scientists more seasoned than he would dismiss as something from the plot of a comic book, government-funded work that was usually of secret variety, with an appropriate cover story. Great work that no one outside of those projects would know he'd done. With no one watching, there were no rules.

He had always been brilliant, always been lauded and respected and awarded special treatment because he was such a genius. If all of that was over, then his life was over.

He stopped pacing. *Don't be crazy,* he thought. *They're not going to ruin your life. They're going to kill you. This has nothing to do with whether or not I have anything to live for. The question is do I want to live?*

He decided he did.

He went to Fara's small closet and searched for a coat he could wear. The only one that was acceptable was a shapeless blob of black corduroy with a fuzzy wool collar and cuffs. He put it on, went to the door and slowly, cautiously pulled it open to see what he could see in the corridor outside.

He heard activity in the direction of the intersection with the main corridor and he could see the bright little spots of light that were the headlamps worn by Ollie's men. Without a light, Corcoran hoped he could blend into the darkness enough to get by them. He stayed close to the wall as he neared the intersection, then hugged it as he rounded the corner. Ollie was talking to his men and all their attention—as well as their headlamps—was on him.

Corcoran couldn't see the double doors that opened onto a foyer, which in turn opened onto the parking lot behind the building, but he knew they were down there at the end of the corridor, only twenty yards away.

No slowing down, no stopping to think. He heard sounds in the darkness around him, things blowing and rattling over the floor, voices in the other direction, but he kept moving forward as quickly as possible without running, hoping there was nothing directly in front of him in the dark, hoping he could cross the span of darkness without interruption, without encountering anyone, without being noticed, and as he hoped those things, he closed the distance and then—

—he was there.

He pushed into the foyer to find one of the double doors to the parking lot blown all the way open against the wall. He leaned into the wind as he stepped through the open doorway and out into the storm.

The wind threatened to knock him over and the rain soaked his coat quickly as he slowly made his way to his parking spot, fighting the relentless force of the wind.

His attention was caught by a pair of headlights below flashing red and blue lights just beyond the gate. A police car. After a moment, he realized it had slammed into the guardhouse.

Two figures were approaching the police cruiser. Once they were close enough to be illuminated by the car's lights, Corcoran recognized the figures as his test subjects. Former test subjects, anyway.

Oh, Jesus Christ, they've gotten out, he thought. But he instantly forgot about them when his eyes fell on an empty parking space.

His Jeep was gone.

"Mother*fuck*!" he shouted, but it was swallowed up by the storm and even he couldn't hear it.

40

The police are here, Latrice thought as she stood in the kitchen, *and you've got blood all over you. Get your shit together, girl.*

She left the kitchen, but instead of entering the living room, she went down the hall and found the bathroom. She closed the door and locked it.

The bathroom was a spacious mess. The clothes hamper was full and more dirty clothes were piled on the floor beside it. An unflushed turd lounged at the bottom of the toilet bowl and towels were everywhere—on the counter, the back of the toilet, the side of the bathtub—except hanging on towel racks.

Latrice inspected herself in the mirror. She was wearing a navy blue sweater and grey slacks. The sleeves of her sweater had been pushed up to her elbows and her right hand and forearm were covered with blood. There was some on her left hand, too, and it was spattered on her face. There were a few speckles of it on the front of her sweater, but somehow, she'd managed to avoid getting her clothes bloody.

She turned on the faucet and let the water get warm, then she grabbed a bottle of liquid soap and lathered up her hands. She scrubbed her forearms and washed her face, found a towel that appeared relatively clean, and dried off. Then she dabbed the spatters of blood from her sweater with some tissue until it was no longer visible.

She'd been watching *CSI* long enough to know they'd be able to find enough blood on her to send her away for good. But she didn't plan to stick around long enough for that to happen.

She leaned on the edge of the sink, looked at her reflection, and took some deep breaths. Then she lifted her right hand and rubbed her eyes with thumb and fingers. A headache was creeping in like a morning fog, gathering behind her eyes. She was beginning to feel achy, probably because every muscle in her body had been so tense for so long.

Turning to the door, she listened for a moment. The storm still raged outside, worse than ever, a nonstop rumble accompanied by loud rattles and clashes. She heard nothing happening inside the house, though—no shouting, no shooting. She took another deep breath, then opened the door and stepped out.

It remained quiet in the house as she made her way down the hall. It seemed even the television had been silenced. She entered the living room without making a sound, hoping she wouldn't be noticed.

Marcus had come back into the house and was frantically cleaning the guns, drugs, and paraphernalia off the coffee table, moving fast as he swept everything into a plastic garbage bag. He wore a dripping raincoat.

Jada was finally awake and sitting up on the love seat, rubbing her eyes with both hands and looking groggy. She lowered her hands and lifted her head and her puffy eyes went directly to Latrice, widening a little.

Giff was at the front door, looking out the peephole. The left sleeve of his sweatshirt had been removed and his arm had been bandaged. A younger man with short, black hair and mocha skin stood beside him, leaning close and talking quietly. Beside him stood a young woman in a long, dark coat.

Her auburn hair was short and spiky and Latrice could see part of a tattoo on the right side of her neck. She looked apprehensive as she ran a hand through her hair. Standing several feet away, fidgeting and smoking nervously, was Tojo.

The tattooed woman turned slightly, spotted Latrice, and turned fully toward her. Her skin was pale and she had piercings in her face. She took off her coat to reveal a blue sweatshirt and green sweatpants.

"Who're you?" she said.

Giff pulled away from the peephole and turned around. "Oh, that's Latrice, she's a . . . guest." Striding toward Latrice, he frowned and said, "There's a sheriff's deputy outside and it looks like he's coming in, but I don't know why. And it looks like he's got some guy and a little boy with him. You know anything about this?"

Latrice assumed it would be unwise to admit that she was the one who'd called the police. Now she wished she hadn't. She should have just gotten the hell out of there while she could, gotten back into her car and driven into the storm. She slowly turned her head back and forth in response to Giff's question.

The headache had gotten worse and was making her ears ring, and her shoulders, arms, and legs ached. She had a sinking feeling she was getting sick. At the worst possible time.

"Well, far as I know, he's got nothing on us," Giff said. He turned around to find that the man and woman were now standing right behind him. "You think he followed Hank? Maybe that's it. He was chasin' Hank. Y'think?"

The man nodded. "It's possible."

"Giff, I think you should sit down," the young woman said. "You're sweatin' like a pig. Shaking, too."

"I'm gonna be okay, Mia," Giff said. "The bullet went straight through, it's just a flesh wound."

"But you look like shit."

"Leave him alone, Mia," the man said.

"Well, *look* at him, Miguel, he looks like he's gonna pass out, or something!" She lifted her hand to Giff's face and placed her palm over his forehead, then his cheek. "Jesus, you've got a fever." She shook her hand a few times, saying, "And you're soaking wet."

"I'm not feeling so good, you wanna know the truth, but I think maybe I'm just getting a flu bug, or something. I'll be fine, don't worry. Shit, this is bad, 'cause the cop's gonna want to *see* Hank. Goddammit, we don't have time to clean up that mess in the kitchen and hide the bodies."

"*Bodies?*" Mia said. "The fuck's goin' on here, you didn't say nothin' about no bodies in the kitchen."

"He's gonna see Jimmy out in the front yard, anyway," Miguel said. "He'll know something's up."

"What the hell are we talking about?" the woman said. "He's going to see *that*!" She pointed at the bloody bandage on Giff's arm. "You gonna tell him you cut yourself shaving?"

"Fuck." Giff turned to her. "Oh, uh, Latrice, this is Miguel and Mia. They live in one of the trailers out front. Guys, this is Latrice." He turned to Mia and said, "Go to my room. Dresser drawer, second from the top, grab me a sweatshirt. Hurry."

Mia ran from the room.

They all jumped at the loud pounding on the door.

"Sheriff's department!" a voice shouted just outside the door.

"Jesus fucking *Christ*," Giff hissed.

"You okay, Giff?" Miguel said. "You do look pretty bad. You got sweat dripping down your face."

He wiped a hand down his glistening face. "Yeah, I'm not feelin' so good."

"What's wrong?" he said.

Giff shook his head. "I don't have time to worry about it now."

Mia returned with a sweatshirt. She helped Giff remove

the sweatshirt he was wearing, with its missing sleeve, and then helped him put on the one she'd brought. It was clean and had both sleeves and concealed Giff's bandage well.

"What do you want to do?" Miguel said.

More pounding on the door.

"Sheriff's department, open up!"

Giff clenched his teeth and growled through them, "Son of a *bitch*." His forehead cut with deep frown lines, he frantically looked around the room, as if the solution might be right in front of him. "Okay, okay. Mia, go to the bedroom and get the kids. Bring 'em out here and put 'em in front of the TV. Turn on cartoons, or something. Do it now."

Mia looked uncertain. She'd had a slightly sickened look on her face ever since she'd learned there were dead people in the kitchen.

"I don't know, Giff," she said, talking fast, "if you got bodies in the kitchen, are you sure you want me to bring the kids—"

"Do it!" Miguel snapped.

She hurried out of the room.

Giff said, "Tojo, go sit on the couch and read your fuckin' book."

Tojo quickly did as he was told.

He turned to Marcus, who stood nearby in his wet raincoat with the garbage bag full of contraband on the floor by his feet. "Marcus, you know where to put that. But take off that raincoat first."

There was more pounding on the door as Mia hurried two young boys into the living room and sat them on the couch, then turned on the TV. Once there were animated spaceships on the screen, Mia sat down on the couch with the boys.

"Latrice," Giff said. "Sit down and watch TV."

She crossed the room and sat down in the recliner. The package she'd delivered, which she'd last seen on the floor beside the recliner, was nowhere in sight. It felt good to sit.

She was aching all over and she was beginning to feel cold. Feverish. Sick. She wished she were at home on her couch, legs tucked up, her elbow propped on a couple of pillows, safe and warm and well, the kids playing in the front yard, their laughter drifting in through the screen door while Latrice laughed with Mama at Ellen DeGeneres.

Giff whispered, "Everybody just try to follow my lead. Whatever the hell that is." He turned with a sigh, his face wet with perspiration, eyes heavy-lidded with sudden weariness, and went to the front door. He leaned against it as he opened it so it wouldn't be slammed in by the powerful wind. The sounds of the storm rushed into the house.

Latrice heard voices but couldn't understand their words. The door was closed a moment later and the house became a little quieter. She leaned forward slightly in the chair and turned toward the entrance, trying not to be too obvious.

"Hey, Giff!" a cheerful, booming voice said. "It's been a while. How you doing?"

Giff backed slowly into the living room with his left hand on his hip and the other scratching the top of his head.

"Hey, deputy . . . is it von Pohle?" he said.

"Right the first time!"

"Yeah, it has been a while." There was a smile on his face, but his voice was chilly and nervous.

The deputy came into the living room with a kind of strut, like a rooster. His big leather belt crackled softly under the pressure of his belly as he walked. A few steps behind him were a man and a young boy, both of whom looked very uncomfortable, even apologetic. All three of them were quite wet from the rain. The deputy wore a menacing grin as he watched Giff closely with cold eyes. He took off his plastic-wrapped cap and dropped it into a chair.

"Far as I know," Giff said, "I haven't got any warrants. Neither does anybody else here."

"That's not why I'm here. No. Somebody called."

"Called you? From *here*?" He chuckled. "No, I don't think so." He turned to the others in the living room and said, "Anybody been doin' any butt-dialing?" He laughed.

"No, it wasn't butt-dialing," the deputy said. "Somebody called about a shooting and some crazy old man? And you know, I couldn't help noticing you got an SUV out there that's slammed into the corner of your house and what looks like a dead man on the ground, shot right in the head. Did that have anything to do with the old man?"

"I don't know what that was. That happened about, uh"— he turned to the others—"when did that car crash into the house? Half hour ago? Forty-five minutes?"

"Something like that," Miguel said. "Scared the hell out of me. I thought one of the trees had fallen."

"Sounded like a bomb," Marcus added as he came into the room and sat down on the broad armrest at the end of the couch.

"Then you don't know anything about the dead body, Giff?" von Pohle said.

"Body?"

"In your front yard."

"You were serious? There's a body?"

The deputy's grin got a little bigger as he firmly shook his head and wagged a rigid forefinger back and forth in the air, saying, "Ah-ah-ah, I never joke about dead bodies. Not on duty, anyway. You're also gonna tell me you don't know anything about the bullet holes in your front door, I suppose."

"Bullet holes?" Giff said.

As he laughed, von Pohle turned to the man and boy who had come in with him and gave them a look that said *Can you believe this shit?* Then his head snapped around and his smile turned into an O for a moment. "Oh, I'm sorry, these are a couple friends I'm giving a ride to, is all. This is Andy and his son, Donny. They're not with me in any kind of official way, not at all, I'm just giving 'em a lift. But I figured since we're, y'know, in the middle of a fuckin' hurricane, they should come inside with me. I knew you wouldn't mind. If you'd like, they can go wait in some other part of the house. Maybe they could sit in the kitchen? You know, I think we could all use some coffee." He turned to the man, who looked deeply worried, and said, "You want some coffee, Andy?"

"Sure," Andy said. "Coffee would be good." He bent toward the boy and said, "Do you want anything to drink, Donny? Some water, maybe?"

Donny nodded, then said, "I'm real hungry, too."

Andy put a hand on the boy's shoulder and gave it a comforting squeeze.

Latrice watched the boy. A handsome young fellow with the same lustrous black hair as his father, big nervous eyes.

Donny made her think of Robert and Tamara. Especially Robert and his poor arm and leg. She had to get home to them.

"Do you have some coffee?" von Pohle asked Giff.

"I'll go make some right now," Giff said.

Latrice said, "There's already coffee made out there. Should still be hot."

The deputy hadn't noticed her before and now, as he turned to her, his face lit up. "Well, look at you!" he said. "Perfect! Why don't *you* get the coffee for us!" He seemed quite happy about it.

"I'll get it," Giff said, smiling as he headed for the doorway.

"No, really," von Pohle said, "I think I'd kind of enjoy being served coffee by your friend, here." He turned to Latrice again.

Latrice realized she was clenching her teeth and relaxed her jaw. This cop was pissing her off. She saw what he was doing. He thought he was being funny. She was surprised he hadn't already called her Mammy or Beulah. But she felt too sick to say or do anything about it.

"I'm not feeling so good," she said. "You should let Giff get the coffee."

"Coming up," Giff said as he left the room.

The deputy took a few steps toward her. "You're sick. What's the matter?"

She shrugged. "I'm feeling fluish. You might want to stay away. I may be contagious."

"Oh, the flu bug doesn't like me. I never get it. Don't even get the shots. I'm tough as nails. Are you, Latrice?"

She hoped she didn't look as shocked as she felt.

Before she could reply, he said, "Dispatch said a Latrice had called. Was it you?"

Her mouth opened, but nothing came out.

Say something say something say something! she thought.

Finally, she simply nodded.

"What's the story? What's going on here? Something about a crazy old man and shooting?"

Once again, she could not find her voice. Even when she tried to speak, nothing came out. And once again, she nodded.

"That SUV out there have anything to do with it? The one that crashed into the house?"

Another nod.

"Why won't you talk? Are you afraid?" He came closer and bent forward, leaning his hands on his thighs. "Are you in some kind of trouble here? Are these people hurting you? Do you—Jesus, you're sweating."

She already didn't like him, and she already felt angry, but when he leaned toward her like that, as if he were bending down to talk to a child, speaking so condescendingly, Latrice felt something hot rise up in her chest. She was suddenly so angry that she wanted nothing more than to drag her fingernails through his face from top to bottom, side to side.

There was a loud crash in the kitchen, followed by the shattering of glass. The sounds startled nearly everyone in the room.

"Hey, Marcus!" Giff called from the kitchen. "Could you come give me a hand?"

Marcus shot up off the couch and hurried out of the room.

The deputy stood up straight and frowned as he turned and watched Marcus go. Then he stared for a moment at the doorway leading into the hallway and, across the hall, into the kitchen.

There was another crash, this time something metallic hitting the floor, like a baking tray, or something. Hushed but urgent voices came from the kitchen, sibilant and hissed.

"The hell's goin' on in there, anyway?" von Pohle shouted.

"Everything's fine!" Giff called. "Just clumsy. Coffee coming up."

The deputy stared at the doorway, clearly suspicious. Then he started across the room, heading directly for it.

No one moved or made a sound, but the air in the room seemed to tense.

If the deputy went into the kitchen and found those two dead bodies lying in that bloody mess, the shit would hit the fan and fly in all directions. Latrice wondered how fast she could get out of that chair and run out of the house to her car. Her muscles ached and she felt weak, but she could not stick around for what was coming. She had to get home to her babies.

Latrice's head hurt so bad, she squinted as she watched von Pohle continue across the room, obviously on his way to the kitchen.

Miguel closed his eyes for a moment.

Latrice watched von Pohle pass through that doorway. She was tempted to dash out of the chair immediately, but she wanted to make sure he wasn't coming right back.

A moment later, von Pohle's laugh bellowed out of the kitchen. "Well, what the fuck have we got *here*?" he said happily.

Latrice's aching muscles tensed painfully as she pushed

herself out of the chair. She resisted the urge to run as she crossed the room. She was afraid that if she ran, somebody might try to stop her. But the second the front door was in sight, she broke into a run and grabbed her coat as she passed the coat tree. When she opened the door, it was almost blown out of her grip. She slipped around its edge and through the opening, then pulled it closed.

Every muscle in her body cried out in pain as she put her coat on while hurrying down the steps. The wind was like a giant fist that just kept punching again and again, threatening to knock Latrice on her ass. Rain pelted her face and stung her eyes, but she put the steps behind her and reached into her coat pocket for her keys as she made her way between a couple of cars to the spot where she'd parked and—

—she wanted to scream.

The deputy's patrol car was parked directly behind her Highlander. She could not get out.

41

One day, Sheriff Mitchell Kaufman would retire and finally devote some time to trying to get his cop stories published, maybe in a collection, stories he'd been writing and rewriting and polishing for years, and he might even start work on a novel. He'd never shown his stories to anyone, not even his wife, but he thought they would be ready when he retired. He knew that this story—the story of what was happening to him at that moment—was going to be a standout. It would be the story people remembered. He didn't even know what the hell was going on yet, and already he could tell it would be memorable.

After driving into the guardhouse, Kaufman sat stunned at the wheel, staring out the windshield. He wasn't hurt, just momentarily flabbergasted.

There'd been a lot of chatter on the radio, and normally he would be tuned to every word that came over that damned thing, but he hadn't heard any of it as words or language, only as garbled background noise. He was too focused on his situation. But he needed that radio and he had to shake the fog out of his head and use it. The radio, the radio, he focused his attention on the radio.

Dispatch was calling him.

The homeless shelter was on fire in Old Town.

A looter had been shot by a civilian, who was now in custody.

Dispatch called him again.

He needed that mike.

Kaufman gave his head a good, hard shake back and forth a few times and rubbed his eyes.

The person who had been on his roof when Kaufman crashed into the corner of the guardhouse had tumbled through the air, slammed into the guardhouse wall, and dropped to the ground like a rock.

Now he was up, and he was shouting and gesticulating wildly as he looked around for a target for all that shouting and gesticulating, and his eyes fell on Kaufman through the windshield and side window.

Getting a firm grip on the handle, Kaufman popped the door open against the blasting of the wind, then pushed it until there was a big enough opening along the bottom to quickly pull the microphone back into the car. But before he could pull the door closed—

"You motherfucker who the fuck do you think you are you mean no-good son of a bitch—"

The enraged and senseless screaming went on and on as two hands pulled on the top of the door. Kaufman saw the fingers curled over the edge, pulling hard. He dropped his gun on the passenger seat and reached his right hand over, grabbed the door handle with both hands and heaved back on it.

He pulled the door closed.

The hands had not let go.

The angry cursing was replaced by a long, ululating cry of pain as the crazy man outside the car stood with eight fingers trapped in the top of the closed door, arms outstretched, elbows out and up at the sides, pale face elongated as the scream went on.

For a moment, Kaufman was paralyzed by the scream and

the sight of the man's white face from below and he just sat there, unable to move. It went on for what seemed a long time, and Kaufman finally coaxed his right hand to inch over to the passenger seat and search blindly for his gun, fingers feeling around, fluttering over the upholstery until they found the cold metal.

The man jerked his hands upward, pulling his fingers out of the door, and he staggered backwards. He was still screaming and because he was unsteady on his feet, the wind slammed him to the gravel. He rolled around on the ground in the rain and wind, wailing in pain, holding his hands to his chest and kicking his bare legs like a lunatic.

Then he was on hands and knees facing Kaufman. Glaring up at him with teeth bared, like an animal on four legs. He got up on his feet, but did not stand up straight. Instead, he squatted low to the ground, pointed a finger at Kaufman, and ranted some kind of gibberish before charging forward like a bull with a loud battle cry, head down, straight for the car.

Kaufman watched in horror as the man slammed his head into the door of the patrol car. Already rocking under the force of the wind, the car jolted with the impact and the man dropped to the ground again. But he didn't stay there.

Still gibbering, the man crawled over the ground away from the car, then got up again, hunkered down, let out another hoarse cry and charged the car again. But this time, he didn't crash his head into the door. It hit the window.

"Oh, shit," Kaufman said as several cracks appeared in a sunburst formation branching out from the point of impact.

The car's engine was still running and Kaufman shifted to reverse. He looked in the rearview mirror and saw the black man who'd crossed the road in front of the car earlier. Now he was staggering toward the rear of the car, having trouble remaining upright under the storm's assault, holding something in both hands, something long and heavy. It was a large tree branch. If Kaufman backed up, he'd run over the guy, and he didn't want to do that again. He backed up just enough to disengage the front of his car with the corner of the guard-house, then put it in park.

Meanwhile, the other man was preparing to charge the car a third time. He'd crawled away again and now he was bend-ing over once more, a look of determination on his face. His forehead now had dark stripes where blood was running down to his face from the wound on top of his head.

"What the hell am I doing?" Kaufman muttered when he realized he had the radio mike in his lap and was just sitting there staring dumbly like a cow in a field. He picked it up and depressed the button with his thumb, but before he could speak—

—the crack of a gunshot broke through the sound of the storm.

The man charging toward the car went down heavily and lay sprawled and unmoving on the ground.

Something heavy struck the back of the car with a loud bang once, then again, and Kaufman looked in the rearview. The black man was beating the trunk of the patrol car with the fat tree branch. Then he hit the left rear fender and started working his way up that side of the car, pounding the rear door, then the driver's door. He clubbed the side mirror twice until it was dangling from the side of the car, and he would have finished the job, but there was another gunshot. That distracted him and he looked in the direction of the sound. The next gunshot put him down.

As Kaufman looked around for the shooter, squinting to find a figure in the darkness that surrounded him, he lifted the mike to his mouth and said, "This is one-oh-one, one-oh-one." He was surprised how winded and frantic he sounded and stopped to take a steadying breath. His heart was hammering rapidly in his chest. "I need backup immediately at the old Springmeier mental hospital in Batten. Shots fired, two people have been shot. I'm in my car at the rear of the building. Do not go to the front gate, it's closed. Go farther east and turn left on Ogden Pass. It's closed, but I removed the barrier earlier. About a quarter of a mile in there's a new gravel road on the left that's been cut through the woods. Take that road, it'll bring you right to me."

He spotted unusual movement beyond the crashed gate. A dark shape was moving in the darkness toward him. It wore a black mask and black clothes. It carried something in the right hand that looked like it might be a gun.

"The shooter's approaching my car," Kaufman said. "I see one, but there may be more. He's wearing a black mask, like a ski mask."

The dark man kept coming.

Kaufman reached down with his right hand, the hand holding his gun, and flicked a switch. When he spoke into the mike, his voice echoed outside the car from the speaker.

"Stop! Do not come any closer! Put the gun down!"

The figure stopped advancing, but he made no move to put down the gun. He simply stood there and stared at Kaufman.

Beyond that dark shape, another emerged from the blackness. Then another. They all looked the same—black masks, black clothes—but something hung from the right shoulder of the second figure.

"Son of a bitch," Kaufman said as he flipped the switch. "This is one-oh-one. There are several people here approaching my car and they're all wearing black masks. One of these guys looks like he's got an Uzi."

"Backup's on the way, one-oh-one."

The storm was growing worse. There was a sudden increase in the severity of the car's rocking motions as branches and bits of debris clattered against it in a constant barrage.

"In a hurricane?" he muttered to himself. "They're not getting here anytime soon."

He was on his own and he was going to have to make the

best of it. He put the mike on its hook, then tightened his grip on the gun as he reached for the handle to open the door.

The cracked window in the door exploded inward and the howling wind drove the broken bits of glass into his cheeks and chin and lips and eyes.

The endless roar of the storm swallowed up Sheriff Kaufman's cry of pain.

42

When Emilio looked at Fara's face, he knew she wasn't going to help Ollie and his men kill anyone. She turned to him, her features sagging with exhaustion and disgust, and said, "I can't. I just can't, I'm sorry."

Emilio said, "I think we're gonna hole up in the office, Ollie."

"I need to know exactly how many infected people we're talking about here," Ollie said. He turned to Fara and said, "Can you give me a number?"

"Dr. Corcoran could."

"And where is he?"

"He was in my office when we left."

Ollie turned to one of his men, pointed down the side corridor in the direction of Fara's office and said, "Go fetch the good doctor, will you? Fourth door on the right." The man hurried away. He turned to Fara again and asked, "Is he going to cooperate?"

"He doesn't like confrontation," she said. "If he doesn't want to cooperate, I'm sure you can change his mind quickly with a little yelling and threatening."

Ollie nodded once. "Happy to do it."

She turned to Emilio and said, "I'm starving all of a sudden. I've got food in the office. Let's go."

As they headed toward Fara's office, one of the headlamps approached them through the dark.

"He's not there," the figure said. It was the man Ollie had sent to get Corcoran.

"He's not in the office?" Fara said.

"There's nobody in the office."

Emilio asked Fara, "Where would he go?"

"I have no idea. I'm amazed he would leave the office at all knowing what's out here in the dark."

"What's the deal?" Ollie said, approaching them.

A voice shouted urgently from down the main corridor: "Hey! Hey! They've gotten out! You hear me? They got out down here and they're loose! Outside!"

It was Corcoran's voice coming from the rear entrance. His footsteps sounded as he jogged toward them.

"Two of the test subjects are out there attacking someone in a car," he said.

"Who the hell went out and got in their car?" Ollie barked.

"No, no," Corcoran said, shaking his head hard. He stood rigid, fists clenched at his sides. "It's someone who's driving here, to the hospital. A *police* car. They're outside the gate, but the gates are open, for some reason. Crashed open. From inside. And *somebody stole my goddamned Jeep*!" As he shouted the last sentence, his whole body quaked.

"Did you get that coat out of my closet?" Fara asked absently. It sounded more like a thought inadvertently spoken aloud than a question in search of an answer.

"I bet Ivan called the sheriff," Emilio said.

"The sheriff," Ollie said. "Fuck." He turned to his men and shouted, "Did any of you hear *that*? While we're standing here contemplating our fuckin' navels, those people are gettin' out of the fuckin' *building*!" He called out, "McCoy! Baker! Axelrod! Come with me!"

They followed Ollie down the corridor, the light from their headlamps bouncing and swaying through the dark ahead of them.

"What were you doing out there, Dr. Corcoran?" Fara said, shining her small Maglite directly in his face. "Trying to leave?"

Corcoran squinted and turned his head away. He made a sound of disgust as he held up a hand to shield his eyes from the light. "I . . . I wanted to get something from my car."

Fara nodded. "Uh-huh. A new location. I so admire a man who stands behind his work."

Corcoran looked down at her right hand, which hung at her side, then at her, with disbelief. "Is that a *gun* in your hand, Dr. McManus?"

"It is. And I know how to use it. Remember that the next time you think about trying to ditch us. You're going down with this ship, captain. Vendon Labs may be able to step in and save your ass, but I'm going to make it as difficult for them as possible."

Corcoran fidgeted and tried to dodge Fara's light, but like a mean child holding a magnifying glass over an ant on a sunny day, she wouldn't let him. Finally, he straightened his back and looked directly at her with squinting eyes.

"You seem to be forgetting who's in charge here, Dr. McManus," he said.

"It's certainly not you, Dr. Corcoran. Not anymore."

Watching Fara stand up to Corcoran, listening to her talk to him like that—Emilio thought it was sexy as hell. He was glad it was dark because he'd been watching her with an admiring smile and a growing erection.

Then Emilio noticed that Dr. Corcoran was looking at him. Staring at him. As if he expected him to say something. It quickly made Emilio uncomfortable.

"What?" he said, shrugging. "She's right. Looks like Ollie's the alpha male in here now. And outside, the hurricane's in charge. Right here, though, in this corridor?" He nodded his head toward Fara. "She's in charge. And she's got a gun. I'd listen to her."

Corcoran lifted the back of his hand to his eyes against the light. "Put that fucking light down. You've made your point."

Fara lowered the light and Corcoran dropped his hand. He looked back and forth between them with a contemptuous smirk that oozed into a smile.

He chuckled that annoying chuckle of his, then said, "You're in for *such* an unpleasant surprise."

"What does that mean?" Fara said.

He kept smiling, but didn't say anything.

"What does that *mean*, Dr. Corcoran? *What* surprise?"

Another chuckle, then he said, "You've got the light. Let's go."

Corcoran stepped around Emilio and headed for the office.

"What the hell do you think he means?" Emilio whispered.

"I have no idea, but it worries me."

"Are you coming?" Corcoran said.

They followed him down the drafty, cold corridor.

Emilio's stomach growled with hunger, which would soon be followed by acidic burning. He had some Gaviscon tablets in the utility closet they'd just passed, but he didn't stop to get them. He'd do that later. The heartburn and reflux were always worse when he was seriously worried about something, and if Fara was worried, then Emilio was damned sure worried, because she knew this guy a lot better than he did. When Emilio had come to work there, he'd decided pretty quickly that he didn't like Corcoran simply based on his behavior. Fara had much better and far more solid reasons for not liking him, and though he didn't know what all of them were, Emilio trusted them.

The sound of a door gently closing with a couple of clicks was just loud enough to catch Fara's attention. She stopped walking and turned toward the sound with her light—to her left, the beam sweeping along the wall to stop on the door marked STAIRS, and beneath that, EMPLOYEES ONLY.

"Did you hear that?" she said.

"Yeah," Emilio said. "Ollie sent a guy down to the basement earlier."

She aimed the light down the middle of the corridor, swept it back and forth to see if there was anyone behind them. There was no one, nothing. She turned the light back to the door—

—as it finished swinging shut and made that same clicking sound again.

"Hey," she said, "what was—"

"Fucking cunt!" a thick female voice growled as a fist swung out of the darkness and struck Fara in the left side of her jaw.

"Shit," Emilio said, quickly stepping forward to catch her before she fell. The gun and flashlight clattered to the floor. Her body was limp, she was unconscious, and the woman who had punched her babbled furiously as she began pummeling Fara with her fists while Emilio held her.

Occasionally, something coherent emerged from the woman's angry, senseless babbling and ranting.

"You hateful bastard, you never loved me, you son of a bitch, eighteen years, eighteen fucking *years*!"

Her face remained obscured by darkness, but the shape of her head told him she was mostly bald.

He backed away from the woman, tried kicking her but couldn't connect, then backed away some more. He bent down and swept Fara's legs up, then swung his leg up again. This time, his foot connected solidly with her left knee and she stumbled and fell as Emilio turned and ran to the office door. He heard her getting up, though, ranting, coming after him.

"Run away! Run away! That's all you ever do, you useless prick, you liar, you thief, you fucking *asshole*! *I'm finally gonna kill you!*" Then she became incoherent again, making more sounds than words.

The office door stood open, with the soft glow of candle-light coming from inside.

Hands grabbed the back of Emilio's shirt and the woman's angry, incoherent babbling was suddenly in his right ear as she latched on to his shoulders and wrapped her skinny legs around his waist.

"Goddammit, lady!" Emilio croaked, panting as he turned around and slammed her against the wall, throwing all his weight into her, trying to crush her.

She grunted and wheezed as her lungs emptied and he felt something crack against his back—a rib? Her hold on his shoulders and waist weakened until her legs slipped off of him and her arms dropped down to her sides.

Emilio stepped forward and the woman dropped to the floor with a whimpering sound. He sidled through the door, pushing Fara's feet through first, then kicked it shut behind him. He spun around and turned the lock on the doorknob, then carried Fara into the office and gently placed her on the couch.

"What the hell was that?" Corcoran said. He was already seated at her desk again, smoking a cigarette. "What's wrong with her?" He pulled his feet off the desk and stood, went to the couch and stood behind Emilio.

Emilio ignored him and knelt on the floor beside Fara. A bruise was beginning to darken on her cheek as it became puffy with swelling.

She coughed and sniffled and opened her eyes only slightly.

"That's twice you've been punched in the face in one night," Emilio said.

She closed her eyes again. "Yeah, but I don't think it's the kind of thing you get better at with practice."

"The door's locked and she's in the hall not feeling very well, I think. We're safe for now."

"Who clocked you?" Corcoran said, peering over Emilio's shoulder with a smile that he was managing to hold down to a smirk.

"I think it was one of the survivors," Fara said without opening her eyes. She sat up and put her feet on the floor.

Emilio stood and said, "I'll get some cold water for that—"

"No, not yet," she said. "I don't want to touch it yet. Half my face is throbbing and my headache's back."

Emilio sat beside her on the couch.

Corcoran paced while he smoked.

The storm continued to assault the building with a howling rage.

43

Ollie felt as if he were moving through a dream because the simple act of walking in the storm was like trying to walk through water against a strong current. He saw the car's lights as soon as he stepped outside.

He did not want any trouble with the police, but at this point, it was inevitable. Ollie could not remember ever making a bigger mistake than he'd made by bringing his men here to rescue a bunch of homeless people. It didn't seem so at the time, of course, but now? It gave new depth to the word "cluster fuck." And now, they were going to have to kill the people they'd come to rescue.

He *was* in a bad dream. But he wasn't dreaming.

But it didn't end there. Now somebody had stolen Dr. Corcoran's Jeep and it looked like the thief drove it through the gate. Ollie wondered if it could have been one of the test subjects. That was a frightening thought and he wondered if it had occurred to either Dr. Corcoran or Dr. McManus. Just in case, he'd bring it up when he went back inside.

While he would like to be able to blame all of this on Dr. Corcoran and his team from Vendon Labs, Ollie could not sidestep his own responsibility. He had gotten too wrapped up in his cause and had not been practical enough. He hadn't thought it through. He hated to admit it, but Ivan had been right about it being a mistake. It was worse than that. Ollie had fucked up by allowing his anger about the ends to cloud his judgment of the means.

A thin figure rammed the driver's-side door of the car with his head. Ollie recognized it as a Humboldt County Sheriff's car—white with green and black stripes. He saw another darker figure emerging from the night just beyond the car. He was black and carried a large, heavy tree branch.

The first figure crawled away from the car, then turned around and charged again, bashing his head into the window.

It was a struggle to walk across the parking lot. Ollie heard a lot of cracking and popping all around him and assumed it was the sound of trees losing branches or coming down under the violent force of the storm.

It was like the planet was throwing a tantrum. It seemed much too angry to be mere weather.

Ollie drew his gun when he got to the gate and figured he was close enough. He was surprised when the first shot put the attacking figure on the ground. He thought the storm would be more of an interference.

The black man started beating the trunk of the car with the tree branch, then the side as he made his way to the driver's door.

Ollie moved in even closer and aimed his gun. He fired once, and when the man kept pounding the car with the branch, he fired again.

The second shot took him down.

Ollie continued toward the car, but stopped when it spoke to him.

"Stop! Do not come any closer! Put the gun down!"

Ollie stopped walking and stared at the car.

He was happy to go back inside and let the cop fend for himself, but there was no way in hell he was putting his gun down while there were test subjects running around on the premises. When no further instructions came from the car, Ollie decided to keep advancing. As he drew nearer, he heard something else.

The man at the wheel was screaming.

Ollie hurried the rest of the way as best he could and found the window in the driver's-side door gone. The beam of his headlamp fell on the bleeding face of Sheriff Mitch Kaufman.

Ollie resisted the urge to curse loudly. He and Sheriff Kaufman did not get along. He was pretty sure Kaufman had disliked him from the moment they met and had not altered that policy since. Ollie had nothing against the man personally, even though he was a goddamned liberal and a Roman Catholic, which, he supposed, was neither here nor there, but as a sheriff, he was as useless as tits on the pope. Ollie had expressed that opinion generously in Kaufman's presence, which might have had something to do with the sheriff's opinion of him.

But none of that mattered right now because the man had a face full of glass shards, which probably had something to do with that test subject bashing his head into the window.

Ollie reached in and put a hand on Kaufman's shoulder and the sheriff jerked away, frightened. "Sheriff, it's Ollie Monk," he said, shouting to be heard through the wind. Kaufman stopped screaming. Ollie glanced over his shoulder and saw that his men had followed him. "We need to get you inside. Can you walk if we guide you?"

Kaufman tried to pull himself together and absorb the pain. He made an affirmative sound.

"Okay, I'm gonna open the door and help you out. Can you handle that?"

He made another sound that seemed to say, *Just do it*.

As Ollie helped ease him out of the car, Kaufman sucked air through his teeth sharply. Once he was standing, he bowed his head—Ollie was sure that the rain being blown into his swollen, bloody face was painful.

"Kill the engine," Ollie said to the others, "then use the keys to open the trunk. Bring in any weapons you find." He nodded toward the nearest body on the ground. "And make sure he and the other one are dead."

"There's another one," Kaufman said, his voice thick and shaky. "I ran over him coming in. I don't know if he's dead."

"Get to it," Ollie said. "Leave the bodies where they are and come in when you're done. I'm taking him inside."

Once they were inside, Ollie wasn't sure where to take the injured sheriff. The only place he knew of where Kaufman could lie down was the couch in Dr. McManus's office.

As they approached the office, Ollie heard a sound—the slapping of bare feet on the floor moving around them, avoiding their light, and fading away behind them.

The couch was already occupied by Dr. McManus, whose face was bruised and swollen. She was reloading her revolver.

Test subjects, Ollie thought, *I've gotta remember that. Test subjects. Test subjects.*

It made them easier to kill.

"Oh, my God," Dr. McManus said, getting up from the couch and putting her gun and box of ammo on her desk. "Put him on the couch."

Once Kaufman was stretched out on the couch, Ollie said to Baker, "He's gonna need some first aid." Then he turned to McManus and said, "Where should we put the dead bodies?"

"Dead bodies?"

"The test subjects. There are at least two outside, and we've got others scattered around. I don't know how many. But what do you want us to do with them?"

"Put them in the hydrotherapy room. It's at the other end of this corridor on the right."

Ollie watched Corcoran, who was quietly pacing and smoking.

"What's wrong with him?" he said.

"I'm . . . not sure. Could we step outside for a minute?"

They left the office and stood just outside in the dark, windy corridor.

"Earlier," she said, "Dr. Corcoran said we were in for an unpleasant surprise. Before that, he was talking to someone on the phone. I think it was someone from Vendon Labs."

"What do you think he meant?"

"I don't know, but I think we should keep it in mind. If Vendon Labs decides to step in and clean this mess up before it gets out . . . well, that probably wouldn't be good for us."

Ollie needed no encouragement to believe that Vendon Labs would do anything it needed to do to protect itself and its relationship with the government. He nodded slowly and said, "Thank you for telling me that. Smart of you. I think you know as well as I do, don't you, Dr. McManus, that if they have the chance, Vendon Labs *will* come in here and make all of this disappear."

"Yes. That's why I mentioned it."

He smiled behind his mask. "Nice to know we're on the same page when it comes to Vendon. Got any ice for your face?"

"I think we used it up after you hit me."

"Too bad. You need to learn to duck."

He left her in the office and went to join his men in the hunt.

44

Andy kept his hands on Donny's shoulders as he stood rigidly near the living room's entrance, watching the others. He wasn't sure what was happening, but tension filled the air like an odorless toxic gas. They did not belong there. Andy had the sickening sense that something bad was about to happen. He had to get Donny out of there as soon as possible, but he had no idea where to go.

Everyone in the living room became silent as they stared at the doorway through which Ram had just passed, waiting tensely for . . . something. Then the moment was shattered by Ram's voice from the kitchen, which somehow sounded at once happy and menacing.

"Well, what the fuck have we got *here*?"

The question was chilling because from the sound of Ram's voice, he'd found something bad but not unexpected.

Latrice, the black woman seated in the recliner, got up slowly and walked through the living room. She suddenly broke into a run and grabbed her coat before rushing out the front door.

Donny watched her go, then looked up at Andy curiously. Andy shrugged.

Voices argued in the kitchen and heavy footsteps stomped over the floor.

"I can't handle this shit," Giff said as he stalked into the living room.

"Where the hell you think *you're* going, Giff?" Ram said, following him. He reached out and grabbed the upper part of Giff's left arm to stop him and turn him around.

Giff roared like a bear as he pulled away from Ram and spun around, instinctively reaching with his right hand to grab his injured arm. When he did, he only hurt himself more and instantly pulled his hand away. But he continued to wail, bending over for a moment, then walking in a small circle as the features of his face all pulled toward the center in a mask of pain.

"Uh-oh, got a little owie, there, Giff?" Ram said, grinning like a little boy given free reign of a toy store. "How'd *that* happen, huh? Is it bad?" He stepped over and punched Giff's wounded arm in an amiable fashion.

Giff screamed as he dropped to his knees, then fell forward and propped himself up with his right hand on the floor, arm rigid. He held his left arm close to his body.

Andy could not stay here and subject Donny to this sadism. They could at least go outside and sit in Ram's car. They'd be out of the wind and rain and away from this horror show. It suddenly occurred to Andy that he could use the radio to call for help.

Mia stood up from her seat on the couch with the children and said firmly, "He's *sick*! Stop hurting him."

Ram turned his grin to her and his eyes glared for a moment. "Well, if he's responsible for the bloodbath in the kitchen, then, yeah, you're goddamned right he's sick." Ram hunkered down beside Giff. "Did you do that? Huh, Giff?"

Giff was groaning and whimpering, head hanging low from his shoulders.

Ram spoke louder, nearly shouting, when he said, "Did

you finally get around to killing your daddy like everybody in town's been waiting for you to do, Giff? Huh? Is that what you did?"

While Ram was still speaking, Giff's groan became a growl.

"He's got a fever," Mia said. "He needs to be in bed."

"What are you, his *doctor*?" Ram said as he rose to his feet. "This boy won't be goin' to bed, he'll be goin' to jail because he's under arrest. In fact, everyone in this room is—"

Giff roared like a bear as he lunged forward on his knees, mouth open wide, and closed his teeth on Ram's crotch.

Ram's scream was shrill as he stumbled but instead of letting go, Giff moved forward on his knees, his teeth hanging on to the crotch of Ram's pants. He finally let go as Ram fell over backwards.

He had not yet hit the floor when Marcus jolted from his chair. As soon as Ram was down, Marcus bent over and took his gun from its holster.

Andy leaned forward and whispered into Donny's ear, "We're going back out to the car now." He kept an arm around Donny and hurried him toward the front door. There was nothing but screaming and shouting behind them, and he wanted out before it turned into gunfire.

"It's going to be windy," Andy whispered as he reached for the doorknob, "so hang on."

The door flew open before Andy could reach the knob and it thwacked his hand before hitting the wall with a bang. Andy pulled Donny backwards as pain exploded in his hand.

Latrice stomped into the house almost at a run, shrieking at the top of her lungs as she swung a fist and connected with Andy's cheekbone.

The world flashed white and the house turned on end and the floor flew up and crashed into Andy. He quickly tried to get to his feet, but the house would not stop tilting and swaying as the room rapidly grew darker.

Andy suddenly found himself on his back staring up at the ceiling. Had he lost consciousness for a moment? Longer? Probably not long. Nothing had changed. He could still hear Ram bellowing, and now Giff was shouting a long stream of obscenities and threats, and Latrice was still screaming, and all he could think about was getting Donny out of there.

Donny! he thought as he sat up. He was still a little dizzy, but he tried to ignore it as he looked around for Donny.

Latrice's hands were on Donny's throat and she had him pinned to the wall with his feet a couple of feet off the floor. He tried to kick his legs, but she was standing too close, pressing her body against him to hold him to the wall. His face was red and his eyes were bulging as they turned to Andy and silently begged for help.

There was a frenzied storm raging inside Latrice's head that was every bit as powerful and chaotic as the one battering the house outside. It was made up mostly of directionless rage that swirled like a tornado inside her, looking for some outlet, *any* outlet, and some of it flew into her hands as she squeezed the throat of a small eight-year-old boy, pressing him against the wall with her body, a stream of profanity-laced gibberish coming through her clenched teeth. As she squeezed his throat, she pounded the back of his head against the wall.

In the very center of the storm that was erupting inside Latrice's head stood Latrice herself, calm and confused and isolated from the world by the swirling, roaring tempest. But there was a moment when the inner Latrice had a window on the outside world and she saw Donny's small, frightened, discolored face, mouth open, tongue sticking out, bulging eyes rolling around in their sockets, and in that moment, when the inner Latrice saw what the outer Latrice was doing, she connected with that inner self in a galvanizing instant of awareness and horror.

In that instant, Donny's face melted into Robert's.

She released her hold on the boy.

He dropped to the floor in a gasping, coughing heap.

Latrice was paralyzed for a moment and stared at the wall as the horror of what she had been doing dug into her with barbed hooks.

Someone standing close was shouting at her: "—him alone you fuckin' nigger what the fuck you think you're—"

Latrice turned to see yet another gun pointed in her face, this time by Marcus, who was shouting at her.

Then a hand came down on the gun and shoved it downward as Miguel said, "Don't we have enough fucking trouble as it is? Shut up and calm the fuck down!"

"Did you see what she was doin' to that kid, Miguel? Jesus Christ, what the fuck am I supposed to—"

"Give me that goddamned gun and go sit the fuck down."

"Why do I gotta give you the gun when *she's* the one who was—"

Miguel grabbed Marcus's wrist with his left hand and wrestled the gun from him with his right, shouting, "Will you shut the fuck up and go sit the fuck down *now*!"

Latrice was vaguely aware of her own relief that the gun had been taken from Marcus, but she was too sick and confused to care much and part of her wanted nothing more than to lie down and give her aching muscles a rest.

She turned enough to scan the room with her eyes and found that, other than Giff and the sheriff's deputy struggling and shouting on the floor, everyone else had left the room.

Marcus looked at Miguel with slack-jawed shock. He looked betrayed for a couple of seconds, then his expression hardened as he nodded slowly and said, "Yeah, okay, I see how this works, I see how this works. It's the spic lookin' out for the nigger. Yeah, sure, why not, it's happenin' all over the fuckin' country, so why not here, huh? You people come to this country and we give you everything, and you decide you wanna take the fuck over!"

With a look of disgusted contempt, Miguel said, "I was born in Yakima, Washington, you dumb fuck."

Marcus's eyes widened and he smiled and nodded faster as he pointed a finger at Miguel, poking it repeatedly in his direction, and he opened his mouth to say something, but he didn't get it out.

Something black and heavy swung through the air and struck Marcus's face with a sharp *crack* and blood erupted from his forehead and flowed from his nostrils as he fell backwards. When he hit the floor, his legs began to kick spastically.

It was the iron shovel from the set of fireplace tools on the hearth and Mia held it in both hands like a baseball bat, already drawn back and ready to strike again. But Marcus had gone down. She dove for him as if he were a pile of money and started pounding with the shovel.

"Jesus Christ, Mia, *what the fuck are you doing?*" Miguel shouted.

As Latrice watched Mia bludgeon Marcus with the shovel, then turn the shovel so that she was stabbing him with it like a knife, she began to regain her bearings and that inner storm surged once again, isolating her from herself. She felt rage consume her, as if it were a substance pumping through her veins.

The inner Latrice had just enough of a connection left to wonder if Donny was safe from her. She turned to the place where he'd collapsed on the floor after she released him. The spot was empty. She turned toward the front door just in time to see father and son hurrying out into the storm.

She was relieved to see him getting away. The hurricane was safer for the boy and his father than the storm that was going on inside Latrice.

And inside Gifford Clancy's house.

45

After plucking the last piece of glass from Kaufman's face—the last piece she could find in such poor light, anyway—Fara set her tweezers on the end table. While she had been sitting in a chair beside the couch removing the shards of glass, Ollie had been standing beside her holding his headlamp on Kaufman's face and catching the sheriff up on everything that had been happening there. He had finally removed his ski mask and the headlamp was centered in his forehead like an alien eye. It wasn't the best light for the job, but the headlamps were the brightest they had.

"How are you doing, sheriff?" she asked.

Kaufman lay on the couch with his head propped up on a couple of throw pillows, puffy eyes closed. His face was bloody and lumpy with swelling. Fortunately, the glass had not gone into his eyes, but a few tiny pieces had lodged in his eyelids.

He licked his lips slowly and said, "I've been better."

"I'm going to clean you up now. I've got soap and water and rubbing alcohol. And I'm really sorry, but it's probably going to hurt some more."

"It's going to hurt whether you do that or not. Look, before you do that, I'd like to make a call. But I'll need some help."

"Sure," Fara said. She went to her purse and got her phone. "Who would you like to call?"

He gave her a number. "It's my office. I need to tell them where I am and request backup."

She keyed the number in, then placed the phone in his hand.

"Thank you," he said. Then he turned away from her onto his side for some privacy.

Fara looked around for Corcoran. He'd moved a chair over to a far corner of the office and was making a call. That's what he'd been doing the last time she'd noticed him, trying to make a call. Apparently, he was having no success and was frustrated to the point of anger. His face had that tight look he got when he was angry, with his small mouth compressed into a tiny, white-lipped cut below his nose.

"Dr. Corcoran, do you have anything Sheriff Kaufman can take for pain?" she said.

He glanced at her with the phone to his ear. "Not on me," he said.

"I didn't mean *on* you. Do you have *access* to something that will dull his pain?"

He held up a forefinger and turned away from her as he said something quietly into the phone. A moment later, he punched a button on the phone and scrubbed a hand downward over his face as he sighed and muttered, "Damn."

"Something wrong?"

"I'm trying to make a call," he said, irritated. He looked down at the phone again and poked at the keypad, then he put it to his ear.

"Well, how about getting something we can give Sheriff Kaufman for pain? I don't even have any aspirin here in the office."

He nodded toward the door. "I'm not going out there."

Ollie walked slowly toward him, saying, "I'd be happy to

send a couple of men with you. They'll both be well armed so they can protect you from your work."

Corcoran's eyes narrowed and he cocked his head sneeringly at Ollie. "And who's going to protect me from them?"

"Who are you calling, Dr. Corcoran?"

"I don't see how that's any business of yours."

"Maybe you forgot. I'm the guy with the gun who's in charge of all the other guys with guns. It's my business. I'd rather you don't call anybody, but since you're already doing it, I want to know who you're calling, and don't give me any shit. You're lucky to be alive, you pompous prick."

Corcoran sighed. "I've been trying to reach a couple of associates."

"Vendon Labs associates," Ollie said, nodding. He stepped a little closer and snatched the phone from Corcoran's hand.

"*Hey!*" Corcoran shouted, jumping to his feet.

"It seems to me that Vendon Labs isn't going to be very happy about this situation, and the first thing they're going to want to do is make it disappear. I know enough about Vendon to know they'll do whatever's necessary to make that happen, and anybody standing in the way will disappear, too. Like us. You think I have a legitimate concern?"

He shrugged. "You seem to think you do. Maybe you know more about Vendon Labs than I do."

"Oh, you know plenty. They're going to come here as soon as they can, aren't they? To make their problem disappear. Along with anybody who knows about it. You'll be safe, of course. Hell, they'll probably give you a raise. But everybody else . . ."

Corcoran folded his arms across his chest, but said nothing.

Without taking his eyes from Corcoran, Ollie said, "Emilio, get Ivan on the phone and tell him what's going on here. Tell him to call every media outlet he can think of and pass on the story."

Although she didn't think she ever would, Fara had to admit to herself that she rather liked Ollie in spite of everything.

He turned to Emilio this time and said, "Does Ivan have any media connections? Does he know anybody?"

"Yeah, quite a few."

"Tell him to start calling in favors. He needs to get all the cameras and microphones over here that he can as soon as possible."

"Well, the hurricane—"

"Yeah, I know, that's gonna slow 'em down. But tell him to get 'em here, anyway." He smiled at Corcoran. "You think your bosses are gonna like that?"

"I'm sure they won't. If it comes to anything. And I doubt it will. Your friend may have some media connections, but Vendon Labs is owned by DeCamp Pharmaceuticals, a very big and powerful corporation, and DeCamp doesn't have *connections*. It has friends and associates who *own* media outlets. TV and radio networks, and cable news channels, and whatever newspapers and magazines are still hanging on. They own the media. Do you see what I'm saying?"

Ollie's smile was gone and his face was grim as he nodded. "Yeah, I see. You're saying it's a lost cause, a no-win situation. Except for you. You don't have anything to worry about, do you?"

"That's where you're wrong." Corcoran lowered his eyes and dropped his arms at his sides.

Fara was surprised. "Have they threatened you?"

"The equivalent of a threat."

"What do you think they'll do?"

"I strongly suspect termination."

Fara started to speak, but snapped her mouth shut when she realized that "termination" did not necessarily refer to Corcoran's job.

Ollie laughed, shook his head, then laughed a little more.

"And you've been trying to call them to plead for mercy, right?"

Corcoran didn't look at him. "Something like that."

"Then I guess we're all in the same boat," Ollie said with another laugh. "And it's sinking."

Mike began to snore softly as he lay on the couch with his head in Julie's lap.

"I guess nothing's bothering him now," Ivan said.

"At least he's not fidgeting all over the place."

"It sounds worse out there."

"I'm trying not to think about it. But I can't get rid of the feeling that we should be doing something."

"What?"

She said nothing, and they didn't speak until Ivan's phone chirped.

"Emilio!" Ivan said, so loudly that it made Mike sit up.

"Listen, Ivan, there's some stuff I need you to do. Some stuff *we* need you to do—including Ollie. But first, a question. You know some people in the media, don't you? I mean, you've got friends in, like, the news business, that kind of thing?"

"Just a couple of local people and a guy in San Francisco, but that's all," Ivan said.

"That's all we need. These days, everything's local and national at the same time. More important—do you know someone in the media who could get over here sometime in the next, oh, hell, I don't know, let's say—"

"Wait, you want me to send local news people there? Are you crazy? The people who know me will never *believe* me. I mean, we're friendly, they're good people, but they don't take any of my information seriously."

"They will after this."

46

Corcoran wanted to get this over with as soon as possible and walked at a brisk pace down the dark corridor with two of Ollie's masked men flanking him, their headlamp beams shining ahead of them.

If he'd had his way, he never would have left Fara's office. It was a relatively safe place to wait out the storm and avoid the remaining test subjects roaming the dark hospital. But he knew that the end of the hurricane held nothing good for them. He was not optimistic about facing whoever Vendon Labs would send to clean up this mess.

As they walked through the windy main corridor and continued straight ahead, he heard the crack of a gunshot somewhere in the building, quickly followed by another. Corcoran hoped it meant at least one fewer test subject, possibly two, to worry about. But he had little confidence in Ollie and his men, whose rescue mission had rescued no one and endangered *everyone*. And it had destroyed his project.

If Vendon Labs chose to blame him for this, there was little he could do about it, but that would not change the fact that things would have gone along swimmingly if they hadn't been invaded by Ollie's bloodthirsty circus act. Even the hurricane wouldn't have been a problem. Sure, the building had been damaged by a falling tree, but they could have worked around that. Even Dr. McManus, for all her effort, had been unable to derail the project by tattling on him like a teacher's pet in the third grade. And it had backfired on her when Vendon Labs had simply done nothing in response, giving Corcoran their tacit support. That was what the company had *always* done.

Until now.

He couldn't think about that at the moment. It was too distracting and stressful. He was on his way to his quarters to get Sheriff Kaufman something for pain. He had a virtual pharmacy in his bathroom, a wide variety of narcotic painkillers from which to choose. He'd seen Kaufman's lacerated face and decided to take him some Oxycontin.

He was curious to see how his party had been doing since he'd left. It seemed like a long time had passed since he'd been enjoying himself with Holly and his friends. He hoped they hadn't been in the hands of bullies. He wanted to believe that they had managed to get Ollie's men stoned and the party hadn't ended, but he knew better than that.

On Corcoran's right was a young man named Zach and on his left, Nagesh, who had an Uzi strapped to his shoulder.

"They'll go with you," Ollie had said. "But don't give them any crap, okay? They're protecting you—"

"From my work, yes, I know," Corcoran finished for him. "I would be a lot more comfortable if I were carrying a gun."

"I'm sure you would, but that ain't gonna happen, so quit asking, it's annoying. You're being tolerated for your usefulness, Dr. Corcoran. Nobody here likes you. In fact, to be honest . . . well . . ."

Smiling sheepishly, Ollie crooked a finger at Corcoran, who stood about eight inches taller. Corcoran bent forward so Ollie could whisper in his ear.

"I kinda had my heart set on killing you myself," he said.

Corcoran's back stiffened and he glared down at the squat little fascist, who kept smiling.

"You'll find everybody on my team feels the same way. Keep that in mind, Dr. Corcoran. Don't give them any reason to act on it."

When they reached the top of the stairs, Nagesh moved forward, opened the door, and stepped through it first. A moment later, he said, "Looks clear."

Corcoran went through the door, followed by Zach.

"It's this way," Corcoran said, gesturing to the right.

Two headlamp beams cut a path through the dark as they went down the corridor. The wind sounded like a pack of wolves surrounding the building.

"How close are we?" Nagesh said. He was standing on Corcoran's right side.

"There's another corridor coming up on the right," Corcoran said. "It's not far beyond that point."

As they passed that corridor, Nagesh turned his head to the right. The headlamp beam shone down the narrower corridor and sparkled in the eyes of two gaunt faces that rushed forward out of the dark. Nagesh released an abrupt cry of surprise as he attempted to lift the Uzi and turn it in their direction.

The headlamp beams danced wildly as the two figures, suddenly chattering angrily and incoherently, pounced on Nagesh and knocked him to the ground before he could get a grip on the submachine gun. As Nagesh's voice rose in a quavering bawling sound, Zach shoved Corcoran aside. He already had his gun in hand and raised it to fire, but the two test subjects were on top of Nagesh. If he fired, there was a good chance he would hit Nagesh. As he waited for an opening, there were soft slapping sounds in the side corridor rapidly growing closer, until—

—another of the test subjects lunged from the dark and tackled Zach to the floor. The two of them slid a few feet over the tiles and Zach's gun went off, but they continued struggling.

Nagesh began to scream in pain.

Corcoran stood frozen in the corridor and watched the headlamp beams. Nagesh's shone upward and jiggled back and forth as the two test subjects beat and tore at him. Zach's flew back and forth wildly as he fought his attacker.

They left Corcoran in the dark, alone, unprotected, and he quickly looked around, half expecting another of the slender figures in a hospital gown to come flying out of the darkness at him.

He turned and ran in the direction they'd been going, toward his quarters. His shoulder bumped into the wall and he reached out and felt his way along as he hurried forward, stumbling, groping, feeling for the door.

Behind him, a voice rose in a gibbering frenzy, then broke into a laugh that was followed by the rattling fire of the Uzi.

Oh, Jesus, Corcoran thought, nearly breaking into a run, *one of them has a machine gun.*

He reached the door, found the handle, and pushed his way inside as the ripping bursts of machine gunfire echoed down the corridor.

PART SIX
Survivors

47

During the hurricane's peak, the Samoa Cookhouse was reduced to a pile of barn-red wood that was quickly underwater. The entire community of Samoa and the whole northern peninsula on which it was nestled were submerged, as were the sparsely populated Indian Island in Humboldt Bay and Woodley Island adjacent to it. On Woodley, the bar and restaurant that looked out on the marina were flooded and destroyed. So was the National Weather Service station and the nearby Humboldt Bay Harbor Recreation and Conservation District.

Most of the boats in the harbor had been moved or put in dry dock in preparation for the storm, but not all. Some had simply been tied down. But none were safe from the storm. Many of them would next rest on dry land in the middle of town, or in someone's front yard.

Beyond the two islands, Humboldt Bay opened into Arcata Bay, but now there was no discernible difference between the two because both had expanded and flooded inland, covering the Eureka-Samoa Bridge and flooding into Old Town.

The proud turret on the Carson Mansion was ripped out like a tooth by the storm and came to pieces as it tumbled through the air. Not long after that, the mansion was hit by the storm's main surge, a rushing wave of water that viciously attacked the beautiful old house. But it moved in well beyond the historic mansion, flooding streets and parks and lots.

It flooded the cocktail bars and coffee shops and restaurants and gift shops and art galleries in Old Town. It flooded the Humboldt Bay Maritime Museum, the Clarke Historical Museum, and the Redwood Discovery Museum. It rushed up to embrace the California Department of Fish and Game, the Public Defender's office, and the county library. The storm flooded the town all the way up to Fifth Street, making worse a situation that already was severe thanks to the hurricane's bludgeoning winds.

The fire in the Old Town Shelter did not last long. It was snuffed out by the flood, which followed not long after the power pole crashed into the shelter.

By the time Hurricane Quentin moved on, it had destroyed most of Eureka.

48

Andy had never experienced such menacing weather in his life. As he walked down the front steps of Giff's house, his arm wrapped protectively around Donny's shoulders, it felt as if the storm had noticed them, turned its attention to them, and was deliberately trying to knock them down.

Andy's right foot sank into the thick mud of the driveway and it took some effort to pull it out. Before Donny could do the same thing, Andy grabbed him and swept him up in his arms. He carried him as he made his slow, clumsy way to Ram's patrol car.

The world was exploding all around them. There was no safe way to move through the storm because of the debris, large and small, constantly flying through the air at dangerous speeds. All around them, Andy could hear the cracking and popping of trees straining against the force of the wind, and more than once, he heard what sounded like a tree going down. He had the unnerving fear that one would fall on them before they could take cover.

Andy put an arm over Donny's head and lowered his own as he battled the wind to stay on his feet and move forward. The wind felt like a wave of meaty fists that never stopped punching him. The car seemed a long distance away and

Andy felt exhausted. His feet seemed made of lead and the mud made them even harder to lift.

The car loomed out of the murky darkness, slowly appearing larger as Andy pushed forward, gradually getting closer. The mud sucked at his feet, tried to swallow each one up with every step he took.

Donny was tense and stiff in his arms, scared to death.

A white gate, the kind that might be found in a picket fence around a front yard, cartwheeled through the air, slicing across Andy's path less than three feet in front of him.

Donny shouted something, but even though his head was next to Andy's, he couldn't understand what the boy said. It didn't matter. They were almost there.

Andy reached out his right hand as he approached the driver's door, grasped the handle, and pulled it to open the door, but the handle snapped from his grip and the door didn't open.

It was locked.

Ram had the keys.

There were other cars parked in front of the house. Andy just wanted shelter from the storm. One of the vehicles there had to be unlocked. None of Giff's friends struck Andy as especially responsible people and it seemed unlikely that they were all conscientious enough to lock their cars.

The closest vehicle was the Toyota Highlander parked behind him. He wrapped both arms tightly around Donny and turned, slowly making his way to the dark SUV. It was parked next to another SUV and standing between them provided some shelter from the wind, but they were still getting soaked by the rain. He tried the door.

It was locked.

"Goddammit!" he shouted, frustrated and weary, but the word was blown away even before he heard it.

He turned around and looked at the dark green SUV parked next to the Highlander. It was a Ford Explorer that had seen a lot of wear. There were dings and scrapes on the passenger side of the vehicle. Andy tried the door.

It opened.

His knees almost gave way under the heavy weight of relief that fell over him. He was about to bend down and lift Donny into the Explorer when he heard a loud pop, like a gunshot, followed by several more, and behind those sounds was a steady, ongoing crackling and groaning sound, like something large breaking. It was coming from behind them. He looked over his shoulder, but could see nothing in the stormy darkness. He knew what the sound was, though. A tree was falling, a *big* tree, and it was falling dangerously close.

He swept Donny up and shoved him into the SUV, almost *threw* him, shouting, "Get in, get in, get in!" He climbed in after the boy, then plopped his butt in the seat and pulled the door closed.

The crackling and groaning became deafening, over-whelming the sound of the storm for a moment, and Andy instinctively leaned over and covered Donny with his body. The sound continued to grow until it ended in a tremendous crash filled with shattering and snapping and crushing, including something hitting the SUV.

When Andy realized it was over and they were safe, he rose up and looked around. Tree branches were pressed against the windshield making it impossible to see anything.

They sat in the Explorer, Donny behind the wheel and Andy in the passenger seat, and just breathed for a while. The windows fogged up as the SUV was rocked and jostled by the storm.

Through the branches, Andy could see a glimpse of the grey trunk of an old redwood. It had fallen on Giff's house. He realized that every inch of his body was shaking.

"I'm sorry, Donny," Andy said, shifting in the seat, trying to get comfortable, but there was a lump in the seat. "I'm sorry for getting you into this. I just wanted to get you out of that house because I knew you weren't safe there, and now . . ."

"You didn't get us into this, Dad. Your cop friend did. You got us out of the house before we got smashed."

Andy laughed gently and turned to Donny. He looked at him for a while, such a tough kid to have held up so well while living with his drug addict mother and her pimp-daddy friends. He hoped Donny was holding up well, anyway. It was always possible that any damage done wouldn't show up until later. But he had to give the boy credit for having a thick skin.

"I guess you're right," Andy said. "Ram is the one who got us into this. But I should have known better than to trust him. And by the way, he's not my friend. I grew up with Ram. We went to school together."

"You mean, you knew him when you were my age?"

"Yeah. I'll tell you about that someday."

Andy shifted in the seat again, but he could not get comfortable. Something hard and jagged was poking him in the ass. He lifted his hips, reached under them, and found something that jangled.

It was a key ring with about twenty keys on it. Attached to the ring was a silver skull. Of all the keys, only one had a plastic bow that bore the Ford Motors emblem. The keys jangled in his hand.

"Is that the keys?" Donny said.

"You know what? These *are* the keys. The driver left them here." He got up from the seat as much as he could and turned toward Donny, waving the boy toward him. "Come on, we've got to switch places."

"Can you drive in this storm?" Donny said as he climbed over the console to the passenger seat.

"Maybe not far, but we can get away from here."

He slipped the key into the ignition and turned it. The engine started without hesitation.

"Seat belts," Andy said as he put on his own, then looked to make sure Donny's was secure.

He backed slowly away from the house and the tree branches scraped and whined against the windshield and trunk. He turned the wheel to the right as he backed away. With distance, he could see that the tree had fallen diagonally over the house. Windows were shattered and the trunk had demolished most of the roof and fallen inside the house.

"Where are we gonna go?" Donny said. His voice was higher than usual and thin with fear.

"I don't know," he said, "but we'll be away from here."

Andy pulled away from the house and drove down the road that led back to Emerald Canyon. As they passed the trailers on either side, he noticed that two of them had been knocked over and one of them appeared to be gone. Before they passed through the cluster of small mobile homes, Andy had to step on the brake because one of the trailers rolled from left to right across the road like an angular barrel, until it slammed into the fat trunk of tree and casually embraced it.

Between the wind and the potholes, the SUV felt like a boat on stormy waters. Andy had to drive around branches and one fallen tree to get to the main road, where he turned right. He drove slowly down Emerald Canyon until he had to slow down even more because a long stretch of the road was mostly underwater.

"I'm scared, Dad," Donny said.

"Nothing wrong with that, Donny. So am I."

49

Corcoran fell into his temporary apartment and hit the floor facedown. He kicked at the door as he scrambled to his feet, then threw himself against the door, slammed it shut, and locked it. He spun around and leaned back against the door.

His eyes squinted against the candlelight. There were candles everywhere—on shelves, the sideboard, the coffee table—and each flame seemed bright. The candles sent shards of golden light dancing over the faces of his party guests. Some stood and some were seated in the deep, shifting shadows. All of them faced him. Stared at him.

Corcoran stood and took a few deep breaths, trying to calm his wildly hammering heart. Once he'd caught his breath, he said, "I think it would be prudent, under the circumstances, to keep the door *locked*."

"But then you couldn't have gotten in," someone said.

There was more machine gunfire in the corridor outside.

"Jesus Christ," Corcoran whispered, rubbing his face with both hands. "Don't you hear that? One of those people out there, one of the *test subjects* actually has a machine gun. A fucking *machine gun*!"

They continued to stare at him, unmoving dark figures in

a dark room. They were little more than shapes robed in blackness, as if he'd walked in on the middle of some kind of occult ritual.

Corcoran's stomach made an unpleasant belching sound.

"Is there any food left?" he said, going toward the coffee table, where finger foods had been set out earlier.

No one spoke as they watched him cross the room.

He grabbed a handful of potato chips and started eating them as he looked for something else to eat. After spending about a minute munching on cold cuts and crackers, he noticed the room was silent. He stood up straight and faced them.

"Well, how have you been, uh, holding up?" he said.

The silence that followed went on for an uncomfortable length of time before Todd Hinkle said, "We've managed."

"Good. That's good."

"Our friend Ziggy has been catching us up on everything," Caleb Tan said.

"Ziggy? Who's Ziggy?"

With a click, Ziggy turned on his headlamp as he rose to his feet from a chair. "I was the guy who stayed here when you left."

Corcoran nodded. "Ziggy? That's your real name?"

"Of course not. But they had to have something to call me because we were talking, so I gave them my childhood nickname."

He nodded again, ate another potato chip, then said, "And what have you been talking about?"

"Ziggy's been telling us what *you've* been up to," Caleb said.

"Me?"

"Yes. About your method of finding test subjects."

Corcoran ate another potato chip and chewed slowly to give himself time to think. He wondered how many of them would stop being scientists and become moralizers thirsty for his blood. Maybe all of them.

He found it galling that they would have the audacity to suggest his use of homeless people somehow made him a bad person worthy of their judgment and scorn. They put no thought into the conclusion, gave it no consideration. They'd simply reacted as they had been trained to react, according to the morals they had been taught as children. It was a knee-jerk reaction. Corcoran had seen it before many times, but never in a situation quite like this.

"Yes, I'm afraid it's an unpleasant reality," he said. "But I refuse to believe it's one that did not occur to any of you until now. You had to know that this project could not be completed without human testing. You also knew what this project was when you joined it and you don't seem to have any moral struggles with it or else you wouldn't *be* here."

"We've all done government work," Ira Goldman said. He was still seated in the recliner, although Eileen Waxner was no longer in his lap. "We know most of it is dirty work that it ends up doing harm to others. We could sit on our hands and avoid the jobs, but they pay well and it's good work, and if we didn't do it, somebody else would. It would get done, and any harm it could do would be carried out. We console ourselves with the fact that it will be used on our enemies, on people determined to hurt us."

Corcoran smiled. "I see you have all your justifications nicely lined up. But somehow, *I'm* the bad guy? *I'm* the villain?"

"You took people off the street, Jeremy," Eileen said.

"*Kidnapped* them," Caleb added with disgust.

"I worked on a couple of projects that tested on prisoners," Eileen said. "They volunteered and were fully aware of the risks, and most of them were on death row, so they didn't care much about the risks. But we didn't kidnap them and imprison them and intentionally make them sick against their will."

"What have you been doing with them?" Todd said. "Infecting them with the virus?"

"And recording the results," Corcoran said with a nod.

Todd turned his head slowly from side to side. "That's . . . horrible."

"Where's Holly?" Corcoran said.

Eileen said, "In the bedroom. She wasn't feeling well."

"That's a shame. Holly has been assisting Dr. McManus and me in the entire testing process."

Corcoran sighed as he spread some more cream cheese on a Ritz, slapped a slice of salami on it, and ate it. He took a napkin from the stack on the coffee table and slowly wiped his fingers as he spoke.

"You have no moral difficulty helping to build weapons that kill and maim countless human beings," he said to Ira. "You have no ethical qualms about experimenting on human beings who volunteer only because it's marginally more interesting than sitting in their cells knowing they're one day closer to being electrocuted," he said to Eileen. To Ira: "You say the weapons will be used against our enemies, and that makes the work acceptable for you." To Eileen: "You say the death row inmates volunteer and are fully informed and will be executed, anyway."

He took a handful of olives from a bowl and ate them slowly, one at a time.

"Well, I have chosen the homeless on whom to experiment. These are people who have been reduced, for whatever reasons, to living on the street. And that's where they will die. They're addicted to drugs, alcohol. Most of them suffer from any number of diseases, and if they don't, they will soon. They'll die in alleys and gutters and in homeless shelters."

"That *excuses* it?" Eileen said.

"I haven't said that. And I'm not finished. These people will die meaningless deaths, most of them slow and painful. I'm giving them a chance to add meaning to their lives and their deaths by contributing to the development of a weapon that will save the lives of untold numbers of American troops and effectively disable the enemy by turning its people against each other."

Eileen said, "And . . . *that* excuses it. Right?"

"I'm not trying to *excuse* it. I'm simply explaining to you how I see it. The same way you've explained to me how you choose to see something you've done that might be met with . . . disapproval from others. And I am suggesting that you look at this the way I look at it, just as I'm choosing to look at the things you've done the same way you look at them. At the very least, it certainly would make our current situation a little more tenable, don't you think?"

They watched him eat his olives. He waited for Ira or Eileen or Caleb or Todd to say something, but they didn't make a sound.

"They were human beings," Ziggy said quietly. "They may be homeless and at the end of their ropes and living on the street, but they're still human beings, most of them are fathers and mothers, sons and daughters, they have families. They're human beings who are *supposed* to have all the same rights and freedoms as everyone else."

Corcoran nodded. "Yes. I fully agree with all of that. I've simply told you how I choose to look at it, and suggested that everyone adopt that view because we're going to have to cooperate. We're going to need each other. We have a problem that is much more urgent and dangerous than moral dilemmas, I'm afraid."

"Something that directly affects *you*, I would imagine," Eileen said.

"No, something that affects *all* of us. The powers that be . . . uh, Vendon Labs, that is . . . they're very unhappy with what's happened here. Uh, by the way, do all of you *know* what's happened here?"

"I've gotten a couple calls," Ziggy said. "Last I heard, all your infested test subjects are loose."

"Infected," Corcoran said.

"Whatever. I've been advised to keep them here for their safety, so that's what I've done. Have *you* been infected, Dr. Corcoran?"

"Me? Of *course* not! Ollie's men are hunting them down."

"To kill them," Ira said.

"Yes, of course. We have no choice."

"What were you saying about Vendon Labs?" Todd asked.

"The people in charge are pretty upset about this situation and—"

"Which is your fault," Ira said.

"No. This is *not* my fault. I had nothing to do with Ollie and his men—"

"Better security would have helped. We weren't even prepared for the hurricane, which you knew was coming. You were responsible for buying the generator. Is it used? Rebuilt? Did you pocket the difference? That's why you do jobs like this, Corcoran. You'd do a lot worse than kidnap homeless people if it meant a job with good pay. You need the money for drugs, don't you? Pretty desperately, I'd guess. You'd experiment on your own mother if they told you to, and . . . like all of us . . . you'd find some way to justify it."

"I'm willing to admit I've been . . . lax . . . in some ways . . . and that I could have handled this project better. But I will not take responsibility for a group of paramilitary zealots that manages to break in here and—"

"Zealots?" Ziggy said. "Hey, that's not true. We got some Baptists and Methodists and Catholics, a few Mormons, a few Muslims, we got a couple atheists, and we even have an Amish guy. We're *all* religions in Ollie's group. But . . . now that I think about it, I don't think we've got any Zealots."

"Oh, Jesus," Corcoran groaned as he let his head fall forward. He stayed that way for a moment, staring down at his feet. Finally, he lifted his head and said, "As I was going to say, Vendon Labs will be sending a team out here to clean this up. They'll come as soon as the weather calms down a little. Maybe sooner. They're going to be eager to remove all evidence of the project, make sure all the test subjects have been eliminated, and they'll want to make sure word doesn't get out. They *definitely* want me, but it will be in their best interests to wipe you out, too. All of you. Everyone here. But I could give you some leverage."

"Leverage?" Eileen said. "Why would you give us leverage? Against what?"

"Did you hear what I said? They'll probably come in here with machine guns and flamethrowers. Maybe gas, I don't know. If you have something they want, you might be able to bargain with them. Or at least slow them down until you can come up with a better idea."

"That's not going to happen," Ziggy said. "It won't get that far. We won't let it. Ollie won't let it."

"You have a lot of confidence in Ollie, but you have no idea what you're dealing with."

Caleb said, "You're telling us that Vendon Labs is going to send a team in here to kill all their employees?"

"Haven't you been listening?" Corcoran said. "You've all become liabilities. It won't be the first time Vendon has done something like this, and Vendon sure as hell isn't the only company that does this sort of thing. I'm telling you in advance so you can prepare, come up with a plan, so when they get here—"

"I think you're just trying to come up with reasons for us to protect your ass," Caleb said.

"I'm saying that if you do it right, you could use me to—"

Eileen said, "That's what it sounds like to me, too, Caleb."

"I don't think you should be in here, Corcoran," Ira said.

"I think you should be out there with them. With the people you've infected. The people who now have to be killed because of what you did to them."

"Don't be ridiculous," Corcoran said.

Ira stood. "I'm not being ridiculous."

"I'm inclined to agree with Ira," Todd said.

Ziggy unholstered his gun. "I think you should leave."

"And go out *there*?" Corcoran said, pointing at the door. "Are you *insane*?"

"I don't think it's fair for you to be in here," Ziggy said, bending his right arm at the elbow and aiming the gun at Corcoran. He started to move toward him, saying, "Not after what you've done to them."

"You're crazy," Corcoran said, backing away from him. "Crazy."

Ziggy arced around the coffee table, then came toward Corcoran again, sending him in the direction of the door.

"You want me to go out there . . . or you'll *shoot* me, that's what you're saying?" Corcoran said, still moving backwards. His heart was pounding furiously again and he felt nausea rising in his stomach.

"That's right."

He turned to the others. "Jesus Christ, are you going to let this happen? I'm trying to tell you, dammit, you can *use* me when Vendon Labs gets here."

"I don't think they want to use you, Dr. Corcoran," Ziggy said. He had not stopped advancing.

Soon, Corcoran was backed against the door.

"I'll count to three," Ziggy said. "If you're not out by then, I'll shoot."

Corcoran feared he would hyperventilate if he did not calm down.

"One."

"You don't understand, they'll kill *all* of you!"

"Two."

He reached behind him and found the door's handle. He unlocked it, pushed it down, then stepped forward as he opened it.

"Three."

Corcoran slipped out the door, alone and unarmed, and into the blackness of the windy corridor, resisting the urge to scream.

50

The subbasement of the Springmeier Neuropsychiatric Hospital was like a horror movie set and Ollie didn't like it, but he shoved that deep down inside of himself and ignored it. After finding Delgado in the stairwell, he'd gotten three of his men to accompany him down to the basement, and they weren't going back upstairs until every test subject down there was dead.

He'd brought McCoy, Baker, and Axelrod because they hadn't hesitated to follow orders when they were outside getting the sheriff. When Baker had found the test subject lying in the road—Kaufman had later told Ollie he'd run over the man with his car—trying to crawl away, he'd shot it without pause. He needed men like that with him down in the basement, especially the subbasement, which he had expected to be everything it turned out to be.

Axelrod had already shot one of the test subjects in the basement and their adrenaline was pumping. They were ready for more.

Ollie tried to keep his adrenaline under control as they slowly made their way through the damp darkness, their feet crunching over the rocky dirt floor. He had put his ski mask back on and was glad of it because the light from his headlamp kept glinting off of cobwebs, and with the mask on, he could walk through them without feeling their tingling, sticky touch on his face.

Ollie was about to tell the men to break up and cover more ground, but not to get *too* far apart, when there was a loud crash that made all four of them jump. The sound was immediately followed by an angry voice, and it was coming from somewhere in that inky darkness ahead of them, a darkness so thick that it was heavy and created an almost physical pressure as it closed in from all directions.

They walked around damp pillars and stacks of rotting cardboard boxes and old wooden crates and decayed office furniture and piles of unidentifiable material that formed menacing shapes in the murkiness.

Ollie spotted the source of the noise up ahead. One of the piles of junk had collapsed and someone had been in the way. Even a filing cabinet had toppled over onto the mess. Now there was movement as someone crawled out, chattering angrily.

They gathered on one side of the pile, where an arm was reaching out, pale, bare, and covered with cuts and scratches. Then a head. It was a woman, short and stout. As she rose from the mess in her grimy hospital gown, their headlamp beams revealed a horrible wound in her neck where flesh had been torn away. It had been there a while and was swollen and infected.

"Oh, Jesus, Vera," Ollie said when he recognized her.

She held up a hand against the light and said, "Who's that?"

Vera Washington had been homeless for years. Her story was a heartbreaking one, but not uncommon. She'd lost everyone and everything in her life by the time she was forty—her husband, her two children—and after that, she'd forgotten how to live life, how to function properly throughout the day, and she kind of fell apart. She hadn't spoken to her aging parents for years because they'd refused to attend her wedding and acknowledge her husband, who met with their disapproval. They had no interest in helping her. She lived on the street for a while, then started taking advantage of the local shelters. But she did more than eat and sleep at the shelters; she started pitching in and working at them, helping out, doing whatever needed to be done. Now, that was her life. Working mostly from the Bayview Homeless Shelter, she organized blanket drives and food drives and fund-raisers for all the local shelters. The homeless shelter had become her home and her life. It had given her something around which to build a new life. She had become productive and was the busiest person Ollie knew besides himself who worked for the homeless. She still considered herself a homeless person and always looked like one as she roamed the streets in third-hand clothes looking for new people to bring to the shelter.

"Who *is* that?" she said.

"Oh, Jesus, I'm so sorry, Vera," he said, shaking his head.

"Ollie?" Her face screwed up as she craned her head forward and squinted at him, shading her eyes from the light with her upheld hand. "Is that *you*, Ollie?"

He turned his head away from her for a moment. He was afraid she might recognize his eyes. He didn't want her to know it was him because she'd think he was there to help her.

"You!" she said, pointing a finger at him. "*You*, Ollie! *You* were the one who did this to us! *You* were behind this, *weren't* you?" Spittle flew from her mouth as she spoke.

"What?" Ollie whispered as he watched her face turned into a mask of hatred that was focused on him alone. "I didn't—"

"You son of a bitch *bastard* you should *die* for doing this to us you *fucker*!"

As she launched into a screaming rant, she swung her left arm back. Her hand was clutching something as she lunged forward and swung the arm in the other direction, slashing at Ollie. It caught his upper arm as he lurched backwards, and hot, searing pain rose in that spot.

Vera kept slashing so fast, he couldn't see what she had in her hand, but it was sharp enough to draw blood. He felt hot moisture spread immediately on his arm as she caught him across the chest.

The others raised their guns but Ollie shouted, "No!" as he kept jumping backwards to avoid her hand. But he wasn't talking to them. "I did *not* do this! I came to *stop* it!"

"Lying sack of shit," Vera growled as she stabbed and slashed at Ollie with what he could now see was a filthy, rusted, old box-cutter. "Fucking *killer* and a *liar* and a—"

Ollie watched her mouth move furiously to form the words, her round, flat face twisted into a venomous look of hatred. For a moment, he was with his father, his gibbering, wasted father who would not let Ollie help him, who would not accept a home, food, money, who angrily rejected everything in favor of his own addiction and insanity. A burning rage rose up in Ollie, hot, bilious frustration and disappointment and guilt lodged in his gullet and he fired his gun. But he fired it again, and again, shouting, not forming words, just releasing all that anger and frustration.

Three bullets put her down.

Ollie said nothing, just stared down at Vera's body.

"You okay?" Axelrod asked.

Ollie was glad, once again, that he was wearing his mask. They couldn't see the hot tears running from his eyes.

A rumbling, crashing explosion occurred somewhere in the hospital. It was big, though, big enough for Ollie to feel it in the dirt floor under his feet. It went on for a while and all four of them stopped to listen, looking at each other with concern.

"Sounds like this place is falling apart," Baker said.

"Jesus Christ," Ollie said. He coughed, took a deep breath, and said, "I'm gonna have to go up and see what that was. Get the rest of them that are down here and come back upstairs when you're done."

"What about Bursell and Castillo?" McCoy said.

"If you find them and they're okay, bring them up with you. If they're not okay, then . . . do *not* bring them up with you."

"What the hell was *that*?" Emilio said after the rumbling and crashing stopped. He was seated in a chair in Fara's office.

Fara was getting a blanket from her closet for Sheriff Kaufman when it happened, whatever it was. She stepped out of the closet and said, "That was in the front part of the hospital. It sounded a lot like the last one. A tree."

"Are there trees in the front?"

"Two huge oaks. One is in the middle of the parking lot, the other's right in front of the hospital."

"Sounds like the storm is worse," Emilio said, listening to the noise outside. "How long does one of these things last, anyway?"

"I don't know." She took the blanket to the couch and spread it out over Sheriff Kaufman.

His face was a lumpy collection of small wounds, but they were clean. He stirred occasionally and Fara suspected he was awake, but he kept his eyes closed and said nothing. He didn't have a fever, but he was feeling cold.

"If that's not warm enough," she said, "let me know and I can put some coats on you."

Fara was wearing her own coat now because it had gotten so cold.

"Are you sure you don't want a coat, Emilio?" she said. "I can probably find something for you in the closet."

"No, thanks. When I'm anxious like this, I always feel hot. If I had a coat on, I'd be burning up."

There was more gunfire in the building, some of it machine gunfire.

"Where the hell is Corcoran?" she said. "He's been gone

too long. He'd better get back before Ollie, or—" She stopped and listened as more rumbling and crashing came from the front of the hospital.

"Another tree?" Emilio said.

"No, that just sounded like . . . something collapsing."

"Yeah. This building."

Eddie Loomis lay screaming in the water in front of the dead, black Springmeier Neuropsychiatric Hospital, but no one heard him.

He'd been in the tree for a long time, listening to the creaking and crackling sounds coming from the trunk as it was battered by the wind. The sounds came and went and didn't sound too severe, so he'd stayed there and kept scanning the long-dead parking lot through his infrared goggles, looking for movement or something suspicious. He hadn't seen any since the shooting outside had stopped and that had been hours ago. He was cold and wet and his ass ached from sitting on that branch, but he was determined to follow Ollie's orders and do his job, which was to sit there and keep watching until they came out of the hospital and headed for the fence. Then he was to climb down and join them. Ollie was the father and brother and coach and friend he'd never had and Eddie wanted to make him happy and help him get his homeless friends out of there.

He'd been sitting there with his left arm hooked around another branch next to him, hanging on tightly as he listened to those creaking and crackling sounds, when he realized the sounds weren't stopping and the tree was moving in one direction.

He started shouting, "Oh, shit!" over and over again when he saw the broad concrete steps that climbed up to the hospital's entrance and then the building itself growing larger and realized the tree was going down.

Eddie had frantically started to climb down, but immediately knew that was pointless. With both feet on a branch, he'd launched himself away from the tree as hard as he could. The sound of the tree crashing through the front of the hospital was like the end of the world as he flew through the air, buffeted by the powerful wind, flipping head over heels at some point, all sense of direction gone.

When he made contact with the ground, all he knew was the pain that exploded in his right leg. He could not move the leg, and even moving other parts of his body intensified the pain. It filled his head with explosions of reddish-purple light and moved up his leg like a hot, electrified spike, so excruciating that he was no longer aware that he was screaming.

He lay there alone, screaming in the six inches of water that stood in the old parking lot, as sounds of further collapse continued to come from the damaged building.

Latrice lost consciousness, but it didn't feel like she'd been out long. It was like several consecutive frames had been cut from a movie, making it jump ahead in time just a little in a split second.

She'd been standing in Giff's living room watching the chaos and violence.

Giff and the sheriff's deputy were still fighting on the floor, but now the deputy had the upper hand and was hunched over Giff, pounding on his face like he was tenderizing a steak.

Miguel was trying to make Mia stop using the fireplace shovel to stab and beat Marcus, who was a bloody, twitching mess. He kept shouting her name as he grabbed her arm, then she would jerk her arm away and go on bludgeoning Marcus until he grabbed her arm again. Without warning, she turned around and lunged at Miguel, rising up from Marcus's body like an angered cobra and striking by leaping onto Miguel with a shrill scream, knocking him to the floor. Then she took the shovel to him, first pounding his face with the flat back of the spade, which made an ugly, thick, clanking sound against his skull. Then she turned the shovel over in both hands and stabbed with the sharp, straight edge, concentrating on his throat and neck.

And through all of that, Latrice heard another sound, one she did not recognize. It was a high, quavering wail, like an animal in pain, or sick with rabies, or both. Seconds after she recognized it as her own miserable voice, it was all swallowed up by the roar of an approaching monster that stomped on the house with a giant foot made of wood and bark and slapping, clawing branches. The world went dark and fell in on top of them.

That was when everything blinked out for a moment.

Next thing Latrice knew, she was flat on the floor, face-down, coughing because of the dust that filled the air. There were still small sounds of collapse around her. Something made of glass broke.

From somewhere in the house, someone was howling in pain, the voice rising to an agonizing cry. A child cried, and some distant part of Latrice feared for that child's safety but was unable to voice that fear or act on it.

Someone in the darkness—it sounded like the sheriff's deputy—laughed long and loud, then said, "Oh, man, fuck *me*, I am havin' the weirdest fuckin' night," and continued laughing.

She tried to get up on her hands and knees, but something big, solid, and heavy prevented her from rising more than six inches off the floor. She crawled forward and was able to move freely. When she tried to get on hands and knees again, she succeeded, and she kept moving forward, shoving things aside when she could, moving around or over them when she couldn't, but moving slowly.

Somewhere in the collapsed beams and crushed walls and broken furniture, she heard the deputy shout, "Now I gotta get outta *this* shit? Oh, *fuck*! Why can't *something* be easy tonight, goddammit?"

The wind and rain were now inside the house, blowing things around and getting Latrice wet. But she kept moving forward, arms and legs shaking, muscles aching, and the inside of her head burning a deep-red rage.

What had begun as Tropical Storm Quentin made landfall as a hurricane and swept through Humboldt County like the rage of an angry deity and laid waste to neighborhoods and malls and bowling alleys and schools and churches and anything else that stood in its path.

Roofs were sheared from buildings large and small and trees and power poles were tossed around like Tinker Toys, flung into homes and shopping centers and churches. The storm surge took out most of the Eureka-Samoa Bridge, all of the Railroad Bridge, and both the North- and Southbound Highway 101 bridges that crossed the bay.

A category 4, Quentin made landfall at Eureka and pounded and slashed and ripped its way northeast, and as it moved on, it left nothing in its wake untouched.

In a quiet, darkened office, a man seated at his desk placed a call, then turned his chair around to look out the window at the sparkling view of San Francisco on a stormy night from the thirty-second floor of Four Embarcadero Center.

It was a spacious, expensively decorated office with lots of onyx and chrome, but the always shiny surfaces were dulled now by the lack of illumination. The only light in the office was a gentle, golden glow that came from behind the large corporate logo on one wall. It was a brass representation of the atomic symbol in which the oversized nucleus was the planet earth with a large gold V emblazoned on it.

The tinny squeak of a voice at the other end of the line came from the small cell phone the man held to his ear.

"Yes, our information says the storm is moving northeast and it's on its way out of Eureka."

More tinny sounds from the phone.

"I think we should get a team in there immediately and clean up this mess while we can. It's a disaster, but it can be handled if it's handled immediately. . . . Good. Do it now."

He severed the connection, then turned his chair around and stood. He slipped the phone into his pocket, walked around his desk and crossed the room to a small closet. He got his coat and put it on.

He could go home now. He was done for the day.

51

For the first time since he was small boy, Dr. Jeremy Corcoran wet himself. He stood in the black corridor with his back pressed against the wall, unable to see anything in the dark. Wind howled down the corridor like angry ghosts, much louder and stronger since the loud rumbling he'd heard in the front of the building earlier. He was paralyzed with fear, unable to move, barely able to breathe, and his bladder, which he hadn't even known was full, suddenly released and he felt the hot urine run down his thighs.

Only a minute earlier, he'd been waiting in what he was almost certain was a restroom. He'd paid little attention to anything in the old hospital that he did not use himself, and the only bathroom he used was the one in his quarters. But after being ejected from his quarters into the darkness of the corridor, he'd panicked. He'd walked and jogged along the wall, never losing touch with it, keeping one hand on it at all times, sometimes stopping to listen when he heard something close. When he'd heard footsteps hurrying toward him, he'd panicked and started groping for a door, any door, and he'd gone into the first one that came long. He'd assumed it was the restroom because of the tile wall, but it didn't matter. He'd stayed there, just inside the door, for a long time, waiting, listening, trembling, trying not to breathe too loudly, trying to will his thundering heart to calm down. After hearing nothing for a while, he'd opened the door and listened, then stepped outside and listened. Nothing. He'd continued again, hurrying back the way he'd come, back toward Fara's office. Until he'd heard something within the wind, movement that was steady and human, and . . . a voice. He'd frozen again and pressed his back against the wall.

And now, having wet his pants, he tried to determine if the sound warranted such a response. Was it just the wind?

He heard a gunshot somewhere in the hospital—there had been a few of those—and the clatter of detritus being blown along the corridor floor by the wind. He thought he'd heard the slap of bare feet on the tile and the secretive grumble of voices. But now, all he heard was the wind.

He continued along the wall, more cautiously now, and thought about what he would do once he got back to the safety of Fara's office. He would get out of here. Somehow. He would pay money to someone to drive him away from Springmeier. He would *scare* someone into doing it if he had to, telling them that if they stuck around, they'd be cleaned up with the rest of this mess once Vendon's team of problem-solvers arrived. He would *threaten* someone if he had to, steal a car, but he was getting out of and away from that building no matter what, storm or no storm.

Shouting. Someone was shouting angrily farther down the corridor. No, it was two voices. And footsteps running in the dark. Toward him. It was two men, and they were fighting. One seemed to be chasing the other, then they would stop and the shouting would go on. After some sounds of struggle, the chase continued, coming closer to Corcoran.

He pressed himself against the wall again and stopped breathing as they came closer. They stopped and began fighting again, shouting about something that made no sense to Corcoran. They were right in front of him now, in the dark, hitting each other and shouting at each other like children, moving around as they struggled, until—

—they slammed directly into Corcoran and he screamed.

In a hoarse voice, a man said, "Hey, who's this? Huh? Who're you?"

Corcoran slid along the wall to his left, trying to get away from them and move along, trying not to whimper, although small sounds were coming out of him involuntarily as he sidled along the wall. But they were aware of him now.

Two hands slapped onto his body, groping for purchase until they clutched the front of his corduroy coat.

"No," Corcoran said in a high, breathy voice. "No, please, no."

"I got him!" the man shouted. "I got the son of a bitch! *This* is the cocksucker! *He's* the one, I bet! Mother*fucker*!"

The man slapped Corcoran's face once, then again, repeatedly, back and forth, and Corcoran began sobbing as he slid down the wall, trying to block his attacker by lifting his arms.

Another hand grabbed Corcoran's hair and pulled him away from the wall, flinging him to the floor. Corcoran immediately began crawling on hands and knees, even though he was no longer sure in which direction he was going. He just wanted to get away.

He crawled as fast as he could, nearly panting as he heard them closing in again.

"Where the fuck you think you're goin', asshole?" one of them said as he jumped on Hal's back, straddling him like a horse and flattening him to the floor. "Come on, boy, *giddy up*!" One hand grabbed Corcoran's hair while the other hit him repeatedly about the neck and shoulders. "Come on, there, boy, whatcha waitin' for, anyway?" the rider said.

When the other man kicked Corcoran in the face, the world cartwheeled a few times and he found himself teetering on unconsciously. Blood ran from a cut on his upper lip and dribbled over his mouth and chin.

The rider got off of him and kicked him in the ribs. Both men were talking now, ranting about something Corcoran had done, or was going to do—none of it made any sense and he couldn't follow it, anyway, because they were both kicking him now.

He felt a final surge of fear and panic and he willed himself to move, to flee. With speed that surprised even him, Corcoran rose up on hands and knees, then screamed his rage as he began to hit back, flailing his arms indiscriminately, hitting and scratching as he got to his feet, then ran forward. He stumbled, but he kept running.

They stayed with him. One of them shouted, "You wanna play, dickhead, huh? Is that it? You wanna play?"

One of them tripped him and he fell hard. His chin hit the floor and started bleeding. Then both of them were on him, but they didn't just hit him.

Corcoran felt something hard and sharp pierce the flesh of his back just below his right shoulder blade. He let out a long scream of fear and pain that became words.

"Help me somebody! Help! Please!"

But that hard, sharp object stabbed into him again. And again.

They laughed and cursed him as they rolled him over onto his back. One of them straddled his legs and began to stab him repeatedly in the abdomen and chest.

Corcoran could not scream anymore. He could only make an involuntary grunting sound with each thrust of the weapon. He felt his blood leaking out of him, soaking into his clothes, warm against his skin.

He wondered how all of this would be reported in the media just a couple of seconds before he died.

52

Latrice's right hand ached from pounding it on the steering wheel of her Highlander, but she was only vaguely aware of it. Her windshield wipers made rapid smacking sounds as they swept back and forth at top speed and the wind jostled the SUV as she drove, but all Latrice could hear was the grinding of her own teeth.

She had crawled and climbed out of Giff's demolished house, reminding herself over and over that she wasn't in a nightmare. But that was what it had felt like, a frustrating nightmare that was enraging her, making the inside of her skull vibrate with anger. Crawling through the rubble and climbing over beams and collapsed walls, soaking wet from the rain, she'd tried to ignore the agonizing screams of one of the children coming from somewhere in the wreckage.

Instead, she focused her thoughts on her own children and her mother waiting for her at home, probably worried sick, maybe following coverage of the hurricane on the news. Tamara and Robert were the reason Latrice had come to Eureka, especially Robert. If it weren't for them, she wouldn't have to crawl out of a tree-crushed house in a hurricane. She'd be safe at home, warm and dry, nice and relaxed in front of the TV, or sitting at the kitchen table talking quietly with

Mama over tea. The kids should be in bed now, but they weren't, she was sure, because Mama hated to be the villain by prying them away from the TV and making them go to bed.

If it weren't for Robert's mystery condition, she wouldn't have needed that five thousand dollars Leland had promised her. It would have been useful, sure, but it wouldn't be so desperately needed. She would have been able to pay so many bills with that money, would have been able to get some nasty, tenacious bill collectors off her back, have some much-needed repairs done on the Highlander and around the house. But it would have to go toward whatever tests Robert was going to need. And medical costs were so outrageously high that even then, five grand probably wouldn't be enough.

If she'd never had the kids, of course, her life would be very different. Less stressful, for one thing. She wouldn't be under such a load of debt. She'd have more time—hell, nothing *but* time for herself. And most important of all, she would not have to crawl out of the remains of a demolished house in a fucking hurricane! She would have a life, her own life, and she could do just about anything she wanted. She'd have no one to worry about but herself.

She'd thought of all the money and time spent catering to them, wrapping her whole life around them. Then what does Robert do? He gets sick with some kind of mystery illness and she would have to spend even *more* money on him.

"Little shit," she'd muttered. "Don't know who the fuck he thinks he is . . . like I got nothing better to do with my goddamned time and money . . . Jesus Christ."

She had climbed out of what was left of a window. As strong as it was, the wind felt good on her face after crawling through that nightmarish obstacle course. She looked around and spotted her Highlander. The deputy's car was still parked behind her, but she didn't care. She'd take care of that.

She'd gotten into the Highlander then and fished the keys from her pocket. There was an unpleasant sound inside the SUV, a thick crunching sound. She was grinding her teeth together. When she became aware of it, she stopped, but seconds later, she was doing it again.

She'd started the engine, put her seat belt on, then put the Highlander in reverse and stomped on the gas pedal. The SUV rocketed backwards and slammed into the deputy's patrol car. With the gas pedal on the floor, the Highlander shoved the car over the mud. She'd turned the SUV around as soon as she had room, but not without hitting the rear of one of the other SUVs parked in front of the house.

"Cocksucker!" she shouted as she headed down the bumpy, narrow road. There was devastation on each side—trailers overturned, trees down. She had to drive off the road to go around a fallen tree. When she reached Emerald Canyon, she turned left.

She decided she would go home. Just drive back to Sacramento. She didn't get the money, she'd nearly been killed, the whole thing was a waste of time and energy and money and it was all because she'd needed the money for that sick little fucker who was probably sitting on his ass in comfort right now while she risked her goddamned life to scrape up some money for the fucking tingling and numbness in his leg and arm and—

"You little shit box!" she shouted as she pounded a fist on the steering wheel repeatedly. "I'll be home soon, fucker, and *then* we'll see who gets to be comfortable, you goddamned waste of space!"

Memories flitted through her mind of the days when she had only herself to worry about, before she had children, when she had so much time and energy. She pressed harder on the gas pedal, telling herself she would have that again. Very soon.

* * *

"That looks like the end of the road for us," Andy said as he stopped the SUV. He peered through the windshield at the mess up ahead. "In this direction, anyway."

Just ahead, the road disappeared in what looked like a large pond. Just beyond that, a huge tree had fallen across the road.

"What are we gonna do, Dad?" Donny asked.

Andy was struck by how calm Donny was, while his own heart was still beating too fast and he was jumpy with tension. He put the SUV in park and it idled as he looked all around them through the windows.

The wind was still blowing detritus over the road and tossing the trees in what looked like throes of agony, and the rain was still pouring hard enough to decrease visibility, but the storm had lost some of its intensity.

"We passed a side road just a little bit ago," he said as he put the car into gear again, made a U-turn in the road, and headed back.

"Where do you think it goes?"

"I don't know, but it would be a good place to park for a little while. What do you think? Shall we park and wait for the storm to die down a little more, then we can go back the way we came."

Donny's back stiffened and, with a note of alarm, he said, "You mean back to that house?"

"No, not there. We'll go home."

The boy slumped in the seat and smiled a little, relieved. "Oh. Yeah. That'd be nice."

Up ahead, a set of headlights was driving toward them, with another set right behind it. The first car crossed Andy's lane to turn onto a side road, followed by the second. They were two large, black SUVs, luxury gas guzzlers.

"That's the road," Andy said. "Where those two SUVs just turned in."

Andy slowed as he approached the road. He turned right and his headlights passed over a road sign that read OGDEN PASS. He was just in time to see the two SUVs turning left up ahead and driving into the woods.

"Maybe they live here," Donny said.

"There are no homes in those woods. There use to be an old mental hospital somewhere in there, but it's been abandoned for a long time. I don't even know if it's still standing."

"I wonder why they're going into the woods."

"I'm sure they have a reason." Andy made a U-turn on Ogden Pass before reaching the road the SUVs had taken, then pulled over onto the shoulder. He turned off the engine and killed the lights. "Okay, we're just going to sit here for a little while."

"Why don't we just keep driving?"

"Well, to be honest, I'm a little nervous about passing by that house again. Ram is going to be coming out of there, if he hasn't already. I'm probably being too cautious and a little cowardly, but I'd rather wait here. For a little while, anyway. The storm is receding, and if we wait awhile, driving will be easier and safer. Okay, buddy?"

"Yeah, sure. Can I turn on the radio?"

"Yeah, let's find some music."

Donny found an upbeat song that he knew and sang along to. But Andy didn't know it, and he didn't feel like singing, anyway. He didn't want Donny to know, but he was still feeling quite nervous. No, that wasn't true. He was still afraid.

Ram couldn't stop laughing as he crawled through the rubble with his flashlight guiding the way, because what else could he do when the night had gone so crazily wrong? It had started out with Ram trying to do a favor for an old friend, and somehow, it had collapsed into nightmarish slapstick comedy.

He found his gun on the floor. It was near the bloody body of the man named Marcus who had been killed by a shovel. He picked it up, shoved it in the holster, and moved on.

Somebody was hurt somewhere. It sounded like two people—an adult and a child. But he wasn't interested in helping them, only in getting out of there. He wondered what had happened to Andy and Donny. Ram had promised to drive them home and he was a man of his word, so he intended to follow through.

With considerable struggle, after hefting aside pieces of the shattered house, Ram finally got out by climbing through what was left of the same window through which Latrice had exited. He stood up straight and got his bearings.

When he saw his car, he shouted, "Son of a *bitch*!"

One of the other vehicles obviously had gotten out by backing into his car and moving it. Most of the driver's side of the car had been smashed in. It made Ram angry, but it was to be expected from the subhuman trash that lived here. He didn't have time to worry about it now.

Standing in the rain and wind, he turned around, faced the house, and shouted, "Andy! Hey, Andy, are you in there? Donny? Andy?"

No answer. But he hadn't really expected one. They'd probably been crushed inside the house.

He slopped through the mud to his car, went around to the passenger side and unlocked the door. He got inside and grabbed the radio microphone.

"This is one-oh-three, one-oh-three," he said. He gave his location and said, "The Clancy house has been mostly flattened by a tree with people inside. I'm going to need an ambulance, and a ride out of here because my vehicle is out of commission."

He listened for a moment and the reply came: "Copy, one-oh-three. We have a unit nearby on the way to Springmeier. One-oh-one has been injured at Springmeier and needs backup."

"Springmeier? The hospital?"

"Ten-four. There's trouble over there."

"Well, have someone come by and pick me up and we'll go over there."

A moment later: "A unit should be there in minutes, as long as the way is clear."

"Ten-four. I'll be here."

He replaced the mike and stared at the radio. What the hell was Kaufman doing at Springmeier? And what was going on over there?

He settled back in the seat and waited, searching the darkness for the oncoming headlights of his ride.

53

"You understand that if this turns out to be nothing, our relationship is over," Jack Bembenek said. "No more appearances on the news to comment on weird stories."

Ivan and Bembenek sat in the backseat of a KIEM news van being driven by Bembenek's camera man, Leon. Ivan had told him everything on the phone, from the initial suspicions to getting Emilio into Springmeier, and everything they'd learned since about what Vendon Labs was doing in the old hospital.

Bembenek was in his late twenties, with thick black hair and a long face. He seemed unusually nervous.

"Yeah, I understand that," Ivan said. "But it's not nothing. You'll see."

"I'm not on great terms with my boss right now. I don't need any trouble. I like this job. And this area. I'd like to stay here. If I get fired, I could end up anywhere. I don't want to have to move to some town in Wyoming or Nebraska."

Ivan laughed. "Jack, you've got nothing to worry about. This story is going to make you famous. But you're not the only one coming."

"What? You called someone else, too?"

"I had to. If it's just you, me, and your cameraman, we may

never be seen again. The more newspeople, the better. It's protection."

"Who else did you call?"

"An old friend of mine works at KGO in San Francisco. I talked him into sending someone. But it's a four-hour drive from there, so I also called other local stations. KVIQ, KBVU, and KAEF in Arcata."

"Jeez, that's *everybody*."

"But I don't know who will show up."

"You didn't call the police?"

"Didn't have to. Like I said, Sheriff Kaufman's there and he's pretty badly hurt from what Emilio said. They'll have cops out there soon enough, if they don't already."

"I hope you're right. We didn't check the van out, we just got in and left. If this turns out to be nothing, some people are going to be pretty pissed about us going out after midnight in a hurricane."

"The storm is passing."

"*Look* at it out there!"

"It's not as bad as it was."

Bembenek nodded toward the driver. "Well, if it weren't for the fact that Leon, here, owes me a lot of favors, I probably wouldn't have managed this."

Leon was a rotund man with long brown hair in a ponytail under his baseball cap. "I didn't come because I owe him favors," Leon said in a deadpan voice, glancing over his shoulder at Ivan. "I'm a rebel."

"I don't think you guys have to worry about getting in trouble for this," Ivan said. "You'll probably win an award for it." After a moment, he added, "If we live through it."

It occurred to Fara as she sat at her desk, listening to the sound of occasional gunfire in other parts of the building and watching Emilio doze in his chair with his feet on the desk that she had agreed to go on a date with him when this was all over. She didn't date often because she found it to be an odious ritual. Simply calling it a date gave rise to a host of expectations and worries. She liked Emilio and probably would enjoy going out with him, but after their experience at Springmeier, she wasn't sure she would ever be entirely comfortable with him.

She wanted to put this whole experience behind her. It was the only way she would be able to live with herself. That would be impossible, of course, once Emilio's recording and the details of what they were doing the night of the hurricane— hunting and killing kidnapped homeless people they'd deliberately infected with a deadly virus—were made public. She was afraid that Emilio would be a vivid reminder of all of it, that every time she looked at him, her mind would flood with horrible memories and strangling guilt. She was fairly sure that Emilio would not hold it against her—that was one of the reasons she liked him so much—but *she* would. Forgiving herself felt like an impossibility.

Of course, if Ollie was right—and in the part of her mind where she kept the things she did not directly admit to herself, she knew he was—Vendon Labs was sending a team of thugs to kill them all, making the details of her social life quite irrelevant.

She heard a loud crashing sound somewhere in the building. It wasn't the first. She'd been hearing sounds like it for a while, and they seemed to be coming from the front of the hospital. Had another tree fallen on the building? Maybe the initial crash they'd heard in front—the one that sounded more like an explosion and then went on for a while—was the cause of it. The oak tree in front of the hospital was an enormous old thing with fat branches that reached out in all directions. And the building, of course, was old. Well over a hundred years.

The door opened and Ollie stomped in. He carelessly

slammed the door behind him and Emilio jerked awake and dropped his feet from the desk. Ollie approached the desk, looking at the sheriff as he passed the couch.

"How's he doing?"

"We're still waiting for Corcoran to come back with a painkiller," Fara said. "For all I know, he's left the building."

"He's not coming back. He's dead."

Fara leaned forward in her chair. "Corcoran?"

Ollie nodded. "One of the test subjects got him. Probably more than one, I'm guessing. Really tore him up. A great loss to humanity. Is the sheriff going to be okay?"

"I think he might be asleep. I hope. He could probably use a couple stitches."

"By our count, there are three of them left," Ollie said. "And one of them's got a goddamned Uzi."

"*What?*" Emilio said, standing.

Ollie went on talking, but Fara didn't hear him. She thought about Corcoran. Done in by his own lab rats. She agreed with Ollie's sarcastic remarks. A great loss to humanity, indeed. He was a sadistic bastard, a narcissistic drug addict. It was a well-deserved death.

But for the past year and a half, Fara had been standing by his side, working with him. Helping him. Being like him. With a deep chill in her bones, she thought she deserved to be next.

"We need to start thinking about getting the hell out of here," Ollie said. "The storm's not as intense as it was, I think it might be subsiding. I've got vans outside the fence. Now that the gate's open, I'll have them brought to the back. My men will be getting into them. I strongly suggest you join us."

"You're going to leave those test subjects here?" Emilio asked.

"Don't worry, they'll be taken care of. Probably soon. We need to get out of here so we aren't taken care of, too. Get everything you need together and be ready to leave."

"I have a car here," Emilio said.

"So do I," Fara said.

"Then what the hell are you doing here? Get in your cars and go. Before you wish you had but can't."

After Ollie left the office again, Emilio said, "I think he's serious. You ready to go?"

"Are you kidding? I've been ready to go for the last eight hours." She gestured toward the door. "I'm just not sure I want to risk going out *there* to get to my car."

Latrice was unaware of how fast she was driving. She was too lost in her own thoughts, too busy telling herself what she was going to do when she got home. She hardly decreased her speed at all as she drove around branches and splashed through large puddles.

"Gonna be some fuckin' changes, I can tell you *that* right now. No more of this shit, drivin' all over the goddamned country because that fuckin' little shit's got some tingling, like I got nothing better to do with my time and money, money *I* earned, money *I* worked for, money—"

She interrupted herself to start pounding her fist on the steering wheel. She hadn't noticed yet how swollen it had become, couldn't feel how much it hurt. Her whole body ached, but she'd lost track of that, too. The vibrating rage inside her head overwhelmed everything else.

Latrice would not have noticed the police car going in the opposite direction if it had not turned on its roof lights just as they passed each other. That got her attention.

She looked in the rearview mirror and saw the white car make a slow U-turn, then speed up as it pursued her. Its siren began to wail.

Latrice pressed harder on the gas pedal.

54

"Did you see that?" Ivan said as Leon turned off of Ogden Pass onto the new gravel road that led through the woods to the old mental hospital. "There was a guy with a little kid in that SUV parked back there."

"Yeah?" Jack said. "What about it?"

"Well . . . I don't know, maybe they broke down, or something. I don't like the idea of a kid being here. We don't know what's going to happen."

"What are we supposed to do, stop and tell them to go away?"

"No, but—oh, wow," Ivan said, leaning forward in the backseat to peer through the windshield.

As Leon drove slowly around the body in the road, Ivan looked ahead at the gate. A sheriff's department car was parked by the guardhouse, and the bent, mangled gate was standing open. It didn't look like the storm had done that damage, it looked like someone had driven through the gate in a hurry without bothering to open it first. Leon stopped the van just outside the gate and put it in park.

Leon steered around the police car and the headlight beams shone through the open gate, revealing bodies sprawled all over the gravel parking lot.

"Shit," Jack said. "I don't suppose you brought a gun."

"I was about to ask you the same question," Ivan said.

"We may not want to go in there unarmed."

"Hey, to be honest, I don't want to go in there at all. But . . . we have to."

"Don't worry," Leon said. He leaned over, opened the glove box, removed a snub-nose revolver and held it up so Ivan and Jack could see it clearly. "We're covered."

"Do you have a permit for that?" Jack asked. He didn't appear too happy to see that Leon had a concealed weapon in one of the station's news vans.

"No."

"Then what the hell are you doing with it?"

Leon stared at him a moment, then said, "There's dead people on the ground and that's the thanks I get for being the only one with a gun?"

"That's not the point. You could lose your job. I probably could, too, just for being in the van with you."

"I bet those dead guys on the ground out there would say it's the point. I've also got ammo. You gonna be pissed about that, too?"

"I, for one, Leon, am glad you have the gun," Ivan said.

"Like I said. I'm a rebel."

"You gonna drive in there," Ivan said, "or do we have to walk the rest of the way?"

Leon put the gun back in the glove box, closed it, and put the van in gear.

As they passed the guardhouse and went through the gate, Ivan saw two black Mercedes-Benz S-Class SUVs parked end to end behind the cars parked at the rear of the hospital, blocking them.

"I don't like the looks of that," Ivan said.

"Looks like somebody doesn't want anyone to drive away," Jack said.

"I'm thinking Vendon Labs beat us here," Ivan said, taking his phone from his pocket.

When Ollie came into the office again, he was accompanied by two of his masked men.

"The vans are being brought to the back," he said. "These men will escort you to your cars as soon as you're ready."

Another rattling, rumbling crash came from somewhere in the front half of the building. Ollie's head turned in the direction of the sound.

Emilio's phone chirped. He took it from his pocket and answered quietly.

Fara stood at her desk with her purse and a large canvas bag on the desk in front of her. "Who's going to take Sheriff Kaufman?"

"He'll go in one of our vans and we'll take him to the hospital, if we can get there. I imagine half the town is flooded. If we wait for his deputies to get here, we could be here until Tuesday. If we can't get to the hospital, we'll—"

"Listen up, guys," Emilio said. He placed his phone on Fara's desk. "Go ahead, Ivan."

"I'm in a news van at the gate behind the hospital," Ivan said over the phone. "There are two big black SUVs parked perpendicularly behind the cars parked out here. They've intentionally blocked them. There doesn't seem to be anyone in the SUVs, which makes me think they've gone inside. I think you've got company in there."

"Shit," Emilio said. He turned to Ollie. "You better let your men know."

"I've got two men at the entrance!" Ollie said, taking Fara's phone from his pocket. "They should know and *stop* them!"

Fara's legs became weak and she lowered herself into her chair. She felt like she was in an elevator that was falling from the very top of the world's tallest skyscraper. Suddenly, her lungs felt tiny and her heart felt huge.

"Hey, hey," Emilio said, hunkering down beside the chair. "You okay? You're not gonna pass out on me, are you?"

"They're here," she said, merely breathing the words. "They're here and we're still here. We should have left earlier. We should have risked the storm and left *hours* ago."

"Whoa, no, we don't know that yet."

She looked all around her office. She was cornered in that room. There was no way out but the door.

"Son of a bitch, they're not answering," Ollie said, raising the phone to his ear on his third call.

"I have to get out of here now," Fara said, standing. She slung her purse strap over her right shoulder and the strap of the canvas bag over her left shoulder, her flashlight in her left hand, and hurried around the desk.

"Wait a second, hold it," Emilio said, quickly stepping in front of her and putting his hands on her shoulders. He nodded toward Ollie.

He was talking on the phone. "When did they get here? . . . How many? . . . Jesus Christ, why didn't you call me?"

Fara felt muscles tightening all over her body. She could not hold still. She stepped around Emilio and went to the door.

He came after her, whispering, "Hey, hey, hey."

She opened the door and heard what she first thought to be the wind. But it wasn't blowing as hard as it had before and this sound was something else.

A rapidly growing scream.

Fara stepped outside the door and Emilio followed right behind her. Both of them turned to the left, toward a shimmering orange glow in the corridor.

A fire in the shape of a person was running through the darkness toward them, screaming in agony, burning arms flailing.

* * *

"What the hell happened back there?" Deputy Olivia Burkett asked as she drove along Emerald Canyon slowly.

"Long story," Ram said. "Buncha subhuman trash. Fuckin' drug dealers and spics and niggers."

Burkett frowned as she looked back and forth from the road to Ram.

"You feeling okay, Ram?"

"Me? You kidding? Never been better. Hell of a night, though. Hell of a night."

"We're supposed to turn up here on Ogden Pass."

"Ogden Pass is closed."

"Supposed to be, yeah. But there's a new road there that leads to that old hospital. That's where the sheriff is."

"What the hell happened, anyway?"

"I don't know. I hope we're not the first ones there. Some kinda trouble."

"Fuck. More trouble."

She turned right onto Ogden Pass.

"Hey, what's that?" Ram said, nodding past Burkett out her window, where a dark SUV was parked beside the road on the other side. "Stop a second."

She stopped the car.

"Shine your light over there."

She turned on the spotlight on her door, manipulating it with a toggle so it pointed directly at the SUV.

"Well, I'll be a son of a bitch," Ram said with a grin. He opened the door.

"What are you doing?"

"Give me a second. I know this guy. Keep the light on."

He got out of the car, ducked his head against the wind and rain, and jogged across the road to the SUV. He knocked on the window, grinning.

"Hey, Andy!" he shouted.

The window slid down slowly and Andy squinted against the rain. "Ram," he said.

"What the hell're you doing here, anyway? And where'd you get—" He laughed loudly. "Did you *steal* this vehicle, Andy?"

"Well, uh . . ."

"Why didn't you just *wait* for me? I was gonna drive you home when we were done there. I'm *still* gonna drive you home. Come on, get into the patrol car."

"I think I'll just drive us home myself, Ram," Andy said.

"In a stolen vehicle? You're not gonna make me arrest you for stealin' a car, are you, Andy?"

"Arrest me?"

"Well, *yeah*! It's against the law, y'know!" Ram looked beyond Andy and saw Donny pressing himself into the back of the passenger seat. "Hey, Donny! How ya doin', buddy?" He looked at Andy again, still grinning. "C'mon, get out. I got one more call to answer, then I'll take you guys home. Just leave this thing here and it'll be found later. The owner'll get it back." He laughed. "'Course, if the owner was one of the assholes in Giff's house, he probably ain't gonna need it anymore." He laughed as he opened Andy's door and stepped back so he could get out.

"Ram, I'm not sure I want to—"

Smiling as he shook his head, Ram said, "I'm not asking, Andy." When he saw that they were going to get out, Ram turned and went back to the patrol car and knocked on Burkett's window, then opened the door a crack. "Can you step out here for a second, Olivia?"

He stepped aside and she pushed the door all the way open. As she got out of the car, Ram took his gun from its holster, leveled it with the back of her head and fired.

The crack of the gun sounded thick and insulated in the wind and rain.

Deputy Olivia Burkett fell forward, hit the car door, then collapsed to the ground.

Ram looked across the road at Andy and Donny standing beside the SUV, gawking at him.

"C'mon, chop-chop!" Ram shouted. "Get in the car!"

He bent down and grabbed Burkett's hair and dragged her away from the open door. He looked across the road again and saw that they were still standing there.

Ram hefted the gun in his hand and said, "Am I gonna have to come over there and get you?"

Andy put a hand on the back of Donny's head and they started toward Ram and the patrol car.

55

At eighteen minutes after one on Saturday morning, the town of Eureka, California, was dark. Normally a bed of diamonds at night on the dark Pacific coast, it now seemed to have disappeared from the face of the earth.

A storm was still raging, but it was no longer the destructive force that had passed through town that night.

The only lights were those of emergency vehicles trying to make their way through the storm and the damage it had done—flooded roads, fallen trees and power poles, piles of rubble. Some roads that weren't flooded were piled with debris—the remains of homes, entire mobile homes, even some small vehicles, as well as trees and power poles had become roadblocks that resembled giant beaver dams.

The tree that had fallen on the dark front of the long-abandoned Springmeier Neuropsychiatric Hospital had crushed the reception area with its three-story-tall vaulted ceiling. But the damage continued to spread well after the tree had fallen.

Eddie Loomis had been crawling slowly through the water and mud toward the spot where they'd entered the grounds. He knew they would return to that fence when they were done, and he wanted to be there. Each time he used his hands and left leg to pull and push himself forward, the movement sent jolts of hot electricity through his right leg. He clenched his teeth and let the pain out as a big breath with a little groan behind it. Then he would have to rest a bit and recover from that before doing it again.

As he made that painful journey across the flooded parking lot, Eddie kept hearing sounds inside the building. He still wore his night-vision goggles and each time he looked over at the building, something was collapsing. Wood crunched and glass shattered.

But those sounds were overwhelmed by the pain in Eddie's leg, pain that chewed through him like fangs. He tried to ignore everything else and focus on getting to that fence.

Emilio grabbed Fara and pulled her back into the office as the flaming screamer ran by, close enough for her to feel heat radiating from the flames. He shoved her farther into the office and ran out again, hurrying across the corridor.

Fara remembered the fire extinguisher hanging on the wall across the way. She went to the open door—Ollie's two men stood just behind her—and watched Emilio run to the flames. Ollie shoved his way to the door and stood beside her. The person had fallen to the floor. Emilio sprayed the flames with the extinguisher, moving the nozzle back and forth to cover the burning body. The flames flickered in the billowing white cloud, but not for long.

Screams came from the main corridor and Fara and Ollie turned their heads toward it. The beam of Ollie's headlamp illuminated the corridor for a surprising distance, but it still ended at a wall of darkness. Another burning person ran down the main corridor, heading for the front of the building and the collapsed cafeteria. The person passed their view in a heartbeat, screaming along the way.

"Shit," Ollie said. "Flamethrowers. Get in here, Emilio, *now*." He roughly grabbed her shoulders—

"Hey!"

—turned her around and shoved her back in the office. "You need to come in here."

"No!" she said, shoving past him to the door. "I have to get out of here now. We all do. Flamethrowers, they've got *flame-throwers*? I hope they keep in mind that we've got oxygen tanks upstairs."

Ollie grabbed her arm and pulled her back in. "Look, you can't go out there because they're gonna—"

Fara spun around and swung her fist as hard as she could. It connected with Ollie's face and he stumbled backwards with a yelp.

"Leave me alone!" she said. "I'm going out to my car and I'm leaving."

Emilio stood in the doorway. "No, you're not."

Fara kicked him between the legs.

Emilio doubled over with a cry of pain, then fell forward onto the floor.

Fara stepped over him and left the office, ignoring the burned body.

Cold wind still blew in the corridor. She stayed next to the left wall, close enough to touch—which she frequently did—and walked fast. She reached into her purse and removed her gun.

There were sounds everywhere, including more rumbling crashes deep in the building, but she focused on getting out of the building safely. Anything else would merely distract her, frighten her, slow her down. She didn't listen to her pounding heart or her rapid breaths. She only moved forward quickly, steadily, possessed by the need to get outside that building and then as far away from it as possible as soon as she could, that was her goal, the focus of her concentration.

She rounded the corner to the left without hesitation, and

her flashlight beam leapt ahead of her and fell on what looked like a gorilla.

Fara gasped and stopped, staring at the creature.

No, it wasn't a creature—it was a man dressed in black, including a black helmet over his head, and his clothes were bulky with body armor, just as Ollie had predicted. In his arms he held a pipe. No, it was some kind of odd-looking gun, more like a nozzle of sorts, and his finger was on a trigger.

Flames exploded from the nozzle and turned the world into a conflagration. The flames clung to Fara and filled her eyes and lungs and ears so that she could not hear her own screams.

"What the fuck!" Ram said. "Looks like it's really hit the fan here."

He drove slowly along the gravel road, the headlights illuminating bodies on the ground, a smashed gate, an abandoned police car. The right side of the car jumped twice as Ram drove over one of the bodies.

"Speed bump!" he shouted, then he bellowed laughter. "Oh, shit! A goddamned TV van. What are *they* doing here?"

Andy was relieved to see the KIEM van. There were other cars in the lot, as well . . . along with dead bodies on the ground.

Ram had wanted Donny to sit up front with him while Andy sat in the back, but Andy had flatly refused. "Go ahead and shoot me, if you want, but he sits in back with me." Ram had laughed then and claimed he was only joking around.

Andy had no idea why they were at the old hospital or what to expect next, but he knew he had to get Donny away from Ram at the first available opportunity.

"Look at *that*!" Ram said when a blast of fire exploded out of a second-floor window

"Whoa," Donny said, leaning forward in the seat. "What kind of place is this?"

"This is the old mental hospital I've told you about. Remember?"

He nodded. "Is it going to blow up?"

"I really don't know."

"See, my problem is, my boss is in there somewhere," Ram said. "The sheriff. He's in there and he's hurt and we've gotta get him out." He laughed. "Well, not we as in me and *you* guys!" Another laugh. "I mean we deputies." He got on the radio. "One-oh-two at the location. Please advise."

"Who else is on the scene?" the female voice on the radio asked.

"A TV van. KIEM. No other units. There are explosions in the building."

"Explosions? Is that what you said?"

"Yep, affirmative. A window blew out and—*whoa!* Another one just blew!"

Another fireball blew through the glass pane just two windows down from the first.

"I'm gonna get out and have a look around," Ram said. "Tell those other units to pick up some speed."

He racked the microphone, then unfastened his seat belt and opened the door. He looked over his shoulder and said, "You guys stay here, okay? I'm gonna see what I can see."

He got out and closed the door.

The news van wasn't very far away, maybe forty feet ahead of them. It was idling and its lights were on, there were people inside. Andy watched to see if that was where Ram was going. If it was, he decided he would get out and warn them. But instead, he walked toward the hospital, past the van.

"What're we gonna do, Dad?" Donny whispered.

Andy got his phone from his pocket and called 911. The call was answered by a recording that explained he would have to wait his turn due to a heavy calling load. He cursed under his breath as he put the phone away.

"I'm going to run over to that van and tell them what's happened to us," he said. "I can't leave you here in case he comes back, so you're going to have to come with me. I'm gonna hold your hand, but if I let go for some reason, I want you to stay right beside me, okay? Can you do that?"

Donny nodded. They removed their seat belts and Andy opened the door.

"Let's go." They got out, he grabbed Donny's hand, and they hurried toward the van. Andy kept glancing at Ram to make sure he still had his back to them. He led Donny to the passenger side so the van was between them and Ram. He knocked on the window.

The passenger seat was empty. The driver, a fat man wearing a cap, flipped the switch on his door that rolled down the window in front of Andy.

"Look, you've got to help us," Andy said. "My name's Andy, and I've got my little boy Donny with me. We've been kidnapped by the sheriff's deputy parked behind you. His name is Ram von Pohle and he's killed several people tonight, and—"

"Whoa, whoa," the driver said as two heads appeared, leaning forward from the backseat, "slow down. You've got a little boy with you?"

Andy bent down and picked up Donny so they could see him.

"You've got to let us in," he said. "This guy is going to kill us. He's insane, I'm serious, that's all he's been doing tonight, killing people. He killed a house full of people tonight that included my—" Andy stopped talking when he realized that Donny did not know his mother was dead. "You have to let us in."

Light flashed in the side-view mirror on the driver's side and the fat man turned to look at it.

348 *Frankenstorm*

"Looks like we've got some company coming," he said.

Ram's smiling face appeared in the driver's side window and he rapped on the glass with his knuckles, shining a flashlight into the van. "Roll it down," he said.

There were eight of the bulky, helmeted men in black and they moved through the hospital quickly and efficiently, leaving behind them rooms in flames. They knew where the oxygen tanks were kept and were counting on them to spread the fire.

They were to leave nothing and no one behind.

56

Latrice was lost, but she didn't let that slow her down. She continued to drive down Emerald Canyon, swerving around fallen trees and power poles, sending plumes of water up on either side of her Highlander as she drove through puddles and flooded sections of road.

Behind her, the police car kept up, its red and blue lights spinning, siren wailing.

"No, no, no, no, I'm not stoppin' for *you*, Mr. Policeman, I've got shit to do! The fuck you think I am, stupid?" Latrice shouted at the rearview mirror.

The road curved to the right, and her headlight beams cut through the rain as she followed it around, and the beams fell on a large redwood tree across the road a hundred yards ahead. Lodged against the tree was a large, half-crushed truck camper without a truck.

"Shit!" Latrice said as she hit the brake.

The Highlander went into a sideways skid over the wet road and slammed broadside into the tree. The airbag deployed and Latrice was momentarily stunned once the SUV stopped moving. Then she began struggling against the bag. She groped for the door handle with her left hand, found it, and shoved the door open. She squeezed out of the seat and fell from the SUV, hitting the pavement hard below.

She climbed to her feet and saw the police car parked several yards away, facing her. The car's door was open and the police officer was heading toward her.

Latrice began to stomp toward him, her right arm outstretched, finger pointing at him as she shouted, "Motherfucker, you *made* me do that! You fucking asshole, what were you chasing *me* for, motherfucker!"

As Latrice continued to shout at the cop, advancing on him while pointing at him, the officer quickly drew his gun and aimed it at her between both hands.

"Drop it!" he shouted. "Drop it now or I will shoot! Drop it *now*!"

She did not lower her arm and continued to shout at him as she drew closer.

The cop fired his gun twice.

A huge invisible fist punched Latrice in the chest, then in the gut. She found herself on the wet ground, staring up at the black sky.

She was vaguely aware of pain, of a shortness of breath that rapidly grew worse, but she quickly got to her knees, then her feet. She pointed at the cop again, screamed at him again.

"I told you to put it down, goddammit!" the cop shouted.

He fired again.

This time, fire began to spread through her abdomen. She went down again. The next time she tried to shout, she made only a gurgling sound as blood rose up in her throat.

She tried to get up again, but her strength was draining from her fast and she dropped back onto the pavement and closed her eyes. Rain fell on her face.

"I gotta get to my babies," she said, spitting blood, tasting it in her mouth, shallow breaths coming rapidly. "I gotta . . . get to my . . . my fuckin' babies . . . so I can . . . make them . . . pay."

When she opened her eyes again, the cop towered over her,

head forward, looking down at her. "Aaawww, *shit*," he said, staring at her hand. He bent down, pulled up the cuff of his right pants leg and produced a small gun. He put it in her hand, then closed her fingers around it.

Blood bubbled up from Latrice's mouth and dribbled down her cheeks when she said, "Fuck you." Then she died.

Emilio's testicles throbbed with pain that extended into his gut and made him severely nauseated. On hands and knees, he stared at the floor and waited to see if he was going to vomit. When he didn't, he slowly got to his feet with a grunt.

Ollie was rubbing his jaw. "That woman is dangerous," he said.

Then they heard her scream.

"Oh, Jesus," Emilio groaned, limping to the door. He stepped outside and looked down the corridor in the direction Fara had fled, but he saw nothing.

He heard something, though. Rumbling. And crashing. He'd been hearing it occasionally for a while, but now it was becoming steady. He went back into the office and said, "What's that noise?"

"Holy shit," Ollie said. He went to the couch and clumsily, roughly pushed Sheriff Kaufman into a sitting position, saying, "C'mon, sheriff, we've gotta get outta here. Now. Everybody. *Now*! I think this fuckin' building is coming down."

Emilio didn't stop to think about it. In spite of his aching balls, he helped Ollie. Flanking the sheriff, the three of them left the office and hurried down the corridor with only Ollie's headlamp to guide them.

They turned left down the main corridor. Sections of the walls on each side were in flames.

The rumbling grew louder, like the whole world was falling in on itself.

* * *

Ivan turned to the man and his son and put a finger to his mouth, signaling them to be quiet. Then he leaned forward along with Jack as Leon cracked the window a couple of inches. Wind and rain blew into the van.

"Can I help you, officer?" Leon said.

The deputy grinned and said, "Yeah, you can let them out of the van for me, okay? My friend Andy and his son. They're coming with me."

"Well, I don't think they want to get out of the van," Leon said.

The deputy reached for the door handle to open it, but Leon quickly hit the lock. The grin did not go away as the deputy said, "You can be arrested for that, you know."

Lights grew brighter on both sides of the van as more cars drove into the parking lot. One of them pulled up behind the deputy. It was another sheriff's department patrol car. The passenger door opened and a deputy got out. He had a mustache and a puffy face.

"Hey, Ram, what's going on?" he said.

"This man is holding a friend of mine and his son in his van," Ram said.

The mustached deputy looked at Leon. "You want to explain?"

Leon said, "The man in the backseat says this deputy has kidnapped him and his son and he's going to kill them. He also says this deputy has killed a lot of people tonight. Says he's unbalanced. He's asked us for help."

Ram's smile disappeared and was replaced by a look of outrage.

The mustache turned to him and said, "What's going on here, Ram?"

Ram ignored him and continued to glare at Leon.

The mustache said, "Ram, what's the—"

Ram suddenly bared his teeth as he lifted his gun to the window and pointed it at Leon, saying, "Let them out of the fucking van, asshole."

"Hey, hey, Ram!" the mustache said, putting a hand on Ram's gun arm and pushing it down. "What the hell's the matter with you? Come here, come on, step over here with me."

The mustache led Ram over to the car he'd gotten out of and began talking to him, standing close.

"Jesus Christ," Leon said with a sigh. "I may have wet myself."

"I'm telling you, he's insane," Andy said.

"What should I do when they come back, Jack?" Leon said.

"Just do what you're doing. Answer the questions."

"You don't understand," Andy said tremulously. "He's dangerous. He's got a gun, he'll shoot you. Without batting an eye, he'll shoot you."

"We're wasting time," Jack said. "We should have a camera set up so we can catch this."

"Maybe you should just go about your business," Ivan said.

"You think?" Jack said.

"Yeah, just get out and do the stuff you'd normally do. Set up for your piece. And I should be getting this," he said, taking his cell phone from his pocket as he watched the flames still burning in the two third-floor windows.

There was a gunshot and Ivan leaned forward to look out Jack's window again, absently fumbling with his phone.

The mustache lay on the ground and Ram was heading toward them again, gun in hand, chin jutting, eyes narrowed.

"Holy shit, he shot the other cop!" Leon said.

"I told you, *I told you*!" Andy said.

Leon rolled the window all the way up as Ram approached, and the deputy shouted something at him.

Ivan raised his phone and started taking video.

Ram raised his gun, aimed it at Leon, and fired. The

window shattered, and so did the back of Leon's head as he was thrown to the side, into the boxes on the passenger seat. He rolled limply forward and his bloody head dropped toward the floorboard in front of the passenger seat.

"Jesus Christ!" Ivan shouted in horror.

Donny clutched Andy's arm with both hands and said quietly but frantically, "Let's go, Dad, please, let's get out of here, let's get away from him."

There was an explosion of activity outside the van. Voices were shouting Ram's name as car doors slammed.

"Ram!" someone shouted. "Drop the gun!"

Ram shouted something.

"Get out, get out," the other man in the backseat said. "Now, now, get out and get away from the van."

Ivan slid the door open and they quickly piled out as a flurry of gunshots erupted on the other side of the van. Andy held Donny in his arms as he hurried away from the van, running toward the gate. Ivan followed them. Once they were several yards away, they turned around.

Just in time to see the fiery explosion on the second floor.

A bright ball of fire blossomed out of the window and took the window with it, along with a hefty part of the wall. Plaster and wood and glass and more fire exploded into the night and rained down on the ground below.

Halfway through it, Ivan turned his cell phone toward the flames.

Debris rained on several people who came running out of the entrance, shouting and waving at them.

A rumbling sound grew after the explosion had fallen silent, a low, pounding, crashing sound from somewhere in the building.

"Whassat noise, Dad?" Donny asked.

"I'm not sure but I think we should stay back here."

Still aiming his phone at the building, Ivan said, "I think we should get farther back than that."

The rumbling grew to a crescendo as, from apparently nowhere, clouds of dust billowed upward, swirling in the wind, some of it rolling toward them.

"Jesus, the building is collapsing!" Ivan shouted as he turned to Andy and his son, throwing an arm around each and pushing them away from hospital and toward the gate. He vaguely noticed that three other cars had just arrived, all sheriff's department patrol cars.

As the old hospital's collapse grew louder, dust and smoke and fire billowed outward in all directions.

Everyone in the parking lot turned and ran toward the gate, away from the burning, collapsing building. They gathered there as all the noise died down.

All they saw was a pile of rubble where an empty mental hospital was supposed to be.

Epilogue

"Welcome to this special Red Pill Radio podcast. I'm Ivan Renner.

"What you're about to hear is a recording of Dr. Fara McManus. She was part of the team working in the old Springmeier Neuropsychiatric Hospital for Vendon Labs. This recording is a confession. In it, she explains what they were really doing at Springmeier. The official story was that they were developing new antibiotics to fight antibiotic resistant infections. That was not true.

"I have given this recording to Jack Bembenek of KIEM News, and it will be picked up by other news outlets, I'm sure.

"Some of the people who died during last night's hurricane did not die because of the hurricane. They died because of what was done to them by others. When you hear why, I hope you'll get angry. It's happened before. And if you don't get angry and do something about it . . . it probably will happen again."

Hurricane Quentin had torn its way up the coast through Del Norte County and into Oregon, all the way up through Lane County, past Eugene, before it began to dissipate.

The official death toll had not yet been tallied when news of Ivan's recording and the story behind it began to spread the next day. The story was picked up by every major news outlet in the country, and soon, in the world.

Two days later, the Humboldt County Sheriff's Department released a statement expressing suspicion that Deputy Ram von Pohle had somehow contracted the virus created in Springmeier. Sheriff Mitch Kaufman stated that it was the only reason he could imagine for such an upright family man and a sheriff's deputy of long standing to suddenly murder his wife, his children, and a neighbor, then do the other things he apparently had done.

The day after that, Andy Rodriguez's attorney held a press conference to announce that the sheriff was mistaken, that Ram von Pohle was a cold-blooded murder.

The story captured local attention immediately and became a preoccupation.

Ollie had taken twenty-four men into Springmeier Neuropsychiatric Hospital. It seemed like too many at first, but he wasn't sure where the homeless people would be inside that big hospital and he figured more men would find them faster.

Nine of his men came out of the building.

Ollie quickly became a TV personality, thanks to his appearances on the news. When asked by a CNN reporter why he'd risked his life and the lives of his men to rescue the homeless people being held inside the hospital, he said, "Because that's the kind of thing a good American does, and whatever you might have heard, I'm a good goddamned American."

* * *

The work done in Springmeier Neuropsychiatric Hospital quickly overshadowed the story of the hurricane and became the topic of conversation in and outside the United States.

Vendon Labs denied that they knew what Corcoran was doing and expressed outrage over the revelation. A statement was released admitting that Dr. Corcoran had been having difficulties with addiction lately, but no one at Vendon Labs knew how severe the problem had become. The company maintained that the aim of the project had been to develop new antibiotics to fight antibiotic-resistant infections and at no time were they working on a weaponized virus.

No one believed them.

The White House released a statement claiming that Vendon Labs had no connection whatsoever to the Pentagon or military.

No one believed them.

But the only evidence that such a government-funded project had taken place was Dr. Fara McManus's recorded statement. She could not back that up because she was dead.

No one believed Vendon Labs or the government . . . but no one knew what to do about it.

Donny had nightmares. Andy was sure he would for some time. Maybe the rest of his life. He had explained to the boy what had happened to his mother. Donny took the news quietly, then dismissed himself and went to his room.

It would take time. But Andy had plenty of that, and he was willing to give all of it to his son.

Early Saturday morning, Latrice was placed in the morgue of St. Joseph Hospital in Eureka as a Jane Doe. She was put there with the other Jane and John Does who had been left behind by the storm. Statements were released asking anyone who may have information about the Does to please come forward.

Latrice had left her purse in Giff's house, so she had no identification on her. No one knew she carried a deadly virus. She had been shot to death.

She lay in her drawer, waiting for someone to come take her home.

The Guy Down the Street

Once again, this is for
Dawn
25 years and counting

and for
Grey, Lamont, Yuki, Pywacket,
and Mina,
whom we miss every day

1

Look at her. Bare ass up in the air, feet apart. A big smile on her upside-down face as she looks back between her thighs. Now she reaches down and moves her fingers between her legs. I can't believe it. She's laughing, having fun. She's not being forced to do anything against her will. She's *enjoying* herself!

The man shooting the video tells her to get on the sofa. He has a friendly voice, not exactly effeminate, but hardly masculine. Soft, gentle. And familiar. I've heard it before, but cannot pin it down.

"Beautiful," he says as she spreads her legs on the sofa. "Yeah, that's hot. You wanna tell us a little about yourself, Tiffany?"

Tiffany? What a repugnant name. I bet that was his idea. She would never choose to be called something as precious and tiara-friendly as *Tiffany*. But I could be wrong—it seems there is a lot I don't know about her.

"Well, what do you want to know?" she asks.

"Tell us what kind of boys you like."

"I don't like boys. I like *men*." She laughs again, fondles herself as she talks.

"And what do you like to do with your men?"

"Well, I like to . . ." She pauses, giggles. She is embarrassed. Sitting there naked, masturbating on the Internet in front of anyone who wants to watch, and she's embarrassed to talk about what she likes to do with her "men." I don't know whether to pull my hair out screaming, or to laugh.

"Go on, you can say it," the man says. "They all wanna know."

"Well, I like to . . . y'know, give head. Some girls don't. They're all, '*Eeewww*!' and like, 'It's so *gross*!' Some won't do it at all. But I'm totally into it. As long as he, like, goes down on *me*, y'know?"

"So, you're very oral."

"Yeah."

I feel a chill, and my stomach begins to churn.

They go on talking until she becomes distracted and quiet. He says nothing for a while and lets her masturbate.

I have to look away. Horror and rage and guilt mix badly in my stomach, like three kinds of cheap liquor. I am not supposed to see what's on the screen. I don't *want* to see it. But there she is, for all the world to watch. I clutch the small plastic armrests of the chair, squeeze and pull them so hard they creak. My fingers become numb, wrists hurt, but it keeps me from crying out. From throwing up.

They're talking again. I turn my head slowly toward the screen—not all the way, though—eyes narrowed down to razor-thin slits, hand ready to cover them. The way I used to watch scary movies as a kid.

"You look like you're really into that," he says.

She turns on her side with a shrill squeal, presses her legs together. Says something into the cushion.

"What?"

"I said I forgot you were there."

"Well, don't stop now. Looked like you were getting close."

She sits up, tries to continue, but is overtaken by giggles.

The camera wobbles as he approaches her. "You just need something to take your mind off the camera," he says.

"Like that big bulge in your pants?" she asks with a laugh, pointing at his crotch.

He turns the camera down so we can see his erection pressing against denim.

"Well, you said you like doing it, Tiffany."

"I do." As she leans forward, she looks up at the camera with a naughty, teasing smile. It's a face I have never seen before. A face I was never meant to see.

She unfastens his jeans easily, pulls them down, and when his penis springs free, she takes it in her mouth.

My jaws burn from clenching my teeth. I turn away again and stand, walk around the desk. My voice is hoarse and unsteady as I say, "I can't watch any more of this."

"He shows himself pretty soon," Wylie says. He stands against the wall next to the window, behind the chair I was sitting in a moment earlier.

It is his office, his computer. With the exception of shopping for Christmas presents, I have managed to stay away from the Internet. I waste enough of my time as it is; I don't need a new distraction. But over the last year or so, he had become an Internet junkie.

Wylie lives with his wife, Nadine, and their two teenage daughters, Erica and Cherine, across the street from us. "Us" being my wife, Renee, our daughter, Melinda, and myself. He is an officer of the Redding Police Department. Gregarious, generous, always asking us over for drinks or a barbecue. Sometimes we go, sometimes not. Wylie can be moody, temperamental, quick to anger. This is sometimes, but not always, connected to alcohol. He's fine as long as he sticks to beer, but as soon as he switches to Jack Daniel's, it's time to leave, or at least lay low. Sometimes something will set him off while he's sober as a judge. But for the most part, we enjoy his company, and Renee and Nadine are good friends. But if Wylie and I were kids, he'd be the kind of kid I would avoid, knowing that sooner or later, there would be trouble, whether we got into it or Wylie caused it. Trouble just seems to be a part of Wylie Keene, like the smell of his cologne.

Wylie called me over earlier, said he wanted to show me something. He kept smiling. An odd smile, not friendly in the least. The smile of a crocodile.

"This isn't going to be easy to watch," Wylie said as he clicked his mouse a few times. He stood and told me to take the chair.

Wylie was right.

"Can't you fast-forward it, or something?" I ask, pressing fingertips into my temples.

"Nope. Can't fast-forward the Real Player."

"Then just tell me who it is, Wylie. I'm assuming you know, right?"

"Yeah, I know. But it's important you *see* it."

"*Why*? See what?"

"In a minute. Okay, here it is. Come on." He beckoned me impatiently and I returned to the chair.

The camera apparently is mounted on a tripod now. Naked, the man kneels in front of her and puts his face between her thighs. She makes breathy sounds of pleasure. He is small, lean, and wiry, pale as milk. His back is covered with freckles, moles, and a patch of acne between the shoulder blades. He has rusty hair, pulled back tight in a ponytail.

I don't need to see his face. I recognize him immediately. The name of the man having sex on the Internet with my sixteen-year-old daughter Melinda is Teklenburg. Charles Teklenburg, but he likes everyone to call him Chick. For short. Maybe forty-five, a bit of a relic with his long hair, ponytail, and hippy clothes. He even drives an old Volkswagen van from the late sixties. He lives alone with his two chows. Just down the street, at the very end. People sometimes use his driveway to turn around when they realize Gyldcrest goes nowhere. They never see the sign.

I stand so suddenly, the chair wheels away and Wylie catches it before it hits the wall. "My God, Wylie, why aren't you *doing* something about this?" Tears burn my throat and eyes, and my crippled voice is all over the scale.

"What do you mean?"

"I mean, you're a *cop*! Why is that son of a bitch still living comfortably in his house at the end of the street? Why are you coming to *me*, for Christ's sake, you're a *cop*. Why haven't you—"

He puts his hands on my shoulders, squeezes them hard. "Whoa, hold it down, okay? I haven't told Deeny about this yet. Cherine's on the website, too, Clark. So are other girls from the neighborhood. Our neighbors' daughters."

"Oh, Jesus."

"Yeah, I'm a cop, and yeah, we're gonna do something about this, that's why you had to see it. But the two don't have anything to do with each other, okay?"

"What . . . what do you mean?"

"I mean, we're gonna kill the bastard."

2

There will be no sleep until we talk, but I get into bed anyway in my T-shirt and boxers.

I was unable to concentrate enough to hold a conversation at dinner, and Renee noticed. I snapped at her, she snapped back. A couple of martinis before dinner probably didn't help, something I normally do only on weekends. On top of that, Renee tried Deeny's recipe for spinach-stuffed chicken breasts tonight and thought I hated it because I only took a couple bites. I did not eat it because I could not eat.

"I can't tell you what to do," Wylie said that afternoon in his office. "But I think telling Renee'd be a bad idea. I'm not telling Deeny. Not till we're done. Then I'll tell her and we'll deal with Cherine. I wouldn't tell Melinda, either, I was you. Keep her the hell away from Teklenburg, but wait till we're done with him before you sit her down. Like I said, it's up to you. But I wouldn't. Women just can't keep their damned mouths shut."

I know Wylie is right—about keeping it to myself, anyway—but I don't know how I can keep it from Renee. And how can I not confront Melinda? I want to shout at her and vent my rage, my confusion. I want to hold her tight in my arms and never let her out of the house again.

Doesn't she feel *any* kind of repulsion at the idea of having sex on the Internet with a man almost three times her age? In front of the whole world? That's not the girl we raised.

I punch my pillows a little too hard as I try to get comfortable in bed.

Could Melinda be taking drugs? That would help explain it. But how could I miss that? How could Renee and I not notice something like that? We know what the warning signs are, but we have not seen any of them.

Fortunately, Melinda ate dinner in her bedroom, where she spent the entire evening. Summer vacation ends in a few weeks. She will go back to school, and I will go back to work teaching English at Shasta College. But those weeks will be an eternity if I do not deal with her soon. First, I have to tell Renee.

People usually laugh when I say I tell my wife everything, but it's true. Renee does the same with me. Not as a duty, but because we want to. We married a few years out of college, each with two lovers under our belts, and have been faithful to our vows for almost twenty years (more than twenty-three if you count the years we lived in sin before marrying). Adulterous opportunities have arisen for both of us, and we have turned them down. Not as a duty, but because we wanted to. We always tell each other about them later and laugh together. I was taking my problems to her even before we started dating. Renee is smart—a lot smarter than I—and level-headed. She approaches problems with confidence, fully intending to best them. She almost always does.

But I'm not sure how she will approach *this* problem. We already lost one child—our first, at the age of four, before Melinda was born—and I know if she sees the video I watched at Wylie's, she will fall apart as completely as if she's lost another. That cannot happen. I have to tell her, and now. It seems I've had this bottled up inside me for weeks, months, not just a matter of hours.

Renee comes to her side of the bed and stands there in
her lavender robe, arms interlocked over her breasts. "Are you
going to tell me what's wrong?"

I smile, pat her side of the bed. "Yes, I promise. Come to
bed." My lips won't stop trembling as I smile, so I stop, bite
my lower lip.

Renee does not fall apart at the news as I expected. I
thought there would be tears, sobbing. Instead, her response
is one of ferocious anger. I have never seen her so enraged.
Her eyes become dark and her chin juts, lower teeth visible
between her lips. Rigid cords of muscle stood out in her neck
and her voice becomes a low growl.

"How long have you known about this?" she asks. "Why
didn't you tell me sooner?"

"I told you, I just found out this afternoon, and I—"

"And you're telling me *now*?"

This is going to be more difficult than I anticipated.

When she was a little girl, Renee was sexually molested by
her father. She sometimes jokes about killing him, and sometimes I wonder how serious she might be. I did not consider
this before telling her about Melinda and Teklenburg. I should
have. She is seeing this not only from the viewpoint of a
mother, but from that of a cruelly abused child. I wonder if
now, along with her father, she wants to kill Chick Teklenburg, too.

I hold her close and she shivers in my arms as I tell her the
rest. About Cherine, and that other young girls in the neighborhood are on Teklenburg's website. Other daughters.

Renee bounds from the bed and paces the floor, fists
clenched at her sides. "I want to kill him," she says, voice low
but trembling. She stops pacing at the foot of the bed and
faces me. "Give me your gun. I want to kill him now. Right
now, tonight."

I get out of bed and go to her. "Wylie feels the same way.
And he wants me to help."

"He's a cop. Why does he need your help? He should take care of this himself, right away, Goddammit. Why hasn't he already, why hasn't—"

"He wants us to *kill* this guy, Renee."

She looks at me for several seconds, teeth clenched and eyes wide. "Then do it. No jury in the world would convict you." She is very serious.

I shake my head. "Honey, that's premeditated murder. The reason behind it won't make much difference, if any at all."

"He's a cop," she says again. "Do you think he's going to let you two get caught? Don't you think he knows what he's doing?"

Yes, I do think he knows what he's doing. That makes it all the more appealing. I *want* to kill Chick Teklenburg. I want to dismember him with my bare hands. But it would mean life in prison, maybe the death penalty, if we're caught. Who better to keep that from happening than a friendly, like-minded cop?

I stroke Renee's hair as I hold her. "We can't say anything about this to Mel yet."

"Are you out of your mind? I'd like to go to her room right now and—"

"She might warn Captain Video that we know what he's up to," I whisper.

She pulls away and frowns at me. "Do you really think she'd do that?"

"Did you think she'd do *this*?"

I pull Renee close again. She trembles rigidly in my arms, as if feverish. Her tears fall on my neck, but she is not really crying, not screwing up her face and sobbing. She's too angry for that. I can hear her anger boiling just beneath the smooth surface of her low, level voice.

"I want to help you," she says against my shoulder.

"What? Help me—"

"I'll do whatever you want. I'll cut him up into tiny pieces for you. I'll even kill him, if you want. I think it should be something slow. And painful."

The even, serious tone of her voice chills my blood. I tell myself she's just not taking this well, that's all; she'll feel differently once it sinks in. But I'm not so sure. Without comment, I lead her slowly back to the bed. I am exhausted and want to sleep, but I know I won't until Renee calms down.

She takes a Xanax and we go back to bed. Renee talks in whispers, partly to me, but mostly to herself, I think. About torturing Teklenburg, killing him. I stroke her neck and make small sounds of acknowledgment in my throat as she talks, and try not to visualize the things she is saying. Her whispers fade, words become garbled and farther apart. I am relieved to hear her quiet, purring snore. But sleep does not come as easily for me, and I spend most of the night staring into the bedroom's darkness. Watching that stringy old hippy fuck my daughter.

3

Chick Teklenburg moved into the house at the end of Gyldcrest just short of a year ago. Like the family of strict Jehovah's Witnesses who lived there before him, he keeps to himself. He's friendly enough if you meet him on the sidewalk, even calls hello from across the street. But he makes no effort to get to know anyone in the neighborhood. He put up no decorations last Christmas, which pissed a lot of people off because it probably cost Gyldcrest a special color photo spread in the Christmas Day edition of the Redding *Record Searchlight*. Gyldcrest won that honor four Christmases in a row—but then the Jehovah's Witnesses moved in. Chick was the only one on the street who did not participate in this year's Gyldcrest Spring Yard Sale, an event that grew bigger and drew more attention from around the state each year. Those who gave him a pass at Christmas were not so charitable about the big yard sale weekend.

If everyone on the street were to find out about *this* . . . I'm not sure what they would do. But it would not be good for Chick Teklenburg.

Minutes after Renee leaves for work this morning, Wylie calls. Says he wants me to meet a friend of his. Deeny and the girls went shopping, so I should just let myself in the front door. So I do.

His friend is a nervous little guy he introduces only as Ricky. A colleague, he says. He looks more like one of those guys who washes your windshield without asking at a red light and then expects a tip for it. He wears a dirty white T-shirt beneath an open blue chambray shirt, torn jeans, dilapidated sneakers. He looks in his mid-thirties, but that stubble on his face might add a couple years.

"Nice to meet you," I say as I sit on the sofa.

Ricky sits hunched forward on an ottoman and Wylie wanders around the living room with a tall glass of orange juice.

"See, I own Ricky," Wylie says, then laughs. "I've owned Ricky since 1993. Ain't that right, Ricky?"

Ricky shrugs a shoulder and smirks, but it is not a pleasant smirk.

"Ricky's my snitch. When he's not in jail, of course. He's a pyro. A firebug. I got a couple things on Ricky, here, could send him away for a long time. But I look the other way as long as he keeps his eyes and ears open for me. And helps me out if I happen to need it every once in a while. Like today. He's gonna help us out."

A few of my internal alarms go off, and with a jerk of my head, I silently ask Wylie to accompany me to the kitchen.

"Something wrong?" he asks. He gulps the rest of his orange juice, puts the glass on the counter. I can smell no alcohol on him, so I guess the juice was nothing more than juice. I hope.

"Look, Wylie, I haven't exactly said I'm going to do this."

He grins. "Well, y'gotta do it now, Clark."

"What do you mean?"

"Because you know *I'm* doin' it. If you don't do it, then I gotta kill you."

Before I can stir up enough saliva in my suddenly dry

mouth to respond, Wylie slaps me on the back and roars with laughter.

"You got any plans for dinner this evening?" he asks, still chuckling.

"Just the usual. Eating."

"Don't make any. I'm throwing a little barbecue for our flower child down the street. Think Renee would mind making her potato salad? She makes the best damned potato salad."

"She's working today. I doubt she'll have time."

"Too bad. Which do you like better, chicken, or burgers and dogs?"

"I always prefer burgers and dogs," I say, patting my softening belly.

"Burgers and dogs it is. Let's go." He puts his arm around me and leads me back into the living room. Says to Ricky, "You ready?"

Ricky stands, nods.

"Where are we going?" I ask.

"We're gonna walk down to Teklenburg's house," Wylie says.

"To invite him to the barbecue?"

"Yeah. Just making a friendly visit. Give Ricky a chance to look the place over, see what he's working with. Just go along with whatever I say, Clark."

"What are you going to say?"

"I don't know."

Dread constricts my throat. "Look, Wylie, I'm no good at this kind of thing, okay? I'm a lousy liar, I can't—"

"What's to be good at? Just smile and be friendly, Clark, that's all. You can do that—I've *seen* you!" More laughter.

An unfamiliar Volkswagen Jetta is parked at the curb in front of Chick Teklenburg's house. His old van is in front of the closed garage. Loud music plays inside.

On the front porch, Wylie knocks hard on the door. Several

seconds pass before he pounds harder, longer, then says, "He can't hear us. Let's stroll around to the backyard."

I quickly say, "Wait, do you think that's a good idea?"

"Sure, we're neighbors, aren't we? Why?" Wylie lowers his voice. "You don't think good ol' Chick's doing somethin' back there he'd be *ashamed* of, do you?" He laughs as he goes back down the steps and crosses the lawn.

I start to follow, but look back when Ricky doesn't move. Just stands on the porch looking the front of the house over carefully.

"You guys coming?" Wylie calls, and we jog across the lawn to catch up with him.

"He's got a couple of big chows, remember," I say as Wylie opens the gate in the tall, weathered, old wooden fence that surrounds the backyard.

"Chick!" Wylie calls as we walk along the side of the house. "Hey, Chick!"

The music's volume drops by half. There is movement in the house, just beyond the wall to our left. The curtains in the window just ahead of us part. Teklenburg lifts the sash, smiles at us through the screen, wearing jeans and no shirt.

"Hi, guys. What can I do ya for?"

"Hey, Chick, how goes it? We catch you at a bad time?"

"Kind of. I'm working."

"Working? Yeah, that's right, you said you're self-employed. What kinda work you do, anyway?"

"I'm an artist."

"An artist!" Wylie turns to me for a moment, eyebrows high. "Hey, Chick, you've met Clark, haven't you? Clark Fletcher from up the street. And this is Ricky, a buddy of mine. So, Chick, what kind of artist are you?"

His ponytail flops as he glances over his shoulder, preoc-cupied. "Um, the digital kind. My art is computer generated. It's, uh, kind of like—"

The high laughter of a young woman comes through the

open doorway behind him, followed by the young woman herself. Through the screen she is little more than a silhouette, but a shapely one.

Teklenburg turns to her and says, "I'll be there in a sec, okay? Just go back and wait for me."

"I suppose she's a professional model posing for you? Huh?" Wylie asks with a devilish grin.

Teklenburg smiles and nods. "Yeah, she is."

I cock my head to one side and say, "You need a model for computer-generated art?"

He clears his throat. "Well, uh, I've been trying some real world art lately. Sketching and painting. I'm painting a nude right now, and the model doesn't come cheap, guys, so—"

"Hear that, guys?" Wylie says over his shoulder. "How come you haven't invited your neighbors over to watch you work, Chick?" We all laugh then.

The pale, stringy hippy laughs with us, showing only the slightest hint of nervousness. The ease with which he lies makes me want to kill him right now, no waiting around. "I've gotta get back to it. Was there something—"

"Yeah, I wanted to invite you over for dinner tonight," Wylie says. "We're having a few people over for a barbecue. Just people from the neighborhood, here. Nothin' special, really, just a spur-of-the-moment thing. Burgers and hot dogs, potato salad."

"It's nice of you to ask, Wylie, but I'd probably be a bother. I'm a vegetarian."

"No bother at all! We got vegetarian hamburger patties. My wife's mother's a vegetarian, so we've gotta keep the freezer stocked."

"Really? You know, that sounds like just the thing I need. What can I bring?"

"What's your beverage of choice?"

"Usually white wine."

"Bring some. About six-thirty, okay?"

Teklenburg smiles. "See you then, guys." Starts to close the window.

"One more thing," Wylie says. "You mind if I take my buddy here in the back and show him your koi pond? He's thinking about starting one."

"Sure, man. Go ahead." He closes the window and the curtains fall back into place.

My heart is going off like a machine gun in my ears. Walking beside Wylie, I whisper, "How did you know he has a koi pond?"

"He told me. Sometimes I run into him while he's walking his dogs, and we shoot the bull a couple minutes."

As Wylie and I go to the attractive pond with a small wooden bridge arching over it, Ricky walks slowly along the back of the house.

"What's he doing?" I whisper.

"Trying to get a feel for the place. The plan was to go inside so he could look around. Didn't work out that way. You know what he's doing in there, don't you?"

"I've been trying not to think about it."

"Yeah, but that don't stop it. He's got himself another little girl in there. Got her in front of the camera. You think that car out front belongs to her parents? Or maybe it was a gift for her sixteenth birthday."

My fists are clenched so hard, my fingernails dig into the flesh of my palm. "Look, if you want to kill him now, right here, fine. Otherwise, knock it the hell off, okay?"

"Yeah. Sorry, Clark."

We watch the pretty fish in the pond until Ricky says he's ready to go, and we walk back to Wylie's house.

"Since when is Nadine's mother a vegetarian?" I ask. "She makes the best beef stroganoff in the world."

"Since a few minutes ago," Wylie says. "I made it up, figured he'd be more likely to come if we already had veggie burgers in the house. I'll have Deeny pick some up at the store." In the kitchen again, Wylie pours himself another orange juice. "Whatta you think, Ricky? Any good?"

Ricky takes an apple from a bowl of fruit on the small kitchen table, bites into it loudly. "Yeah, no problem."

"Sorry we couldn't get inside, but—"

"Nah, forget about it. That house is no big mystery. I get inside, I'll be fine."

I turn to Wylie. "Inside? When is he going inside?"

"During the barbecue." Wylie smiles. "All you gotta do is keep the vegetarian entertained, make sure he don't decide to go back to his house until Ricky's done."

"Done doing what?"

Wylie's big shoulders sag as he sighs. "You gotta pay attention, Clark, okay? Didn't I tell you Ricky's a firebug? He's a pro. Been doing it since he was a kid. Give him half an hour, he'll set up a fire to start whenever he wants it to, and once it does, nobody gets out." He smiles again. "*That's* what he's gonna do. After tonight, Clark, that fuckin' lettuce-eatin' prick's days of getting the little neighbor girls to take off their clothes are over."

Again, internal alarms are sounding. A brief wave of dizziness passes over me as I wonder what I've gotten into. "Wait, wait, how do you know there won't be someone in there with him?" I ask.

"Is Melinda gonna be over there tonight?" Wylie asks.

"Hell, no!"

"Neither is Cherine. And that's all I need to know."

I get a glass from the cupboard, fill it with ice water at the refrigerator door. Take a few long, hard gulps of it. "What do you need me for, Wylie?"

"Need you? I don't *need* you. I'm doing this no matter what. If you think I'm gonna let that son of a bitch get himself a high-priced attorney and squeak by with probation and some counseling, you're outta your fuckin' mind! I thought you'd feel the same way. I thought you'd *want* to know what he was doing with your daughter. Hell, I thought you'd want to help me with this. Otherwise, I wouldn't have brought it up."

I don't want to say it. It sounds so weak, so cowardly. But it is real, something I cannot ignore, so I say it, anyway. "Wylie, no one wants to hurt that guy more than I do, I swear. But if I get caught . . . I've got Renee and Melinda to take care of. I can't do this if there's a chance—"

Wylie laughs hard, shaking his head. "Renee makes more money with her realty business than you do teaching—whatta you mean, you've got Renee and Melinda to *take care* of ?"

As he laughs some more, I have an urge to punch him right in the face. It was a rotten thing to say, but my anger diminishes quickly. Too many other things eating at me, I guess.

Wylie finishes off his orange juice. "You don't have to worry about that. Won't happen."

"You don't know that. You can't."

He sets his empty glass on the counter hard and steps close to me. "I can't prove it to you, no. But I *know* it. You'll just have to trust me. If that's something you can't do . . . well, I thought we were friends, Clark, but maybe I was wrong."

I am surprised and touched, and feel a pang of guilt for not feeling the same way about him. I put a hand on his shoulder and say, "No, of course not, Wylie, you're not wrong about that."

"I mean, you're the only one I *told*, for cryin' out loud. I didn't tell the Hentoffs or the Griffens, and their daughters are on that website. So's the Elliott girl. I figured you and me, we could take care of it for everybody, and they wouldn't have to know. And even if we get nailed, Clark—and that's *not* gonna happen, I'm tellin' ya—but if we do, the shit's gonna land on me, not you. What the hell have you done? All you're gonna do is keep Tofu Boy occupied for a while. I'm the one employing the services of a known criminal. I'm the one playin' with fire here, no pun intended." He puts an arm around me, leads me out of the kitchen and to the front door. "You got nothing to worry about, Clark. You have my word. Now go home and do whatever it is you do. You started preparing for classes this fall yet?"

"I started doing that six weeks ago," I mutter.

He opens the door. "Then you've probably got work to do, huh? Just go home and keep busy till I give you a call, okay?"

"Okay," I say, stepping through the door. "See you later." I cross the street in a kind of daze, wondering what happened to my life. I had it just yesterday and it was perfectly fine.

4

Every summer, I wonder why the hell I live in Redding, California. The summers are miserably hot, and each one seems worse than the last. With August just starting, the worst is yet to come. It's too hot to cook indoors, so summer evenings always smell of meat cooking on grills in the open air.

It is muggier than usual this evening. There is no breeze. The air feels clenched.

"I don't understand why *I* have to do this," Melinda whines as we start across the street together. "Can't I stay home and eat a sandwich, or something?"

My voice is tense as I say, "We're going to eat, you can visit with Cherine and Erica, and then we'll go home. I don't want to hear any complaints. And don't even *ask* if you can go anywhere, because you can't."

"I wasn't going to—okay, what'd I do?" Melinda asks as we start up Wylie's steep driveway. "How come you're so pissed at me. Am I being punished?"

"Watch your language," Renee says.

"You're not being punished. Yet. But tonight, we need to talk."

Melinda stops walking and I turn to her. She looks at me with dread.

"Talk about what?" she asks.

"We'll talk about it tonight, at home. Come on." That will give her something to chew on for a while. She'll be so busy trying to figure out what I'm talking about, she won't have time to get into trouble.

The only guests to arrive before us are Monica and Phil Halprin. Chick Teklenburg is nowhere to be seen. Wylie greets us loudly, then beckons me over to the barbecue, where he stands in a bib apron that reads "Kill My Skillet!" on the front.

It's a standard Weber kettle-style barbecue. None of those pansy-assed gas barbecues for Wylie. At barbecues past, he has proudly claimed the title Master of the Charcoal Briquette. But not this evening. He curses the briquettes as he replaces the lid.

"I invited the Morgans and Elliots," he says, "but the Morgan boy's having a big pool party for his birthday, and the Elliots are helping out. They're probably gonna burn down the neighborhood with those damned torches. People like that even scare the hell out of Ricky."

Wylie refers to the tiki torches the Morgans have been lighting up in their backyard two or three times a week since the luau they threw back in June.

"Why isn't he here yet?" I ask.

"Don't worry, it's early."

"Where's Ricky?"

"In the kitchen cuttin' up carrots and celery."

My heart skips a beat. "Are you serious?"

"Yeah. What, you think he can't cut up carrots and celery?"

"No, I mean, why is he *here*? Shouldn't he be out of sight, waiting for—"

"Would you just calm down? Everything's cool. Jeez, look at you, you look like John Hurt in *Alien*." He laughs. "There's nothing to worry about, Clark, I mean it. You wanna know when you can worry? When *I* get worried. *Then* you can worry. Can I get you a beer?"

I take a couple deep breaths, trying to calm myself. My veins are already pumping with adrenaline and nothing has happened yet. "Yeah, a beer sounds good," I say, but quickly backtrack. "No, wait . . . are you drinking tonight, Wylie? No offense, but I'd really appreciate it if—"

He laughed. "Boy, you're coverin' all your bases, huh? No offense taken. I'm workin' tonight, Clark. I never drink when I'm workin'. But that don't mean you can't. In fact, you need to. C'mon, let's get you a beer, then you can mingle."

I don't feel like mingling. Honestly, I don't feel like being here. And for a while, I thought we wouldn't make it over here.

I told Renee about the picnic when she got home from work, and she groaned.

"Can't we just stay home and have pizza delivered?" she said. "I had a lousy day."

"I wish we could," I said. I told her Teklenburg would be there.

Her mouth dropped open, eyes widened impossibly, and her hands began to tremble. "Clark, you can't expect me to go to a barbecue with that . . . that . . . oh, *God*, I'd put a fork in his throat, Clark, I wouldn't be able to *help* myself!"

I led her to the kitchen, poured her a glass of wine. We went out on the back porch, sat on the swing and I told her Wylie's plan in whispers. Several emotions battled for dominance on her face as she thought about it. Finally, she whispered, "We can't take Melinda if he's going to be there."

"You want to leave her here by herself? No way. She's coming. It'll be interesting to see her reaction when she sees him there. When we get home tonight, we'll sit her down and have a talk."

More seconds passed. "So, you're really going to do this?"

"What do you mean? Last night, *you* wanted to do it."

Suddenly, she threw her arms around me and held me

close. "What did we do wrong, Clark? I mean, if he had forced her . . . if it had been against her will . . . that would be different. But you said she seemed to enjoy it. This is something she's been *keeping* from us. What did we do wrong?"

I could not answer her question, so I said nothing, just held her.

Wylie's stereo plays the Dixie Chicks through speakers mounted around the covered patio. In the center of the patio, a large metal tub of ice holds beer and soft drinks. Melinda huddles with Cherine and Erica in a corner, each with a soft drink in hand. Renee is helping Nadine in the kitchen and I wish she were with me now. I sip a Heineken, smile at Melinda. She turns away, looking pissed. I chat with Monica and Phil for a couple minutes, until Wylie joins us, says the burgers and dogs will be on the grill in no time, and then takes me aside.

He quietly says, "Why don't you go out front, see if that little alfalfa-sprout-eating prick is out there. Maybe he's not sure which house I'm in."

"Sure. Do me a favor and keep an eye on the girls, okay? Renee and Melinda are not to leave the premises."

"I told the girls if they even think of going anywhere tonight, I'll kill 'em, have 'em stuffed, and we'll drag 'em out at the holidays to prop up at the table."

We laugh, then I cross the yard, walk along the far side of the house toward the front. Kate and Barry Murchison are on their way to the backyard and smile.

"Wylie got them burgers cookin' yet?" Barry asked.

"I think the briquettes are giving him a hard time tonight, Barry."

"Oh, shit! Briquettes givin' *Wylie* a hard time?" His laughter sounds like a bad case of hiccups. "Man, that *can't* be good. I bet Wylie's pissed!"

"Why would Wylie be pissed?" Kate asks.

Still grinning, Barry says, "Shut up," and they walk on behind me.

I spot Chick Teklenburg coming up the street on this side. Head down, four fingers stuffed into each pocket of his jeans, something tucked under his left arm. He's not very big. I could overpower him easily. Get him in the shadows beside Wylie's house and kill him. Strangle him, maybe. Or maybe I'd just stomp on his skull till it was flat. It would feel so good.

"Hey, Chick," I say with a smile.

He smiles back, coming closer. "I hope I'm not late."

"Not at all. Wylie's still battling the briquettes." I turn around and we go up Wylie's driveway together.

"I got involved in work and lost track of time," he says. "I couldn't remember what time Wylie told me to come, and I was afraid I was late."

"Must be nice to do something you enjoy so much, you can lose track of time like that," I say, wanting to wrap my hands around his scrawny neck, dig my thumbs into his larynx.

He nods. "It's the only way to live, man. I love my work. It hasn't made me rich and famous, but it's made me very happy."

I want to scoop his eyeballs out of their sockets with my fingers and shove them into his mouth. Instead, I say, "I enjoy my work, but not that much." He is about to ask, but I don't wait. "I teach out at Shasta College. English. I like working with young people." I smile at him. "Of course, the young people *I* work with all have their clothes on."

He stumbles to a stop, turns to me. "Huh? I mean . . . what?"

"The model at your place this morning. You said she was naked."

His head tips back and he laughs, starts walking again. "Oh, yeah. She was, man. And she was beautiful."

He must know Melinda is my daughter. Unless he's an

idiot. For just a second, there, I thought I'd scared him, but now I'm not so sure. He's so relaxed, so casual.

"But when you're working on something," he says, "you really don't notice. I mean, the work takes over and you don't even think about it."

A yelp of laughter gets out before I can stop it. I ignore it and say, "That's interesting."

His head bobs a few times. I'd like to put it on the end of a stick.

We round the corner of the house to the backyard. "Would you like a beer?"

"Wylie told me to bring this," he says, taking the bottle of wine from under his arm. "I had it in the fridge for a while to chill.'"

"Let's go in the kitchen for a glass. I'll introduce you to my wife," I say, thinking, *Oh, yeah, she's just* dying *to meet you, buddy*.

Nadine is laughing her loud, wailing laugh as we walk into the kitchen. Ricky is washing his hands in the sink and Renee is taking a platter of deviled eggs from the refrigerator, setting it on the counter.

"Renee?" I say. "Chick's here."

As she turns, I feel genuine suspense. I have no idea what will be on her face, what she will say.

She is grinning.

"Hey, Chick," Ricky says, drying his hands on a couple of paper towels.

"Chick, this is my wife, Renee. Renee, this is Chick Teklenburg, our neighbor who keeps to himself."

He glances at me and chuckles.

Still grinning, Renee rushes toward him, and for an instant, I fear she's going to pounce on him, take him down to the floor, strangle him, and I almost step forward to stop her when she reaches out for his hand.

"Well, it's so nice to meet you, Mr. Teklenburg," she says

as they shake. "You know, I've wanted to drop by a few times, maybe bring you some cookies, or something, but you're so quiet down there at the end of the street, I'm afraid I'll be disturbing you, or interrupting something."

If it weren't for the fact that I know what is going through her head at that moment, if I weren't in on the whole thing, I would have no idea she wants to kill the man. She is genuinely warm. I married Meryl Streep.

"He's an artist, honey," I say, smiling.

"Really?" She turns to Nadine. "Did you know we had an artist living on the street?"

"I had no idea!" Nadine said loudly. She is even more outgoing than Wylie. I'm surprised she hasn't hugged Teklenburg yet. After all, she has no idea what he did to her daughter. "All this time we've been running into each other at Raley's a couple times a week, and you never said a *thing*." She swiped the dish towel at him. "Self-employed, he says. You're too modest, Chick." She points at the bottle. "Can I get you a glass for that, or are you drinking it straight from the bottle tonight?"

He laughs, nods. Nadine takes the bottle to open it.

"What kind of artist are you, Mr. Teklenburg?" Renee asks. She's giving him the same look she gives her clients, the you-are-the-only-other-person-in-this-room look.

"Call me Chick," he says. "Mr. Teklenburg is my dad, and man, if *he's* here, I'm gone." Renee laughs. "I'm a digital artist."

"That's fascinating," she says.

Nadine hands Teklenburg a glass of wine and we leave the kitchen, go outside to join the others. Renee and Teklenburg chat the whole time.

"Hey, Chick!" Wylie says. "Didn't know if you were gonna make it. I hope you brought an appetite."

"I'm ready to eat."

"Won't be long now. I'm having a little trouble with the

briquettes. Deeny bought a case of some off-brand at Costco and they're not worth a piss into the wind. Lessee, you got your drink. Here comes Deeny and Ricky with the appetizers."

Nadine and Ricky carry the trays to the patio and put them on a table. Wylie heads back to the barbecue and we go to the table, munch on celery, potato chips.

The sun is going down and long shadows are being dissolved. The lights in the covered patio have not been turned on yet, but in spite of the murkiness, I can see Melinda talking with Wylie's girls. They are leaning close, as if conspiring. She has not noticed Teklenburg. Not yet. Suddenly, Melinda stands up, looks around until she spots me. She hurries around the tub of ice.

"Dad, if it's only for a minute, can I go with Cherine and Erica to Target for a—"

"No."

"But we'll only be gone for a—"

"I said, *no*. And I've got news for you. Cherine and Erica can't go anywhere, either. Wylie told me. Have you met our neighbor?" I turn to Teklenburg, who is facing the table, dipping a chip. "Chick? This is our daughter, Melinda."

As he turns, he lifts a chip with a glob of green dip on it to his mouth. It freezes an inch from his parted lips when he sees her.

"Melinda, this is Chick Teklenburg," I say, smiling. "He's a digital artist."

She freezes, too, jaw slack.

As if cued by God Himself, the patio lights come on and they gawk at one another for a second. Finally, he pops the chip in his mouth, wipes his hand on his jeans, and extends it to her.

"Melinda," he says. "Nice to meet you."

"Yeah. Nice . . . to meet you, too." After a single shake, she drops his hand and turns to me again.

"No," I say before she can speak.

With a long sigh that sounds like her whole life is one big torture, Melinda turns and goes back to the corner to rejoin Cherine and Erica.

Teklenburg turns back to the table. To compose himself, I'm sure.

"She's a very obstinate girl," I say, slowly shaking my head.

Renee says, "We're thinking of selling her into slavery. You know anybody who'd be interested, Chick?"

His head turns to her in jerks and he stares at her a moment, mouth open. When Renee laughs, I laugh with her, and Teklenberg's whole body relaxes as he smiles slowly, finally laughs with us.

Lights on the back of the house brighten the backyard. Barry Murchison and Phil Halprin have started a horseshoe game on the lawn. Wylie is hovering nervously around the barbecue. He checks his watch. Ricky joins him and they confer, heads close together.

"Clark says you have a lovely koi pond," Renee says.

"Oh, yeah," Teklenburg says, head bobbing. "The koi. They need a lot of attention, but they're so beautiful, they're worth it."

"I've been thinking about putting a koi pond in the backyard," she says.

"You have?" It's the first I've heard about it.

"Oh, I haven't told *you*, of course, because you'd just say no and complain about what a bad idea it is, and then I'd go off and do it, anyway. I figure, why bother you with it," she says with a smile, puts an arm across my shoulders.

Teklenburg laughs.

"Anyway, I *have* been thinking about it," she says. "I just haven't looked into it. I know nothing about koi, or ponds. I've tried to find information on the Internet, but I just can't figure out those damned search motors."

"Engines," I say. "Search engines."

"Whatever." She turns to him, hooks a thumb in my direction. "He's no help, because he doesn't know any more about the Internet than I do."

I shake my head. "Not interested, thank you. I've got enough distractions in my life."

"Do you have much experience on the Internet, Chick?"

His eyebrows rise above his wire-framed glasses as he puts another potato chip into his mouth. Chews slowly a moment before saying, "The Internet?"

"Yeah. You know, I bet you could sell your work on the Internet. Or, maybe you do. Do you?"

He empties his wineglass with one gulp.

I say, "I've heard a lot of people are making money on that, um . . . what is it?"

"EBay," Renee says, nodding. "I have a client who makes little animals out of hot glue, puts eyes and ears on them. Makes a fortune selling them on eBay. So, do you sell any of your work on the Internet, Chick?"

His head bobs again, but he is tense. "Yeah, I've sold a few things on the Internet. At online art galleries, that sorta thing. Uh . . ." He looked around, eyes darting. "Could I use the—"

"Do you surf the web a lot?" Renee asks. Suddenly, there is an edge to her voice that I have heard before. It means she's getting angry and is about to blow.

"Well, not a lot," he says uncomfortably. "Could you tell me where the—"

"It's nice to know there's *art* on the Internet," she goes on. "I mean, the way people talk about it, you'd think there's nothing but naked girls and people having sex out there." She laughs, but it was a laugh that could cut flesh.

I close my hand on her elbow, squeeze. "Honey, I think you're keeping him from going to the bathroom."

He smiles and chuckles, but it's forced. "Could you point me in the right direction?"

"I'll take you, Chick," I say with a jerk of my head in the direction of the house. I lean close and whisper in Renee's ear, "Keep an eye on Snow White, over there. And calm down. Have another beer."

I take Teklenburg into the house. As I turn to close the kitchen door, I see Wylie hurrying in my direction.

"Right down that hall," I say, pointing. "Second door on the right."

As soon as he's gone, Wylie comes in, speaks in a whisper. "Goddamned briquettes wouldn't burn. I just put the first batch of patties and weenies on the grill."

"Where's Ricky?" Without meaning to, I whispered, too.

He leans close. "Down the street."

"I thought you were going with him."

"I was, but I couldn't get the fucking briquettes going. Figured I'd have a buncha burgers done by now. You wanna take over the grill for me?"

"Not if I'm supposed to keep an eye on him, too."

"Okay, maybe I'll have Deeny do it. But I don't want it to look like I'm sneakin' off somewhere."

"Get a couple veggie burgers cooked. Give him some food, and I'll try to keep him occupied for a while. How long will it take?"

"As long as it takes."

"Come on, Wylie, I can't keep him here forever."

"Shouldn't be more than thirty minutes. Just don't let him leave till we get back."

"You don't know how long it'll take? I thought you had this *planned*."

"Give me a break, I planned this overnight. If it hadn't been for—"

Footsteps in the hall shut him up. Teklenburg comes out of the hallway frowning, a hand on his stomach. "You know, guys" he says, "I'm not feeling so well. I'm thinking maybe I should go home and lie down."

Panic hits me hard for a moment. Ricky is already in the

house, but if Teklenburg decides he really wants to go home, how can we stop him?

"You just need to eat, that's all," Wylie says with booming enthusiasm. "I'll put a coupla yours on right away."

"No, really, I think—"

"You want some Alka-Seltzer?" Wylie asks. "Some Pepto-Bismol? Maalox? I got 'em all."

I put an arm around Teklenburg's shoulders and my insides recoil as I smile. "Can you try to stick around a little longer?" I ask. "This is the first time a lot of us have had a chance to meet you. Nadine would be very disappointed, I think, if you—"

"Oh, Deeny'd be beside herself," Wylie said, going to a kitchen cupboard. He opened it and removed something, handed it to Teklenburg. A packet of Maalox tablets. "Chew up a coupla these. If they don't help, then you should go home. But for Deeny's sake, stick around awhile. I'll get you a burger."

Wylie hurried out ahead of us and I followed with Teklenburg at my side.

A few more people wander in and the music changes from Dixie Chicks to Garth Brooks to Faith Hill. Not my kind of music, but it's just white noise. Nadine brings us hamburger patties and hot dogs on paper plates. We take them to the table where the condiments and buns are waiting.

"You feeling better?" I ask Teklenburg as I apply mustard and lettuce and onions to my burger.

"Yeah, I think so. A little hungry after smelling this."

"Good. You looked pretty sick for a few seconds, there."

He simply chuckles and says, "Yeah." Then bites into his veggie burger.

Nadine is cooking at the grill. Wylie is nowhere to be seen. After we finish our burgers, Renee suggests a game of horse-shoes.

"I know!" Renee says. Her beer is showing. "We can play

in teams." She turns back to the patio and calls, "Me*lin*da! Come play horsehoes with us."

Melinda mutters something grouchy.

"This is neither a suggestion nor a request, Melinda. Come, *now*."

She comes out of the patio with her head down, shoulders slumped.

Renee says, "You and Chick against your dad and me."

"*Mom*!" Melinda says, dragging the word into two long syllables.

Teklenburg smiles and holds up a hand, palm out. "Um, maybe I'll sit this out, 'cause I'm pretty stuffed, and I—"

"Oh, don't pay any attention to *her*," Renee says. "She's just feeling persecuted this evening. Come on, let's play!"

We walk over to the two metal stakes in the lawn and take sides. Teklenburg and Melinda talk to one another quietly, but try to keep their heads down when they do it. Probably hoping we won't notice. As we play, Renee and I whisper back and forth.

"I can't believe you did this," I say.

"I can't either. You should never let me drink."

"Right now, they are two of the most uncomfortable people in the world."

"Yeah. Ain't it a riot?" Her words are cold, without humor. "What do you suppose they're saying to each other right now?"

"I don't know, but the only reason I'm allowing it is that I know that son of a bitch is gonna be dead in a while."

I nearly burst out of my skin when someone claps me on the back.

"All systems go, Houston," Wylie says in my ear. Then he raises his arms high, waves his hands and shouts, "Deeny and I play the winners!"

5

We're smiling and holding hands, Renee and I, as we walk home. Melinda mopes a couple of steps behind us.

Laughter and shouting and splashing come from behind the Morgan house, just two up from us. Obnoxious rap music, too. The glow of their torches hovers over the backyard and tendrils of smoke rise above the roof of the house. Several unfamiliar cars are parked on both sides of the street. A couple of adults stand on the front lawn smoking cigarettes.

"Well, that was a pleasant evening," I say on the way up the front walk.

"Yes, it was," Renee says. "Did you have a nice evening, sweetheart?" No response. "Melinda? Did you have a nice evening?"

"No, the evening *sucked*."

I stop and turn to her. "Hey, you want to watch your language, little girl? Especially when you're talking to your mother. Maybe you talk that way around your friends, but not with your parents, do you under—" I interrupt myself by spinning around and going up the steps to the door. "Never mind, we'll talk inside." I take my keys from my pocket, unlock the door, and go in the house.

Melinda slinks away and heads down the hall for the sanctuary of her bedroom.

"Oh, no you don't!" I say. "In the living room."

Sighing and harrumphing, she turns and goes into the living room. A second later, the sound of a studio audience laughing itself silly comes from the television.

We're still standing in the entryway when Renee whispers, "You sure you want to do this now? I've been drinking."

"That's right. And you're happy and cuddly and a lot less likely to kill her."

She tries to suppress a laugh, but it snorts through her nose as she nods. She smiles, hooks her arm through mine, and leans on me as we go into the living room.

Melinda sits at the end of the sofa, legs curled up beneath her, watching *Family Ties* on television.

"Turn it off," I say.

She aims the remote, turns down the volume.

"I said *off*, not down."

Jutting her jaw, she turns off the television as Renee sits at the other end of the sofa. I sit in my recliner, swivel it toward her. Lean forward with elbows on knees. "Did you enjoy meeting Mr. Teklenburg tonight?"

She fidgets, brings her legs out, hugs her knees to her and stares at the television as if it's still on.

"Didn't you find him interesting?" I say. "I mean, Chick being an artist, and all, I thought he was *fascinating*, didn't you?"

She ducks her head lower, trying to hide behind her knees. Her eyes glisten with unfallen tears.

"I'm talking to you. *Tiffany*."

She buries her face between her knees. Her body quakes a few times, but she does not make a sound.

"I saw your video," I say. "One of them, anyway." I wait for some response. Instead, the phone chirps. Renee, who has been unusually, almost unsettlingly, quiet so far, starts to get up. "Let the machine get it," I say, and she nods. I turn to Melinda, open my mouth to continue, but I cannot. Out of habit, I am unable to ignore the answering machine. After my recorded voice, the beep sounds, then:

"Renee? You there, honey?" Renee's mother, Enid. She pauses a moment. "I been thinking about that neighbor of yours, and I think you'd better have Melinda checked for AIDS, and make sure she's not pregnant."

Melinda lifts her head, face red and streaked with tears, and shrieks, *"You told Grandma?"*

Enid's voice drones on as I say, "Dammit, Renee, I told you—*no* one."

Renee spread her arms wide. "Who's she gonna tell? She lives twenty minutes away in Cottonwood. It's not like she hangs around the neighborhood here."

Dropping her feet to the floor, Melinda grabs a throw pillow from the sofa, puts it in her lap and pounds a fist into it repeatedly. "Jesus *Christ*, I can't *believe* you told *Grandma*!" Her voice is quivery and thick with tears. "Who *else* did you tell, Mom? Did you put it in the *Recycler*?"

Renee's voice gradually raises as she says, "You're in no position to complain, young lady, so I don't want to hear any—"

"Whoa, hold it," I say, "can we quiet down, please? This is not going to be a shouting match. We're going to discuss this calmly and quietly, okay? Now, Melinda. Can you tell us, calmly and quietly, why you've been having sex with Chick Teklenburg on the Internet?"

She pounds the pillow again, then tosses it aside and stands. "You weren't supposed to know, you were *never* supposed to know!" She paces between Renee and myself.

"But we *do* know," Renee says. "And even if we never

found out, how could you live with yourself, Melinda? Why would you do such a thing?"

Melinda shrugged and spread her arms. "Why is it such a big deal? It's *not* a big deal! Nobody was hurt, and it's not like I was some, y'know, innocent virgin he, like, *corrupted*, or anything."

"But on the *Internet*!" Renee's anger breaks through and she stands, and steps in front of Melinda. "My God, why didn't you just do it in the street? Or on television? Don't you have *any* shame?"

"Look, he pays good, and Cherine knew I was saving for a car," Melinda explains, calmly, rationally, as if her words would solve everything.

"He *pays* you?" I ask. "Don't you have a problem with that? Don't you know what that's *called*?"

Renee's voice trembles as she says, "It's called prostitution, Melinda, and it makes you a *prostitute*."

"He doesn't pay for the *sex*!" She rolled her eyes. "He just pays for the right to use my image on his website. I would've had sex with him whether he was videotaping it or not."

Covering her eyes with a hand, Renee says, "Oh, sweet Jesus."

Someone shouts out in the street. Sounds like an angry teenager. I ignore it. My attention is already overtaxed as I try to keep up with the conversation, and at the same time, I'm preoccupied with how angry I am at Renee for telling her mother. My anger seems misdirected, though, because it's unlikely that Enid would be able to— *No!* a tiny voice in the back of my mind cries. *No, it is likely, it is!* And I know the voice is right, but I'm not sure why. It's just beyond my memory's reach.

Melinda takes a deep breath, rubs her hands over her face. Speaks softly in a monotone, never meeting Renee's eyes. "Look, Mom, sex is . . . well, it's just not like it was when you were my age."

Outside, a couple more voices shout at one another angrily. I glance in the direction of the front window, but stay in the chair.

"Don't give me that," Renee says. "You think your generation has reinvented sex because you're doing it on computer screens? You've just found a better way to degrade it, that's all. Sex is still *sex*, Melinda. And it still spreads diseases and gets you *pregnant*! We had this talk when you were nine, Melinda, remember?"

"Yeah, but—"

"No, I don't think you do! We've had a lot of talks about boys, too, haven't we? About how some will try to take advantage of you and—"

"I don't like boys, Mom. I like men."

Renee drops back onto the sofa, leans forward and puts her face in her hands.

Something clangs in the street outside, more voices shout. Frowning, I stand and go to the front window, pull the drapes apart.

The Morgan boy is walking down the street. The Elliott boy hurries to catch up with him. There are others, too, all walking toward the end of the street. My first thought is, *It's happened already? His house has already gone up in flames?* But I know that's not right. The voices would be different if that were the case; they would sound distressed, not angry. And they wouldn't be carrying torches. The Morgan boy and the Elliott boy are carrying burning torches. Tiki torches. And a hammer, the Morgan boy has a hammer. And behind him, Garry Elliott is jogging along, beer gut bouncing, a torch held in one hand, a large gun in another.

"Oh, shit," I say as it comes to me, the thing that's been bugging me about Renee telling her mother about Teklenburg.

"What?" Renee says, and I hear her and Melinda hurry toward me, feel Renee's hand on my back as she pulls the drape back farther. "What's happening? Where's everybody—"

"Your mother," I say as I back away from the window, and turn to her. "When did you talk to her?"

"This morning."

"Was she on her way to a hair appointment, by any chance?"

She turns to me, eyes round. "Yes! How did you—oh, God."

Enid Plummer, Renee's mother, has her hair done at the Golden Orchid, always by the same woman, one Janet Smidden, who lives with her husband and triplet toddlers just up the street and around the corner on Madison Way.

I step forward, jerk the drapes apart and look out the window again. Some are carrying golf clubs, others tire irons. Teenage boys, grown men. And women, too—there's Rita Bartlett, whose daughter recently turned seventeen, and she's carrying what looks like a .22 rifle, and behind her, Kate Murchison, who has two adolescent girls, carries a machete.

I shake my head and say, "Dammit, Renee, you had to tell your *mother*?"

"She can't be responsible for *this*," she says. She's emphatic, but I can hear the doubt in her voice.

"Are you kidding? She told Janet Smidden all about it, then Janet came home and made a few phone calls, word got around"—I point at the people going up the street—"and now they *all* know."

"Oh, my God, what're they gonna *do*?" Melinda asks. There is real concern in her voice, her eyes.

"They're going to kill him, that's what," I say, heading out of the living room.

Melinda moves close to the window, palms flat on the pane. "He hasn't done anything wrong!" she cries.

"You have no idea how idiotic you sound," Renee says as she follows me out of the living room. In the entryway, as I reach out to open the front door, she asks, "What exactly are you planning to do out there, Clark?"

I freeze. I have no idea what I will do out there. Try to hold

them off? Shout at them, *Hey, you people can't kill this guy—*
we're *killing him*! My hand drops from the doorknob and I go
to the phone in the kitchen, call Wylie. Nadine answers.

"Wylie said you might call," she says. "I'm supposed to
tell you not to worry, he's got everything under control."

"Oh. Okay."

"What's going *on* out there, anyway? He told me and the
girls to stay inside."

"That's probably a good idea, Nadine. Thanks." I turn the
phone off, return it to its base at the end of the counter.

"What did she say?" Renee asks. "Where's Wylie?"

"Both of you stay in the house." I go back to the front door,
but this time step outside and close it behind me.

Most of them have passed by now, but I can still hear them,
voices and footsteps fading to my left. I cross the down-
sloping lawn to the sidewalk and watch them. I can't tell how
many there are, but six . . . no, eight of them are carrying
torches.

What do they intend to do, anyway? Drag Teklenburg out
of the house and lynch him in the front yard? Thanks to them,
maybe he will be out of the house when it goes up in flames.

Across the street, Nadine stands at the window, trying to
see down the street from an impossible angle. She turns and
hurries away, probably to go to another window.

Up and down the street, dogs are barking. The air is still
and warm, and still carries the aromas of cut grass and out-
door cooking. It is a perfectly normal late-summer evening.
Except for the angry voices and the jewels of fire bobbing
through the night, all the way to the end of the street.

Wylie's voice rises above the others just before they reach
Teklenburg's house. I cannot understand his words, but the
neighborhood mob has come to a stop. Whatever he is saying,
they are listening to it.

But they do not listen long. Another male voice shouts in
protest. Then another. Some of the torches move forward,

then the whole crowd. More shouting. A gun fires and my feet leave the sidewalk for an instant.

"What's *happening*?" Renee calls from the porch.

"Stay inside," I say.

"Who's shooting?"

Someone is running up the street, away from the mob.

"I don't know. Go inside!"

I recognize the shadowy shape and step off the sidewalk, hurry down the road to meet him. "What the hell is going on?"

"Cat's outta the bag," Wylie says, winded. "Who'd you tell?"

"Renee. And she told her damned mother."

"Yeah, you gotta love women. If their mouths worked as much in bed as they do the rest of the time, we'd be happy men, huh?"

Glass shatters at the end of the road, followed by pounding, pounding. The shouting crescendos as more glass breaks.

"What should we do?" I ask. My voice wavers in time with my heart, which is beating in my throat.

"Well, I did all I could. I couldn't stop 'em."

"Who fired the gun?"

"Oh, that pompous ass Garry Elliott. Fired it in the air. I was hopin' it'd come back down and land right in his brain."

I can only see three . . . no, four torches now. Where are the other four? I turn to Wylie. "What do we *do*, dammit? They're going to kill him!"

Wylie laughs. "You're funny. Well, I'll go inside and call the station, tell 'em I did what I could. Have 'em send a couple cars down. An ambulance and a fire truck."

"A fire truck?"

"Yeah, I really oughtta make that call right away, but I'd hate to miss it. It should be any—"

A heavy *whump*—not quite an explosion—sounded from Teklenburg's house. Windowpanes blew out with a sudden clapping sound and flames belched from a few of the windows. It's impossible to tell where the fire started because suddenly it is everywhere, glowing in all the windows. But I can't hear it burning. Not above the screaming. Men and women screaming as they run from the fire, taking the flames with them, staggering, falling. Burning figures—I don't know how many—scatter and fall and scream.

Wylie chuckles, slaps me on the back. I turn to him, and he's grinning, watching the fire. "Yeah, that was something. Well, I gotta go make that call. You better run inside like you're in a hurry, too. 'Case somebody's watching us." He took off at a jog, disappearing up his driveway.

I realize I'm standing in the middle of the street. Wylie was right—if somebody's watching, they're going to remember me. I turn and hurry back up the lawn, into the house.

As I go inside, the screams fade to nothing behind me. But I can still hear them in my head. I rush to the bathroom and vomit.

6

Three people were killed in the fire—Garry Elliott, his seventeen-year-old son, David, and Chick Teklenburg—and nine were injured, five of them seriously. Fire trucks arrived, but by the time they were done, the house was nothing more than a black skeleton.

Although there was nothing left in the remains of the house to incriminate Teklenburg, police were told about the website. Wylie told his buddies on the force that he knew nothing about Teklenburg's activities until that evening, when people started talking. He helped question everyone on the street, including myself and Renee, which was a lot less stressful than being questioned by an unfamiliar officer in uniform.

The website remained on the Internet, and police confirmed the story. Somehow, Janet Smidden's name never came up, so police never questioned her to learn that she heard about what Chick Teklenburg was doing from Enid Plummer, which would have led them to contact Enid and learn that she'd heard about it from her daughter.

As Wylie predicted, everything went smoothly. No evidence of arson was found—Ricky was as good as Wylie said he was—and it was assumed the fire was started by the torches carried by those who had burst into the house.

But you've probably heard about it all by now. It was in the news for weeks.

Renee handled it all very well. Melinda, on the other hand, became silent and brooding for weeks afterward. We have decided to send her to a private school, and are looking around to find the one that's strictest with its students. We have been talking about taking her to a psychologist as well, maybe a psychiatrist. Her behavior has only gotten worse since the fire. We discovered she's been crawling out her bedroom window at night, going out with friends and getting drunk, stoned. She becomes more unfamiliar every day. I have little hope that counseling will help, but I've put up an optimistic front for Renee.

I don't talk about what happened, not with Renee or Wylie. As far as they know, I'm fine. But it eats at me inside. Probably always will.

Betty Elliott and her two remaining children—both girls, one eleven, one fifteen—moved out of their house on Gyldcrest almost immediately and went to live near Betty's mother in Mt. Shasta City. The FOR SALE sign stood in front of the house for more than three months. Just a few days ago, two men began moving in. I met them the first day, Sidney and Leo . . . I don't remember their last names. Nice guys, both of them in their late fifties. Sidney is an artist, and Leo is a retired florist. They moved up here from San Francisco, tired of city life, looking for a place to relax with their four cats.

The remains of Teklenburg's house were leveled, the lot put up for sale, although I don't know by whom, and do not care to find out. A new house will be built there eventually, and someone else will move in. I have no intention of getting to know the new residents. But even then, with a new house standing at the end of the street, the black and broken bones of the previous one long gone, the fire's scars will remain on the street. In the pink and twisted faces of those burned by it.

"What the hell you doin' out here in this cold, tryin' to catch pneumonia?" Wylie asks as he comes up the back steps to the porch.

I am sitting on one of the two chairs on the porch, beside a small table. The lamp on the table casts its glow on the John Irving novel I'm reading. "It's not that cold," I say. "And this is a warm sweater."

Renee and I have turned down the last few invitations to cross the street to eat or drink. Renee would have gone, but I didn't want to. It would be just like Wylie to joke about what happened. A lot. I knew I couldn't take that. I thought Wylie would get the hint, but no, I doubt it ever occurred to him I didn't want to see him.

"What you been up to, Clark? Haven't seen you in a while."

"Busy with classes."

He's wearing a fat down jacket and removes a Heineken from each pocket, grinning. Hands me one, sits in the other chair as he twists the cap off.

"Are you sure?" He takes a sip. "Look, Clark, if I've done something to offend you, I want you to let me know, okay? I'd do the same for you. I don't believe in holding things in, y'know?"

I'm surprised, but keep it to myself. I'm not sure what to say for a moment. Then: "No, Clark, you haven't done anything to offend me."

"Anything wrong?"

I slip my bookmark into the book, close it. "It's just . . . well, I don't want to talk about . . . about what happened."

"What happened when?"

"You know what I mean."

He leans forward in the chair. "Clark, I've already forgotten it. It's over with, a done deal. You oughtta do the same."

I am tremendously relieved to hear Wylie say that. But it's not something I could ever forget.

"You meet the new neighbors yet?" he asks.

"Yes. Have you?"

"Yeah, I met 'em. Didn't think I'd ever see it. This town's gone right down the shitter."

"What do you mean?"

"I mean I've lived in this town all my life, and it's always been a good family town, a good place to raise kids. But in the last ten or fifteen years, with all them people moving up from the Gay Bay, I just can't say that about Redding anymore."

I sipped my beer and closed my eyes so Wylie would not see them roll.

"It's one thing to see 'em swishin' around in the mall, or in restaurants," he went on. "But I'll be damned if I'm gonna sit by and watch 'em move in on Gyldcrest. Hell, first our girls were being preyed on, now it's our boys who're at risk."

The beer did not sit well in my stomach because suddenly I had a sense of where Wylie was going.

"We're just gonna have to do somethin' about it, Clark. And the sooner, the better. You don't wanna let them fags get too settled."

Suddenly, I am very cold. But from the inside out.

"I'm not sure how we'll handle it yet," he says, "but I'm gonna think hard about it. I wish you'd do the same, Clark." He chuckled. "You're a college professor, you're probably a hell of a lot better at thinkin' than I am. I think it's way too soon for another fire, so Ricky's useless. Maybe we could—"

"Wylie, I-I'm hoping you're joking. You . . . you *are* joking, right?"

"Joking? Shit, no, Clark, I'm as serious as a heart attack.

Just because we don't have any boys doesn't mean we shouldn't be worried about the rest of the neighborhood."

I squint at him as if he's far away, shake my head. "What . . . what the hell are you talking about?"

"Boys! Little boys!" He stands, a little angry all of a sudden. Sips his beer as he walks the length of the porch, then comes back, saying, "You know how them fags are. The older they get, the younger they hunt. Those two'll be goin' after the tender meat we got here on Gyldcrest. And we're not gonna let that happen."

My mouth hangs open as if I've had a stroke. I can't remember ever being this afraid in my own home. On the back porch, anyway. He means everything he's saying, and that angry edge to his voice said he was willing to prove it.

"Wylie . . . Wylie . . ." My tongue feels thick. "I . . . I can't, Wylie. I can't."

Towering over me, he looks down at me the way he might look at a cockroach before he stomps on it with the heel of his boot. "Can't? You can't what?"

"I can't do it again. I just can't. Look, we're friends, right, Wylie?"

He nods slowly, still glaring. "That's what I've always thought, yeah."

"Well, if you're really my friend . . . I know you won't ask me to do something that I . . . that I just can't do."

His face relaxes when he laughs. He hunkers down in front of me, smiling. "Hell, no, I'd never ask you to do something like that, Clark. I'm not askin' you now." He lowers his voice, almost to a whisper. "I'm tellin' you. I don't think you realize how easy it'd be for me to put you behind bars for a long time, Clark. That fire? Those deaths? All them people walkin' around lookin' like dog vomit on two feet? I could pin *all* that on you and make it stick. I'm a cop, remember? I work the law from the inside. I can get you out of a jam . . . or put you into one." He's still smiling, and his voice becomes little more than a breath. "And just in case that don't work—it would, don't worry, it would—but just in case, I can always come into your house in the middle of the night, tie you up, and make you watch while I fuck your wife and daughter. Then I'll kill 'em, and make you watch me fuck their corpses. By the time I get around to killing you, you'll thank me for doin' it."

Wylie stands so suddenly that I gasp in surprise.

"But that ain't gonna happen," he says. "Because, like you said, we're friends. And we're gonna do the right thing. And the right thing is getting ridda them cocksuckers." He takes a swig of beer, then turns and goes back to the porch's doorway. "I gotta get home. Hey, tell you what. Why don't you come over tomorrow night for dinner. Deeny's gonna fix a big stir fry, and there's always way too much. Bring Melinda and the girls can run off shopping after dinner. That's all they ever wanna do is shop."

My mouth still hangs open as I watch him go down the steps.

"I'll see you tomorrow, Clark," he says. Then he disappears into the darkness that presses close against the screened-in porch.

ACKNOWLEDGMENTS

Rhonda Blackmon Walton, Karl Hexean Sumner, Latrice and Kenny, Karen Leonard, Steven Spruill, Jane Naccarato, Ed Kurtz, Cheryl Burcham, Joe Parks, Julie Hamilton, Paul Heinze, Jr., Saranna DeWylde, Hal Bodner, and my agent and friend, Richard Curtis.